The Ruined
Thomas Perkins

Copyright © 2025 by Thomas Perkins.

All rights reserved.

No portion of this book may be reproduced in any form without written permission from the publisher or author, except as permitted by U.S. copyright law.

Huge thanks to everyone who provided feedback for this project:

Nat, Mom, Dad, Amr, Christo, Matt, and Sam

And thank you to Marcos Ramones for the amazing cover art! Check him out at marcosrac.artstation.com

Chapter 1
Partners

Krothus was certain of a great many things.

He was certain that he was destined for greatness. That he was better than everyone else. And, especially now, certain he was doing what was right.

His blunted sword crunched into his opponent's ribs, the resulting cry of pain only confirming Krothus' righteous path. The smaller acolyte needed to be instructed, taught the proper hierarchy of strength. Krothus' training sword swung around for more, the impact sending a jolt up arm, rattling his bones and pinching his shoulder, the sign of a lesson well-struck.

A usual sight during their sessions, this latest blow set little Vyrion crying. The sight of it made Krothus uncomfortable. But this did not stay his hand, instead it only stoked his fury.

"Tears won't help you, Vyrion. Get up."

Vyrion was a pathetic sight even without the steady trickle of tears down his face. Stubbornly scrawny and embarrassingly neat, his mere existence invited torment, his small stature in particular leaving him further and further behind as the other acolytes, Krothus most of all, had passed him by leaps and bounds. But such was life, nothing was truly fair.

"Get up," Krothus said again, delivering a savage kick to Vyrion's side, as if continued abuse were the secret to standing.

Vyrion groaned and writhed in the dusty grey soil, the lifeless wasteland outside the Ascendancy providing only a light breeze as consolation for his struggles. Krothus was about to deliver another kick when the groaning abruptly stopped.

"Bastard!" Vyrion squeaked suddenly, his tear-caked face twisted in rage as he swung his practice blade in a weak attempt at Krothus' legs.

Krothus took a single step backwards and the sword sailed uselessly through the air.

It was pathetic, really, but Krothus couldn't help but smile. Beating Vyrion down always had a habit of boosting his mood, a boost Krothus had sorely needed after one of the Ascendancy overseers had left him thoroughly educated only hours before. It was hardly unusual, scars were key to ensure lessons weren't forgotten.

"The strong rule the weak, Vyrion. You clearly don't understand this," Krothus said, echoing the same words said to him then. Quoting the Ruined Code always made him feel smart, he could see why the overseers did it.

Vyrion likely already understood the concept, for what little it helped him. The weak were simply meant to be ruled. It's just how things were. If through some miracle Vyrion emerged the victor in this private session, then perhaps the measure of weakness would shift and Krothus would see his reputation take a tumble, but the chances of this were slim to none. Precisely why Krothus picked him out. No need to risk more than needed for a bit of fun.

Vyrion had at least pushed himself to his feet, scraped elbows wobbling, bruised knees quaking, as he flopped back into a fighting stance, practice sword held in a tight, white-knuckled fist.

"Good. Getting up means you're ready for more," Krothus said, willingly overlooking the fact that he had just kicked him on the floor.

"Do you ever shut up?" Vyrion snapped, his high voice shrill with a sudden anger, "No one else talks this much when they thrash me, they just do it. Close your mouth and get it over with."

Krothus frowned. He always thought of taunting as part of the process, a tradition that gave meaning to an otherwise senseless beating. Why receive lessons if they are not delivered unto others? But if Vyrion was inferring that his words were compensating for some insecurity, some weakness of character, then Krothus wouldn't stand for it. Weakness of any kind had no place in the Ascendancy, the Empire, and certainly not in Krothus himself.

He felt his face go red hot. Showing a hint of vulnerability at the Ascendancy was inviting trouble. Like a carcass in the desert, it attracted all sorts of scavengers, eager to pick apart any unfortunate soul who garnered their attention, and the last thing Krothus needed was more acolytes trying their luck with him over a blatant lie. Krothus was no weakling, he refused to be. He was going to be the most powerful Ruin Lord the Empire had ever seen. He was certain of it.

"You shouldn't have said that. I was going easy on you before, but now I think you deserve an extra session today."

Vyrion snorted, "You? Thinking? The catacombs' rotting corpses would get better marks than you. No Ruin Lord will want to take a fool as an apprentice, no matter how strong you think you are."

Krothus had been angry before, but as his academic ability was called into question the heat in his face roared through the rest of his body. He knew it was the type of fury that only emerged when the truth was a flaw you refused to accept, but Vyrion hadn't earned the right to poke fun at him. Far from it.

Krothus said nothing in response to the remarks, just clenched his jaw and strode forward. Vyrion's brief spell of snarky courage evaporated as he stumbled back, neck craning around, desperately looking for somewhere to hide. But Krothus knew there was nowhere to go. They were alone, two solitary acolytes in a sea of grey dust, the worn pyramid of the Ascendancy nothing more than a neglectful parent looming coldly in the distance.

"Mercy is a lie, power is the one truth," Krothus said, laying out his lesson in the same way it had been delivered to him so many times before.

First, Krothus swung wide. His blow swept through Vyrion's feeble block, and the backswing easily sent the small boy's practice blade sailing out of reach.

They both watched it flip through the air over and over, a wild still couldn't quite wrap his head around. His glorious journey to the top of the Empire, nearly cut short at the clench of a single fist.

To be slapped down by the weakest acolyte in the Ascendancy, not to mention nearly killed, was nothing short of total humiliation.

A creeping horror crawled across Krothus' skin. If word of this got out, he was finished.

Drums pounded against his aching skull as he looked down at Vyrion, hoping for some idea, some solution to come to him. Of course, he could simply kill the boy, bury the body in the wastes and plead ignorance if the overseers questioned him. Who would even notice Vyrion was gone? The overseers were hardly strangers to acolytes going missing. But was that even necessary? Technically, if Vyrion had knocked himself out, then the victor was unclear.

But before Krothus could finish his creative problem solving, it all became a great deal more complicated.

Vyrion was awake. He was looking up at Krothus suspiciously, no doubt guessing what he had just been planning. For some reason, Krothus felt ashamed, guilty that he had even been considering it.

"Good fight," he found himself saying.

Vyrion said nothing, just kept looking at him with those sad, watery eyes of his.

Krothus swallowed. He reached out a hand, intending to help Vyrion to his feet, for some reason. Vyrion initially flinched back, no doubt expecting some underhanded strike to come his way the moment he took it, but settled with ignoring the gesture and getting up himself, leaving Krothus to awkwardly withdraw his hand.

"Who won?" Vyrion asked.

"I don't know," Krothus answered honestly.

"Right."

The air was thick with awkwardness, confused tension, the leftover feelings of combat left wandering. Krothus felt a need to fill the silence.

"How long have you been able to do that?"

"Not long enough," Vyrion snapped, "Or I would have killed you."

Krothus blinked. All things considered, that was probably fair.

Vyrion, clearly not wanting to continue to be subjected to Krothus' poor attempts at conversation, limped over to his practice blade, its previous twirling performance long forgotten. He yanked it out of the dirt, hissing at some injury on his arm, then started back to the Ascendancy pyramid.

Krothus watched him go, any feeling of his usual certainty washed away in a sea of self-doubt and lost confidence.

"Teach me!" Some idiot shouted.

Surprised, Krothus realized that idiot was himself.

Vyrion whipped around, "What?"

"Teach... me," Krothus repeatedly lamely, the absurdity of his words nearly causing him physical pain as they left his lips.

Acolytes didn't share knowledge. They didn't share much of anything, besides the Overseers' harsh lessons and the Ascendancy's terrible excuse for food. Only a few acolytes made it to the end, and even fewer had enough promise to be selected by a Ruin Lord as their apprentice, so any help you gave, any mercy you showed, it only stacked the cards against you. Krothus knew all of this, and yet for some inexplicable reason he had persisted with his foolish notion anyways.

"Why would I help you at all?" Vyrion snarled, "You have been more than happy to torture me as long as I couldn't fight back, but now that I can you expect me to forget? To help you?"

Earlier that day, Krothus would have happily used Vyrion's words as an easy excuse for a harsh lesson in respect. But with his entire body aching, and a realisation of his own mortality fresh in his mind, for once in his life he chose to resist the urge for violence.

"We could trade our knowledge," he suggested, desperately trying to ignore how close desperate it sounded, "I can teach you proper swordsmanship, train you to defend yourself."

Krothus should have felt shame for the near grovelling he was subjecting himself to, but he didn't. Seeing how effortlessly Vyrion had nearly snuffed his life out, how easily his bones could have been shattered, he could only think of one thing: he needed this power above all else. Who knows how long it would be before the other acolytes tapped into their own abilities? Krothus needed to be ahead of the curve if he was to surpass them, or his grand designs would never bear the fruit he dreamt of.

Vyrion snorted, "This goes against everything the Code represents."

"Name one line that contradicts it," Krothus challenged.

Vyrion just rolled his eyes, "The overseers would still forbid it, even if I did want to help you. Which I still don't, by the way."

"I think you've made that abundantly clear. "

Krothus could feel his agitation building. Vyrion clearly wasn't interested, but that was not an acceptable outcome. So a change of strategy was in order.

What was the one thing Vyrion clearly wanted? To see Krothus dead, of course.

"Then let's have a rematch, whoever loses must teach the victor."

The bait was set. It was clear that Vyrion cared little for the exchange of knowledge Krothus was suggesting, but a chance for the small acolyte to finish what he started and leave Krothus crushed into the dirt was something else entirely. It was a risk, of course, but one Krothus was intent on taking.

Vyrion only took a few seconds.

"Deal."

Krothus nodded, satisfied that had worked. But now the real challenge began.

He rolled the worn leather grip of his practice blade over in his hand, feeling the tough material rub over his calloused fingers, silently wishing him luck. But this fight couldn't be left to chance. If Krothus took his time, tried to wait for the right moment, then Vyrion would kill him. He had to press him, overwhelm Vyrion with enough speed and strength to keep him on the back foot. Krothus had the speed, Overseer Trunol would surely have attested, frequently forcing Krothus to do sprints until he vomited or collapsed. As for the strength, Overseer Bardok had Krothus swing that damn stone pillar thousands of times, until his arms were jelly and his hands so rigid that he could scarcely close them. This was a fight he could win.

Vyrion, of course, had neither speed nor strength, so his confidence must have been entirely within his newfound ability. He only stood there, glaring at Krothus with a warpaint of wasteland dust stuck to his tear-stained face. There was no doubt in those eyes, no more fear, only a determined bloodthirst.

He was learning fast, mercy was for the weak. Krothus was almost proud.

There was no countdown, no gentleman's salute. One moment, they faced one another, completely still. The next, Krothus charged.

He reached Vyrion in only a few strides, greeting him with a heavy overhand strike. Vyrion managed to parry with a raise of his blade, but the force of the blow forced a hesitant step back. Krothus didn't let up, carrying his weapon around, this time aiming for Vyrion's head. Again it was just barely parried, but the force of it left Vyrion unbalanced, exposed. Not one to let an opportunity go to waste, Krothus delivered a swift kick to his chest.

Vyrion grunted out an involuntary gasp of air as he lost his footing and tumbled backwards.

Only seconds into their rematch and Vyrion was already on the ground. Krothus could taste victory only moments away, he was so close now, excitement hushing the painful protests of his sore muscles and aching bones. First, Krothus swept Vyrion's blade out of his grip, sending it scraping across the dirt, before hoisting his practice sword above his head for a final triumphant attack.

Vyrion had never looked smaller, hidden under Krothus' mighty shadow as that blunted sword came down at him. But there were no tears this time.

There was a sudden flash, and Krothus felt his stomach drop, wind running over his face. He desperately stretched out his arms, trying to find something, anything, to hold onto, but managed nothing but fistfuls of air. Then he looked down, and saw the ground rising up to meet him.

"Shit."

There was a crack, then everything went dark.

When Krothus woke, he felt like someone had taken a hammer to his skull. He was a good ten feet away from where he had been, the pain racking across him a vocal reminder of a body very unhappy with his recent decisions.

Had he lost? If he had, then the afterlife looked shockingly similar to the same wasteland where he had just thrown his life away.

Krothus grunted and sat up.

If he hadn't lost ... then maybe he'd won? If Vyrion had knocked himself unconscious, then Krothus could simply claim-

A groan rose up just ahead as Vyrion appeared from behind a dune.

"For Ruin's sake."

"Took the words right out of my mouth," Vyrion said, clutching his head and appearing to be in just as much pain as Krothus.

Through an exchange of pained moans, hisses, and what the average Overseer would have described as an excessive amount of swearing, the pair of acolytes pushed themselves to their feet. Again, they faced one another.

"So what now?" Vyrion asked.

Krothus had no idea. "Best out of three?"

That managed to squeeze a laugh out of Vyrion. "Absolutely not, my head feels like it's about to explode." He brushed his hair back into its uniform neatness.

"Agreed," Krothus said, "Now I know how Hektor must have felt when that Overseer kept throwing him against that wall."

Vyrion laughed again, but quickly stopped himself, as if he was doing something wrong. He glared back at Krothus as he had before, though lacking quite the same venom, injected instead with a fresh dose of uncertainty.

Krothus knew how he felt. The whole situation was strange. Other acolytes weren't someone to share a laugh with; they were rivals, foes to be beaten, hungry wolves who would pounce on the first sign of weakness if you let them. Yet, here they were.

"I don't like this either, you know. The Ruined Code doesn't mention scenarios without victors. It's unnatural," Krothus said.

"It does seem to struggle without the black and white," Vyrion admitted.

"Then you'll teach me?"

Vyrion narrowed his eyes, "That's not what I said."

"Do you want to be selected by a Ruin Lord when the time comes?"

"Yes, like everyone else," Vyrion said, speaking slowly, as if Krothus was trying to spring some trap.

"Then you need my help. No Ruin Lord will ever choose you if your skill with a runeblade is as bad as what I just saw."

Vyrion took the statement as an insult, which the truth often was, "Well no Ruin Lord will select you without a grasp of the Ruin either."

Krothus smiled, an expression he was almost entirely unfamiliar with, "So you agree with my proposal."

Agree was hardly the word that came to mind when looking at Vyrion's frustrated face, but any wall had cracks, and a long drawn out sigh heralded Krothus' hard-fought victory.

"If we do this, we keep it a secret. We'll be the main target of every Overseer and acolyte if we don't."

"Agreed," Krothus said.

"And we aren't friends," Vyrion added, "I still think you are a cruel idiot, and I'm doing this to help myself, not you."

Krothus shrugged, the concept of friends so alien to him that he would have hardly suggested it anyways, "Partners then?"

Vyrion nodded, "I can do partners."

Krothus, satisfied with the terms, extended a hand. Vyrion did the same, his own hand disappearing within Krothus' much larger grip.

They shook, the very act feeling like heresy. But Krothus knew this was the right course of action, merely the next step in his journey to the top of the Empire. He was certain of it.

Chapter 2
Accidents Happen

Vyrion had always hated his room. Cramped, cold, and built with a stubborn habit of retaining dust even after being painstakingly cleaned, he had wished a thousand times over to be rid of this stone prison. But now, sitting on the precisely made bed, facing his muddled reflection in the polished blackness of the far wall, he wanted nothing more than one last night there. He may have hated the place, but it was familiar. Home.

He stifled a yawn. Another night would have been ideal, if only for the extra sleep.

Vyrion had been too nervous to do much else besides lie in bed, his tired mind drifting in and out of consciousness. The comforting embrace of sleep stayed just out of reach, harried away by his usual nightmares - the familiar beatings, the daily punishment, the constant struggle to survive. It had been years since he had been that scared little boy, yet still that boy haunted him.

But this night was too important to spend time dwelling on the past. It required his mind to focus on the here and the now. There could be no room for mistakes.

Vyrion rolled the ornate hilt of his runeblade over and over in his hands, the touch of the cool metal anchoring his mind to the present. The Ruin was with him, he knew that. But it was with the others too.

There was a sequenced knock on his door, two short then one long.

His stomach sank. It was time. Vyrion hooked the hilt to his belt and, after one last adjustment of his carefully tidied hair, stepped out into the dim maw of the hallway, probably for the last time.

There, a familiar man waited, one who could have easily been mistaken for an artist's first attempt at sculpting a square-jawed hero out of stone. Armed with a practiced frown and a suit of glinting, mismatched armor, he stood triumphantly tall, pale grey skin stretched over well-trained muscle and stamped down with an army of scars.

He had certainly played a part in Vyrion's nightmares, once, but Vyrion was no longer the boy he had once been. And neither was Krothus.

"Krothus, did you *polish* your armor?" He had to stifle a laugh.

Krothus's frown deepened as he inspected himself, as if noticing his armor was particularly shiny for the first time. "Possibly."

"The scourge of the Ascendancy, making his armor all nice and shiny for the arrival of the masters," Vyrion prodded, "I'm sure they'll be honored to see such a gesture."

Vyrion was hoping for some verbal joust to take his mind off the upcoming challenge, but Krothus didn't take the bait.

"The masters will be honored when they get to witness my triumph, that much I'm sure."

Vyrion could only wish he had Krothus's confidence. His partner's complete belief in himself was a quality that would no doubt lead to Krothus being selected tonight, it was the type of unwavering certainty that made others doubt their own chances, a scenario Vyrion was only too familiar with.

"What about you? Nervous?" asked Krothus.

"Of course not," Vyrion said, the gnawing in his chest and the trembling of his hands clear evidence to the contrary.

But Krothus saw right through him. "You shouldn't be. I can't think of a single matchup that you should fear."

An easy statement to make for someone as much a stranger to fear as Vyrion was to bravery. But Vyrion was hardly in the mood to convince Krothus of the very valid reasons behind his nervousness; it was a circular conversation that got nowhere, involving anything and everything but the point.

sidestepped it.

The only thing that saved Rythe's arm was his shield. It scraped against the runeblade, changing the blade's arc just enough as another section of it rusted and fell off. The blade nicked Rythe's shoulder. Vyrion didn't even need to check for blood, he knew the fight was over.

Rythe was dragged, kicking and screaming, out of the circle a moment later. Part of his shoulder had simply rotted away, bone and muscle bare for all to see. He'd lost.

Althael was dragged, scratching and shrieking, out of the circle a moment after that. She was still intent on finishing the job. She'd won.

Vyrion had first thought seeing someone else's bout would steady his nerves. But one look at Rythe's ruined shoulder had put that thought to rest.

Several more followed. Hidraga cut off Luthor's hand. Wreth snuck past Saux's dual runeblades to draw first blood. Lewitz and Pauline battled entirely through their mastery of the Ruin, their weapons unused. And Xaz and Yuros knocked each other out when their power runes overloaded and blew up.

Each time the Headmistress called a new name, Vyrion's stomach flipped, anticipating him being dragged forth. But still he waited, yet to be called out of a line of untried acolytes that was rapidly dwindling.

The cane cracked against the floor again, "Krothus. Vadrina."

Krothus stepped into the ring with a great smile, he'd gotten his choice of opponent after all.

Arrogantly beautiful in her long flowing robe, Vadrina followed just behind. A verbal skirmish began the moment they were in position.

"This will be over nice and quick, you great oaf," Vadrina hissed, "For all that armor, the Ruin will crush you into dust like you were nothing."

"I'm going to enjoy watching you die," Krothus said simply, every word oozing superiority.

It wouldn't be a good Kograi without a bit of show.

"Begin!"

Krothus's runeblade ignited first. And when the rest of the weapon revealed itself, it became clear that 'ignite' barely began to describe the process. Even Vadrina seemed taken aback, at least for a single moment.

Most other acolytes had used or iterated upon the standard designs illustrated in the runeforging tomes in the Ascendancy library, but Krothus had decided these weren't worthy of him. Instead, he ventured into the catacombs beneath the pyramid.

Not even Vyrion had any idea what Krothus found down there, only that when he returned, he worked the runeforges for three days straight. And while other acolytes practiced their swordsmanship in the drill yard, Krothus would only do so in the catacombs. Only fools hold a torch to their secrets for all to see, he had said.

Vyrion had called him a fool at the time, but only now did he realize that Krothus's secret was the torch itself.

Krothus's runeblade was a barely contained firestorm, hungry flames crackling off the metal, lepers desperate for a touch. The heat of the blaze was evident even from where Vyrion was standing, caressing his face and forcing his eyes nearly closed as the influx of light shone as bright as day.

Vyrion was impressed. As the fiery sheath burned, he could make out five unfamiliar runes buried within, each feasting on vast amounts of Ruin energy. Krothus was demonstrating his power just by keeping those flames going.

But Krothus's opponent wasn't interested.

"Someone likes to play with fire," Vadrina sneered. Her own weapon was far more subtle, glowing with the soft crimson light of three focus runes, amplifying Ruinous sorcery over any benefit to her swordsmanship.

"I'll show you why," Krothus growled. He leapt forward, runeblade held high.

But she was ready for him. Vadrina's body shuddered with terrible power as she struck, a bolt of crimson lightning shot out from her fingertips. It jolted through the air in a jagged arc.

Krothus chopped at it mid-air, sending the bolt crashing into the ground. He landed with a mighty roar, hurtling his blade down at his opponent.

Vadrina, speed aided by the Ruin, dashed to the side at the very last second, only briefly being licked by the flames. She tried to get in an attack of her own, but Krothus was already on the attack once more.

Their runeblades clashed again and again, Krothus's bloodlust clear as day as he furiously hammered at her defenses. Each strike was an arc of bright light, the flames hissing through the air, singeing parts of Vadrina's clothes, an unrelenting avalanche of heat and fury.

After a monstrous cleave from Krothus nearly knocked her weapon away, Vadrina seemed to realize that staying in melee with him was a terrible idea. With a quick blast of Ruin energy, she sent him skidding to the other side of the ring. Krothus immediately charged after her.

This time, Vadrina thrust a palm forward, the air around it seeming to twist and warp as a great bundle of power erupted forth.

Vyrion held his breath. If Krothus had one weakness, it had always been his mastery of the Ruin. He had a tremendous pool of power to draw on, but his skills were unrefined, and it was difficult for Krothus to direct the Ruin except in the most basic of manners. But Vyrion had prepared him for this.

Krothus didn't break his stride as the blast of Ruinous power zoomed towards him, he didn't even slow down. He swept a hand to the side and a separate wave of energy collided with the oncoming tsunami, not enough to stop it, but Krothus didn't need to.

The shockwave changed its path, rumbling just past Krothus's left. It swept into one of the corners of the platform and, with a great boom, crushed an entire section of black stone to rubble.

Again, Krothus descended upon his prey, but Vyrion could see that maneuver had cost his concentration. The barely contained blaze that had enveloped his weapon was now a dwindled cloak of fire, hugging the blade tightly, the roar of open flame that had filled the air now a softly spoken ember in the breeze.

Vadrina too, noticed this. Now, as Krothus bore down on her, she interlaced her runeblade strikes with blasts of power from her free hand. Whenever Krothus would find an opening, the Ruin would stagger him, giving Vadrina the breathing room she needed to drag out the fight, every second longer dwindling the flames further.

Vyrion could feel worry seep into his gut. That wasn't good - and if Krothus, with all his confidence and all their strategy, couldn't defeat his preferred opponent, then what chance did Vyrion have?

Another web of Ruin lightning burst from Vadrina's fingertips. Krothus brought up a hand just in time to disperse the energy with his own, the lightning sizzling out of existence as it collided with his palm, filling the air with the smell of burnt ozone. But any trace of a grin was wiped off his face as a labored hiss rose up off of Krothus's runeblade.

The flames had gone out.

"Pathetic, all that performance with nothing to show for it," Vadrina spat, "Now we end this." Her red focus runes glowing bright with renewed power

Before Krothus could respond, a net of crimson energy pinned him in place. He twisted and strained, gray muscles bulging, as Vadrina's runeblade sailed down at his head.

Vyrion felt his blood run cold. That was a killing blow.

Vadrina let out a cry of victory as the runeblade sank deep. But not where she intended.

Krothus had only managed to break free a single moment before he'd been struck, not nearly enough time to dodge. So he hadn't.

The towering acolyte had twisted to one side, leading the blade to his single pauldron of shoulder armor. The runeblade had cut into it, but remained there, stuck just far enough to avoid drawing blood, its path slowed by what Vyrion now realized was what little godrium Krothus had.

Vadrina tried to yank her blade back for another strike, but Krothus's pale hand enveloped her wrist. Her arm shook as she struggled in his iron grip, her smug assurance turned to a sudden tragic terror.

Krothus slowly leaned in. "*I* decide when we end this."

One by one, the runes on his blade reignited. It erupted into a pillar of burning heat and light. Vyrion and the other acolytes had to look away or risk being blinded.

Krothus roared. Vadrina had run out of clever words.

One mighty strike separated her head from her shoulders.

The scent of burning flesh filled the air as her body fell to the ground.

Krothus smiled, while Vyrion nervously looked to the Headmistress. He wasn't meant to kill her.

"Krothus is the victor." The Headmistress displayed not a hint of concern. She just raised a hand and Vadrina's body levitated out of the ring.

Accidents always seemed to happen when runeblades were involved.

Vyrion could hear Narvina giggling down the line, the now-twinless twin seeming quite pleased with the result. But the rest of the acolytes were silent, and Vyrion found himself letting out a breath of relief. Mercy was for the weak, Vyrion reminded himself, and Vadrina was the one who had attempted a killing blow first. So why did he still feel like it was wrong?

Krothus extinguished his runeblade and strode back to the line, breathing heavily, smoke fluttering off the pale hand, now blackened, that had dissipated the Ruin lightning. He gave Vyrion a nod, nothing more, as if he had only performed some paltry training exercise. Vyrion didn't return it.

More Kograi followed, but they weren't nearly as deadly. At some point, Althael ran back from wherever she had been taken, shrieking like a woman possessed as she made a run for Rythe, but the Headmistress knocked her out with a swift blow from her cane.

Eventually, the moment Vyrion had been dreading arrived.

"Vyrion. Dorrel."

Vyrion let out a shaky breath as he walked to the ring, feeling the warmth of adrenaline flow through his limbs. Like some internal crusade, his body purged itself of his self-doubt and anxiety, leaving him wondering why it hadn't done that the moment he'd woke that morning.

Dorrel on the other hand, needed no such purge. The Ruin has made its mark on him from an early age; covered head to toe in thick fur, with wide horns that curved out of his skull and strength that put even

Krothus to shame - it was no wonder he stomped into the ring without a care in the world. There was no mystery as to why the other acolytes left him be.

The Ruin was fickle, seeming to dole out its blessings without rhyme or reason. It turned Krothus's skin gray, it made Dorrel stronger than any other, it gave other acolytes a myriad of curiosities and abilities; yet Vyrion had to struggle just to get out of bed in the morning. Couldn't the Ruin have at least made him taller? His stature had made his life a living hell for years, while Dorrel and others had prospered based on nothing but chance.

"Good luck, Vyrion. May the Ruin favor us both," the horned acolyte said, his voice a deep baritone. Dorrel was always pleasant. It was easy to be so when you had a mountain of fur and horns backing you up.

"Good luck," Vyrion replied, swallowing a myriad of bitter retorts.

The strong ruled the weak, but were the strong those with great strength, or those who had persevered despite great weakness? Vyrion might have been biased, but he had an idea.

"Begin."

Vyrion ignited his runeblade, the pair of metal blades curving around each other like a pair of serpents, intertwining around the solid beam of crimson humming at their center. With every beat of his heart, he felt it pulse into his weapon too, like the runeblade were an extension of his own body. Its comforting hum, its tidy grip, he knew it all too well.

He had made specific care to link the focus runes, for them to only ignite in line with the power he wielded at the time. No point bleeding energy like Krothus's blade did. Admittedly twelve total runes was ambitious, if not unrealistic, but Vyrion had never been able to ignite more than a handful. Three seemed fine for now.

Dorrel's weapon wasn't quite a runeblade. In fact, Vyrion wasn't sure what it was at all. Instead of a hilt, he wore it like a gauntlet, wth a set of four claws emerging as it was ignited, the Ruin sluggishly bubbling between each of the talons with a dim yellow glow. Two runes sat at the base of the claws, the source of the golden light.

Vyrion silently swore. Of course Dorrel used absorption runes, why use anything else? Sap his opponent's Ruinous abilities, then beat them down - the last thing Vyrion needed was an opponent with both brawn and brains, but here he was.

Dorrel was the first to move. He crossed the ring in two great strides and thrust his claw at Vyrion like an overgrown child wildly swatting at a fly. Vyrion diverted the thrust with his blade and, feeling bold, grabbed at the invisible but ever-present Ruin around them. He thrust a hand forward. He felt it pass through the air with a slight resistance, like he had moved his palm through a deep pool of water. It sent a blast of Ruinous energy crashing into his opponent.

But Vyrion could have splashed him with water for all the good it did. The blast dissipated against Dorrel's fur, not budging the acolyte an inch, and in a response, a great furred fist swung around. Acting almost on instinct, Vyrion reached out with the Ruin once again. Like he were grabbing it with his own hand, he felt the fur on Dorrels knuckles, the grime underneath his nails, the lines on his palm. He pushed back against it, the Ruin following suit.

The fist froze, a moment away from turning his face to pulp. allowing Vyrion to roll away before he relinquished his hold. Dorrel nearly fell over as his punch flew through empty air.

The absorption runes' lazy yellow glow grew brighter, Vyrion felt something within him dwindle as they soaked in a drop of his energies.

As Dorrel wheeled back around for another go, snorting with frustration, Vyrion held his blade in front of him and crossed one arm behind his back, minimising his profile. Krothus had taught him about dealing with larger opponents, but whether there were size limits to these lessons was yet to be seen.

This time, when Dorrel stomped forwards, Vyrion, like tensing an extra set of muscles, channeled the Ruin into his limbs. The claw again surged forward, but Vyrion jabbed for Dorrel's exposed side with lightning speed. The horned acolyte had to twist mid-air to deflect the blade with his own weapon, losing his momentum and nearly toppling over again. The Ruin surging through him, Vyrion unleashed a series of bothered with - did a boot become well acquainted with the insects it crushed? He clenched his jaw and glared at the masters, hoping for an end to his boredom.

Only when the final Kograi ended with a single cut to the leg did the Headmistress finally speak once more.

"You have presented yourselves for judgement," she rasped, "And now the Ruin and its vessels must decide your fate. You are to remain here, if a Lord decides to claim an acolyte, as is their right, they will return for them. Only these acolytes will become Ruined."

With a wave of her gnarled hand, any unconscious acolytes suddenly came to. Another wave sent the floor quaking as a massive slab of stone rumbled out of nowhere, sliding over the stairwell behind the line of acolytes.

Then she and the masters were gone.

Krothus made his way over to Vyrion, who was just managing to sit up.

The other stirring acolytes did not receive even a passing glance from their peers. Some struck up terse conversations with those that weren't their outright enemies, but most remained silently solitary as they dispersed across the platform.

Vyrion looked up at him from the floor, dazed and confused, "What happened?"

"You won," Krothus said simply.

Vyrion looked pleased, but as usual, it wasn't long before he started worrying. "I heard some voice in my head, right before I passed out. It was ... talking to me, I think. It-"

Krothus had no idea what he was talking about, and his expression must have said as such, because Vyrion stopped mid-sentence to wave a dismissive hand.

"Never mind." He looked at the now empty space where the masters had been. "And where did they go?"

Krothus shrugged. "To decide which acolytes are worth taking, I suppose. The Headmistress had the courtesy of locking us up here while they did."

"How kind. Might as well trap us up here while we wait for our fate to be decreed," Vyrion muttered, starting to push himself up.

Krothus let out an amused snort at the comment, before extending a hand.

Vyrion raised a single eyebrow at him, but Krothus didn't retract the gesture. He knew what such an action meant, he might as well have been asking Vyrion to shout out about their partnership for all to see. But it was the end of the road, what could anyone do about it?

Vyrion grunted as he was hoisted back to his feet. Perhaps some had been suspicious of something between the two before; 'duels' that never amounted to any injuries, coincidentally mutual enemies - there were signs, yes, but this one gesture, performed so blatantly, confirmed it all. So this simple act was followed by glares from every acolyte on the platform, the kind of glares that would have led to trouble had it been any other night.

Yet far from being cowed by the attention, Krothus revelled in it. The other acolytes must be furious. Those fools had done everything in their power to rise above their peers; sabotage, murder, anything that improved their position over others was fair game. But standing alone could only take you so far, even when there seemed to be no other option.

It was by design of course, sharing knowledge would only make your competition stronger, so you didn't. You weren't on anyone's side because no one was on yours. This was encouraged by the code, the overseers, and the very nature of this final night.

But by becoming partners, Krothus and Vyrion had circumvented this process, if not spat in its face. And, as Krothus had just realized, despite the rest of them now knowing the truth, they couldn't do a damned thing about it.

It was too late. They had won.

But Vyrion didn't share his jubilation. In fact, he looked more dejected than ever, wearing that uncertain look he always had when he had thought of something else to worry about, eyebrows scrunched up and his dark forehead furrowed.

Krothus sighed, "What is it now?"

Vyrion looked at blackness beyond, at the faint light of stars looming down at them, "What happens after this?"

Krothus didn't understand the purpose behind the question. "The same as it has always been, we leave the Ascendancy with our new Master to be brought into service of the Empire. We gain in power until we are strong enough to succeed our master and forge our own path." Maybe Vyrion had hit his head harder than Krothus originally thought.

Vyrion shook his head, "Not that. I mean with us, the partnership."

Krothus blinked. In all honesty, he hadn't considered the arrangement beyond getting to where they had this very night. He and Vyrion had learned a great deal from one another in the years since their agreement had been first forged, and while Krothus' opinion of the once pathetic acolyte had grown from tolerance to a grudging respect, he had never thought to maintain anything further. What use was a partner when you were a Ruined? The whole of the Empire would be at your fingertips, the average Imperial nothing but a subject to be ruled.

"Don't let sentiment cloud your judgment, Vyrion. We maintained the partnership to gain an advantage over others, to become apprentices to a suitable Master. We will leave here with that goal fulfilled, thrust into service of Ruin Lords who are no doubt more agreeable than a gang of youthful acolytes. The Empire is a far more civilised place."

Vyrion looked over at the scorched remains of Vadrina, then let out a single snort of laughter. "Civilised. I'm not so sure it's as simple as that." He waved a hand at the angry, isolated acolytes around them. "How different could the Empire possibly be? Why would the Overseers turn a blind eye to all the savagery, murdering and thieving, if they weren't just preparing us for more of the same? We know nothing of how the Empire truly operates beyond whatever inoffensive passages are spoon-fed to us. You're right about one thing, Krothus. Things *will* change, but they'll only get worse."

Vyrion's latest outburst was far from convincing. Krothus had grown used to them. "The strong rule the weak, Vyrion. As we've proven tonight, we are the former. The Ruin favors us, and our strength has no doubt earned us a place among the Ruin Lords for the foreseeable future, what use is there picking apart our accomplishments? I would think you'd be happy."

"You don't get it," Vyrion snapped. He got so easily frustrated that they didn't see eye to eye. Unlike his feeble exterior, Vyrion's opinions were strong, an ancient boulder that refused to budge no matter how strong the long-winded gusts of discussion blew. And he always made sure to remind Krothus of how wrong he thought he was.

"We are strong only *here*," Vyrion continued, pointing a small finger down at his feet. "Only compared to these acolytes, no one else. We are nothing more than the largest bats in a small cave, and the moment we leave this place, the moment we fly into the waiting jaws of whatever new chasm awaits us, we begin again. We start from scratch. We know nothing of the masters, we have no idea how strong they are, how many apprentices they already have, the types of things we will have to do to stay in their favour. We are flying blindly into whatever struggle awaits us without the faintest idea of who to trust."

Krothus frowned. He hated it when Vyrion lectured him, and he especially hated it when he was right.

"Ruin Lords would have rivals within the Empire, enemies outside it. Their apprentices could be targets," he admitted, feeling the high of his victory start to crumble.

"Exactly," Vyrion agreed, "For all we know, our next foes would make these acolytes look like crippled children."

Krothus didn't bother pointing out how many acolytes did, in fact, wind up as crippled or maimed children. He would have found it amusing, but Vyrion would certainly not.

"So you are suggesting the partnership should remain in place?" Krothus asked instead.

"I am," Vyrion said, "At least until we have some sort of idea of what's going on."

"Then I agree," Krothus said. It was hard to fault the logic behind Vyrion's proposal, it would perhaps be wise to keep an ally he could nearly trust. Krothus never trusted anyone fully, to do so was foolish at best and suicidal at worst, one of the many lessons the Ascendancy would leave scarred across both his mind and his skin.

A short while later the floor rumbled as the stone blocking the stairs moved aside, revealing a cloaked figure. Krothus' breath caught in his throat. Was this his master?

"Nardina, come with me," the cloaked woman said.

Krothus and Vyrion both let out a disappointed sigh. It was going to be a long wait.

Nardina, grin wide and stride practically skipping, disappeared with her new master down the stairway. The slab moved back into place.

"What happens to those who aren't chosen?" Krothus asked. He was obviously going to be picked, he was certain of it. His destiny demanded it. But it couldn't hurt to know.

"I hear some are transferred into a division of the Imperial military," Vyrion said, "There, they have the chance to prove themselves as worthy acolytes through battle. Though I also heard one of the overseers say others are forced to power machinery for the Empire, their energy drained for the remainder of their days."

"Which overseer told you that?" Krothus was not happy with that latter option.

Vyrion shrugged, "How should I know? I don't normally make conversation with boots on my neck."

Another rumble heralded another Master's arrival. Her hood was down, her predatory eyes scanning the acolytes like she were searching for her next meal.

"Althael," she called out. Then she retreated back down the steps before her acolyte registered the call.

Althael, conflict with Rythe long forgotten, dashed after the woman on all fours. Krothus made sure to give her a wide berth. Only once she had descended did the slab return to its previous position.

This process repeated itself again and again. There didn't seem to be any pattern or reasoning to the order of the acolytes selected, at least none that Krothus could see. Most had been the winners of their Kograi, but even that didn't ring true for all.

"Dorrel."

One of the horned acolyte's hands was burnt and blackened, his claw destroyed, and the opposite arm a mess of cuts and shards of metal, but still he delivered a bow to his victorious opponent, which Vyrion returned.

Krothus rolled his eyes. How such a fraud was selected was beyond him.

"Good luck, Vyrion. May the Ruin watch over you," Dorrel said, not the slightest hint of malice in his voice.

"And you."

Then Dorrel and his master, a small man who barely went up to Dorrel's knee, disappeared below.

"Should I bow to what's left of Vadrina as well?" Krothus joked.

Vyrion didn't find it as funny as Krothus did. "I guarantee she won't return the favor."

Soon enough, Krothus and Vyrion were among the few still remaining at the top of the pyramid, and of these stragglers, the only two who had won their Kograi. It made Krothus feel uneasy, something he was deeply unfamiliar with. Why had they been left till last?

It didn't take long for others to falsely conflate his agitation with weakness.

"Welcome to the leftovers," Rythe sneered through a cage of black teeth, "Looks like winning doesn't matter when you cheat the system." His decayed shoulder was wrapped in a bandage ripped off his shirt, his godrium-laced shield nothing more than a hunk of rusted metal on the floor.

"Looks like you want your entire arm amputated this time," Krothus snarled. His runeblade hilt flew into his hand.

Rythe, the coward, immediately stumbled back three paces, the color drained from his face as he fumbled around for his own weapon.

Letting out an amused snort, Krothus placed his runeblade back on his belt. Pathetic.

The acolytes all turned as the floor rumbled once more, this time accompanied by a steady tink of metal on stone.

A cloaked man crested the stairs, hobbling along with an uneven gait brought about by a metal contraption in place of his right leg. Despite this limp, his sturdy bulk, shoved into a scarred breastplate, was carried with a practiced march, his retreating hairline an orderly battleline of grey, flanked by a contingent of pepper stubble across his wily face.

Krothus knew this was his master. It would only be fitting that a veteran fighter, a respected, military man had seen his potential. Who else in the Ascendancy could best him in a display of swordplay? Who else had a mind expertly molded for battle? They would be perfectly matched, and his destiny would surely be fulfilled. He could only wait for his name to be called.

The Ruin Lord spoke in a voice like crushed gravel. "Come Vyrion. We are short on time, boy."

Vyrion? Krothus thought the one-legged man had misspoken, as if he would chuckle and reach a hand out to him, begging apology for such an embarrassing mistake. But no such thing followed. Krothus's hands clenched into fists so tight that his fingers trembled.

"Me?" Vyrion said, feigning ignorance, no doubt suppressing the urge to laugh in Krothus' face.

"Unless you've changed your damn name in the last thirty minutes, then yes," barked the old Ruin Lord, "Now come along before I lose my temper."

Vyrion nodded and followed after him. Before he disappeared, his eyes met Krothus' own, brows drawn together and dark forehead furrowed. Krothus just glared at him. What did he have to worry about?

The only acolytes left were those who had lost their bouts, and Krothus. Had that been the final Ruin Lord looking for an apprentice? Krothus was sure there were more. There had to be, there was surely no way he would be held in the same regard as Rythe.

It didn't take long before the slab scraped across the platform once more.

Krothus' heart pounded in his ears. He would not be left unclaimed. It wouldn't happen, his destiny was far greater than any other here, his plans too important to fail.

Bloodshot eyes emerged from the darkness, and the Headmistress climbed back into view.

Krothus nearly fell to his knees. *No.*

But then another arrived.

The woman sprouted up over the Headmistress, looking down at the acolytes with a mocking smile, like they had made fools of themselves and only she knew why. She inspected her prey, prowling towards them like a jungle cat, disobedient black hair ruthlessly cropped short, gracefully menacing and menacingly graceful. But above all else, Krothus could sense her incredible aura of Ruinous energy, like her very presence was a beacon, sending pulsing waves of power rolling through the Ruin all around them.

To have strength like this, to demonstrate your ability by presence alone. This was what Krothus wanted above all else.

So enraptured was he that Krothus barely registered her words when she spoke.

"Krothus, come. The rest of this rabble isn't worth a minute more of your time." Her voice declared each syllable with absolute authority.

"I couldn't agree more," Krothus said, directing his best sneer at Rythe, who only now seemed to realize he had been left unclaimed. Perhaps the Imperial military might actually give Rythe a proper shield before sending him into battle, Krothus mused, or better yet, stick him in some hell-pit for the rest of his life, where no one had to see his foul face again.

As Krothus quickly followed behind his new master's swift pace, spirits so high they threatened to pull him through the ceiling, he could hear the Headmistress behind.

"You acolytes have been ... disappointing. The masters sensed what I do now; no potential, no promise, and a future built on suffering. There are many ways to serve the Empire with your failure, but none of them will be pleasant."

Good riddance. Krothus was relieved beyond belief that he was not still up there. He could hear the Headmistress's ancient cackle fade away

dormant giant, emanating an aura of untold menace.
 Lord Callida put a hand on his shoulder.
 "Welcome, my young apprentice, to Thanaton."

Chapter 4
The Skyport

"Are you even trying?"

Vyrion's arms were jelly, his legs numb, and lungs about to burst. He was barely able to get his runeblade up in time, the coiled blades of his weapon scraping against the oncoming blow and just barely diverting it away. Yes, he was trying, for all the good it did.

"Come, boy. You are being too *predictable*!" Lord Victus roared, already sending his weapon in on the backswing.

As far as Vyrion could tell there were only so many ways you could stop a runeblade from cutting you in two. If his master were bored of his desperate attempts to defend himself, then perhaps he should have gone a little easier on him for once.

Vyrion braced for the shock of the next blow to rattle up his arm, but Victus adjusted the grip on his weapon's curved hilt, changing the angle of his strike just before impact. With a single twist, he sent Vyrion's weapon flying across the courtyard.

"For Ruin's sake," Vyrion gasped, shamelessly leaning down with his hands on his knees, trying to gulp down mouthfuls of air, wishing it would somehow make him a better swordsman. He'd lost count of how many times he'd been easily outclassed in the last few weeks. It was almost like Victus was set on proving how wrong he'd been to take Vyrion in, a notion Vyrion would have absolutely agreed with.

The Ruin Lord shook his head, then took a mighty swig from his hip flask, "You must always be vigilant, Vyrion! If you react the same way to every attack, it will only take a single surprise to catch you unawares, a weakness any competent opponent will quickly capitalise on."

"Yes, master," Vyrion said, silently wishing Victus would heed his own advice, he'd heard this lesson three times now.

Lord Victus retracted his runeblade and looped it onto his belt, looking down at his metal leg as he massaged at his neck with one hand. They both sat for a moment, enjoying what little of the late morning sun managed to press through the gray clouds above.

Victus flicked one of his hands, "One mistake is all it takes to send you tumbling down the hierarchy of the Empire, Vyrion. So when I say to be vigilant-"

Vyrion's runeblade zoomed into his hand from where it fell.

"-listen to this old man's advice."

"I will try to," Vyrion said, "Though I can't imagine I can tumble much further,"

Victus, hands clasped behind his back, gave him a sad smile. "You would be surprised. How are your studies coming along?"

"I've nearly finished going through everything left in my chambers," Vyrion said, declining to mention the dire state the tomes had been in, dusty and falling apart in his hands, "I only have one more chapter left of *The Ruined Empire and Its Provinces.*"

"Good," Victus said with a nod, "I will ensure the next batch is brought to you as soon as possible. Consider this your absolute priority, knowledge is often a more effective protection in Thanaton than any runeblade, its proper application can win many struggles before they even begin."

"Thank you, master," Vyrion said, swallowing awkwardly before continuing, "... and when will I be permitted to leave the compound?"

He had been confined to Lord Victus' compound since he had arrived, told that he would need to gain a base understanding of the Empire before setting out within it. Initially, Vyrion had no problem with such a directive, his room had been many times larger than anything he had ever stayed in before, and the compound's eager servants, bustling kitchens, and expansive library were beyond the harsh conditions at the Ascendancy. But as days had turned to weeks, Vyrion had grown restless. A whole city to explore, Krothus to find, and despite his new rank, he was beginning to feel frighteningly close to a prisoner.

Victus frowned. "Whenever I damn say you can, which I haven't. Finish your readings and I might rethink my position."

Vyrion deflated, his hopes of an early release dashed.

Without waiting for a rebuttal, Victus limped off.

Vyrion sighed as he watched him go. The privileged life of a Ruined was hardly what he had expected it to be.

Hours later, Vyrion was sprawled across one of the courtyard benches in an effort to catch what little sun he could, books neatly stacked all around. He had quickly lost track of time, flipping through countless crumbling pages to the low hum and rumble of the city beyond the compound's walls. Studying was something he had always enjoyed, so much so that he had almost forgotten what he had been annoyed about earlier. One of the kitchen servants had even brought him lunch.

But as he had come to learn, all enjoyment was temporary.

The visitor stomped into the main courtyard of the compound with indignant fury, her cloak billowing behind her. Vyrion, unsure of her intentions, quickly moved to intercept.

"What business do you have with Lord Victus?"

The woman looked important, dressed in fine fabrics and draped in a pleasant perfume, but had eyebrows perched slightly too high on her face, giving her a permanent look of minor surprise. She greeted him with an annoyed huff. "Your master has once again refused to attend a hearing for his latest blunder. He is to report to Highlord Malus *immediately*."

Vyrion frowned, not sure what she was talking about.

"Well? I wouldn't lower myself and come to the outskirts of the Inner City just for a walk," she prodded, her hands on her hips, "Where is the old fool?"

"Who is the young fool asking?" Vyrion asked, annoyed at her brazen tone. He may have thought of himself as the world's worst Ruined, but he was a Ruined nonetheless. "My master doesn't see just any beggar off the street."

He knew full well this woman wasn't a beggar, the runeblade at her waist made that abundantly clear. But he surely had a duty to uphold his master's honor.

"I've killed for less than an insult," she hissed back at him, hand dropping down to her runeblade hilt.

"That seems an odd thing to brag about."

They stood there for a moment, the air thick with the possibility of violence. He might have expected to feel scared, or excited, but Vyrion only found himself wishing to go back to his books.

The standoff was cut short by the sounds of an uneven metal stride.

"Now, now, Saurine, we all know that striking down another Ruined would incur the wrath of their master, do we not?" Lord Victus tutted, limping towards them from a nearby hall.

Whether she was surprised at the Ruin Lord's sudden arrival or not, Vyrion couldn't tell, but Saurine wasted no time in repeating herself. "You are to report to Highlord Malus immediately, as you refused to attend the hearing regarding your unauthorised archaeological expedition."

"I was not made aware of such a hearing," Victus said, his voice ice, "Especially since Highlord Malus was the one who authorised the expedition in the first place."

"The authorisation was revoked when Lord Sanata reported that you returned with nothing but dirt," Saurine sneered, "My master couldn't stand idly by while you wasted the Highlord's resources, you see."

The aged Ruin Lord's grizzled head twitched to the side twice. Then he exploded.

"Sanata and her scheming!" the Ruin Lord shouted, "She knows full well what I discovered, she and Malus aim to seize it for themselves! I won't have it!"

"My master-"

"Silence, woman. Tell Sanata that if she wishes to threaten me, she can come herself! I won't answer to one of her *whelps*. Now get out of my sight."

With a smirk on her lips and surprise on her brow, Saurine swiveled back around and marched out the way she'd come.

"Ridiculous. How dare they even suggest ..." Victus muttered, before falling silent.

Vyrion wasn't quite sure how to react, he had never seen Victus act like this. The sudden burst of his master's anger had sent any nearby servants scurrying away.

"Who are these Lords?" he asked, proceeding only once Victus took a calming swig from his hip flask.

"Malus is my direct superior, an influential Ruin Highlord answering directly to the Council itself," Victus growled, "It's no secret that he despises me, seeing me weak, too focused on the secrets of the past. Utter nonsense, mind you, but he is a powerful man, and such a dislike is easily exploitable, an obvious stepping stone for those who wish to use his strength to protect themselves. Lord Sanata clearly sees this as an open opportunity to gain favor with him and strengthen her power base, so she's played her hand."

Vyrion knew enough from his readings to follow. Ruin Lords weren't just strong by their abilities alone, their power base was key to their position within the Empire. Whatever you controlled; land, soldiers, and even other Ruin Lords, they were all a measure of your strength, your own kingdom within the Empire.

"Why not have Sanata killed?" Vyrion asked, thinking of what Krothus would have suggested in this scenario, "Surely that would solve the issue."

Lord Victus let out a harsh bark of laughter, "the Ascendancy's lax rules do not accurately portray how the Ruin Lords conduct their business, my naive apprentice. Clearly you need to finish your readings. If you brazenly target members of another Ruin Lord's power base, then the retribution is swift, and often deadly. Highlord Malus would ensure my demise was inescapable if it were known that I slayed Lord Sanata. Reputation is everything in Thanaton. So instead, we must be cunning."

"What do you have in mind?" Vyrion asked, desperately hoping whatever his master said next involved something outside the compound.

"You may have gotten your wish after all," Victus said, giving Vyrion a wry smile and leading him out of the courtyard, "My first task for you is to visit Thanaton's skyport. Dock eighteen. I am expecting the results of the expedition to be delivered, and you must ensure it arrives here untouched. Ask for Sergeant Lorren, he and some of my men have already been sent to retrieve it, but with Lord Sanata's involvement clear, they may require assistance that only a Ruined can provide."

"Skyport. Dock Eighteen," Vyrion repeated, unsure of what either of those designations meant. "What is it that I should be retrieving?"

"A trinket of great importance. Do not let it slip out of your grasp," Lord Victus commanded, "Return with my prize or don't bother returning at all."

Vyrion nodded as Victus looked him over, "I will guard it with my life, master."

And with those final words, the one-legged Ruin Lord gave a satisfied nod and plodded off, taking a deep gulp of whatever foul-smelling liquid he kept in his flask as he did.

Vyrion wasted no time. The compound's gate, once a foreboding wall of iron, now seemed like the portal to a wider world, the guards at either side, clad in black plate and adorned with the one-leg tabard of Victus, no longer moved to bar his path as they had before, only bowing and pulling the gate open for him.

"The skyport is to the far east of the city, my lord. Follow the cargo trolleys," one said.

"Thank you, I will keep that in mind."

And with that, he was finally set free. With one more step, he was out on the compound and in the city.

But it was hardly what he expected. He went right from the quiet calm of a temple to the unrestrained chaos of a melee in a single moment. The streets, canyons cut through structures of stone, were a stampede of humanity, packed crowds pressing in on all sides as though now like a sinister shadow, the unknowns beyond setting Vyrion on edge. He wished he had Krothus nearby, just in case.

But Vyrion hadn't seen or heard a single whisper of Krothus yet. Partners or not, in that docking bay he was alone.

"We will simply have to wait and see. Stay alert." Vyrion said.

"Of course, my lord. We will establish a perimeter."

Sergeant Lorren waved a hand and the soldiers fanned out, taking up positions around the dock. The dock workers themselves didn't move an inch.

Vyrion took the opportunity to look out, inspecting the horizon. A wild jungle stretched as far as he could see, a matted net of dark trees that reached out to the skyline while dark clouds lurked to the East, threatening rain. A sharp drop lurked just a few steps away.

"I see the *Donovan* approaching on schedule, my lord."

Vyrion could only make out the smallest speck in the distance. He wasn't sure what he had been expecting, but as it approached, rapidly growing in size, his breath caught in his throat. He was very glad he'd been able to leave the compound that day.

The *Donovan* slowed its descent as it neared, the hatches on either side of the vessel's metal body glinting in the sun as it hovered into the dock. It looked like a floating fortress; bolted down panels, armored plates, and a cockpit of glass peering out at the rear, Vyrion was left astounded as to how it was able to stay airborne. The only clue towards this were two half-orbs on either side of the skyship's hull, expelling jets of some bright energy that Vyrion sensed somehow carried the Ruin's touch.

With a hiss of steam and the screech of strained metal, the half-orbs cut out and the vessel landed on a trio of thick legs that popped out of the skyship's hull. The resulting thud sent a rumble up Vyrion's legs.

The front of the vessel dropped down and one of the crew stepped down the resultant ramp, signaling the suddenly alert dock workers, who, contrary to their previously determined idleness, quickly sprung into action. Sand-crusted crates, boxes, and barrels were rolled out of the belly of the *Donovan* one by one, not one of them catching Vyrion's eye. Where was the prize Lord Victus so desperately wanted?

A woman swaggered down the ramp, uniform jacket unbuttoned, shirt untucked, and hair a mess.

"Lorren, good to see you," she said casually, throwing up a barely passable salute. "And even brought a Ruined with you this time too, eh?"

"Captain Fareese, this is Lord Victus' latest apprentice," Sergeant Lorren said, robotically gesturing an introduction. "Though I must apologize, I didn't quite catch your name, my Lord."

Vyrion gave her a cursory nod, "Vyrion,"

"*M'lord*" the Captain said, delivering an obviously exaggerated bow. Lorren looked nothing short of horrified at the gesture, while Vyrion was rapidly losing patience.

"Do you have what we want, Captain?" he said coldly.

Fareese cleared her throat. "Right here,"

She leaned down and reached into a small crate, rustling her hand around for a moment, before tossing what she had retrieved over to Vyrion. "I'm not sure what it is, but the excavators told me to keep it close."

The thing flipped towards him. Vyrion, taking no chances, enlisted the Ruin to slowly lower it into his hands. But once it was within his grip, Victus' prize hardly seemed worth the trouble. It was no glowing jewel or ancient runeblade, only a small pyramid of metal, covered in unfamiliar symbols and much heavier than it looked. Vyrion had no idea what importance it held, but the metal facets, icy cold to the touch, were sending chills through his fingers, so he quickly stuffed it into a pouch on his belt.

"Everything in order, *my lord*?" Sergeant Lorren asked, emphasizing the title like a parent trying to teach an unruly child. A quick glance to Captain Fareese revealed the intended target of such a lesson.

"I believe so," Vyrion said, hoping Victus would be satisfied with such an insignificant relic. He turned to Fareese, "Thank you, Captain. I'll be on my way, I assume the Sergeant will handle the rest."

"Make sure Victus sends the payment as soon as he gets the rest of the expedition's findings. I'm not running a charity here," Captain Fareese said, gesturing to the rest of the cargo.

Vyrion rolled his eyes, "I'll be sure to mention it."

Sergeant Lorren, seeming to have had enough of the Captain's snark, unleashed a torrent of words at frightening speed, "Forgive me, Captain, but it is *extraordinarily* disrespectful to be speaking to a Ruined like this. If Lieutenant Farke hears of this, then we will most certainly get disciplined and- "

"Relax Lorren, I've said far worse in-" Captain Fareese said, trying and failing to interject.

"- had enough of being disciplined for such absurd reasons. I will not be roped into another hearing as a character witness, *especially* not after-"

"Lorren, I understand, and I order you to calm down and shut-"

"- affair with the missing provisions. I am not going to risk my family's livelihood and my career to -"

"Those provisions had nothing to do-"

But the sound of the bickering Imperial officers bickering faded into the background as Vyrion felt like his head was assailed by a thick fog.

Something was watching him, he could feel its presence at his back, whispering to him, he could feel its murmurs in his ear. The voice, quiet at first, grew louder and louder until a single word could be heard.

Beware, it hissed.

Vyrion knew he had heard this voice before, the same as during his Kograi. Was it Victus, advising him from afar? It sounded nothing like him. But Vyrion wasted no more time on ponderings, this was a warning he couldn't ignore.

"Sergeant? Captain? We've got company." His raised voice carried through the dock.

Lorren and Fareese immediately fell silent, accusatory fingers drooping in defeat. The dockworkers froze, and the soldiers looked up at Vyrion, runeblade already in his hands.

"Assume defensive positions!" Sergeant Lorren commanded.

Captain Fareese rushed back into her skyship, pulling piercers off a rack inside and tossing them to her crew, while Lorren ducked behind the skyship's ramp and drew a piercer pistol out of the holster on his belt, his half-dozen soldiers behind whatever cover they could find.

The dock workers had already fled, the only sign of their presence a half-eaten sandwich and an upturned trolley with a single squeaky wheel still rolling.

Vyrion didn't seek cover, despite very much wanting to. What kind of Ruined would he be if he hid at the first sign of danger? Instead, he strolled into the center of the dock, runeblade at his side, and waited.

He could hear the rapid footsteps of fleeing dockworkers gradually fade away, only to be replaced by a collection of determined, heavy footfalls. It seemed like his master had been right. Though Lord Sanata must have been feeling particularly confident to send such an attack within Thanaton's walls, it hardly seemed like a place to have such blatant power struggles.

But, while Vyrion expected to see battle-ready Imperial guards stride into the dock, sporting some symbol of Lord Sanata on their tabard, the result was not quite as tidy.

A ragtag mob burst into the dock. Vyrion counted twenty or so, all sporting cloth masks over the lower half of their face and ramshackle weapons in their fists.

Most of them, upon seeing Vyrion and his runeblade, took a hesitant step back, but one, a tall woman with flame-red hair, had no such qualms.

"My employer has purchased the contents of this ship," she declared, hands on the two piercers holstered on her belt. "So stack everything you have to one side, and there won't be any trouble."

"If you thought it would be as easy as that, you are dearly mistaken," Vyrion said, trying his best to sound threatening, an attempt that was severely undermined when his voice cracked midway through.

The woman let out a snort, "You must not have heard me correctly. When you hire Jayn Reed, you can purchase anything you want. My employer wants the contents of this vessel, and I'm here to make sure they get it."

"I'm sure you are. Why don't we discuss an alternative payment, one where you tell us who you're working for, then walk away. Like you said, there doesn't have to be trouble," Vyrion asked, desperately hoping that such a gesture would work. He rotated the hilt of his runeblade in his sweaty palm.

"I was paid plenty," Jayn said, clearly not interested, "There's far too many of us, even for a Ruined, so just give us what we want, and we'll be on our way. Or don't, and there'll be hell to pay."

She cocked her head to the side for a moment, "That rhymed, didn't it?"

One of her gang, a rotund man with a rusted axe, gave her an excited nod.

"Oh good, write that down."

"My lord ..." Sergeant Lorren urged quietly, as the large man quickly pulled out a piece of paper and started scribbling.

Vyrion knew he was out of alternatives. He could already feel the calming rush of battle washing over him, the flash of lightning before the thunder of inevitable violence.

Jayn's hand twitched near her holster. The upturned trolley wheel squeaked. Vyrion's sweaty hands danced near his runeblade hilt.

Then all hell broke loose.

Sergeant Lorren's men fired first, each piercer emitting a dull thud as the bowstring snapped forward. Three of Reed's thugs dropped, bolts punching through armor and flesh, while Jayn Reed herself danced backwards, just managing to evade a sweep of Vyrion's runeblade. Those with their own piercers returned fire, pincushioning two *Donovan* crewmembers in the cargo hold as the rest of Reed's crew roared and rushed towards the ship.

Vyrion cut through the man with the axe, sending papers scattering, then ducked under a piercer bolt to thrust his runeblade through another's breastplate. He was no longer thinking, worrying about what would happen next, he was acting, pure instinct guiding his every movement.

Jayn and her crew quickly turned their attention to him, sending a volley of boltfire his way. Vyrion, getting a sudden feeling to do so, opened his palm in front of him. The Ruin heard his call, halting the swarm of bolts mid-air, before Vyrion sent them flying back with another wave of his hand.

Jayn rolled away just in time, but others weren't so lucky. The shards of metal ripped through anyone not behind cover, a bearded man crashed to the floor with a bolt through the eye, a women slowly collapsed, clutching at the river of red seeping out of her chest, while someone dangled lifelessly from a cargo box, a dozen bolts pinning him to the wood like a grim puppet.

Reed's crew quickly made sure to get behind something solid.

But despite Vyrion being the main target, Lord Victus' forces weren't faring well. Another of the *Donovan's crew* met his end, his body hanging limply off the ramp, while two of Lorren's troops had been cut off and struck down.

Vyrion ducked behind some sand-covered barrels, trying to catch his breath.

"Yanis, covering fire!" Sergeant Lorren shouted.

A soldier peeked out from behind the upturned trolley, sending a barrage of bolts downrange, while Lorren used the opening to sprint to Vyrion, sinking behind a crate that already had close to a dozen bolts stuck to the opposite side.

The Sergeant's voice was hoarse, "My lord, we can only hold them off for a bit longer. You should use the first opportunity to escape with the relic."

The soldier who had covered Lorren's advance thudded to the ground, her armor finally giving out. Jayn Reed laughed at her handiwork, before sending a bolt through the helmet of another soldier nearby.

Reed's laughter echoed in Vyrion's head.

"My lord?"

"Stay there," Vyrion growled, stepping back out into the fray.

Someone charged at him with a crooked sword. But Vyrion barely noticed, only felt the Ruin surge into his hand as he blasted them with a web of lightning, filling the air with the choking stench of burning flesh. Some others joined the attack, only to break their weapons and bodies on his runeblade. He tried to carve a path to Jayn Reed.

But for every enemy swiftly dispatched, another would nearly cut in past Vyrion's guard, or send a bolt a hair's width away from his head. The longer he went on for, the more frequent these slip-ups became, the closer each came to putting an end to his struggle. The training earlier that day had still left him drained and sore, and he knew he was rapidly approaching his limit.

It wasn't long before he collapsed against the dock's wall for a moment of respite, surveying the situation as he did. There was blood seeping through one of his sleeves, but he wasn't sure whose, Sergeant Lorren and his two remaining soldiers were hunkered down, and Captain Fareese, crew slain, was lying prone in the *Donovan*'s cargo bay, shooting anyone unlucky enough to catch her eye. Jayn Reed still had nearly half her forces left.

Vyrion wiped sweat and blood off his face and out of his eyes, feeling disgusting and exhausted. He didn't want to continue, but he had to, he didn't exactly have a choice. All of this was his fault anyways, he was the fool who had wanted to leave the compound wasn't he?

Jayn's grating voice rang out from somewhere, "I have to say, this has been fun. But it won't be for much longer, some friends coming along who aren't quite as merciful as I am. Real dangerous types. No ransoms, no prisoners, no negotiating. So why don't you just hand over what we want so we can stop all this before they get here."

One of the remaining soldiers stood up, no doubt thinking Reed was speaking out in the open. A bolt went right through the visor of his helmet.

Vyrion swore. If what she was saying was true, then that was it. He wouldn't be able to deal with another gang all on his own.

He tried to take a quick peek out of cover, see if he could possibly figure out where Jayn was standing. A bolt nearly took his nose off, his Ruin-enhanced senses only just saving him.

"Now, now, I didn't give you permission to move, Ruined," Jayn tutted.

Vyrion racked his brain for some idea, but he was coming up with nothing.

Some kind of commotion could be heard outside, above the skyport's normal crashes that had no doubt shielded the skirmish from outside interference. Distant shouts, a commanding voice, Vyrion could only guess that Reed's reinforcements were nearly there, heralding his imminent demise. He truly was the worst Ruined in the Empire, killed on his very first -

The thoughts of impending doom suddenly halted. Vyrion could sense another Ruined approaching.

The noises outside grew louder, an avalanche of armored footfalls. If Lord Sanata had sent soldiers and a Ruined of her own, then Vyrion knew there was no possibility of his survival. But somehow, he already knew who it was.

The entrance to the dock was suddenly filled with the dark armor of Imperial soldiers, adorned with the mark of a black sun, their weapons trained on what was left of Reed and her gang. At their head was an armored man with a shaved skull, his skin an unnatural grey.

"Who the hell are you?" Jayn asked, her previous confidence quickly evaporating.

She was slammed to the floor with a crashing wave of the Ruin.

"Someone who you should speak to with respect," snarled Krothus.

Chapter 5
In Debt

The excited murmurs that followed his every step, the elusive sun beaming down on his bare skull, the satisfying rap of his column's synchronized marching - Krothus was very much enjoying his victorious trek through Thanaton. His prisoners, on the other hand, bound, gagged, and roughed up, hardly seemed like they shared his sentiment.

Vyrion, too, seemed to be struggling to find any comfort in their victory. He'd been on edge since the moment Krothus had found him, peering round every corner like death lurked just behind, his runeblade passing from one nervous hand to another. Such dramatics had already dampened Krothus's satisfaction towards their reunion.

"Vyrion, you must calm yourself," Krothus advised, knowing it was futile but trying anyway. "Vigilance is a useful quality, paranoia is not."

"It's hardly paranoia," Vyrion snapped.

"Then what is it?"

Vyrion did not answer.

Krothus gestured to the column marching neatly alongside them. "I highly doubt anyone would assault a platoon of Lord Callida's guards in the middle of Thanaton, not unless they want their entire power base ground to dust. It's paranoia."

Vyrion sighed and looked down at his hands, "It's not paranoia. It's just - I haven't had to do this before."

"What, defend yourself?" Krothus scoffed, "Have you forgotten the last decade of struggle, or are you simply-"

"I've never killed someone, Krothus."

Krothus let out a deep breath. Of course that was it. Finally out of the Ascendancy, and still Vyrion was struggling with foolish notions of morality, ignoring the Code's direction and allowing guilt to burrow itself into his heart. Mercy was for the weak, he must know this. Perhaps Vyrion simply needed another perspective.

"They were criminals and murderers," Krothus said.

"I know."

"They killed your master's soldiers."

"I know."

"They were trying to kill you."

"I *know*, Krothus," Vyrion snapped. "But unfortunately, my feelings cannot be dismissed through a barrage of logic. I simply have to deal with it on my own."

Krothus just shrugged, out of arguments. Vyrion's weakness was a stubborn thing, defiantly present no matter how much power he gathered. Krothus was thankful such things had never troubled him.

"At least put your runeblade away. You seem to be frightening the Imperials."

Anyone nearby, once spotting Vyrion with runeblade in hand, acted with a practiced caution, crossing the street or crowding into nearby shops for shelter. It was the type of casual self-preservation that hinted at an acceptance, an understanding that when a Ruin Lord power struggle was on the horizon, the only real course of action was to scurry away like roaches caught in the light.

It didn't take long for Vyrion to heed Krothus' request and return his runeblade hilt to his belt. A half-hearted smile was attempted to coax them out back onto the street, but Vyrion might as well have screamed threats of violence for all the good it did.

"I'm not meaning to give anyone a scare," Vyrion said, quickly abandoning his futile attempts at reassuring the public, "I just don't want to be caught by surprise again. That's all. "

"Nonsense, Vyrion," Krothus said, trying to put such thoughts to rest, "My master does not allow for surprises. Lord Callida's whisperers are everywhere in this city, and there is not a conversation spoken, not a single plan concocted without going through her first."

Vyrion looked at least a little reassured. "I hope so, for our sake."

Of course, Krothus had left out the small detail of how his master had even known about the attack on Lord Victus' expedition in the first place. Such things were not meant to be explained on such open streets.

A spindly officer, one of Lord Victus' few remaining troops, appeared next to them, "Pardon the interruption, my lords, but we have arrived."

Sure enough, a stout keep sat ahead, its walls covered in banners depicting a metal leg. Krothus wondered if Lord Victus had picked his crest as some kind of joke.

The column halted as Krothus turned to address them. Watching as his troops stopped in unison, looking to him for guidance, was enough to set his blood pumping.

"Bring the prisoners and the bodies of Lord Victus' men inside," he demanded, careful to pick the most commanding tone he could muster. "The rest of you remain here until I return."

The troops wordlessly followed his orders, a squad bringing Reed and what remained of her gang to the compound's gatehouse while the rest stood at attention outside, the armored formation enough to make Imperials avoid the street altogether. Krothus followed Vyrion into the compound.

At every turn, Krothus was met with suspicion. Guards and servants alike stopped to watch him enter, their gazes lingering on the bodies his men brought in, before quickly deeming him to be at fault. Even the potted plants seemed hostile. But if their goal was to intimidate, it was failing spectacularly - Krothus ate up their derision and fear like it were his last meal. To fear him or worship him, it was an acknowledgement of his strength just the same.

Only when he found himself face-to-face with Lord Victus in the center of the compound's courtyard, the usual bleak grey of Thanaton's sky looming over them, did Krothus' confidence start to decay. The aged Ruin Lord's watchful eyes seemed to pick up on something

Krothus had missed, this unknown secret emerging out of his beard of black and grey through a knowing smile.

"Lord Callida has my gratitude for intervening at the skyport, I was not expecting such heavy-handedness, or I would have sent more men," Lord Victus began, "Jayn Reed's gang is a notorious name in criminal circles, and they do not come cheap."

Vyrion had already handed over the small pouch he held, whatever prize lurked inside important enough that his master immediately pocketed it.

"For such notorious names they were rather disappointing," Krothus declared, eager to put to rest any false weaknesses Victus had perceived of him, even if Vyrion looked decidedly unappreciative of the comment.

The one-legged Ruin Lord hobbled over for a closer look, that blasted smile still lurking in his beard. "Callida has found quite the weapon in you. But she has many apprentices, all with great potential, and none with your blind arrogance. Now, what do you want?"

Krothus felt anger bubble up inside him, an overboiled pot threatening to burn whoever dared to hold it. But despite this, he forced himself to remain calm - his master had a message for him to deliver, and she did not want him conjuring up new enemies in the process. So he cleared his throat and tried his best to sound neutral.

"My master wishes to inform you-"

"And I wish to hear whatever message your master has for me in private," Victus interrupted bluntly, gesturing to Krothus' troops nearby with his hip flask before taking a swig out of it.

Krothus gave his soldiers a curt nod, and they marched back out of the compound, leaving the Ruined to their own devices in a courtyard emptied of any servants or soldiers. He could hear his heart beating in his ears, such was his rising fury.

"Good. Now, speak."

Using every ounce of willpower he possessed to swallow his growing rage, Krothus cleared his throat and relayed what he had been told. "Lord Callida reminds you of your great debt. It is time that is repaid."

Victus stroked his grey stubble as he stared up at Krothus, who defiantly matched the veteran's gaze with his own, pretending he knew all about this debt. Of course, suffering the disdainful position of a mere messenger, Krothus knew close to nothing, only that Victus would ask a single question, a question Krothus held the answer to.

"Fine," Victus grunted. "Who is it that is such a needle in Callida's side? If she is resorting to cashing in decades-old debts she must be truly desperate."

Krothus answered, repeating a name he knew nothing about, a name that Victus took like a slap in the face.

"Highlord Malus."

"Preposterous!" Victus roared, "Of all people ... Highlord Malus is second to only the Ruined Council, Callida has truly lost her mind if she expects me to-"

With each harsh word that boomed across the courtyard, the ground rumbled beneath their feet and even the clouds seemed to darken in a shared anger. Vyrion had already taken a cautionary step back, an action Krothus was rapidly considering.

But as suddenly as Lord Victus' outburst had started, he grew quiet. The aged Ruin Lord was nodding, each bob of his head accompanied by some muttered secret under his breath. And, with one last gulp of his flask and a sudden hobbled step forward, Lord Victus was now inches from Krothus' face.

"So *that's* why she's sent you parading through my doors. What was your name again, boy?" His breath reeked of some acidic substance Krothus didn't recognise. Whatever Vyrion's master was drinking, it wasn't booze, but it seemed to help his mood just the same.

"Krothus."

The Ruin Lord might have been smiling, but the look in Victus' eyes was hardly reassuring. Some fanatic hunger, some obsession, lurked just beyond his greying brows. Krothus felt a strong need to push him away.

But Victus kept smiling, like they were old friends with nothing amiss. "Yes, of course - the acolyte with the runeblade of flame, I remember now. As for my debt, Lord Callida and I will have similar goals for the moment, and thus, so shall our apprentices. You and young Vyrion will be working closely once more it seems."

"What do you mean, master?" Vyrion sputtered out. His poor attempt at innocence wouldn't have fooled a beggar, let alone a Ruin Lord, but Vyrion had never been a good liar. It was clear as day that he and Krothus were not as hostile as rival Ruined should be.

Lord Victus let out a hearty laugh, "Please, Vyrion, did you think your master blind as well as crippled? Allies, when they can be trusted, are useful. Playing politics in Thanaton will get you many times further than any military campaigns will, as I have spent many years coming to terms with."

Victus took one last glance at Krothus as he capped his now empty flask, "Return to your master. Tell her I will begin preparations at once, and all of us will have their part to play. After this the debt will be paid."

"I will relay the message."

"Come, Vyrion."

Without another word, Lord Victus shambled off, with Vyrion close behind. Krothus barely managed a nod to his partner before he passed out of sight.

The first move in some vast game had been played, a game that Krothus knew he was merely a piece in. An apprentice, a weapon, a messenger; his role mattered not, all of it was no more than a farce, a parade for titles and favour. It was beneath him. His destiny, his glorious purpose, was far beyond any of this nonsense, and if the Ruin Lords refused to see the naked truth, then he needed to show them.

Krothus stomped out of Victus' compound, crashing through some fool servant who made the unwise decision to try and pass in front of him.

The column of his troops remained waiting outside.

"We're leaving!" Krothus shouted, nearly kicking the soldier closest by. The column sensibly marched at double time.

Content to let the soldiers lead the way through the still unfamiliar Thanaton streets, Krothus instead spent his time glaring at any Imperial unfortunate enough to catch his gaze.

Every night spent in the Ascendancy, Krothus had dreamt of being a Ruined; leading campaigns at his master's side, crushing the Emperor's enemies underfoot, and most importantly, being recognised for greatness. Instead, he'd been a hostage in his master's compound for weeks to study and train, only being released to serve as a glorified errand boy. It was unacceptable.

Krothus continued to seethe the rest of the journey back to his master's compound. Only once the blood-red visage of the Dark Pyramid loomed just overhead and the streets shifted from rough cobble to smooth, fine stone did he realize they had arrived. Lord Victus might have been a Ruin Lord by title, but his compound was a spartan hovel compared to how a proper Ruined like Lord Callida conducted her estate. Vast battlements and spiraled towers rose up into the sky like they were clawing their way to the grand height of the Dark Pyramid itself.

The soldiers looked to him expectantly, but Krothus was in no mood for pleasantries. He swept a dismissive hand at them. "You are dismissed."

Krothus didn't bother to check if they followed his orders, he was already striding through the gatehouse and into the fortress beyond. The black suns sewn onto every rich tapestry he passed watched him like a mocking eye, the squeaks of the overly polished stone ridiculing him with every step. His master was going to understand the insult she had delivered to him.

But just as Krothus neared Callida's quarters, two people stepped out from beyond her gilded door. One was a stocky woman, with an ugly face tattoo and wide bat-like ears that Krothus hoped would let her hear every snide comment made about her crooked teeth. The other was a tall man who looked too stupid to realize he had only trimmed his neat goatee, leaving the rest of his hair long and unkempt.

They stopped once they saw Krothus, barring his way.

"Get out of my way," Krothus snarled.

"Ah, the grey brute can speak," the bat-eared woman sneered, before turning to her companion. "Our master didn't mention she had picked up a new pet, did she?"

The tall man laughed and shook his head, "Play nice, Nara - we should introduce ourselves first. You must be Krothus."

The man tried to initiate a handshake, but Krothus said and did nothing, too preoccupied glaring at the woman who had insulted him. He was happy to see the handshake slowly retracted.

"I am Amar," the long-haired man said, remaining cool despite the rebuked handshake, "And this is Nara. We are also Lord Callida's apprentices, though far senior. I'm sure you will be seeing-"

"I don't care. Move."

Krothus saw their runeblade hilts at their sides. Could he cut them down before they had a chance to react?

Amar laughed once more, though not a speck of humor hidden within it. "Beware, Krothus. Growing rivals into outright enemies is a fool's gamble. I've seen far too many apprentices burn their flame too bright, too early. It only leaves you in cinders."

Krothus didn't respond, only letting a long silence drag on and on, each second past drawing the tension out further and further. His two rival apprentices shared an unreadable glance, but remained in place. If they still weren't going to let him through, then they had chosen their fate. He reached out through the Ruin, feeling the metal touch of his runeblade, preparing to send it flying into his hand to cut these fools down.

But before any of them could do anything, an incredible wave of power crashed into them. Krothus was sent to the floor and held there, his head stuck uncomfortably against the cool ground, facing the entrance to Lord Callida's chambers. Two heeled boots of fine black leather stepped out from the doorway.

"My apprentices, as much as I am flattered to see you fighting for my favour, we do not have time for it today," she purred. "Amar. Nara. You have your missions, do not waste time here."

The Ruin's hold, pressing down like it were stood on Krothus' chest, was relinquished with a snap of her fingers.

"Yes, master," Amar and Nara said in unison, hastily getting up and bowing before they left. Amar gave Krothus a wink as he passed by.

Not wanting to look weak, Krothus stood up as well. Callida looked him over, clearly unhappy.

"As for you, Krothus, put your weapon away and calm yourself. Blind rage is as useful as pure cowardice - a Ruined must be able to draw on the power of his emotions, not be led by them. Now come, my power base needs to be unified for what lies ahead, and we have much to discuss."

"Yes, master," Krothus parroted, any previous thoughts of insubordination calmed by her presence as he followed her. He had never been in Lord Callida's chambers; she normally sought him training in the drill yard, or in his own rooms. The gilded doors shut behind him.

While Krothus' chambers were comfortable and spacious, a notable step up from his tiny room at the Ascendancy, his master's were on a separate level entirely. A large window framed the Dark Pyramid as if it were a piece of fine art, painting the rest of the room in a soft crimson glow, the endless racks of potions and vials refracting the light into shadows and back again. In the far corner, some cauldron bubbled and smoldered, casting some bitter taste on the air.

"So," Lord Callida began, sliding behind a fine desk draped in crimson silk, "What was Lord Victus' response?"

"He seemed furious initially, but eventually changed his tune. Preparations will begin at once."

A wide smile stretched across Lord Callida's face. "Excellent. I knew he would need an extra push, hence why I sent you to the skyport today. Not only did it further indebt Victus to me, but it also demonstrated that I knew about his little prize and could have easily taken it from him if I so wished."

Krothus hadn't considered such things, but she was right. Had he been told to take the contents of the ship, Vyrion and his pitiful band of survivors wouldn't have stood a chance. Though he refused to think about the consequences for their partnership if it had come to that. He had better things to ponder over, like the reasoning behind the campaign for Lord Victus' support. What was the goal?

Only then did Krothus feel some itch within his mind, like some creature had crawled in through his ears to pick away at his thoughts.

Callida was smirking at him, "I do suppose you want some sort of explanation as to what's going on?"

The itch ceased. Callida was able to read his mind far too easily, a complication Krothus could do without.

"You enlisted Lord Victus' help for something involving this Highlord Malus," he said, ignoring the blatant invasion of his mental privacy. "But why Victus owes you a debt, and the Highlord himself, are a mystery to me."

Callida nodded, then swivelled round in her chair to gaze upon the Dark Pyramid.

"The Ruined Council is the true prize in this city. Second only to the Emperor, the Council commands every Ruin Lord in the Empire, every army, every soldier. They create the legacy of the nation, and so too can they change it all. To gain a seat among the thirteen, which I intend to, you must possess an incomparable amount of both cunning and power. I will demonstrate both in the coming months."

Krothus could feel the sea of Ruinous energy around them ripple with Callida's words. He felt her determination, her deep desire.

She swivelled back around, "But I have an obstacle in my way. Do you know what it is, my apprentice?"

Recalling his reading the days prior, Krothus answered immediately. "Only Highlords are considered for positions on the council."

"Correct," Callida said, "But one does not become a Highlord without proving you are worthy of the title. And what better way to prove yourself worthy than demonstrate someone else is not?"

"So you intend to take Highlord Malus' position," Krothus said, mulling it over himself. A Highlord was a formidable opponent, they had power bases that dwarfed even the strongest Ruin Lords and were blessed by the Ruin in ways that many could only dream of. To challenge one was an ambition that Krothus could respect.

Callida nodded. "I do, but the Council does not appreciate blatant power struggles. It makes them nervous, concerned about the potential fallout in Thanaton or abroad. So we must be cunning. You have completed the first step today; Lord Victus serves Malus, recruiting him to my cause both strengthens my position while weakening his."

"Won't Victus face consequences for his insubordination?" Krothus knew that if one of the lesser Lords commanded by Callida suddenly had notions of rebellion, she would crush them without mercy. An example to any others with similarly misguided ideas. Vyrion didn't deserve to have his tenure cut short simply because his master was a buffoon.

"He would, if he was to demonstrate it openly. But Victus is no fool, so he will be cautious, ensuring he maintains the image of the Highlord's loyal servant."

"And what of Victus' debt?" Krothus asked, feeling like his window for any further explanations was rapidly closing.

Callida's eyes flitted to her cauldron, simmering its bloodlike contents, lazily emitting fumes. "Let us just say that if not for me, he would have lost a great deal more than a leg."

Krothus opened his mouth to ask another question, but his master waved a hand, and he fell silent.

"A story for another time perhaps, my apprentice," Callida said, clearly finished with their idle chit chat, "I have a more important matter to discuss with you."

"Of course, master."

"I must begin dismantling Lord Malus' power base while also securing my own. You, along with every other weapon at my disposal, will be the tools I use to chop up his forces piece by piece, until he is open and vulnerable."

Krothus nodded. Finally, this sounded like a mission worthy of him, one that would begin his path to greatness.

Lord Callida got up from her desk and looked out the window just behind. "Lord Fira is one of Highlord Malus' longtime allies. She was banished from Thanaton for attempting to storm another Ruin Lord's compound in broad daylight, and now cowers in a jungle fortress outside the city, wallowing in paranoia and fear. Fira is unpredictable, which makes her dangerous."

Krothus couldn't believe it. Did his master intend for him to kill a full Ruin Lord?

"I will strike her down," Krothus declared, masking his uncertainty with bravado.

But Callida just chuckled. "Unnecessary. Nara, who you just recently became acquainted with, has successfully infiltrated Lord Fira's compound, spying upon her for nearly a year. She has uncovered a most startling weakness to be exploited."

Krothus raised an eyebrow.

Lord Callida's serene face became marred by a predatory grin. "Lord Fira has a daughter."

Chapter 6
Ghosts

Vyrion sat in his chambers, his only companion taking the form of a lonely candle, desperately trying to hold back the darkness as it slowly dwindled away. It mirrored his own struggles, trying in vain to keep those anxious voices in the back of his mind tamed.

Sleep was an enticing prospect, but Vyrion's mind refused to consider it. There was too much occupying his thoughts.

The pyramid artifact stood on his table, its metal facets seeming to greedily swallow up the candle's rationed light. There was no reflection, no glint in the dark, the relic was like a hole of blackness darker than any shadow, its true purpose elusive.

Contrary to any logic, Lord Victus had insisted that Vyrion, despite being his most inexperienced apprentice, be the one to unlock the relic's secrets. Vyrion figured the Ruin Lord surely had some idea, or he wouldn't have brought the thing back in the first place, so perhaps confirming his master's suspicions would be enough. But why Victus couldn't do it himself was anyone's guess. He had spent that afternoon barking orders to Vyrion and two of his other apprentices, Lash and Partha, pretending he were some general of some besieged city. Defend this, confirm that, intimidate them; he had issued commands as if he had only hours to live. By the time he had finished, the two women had gone off to secure Victus' holdings, while Vyrion had been given the relic and the seemingly impossible duty of discovering its purpose without the slightest clue where to start.

But even with such a monumental task, his mind had stubbornly refused to commit to the investigation, instead lingering on recent events. Finally seeing Thanaton, committing to his new role as a Ruined, how Krothus had returned at just the right time to save his life - much had changed in such a short time.

And most puzzling of all, there was that voice that appeared in his mind. It was the second time he'd heard it, once in his Kograi, and another in the skyport, and still Vyrion was no closer to finding out its source. Who could have taken such an interest in him? And more importantly, why?

He had many questions and little in the way of answers. The only thing he knew for sure was that sitting in bed wasn't helping anyone. So he got dressed, snatched up the relic, and slipped out into the pitch black corridor, electing to leave the dwindling candle to its fate and instead painted the walls with the crimson light from his runeblade.

The compound was deathly silent at this hour. During the day, the heavy footfalls of patrols echoed from nearby corridors, servants whispered gossip in the doorways, and distant clangs of metal rang out from the drill yard. But now, there was nothing, all except his own quiet breaths and the steady hum of his weapon.

The shadows yawned and twisted as he moved the runeblade to light his way, shady faces and silhouettes lurking in every dark pocket, only to vanish when faced with the brightness of those crimson runes.

A Ruined afraid of the dark. Krothus would have thought it a joke. Vyrion shamelessly quickened his pace.

Before long, he was heaving open the heavy doors to Lord Victus' personal library. Its shelves spiraled up several levels of one of the compound's towers, and to Vyrion's relief, it was protected against the night by a legion of candles, each burning bright and proud, without a hint of the weakness shown by the lone soldier burnt out in his room. Glass in the roof above sent beams of moonlight flickering and dancing across the floor whenever a flock of Thanaton's bats flew overhead.

Lord Victus had collected a vast amount of knowledge during his tenure as a Ruin Lord, though how much of it was actually useful was a different story. Bookcases packed every available space, stuffed to the brim with papers and tomes, none of them labeled or organised with any degree of sense.

He sighed. Maybe this was all he was good for, the only Ruined in Thanaton relegated to library duty. He started dusting off ragged volumes and tugging out lone papers of indecipherable scrawl, looking for anything of use.

It was going to be a long night.

Several hours later, with towers of wasted knowledge piled up around him, Vyrion was on the verge of admitting defeat. He'd learned a great deal about things he didn't need; the vassalage of the orkathi jungle tribes, proper protocol for dealing with Jaykaborian Clans, even the strict laws of the Popularii Republic's warrior monks. But still, the information he sought eluded him.

He gathered what remained of his willpower for one last search of the uppermost level of the library, urging his tired body up the creaky stairs as best he could. A single bat watched him from the window above as his fingers skated across faded spines, only affording them a brief caress as he skimmed their title for anything to go on.

Great Skyship Engagements of the Second War.
The Ruin and The Deus.
Ancient Empires: The Nightmare Lord.

Useless. Vyrion considered tossing these wastes of space over the railing.

Managing to resist the urge to do so, Vyrion instead picked up the pyramid relic, its facets of strange symbols nearly buried under a cocoon of crumpled diagrams. Turning the cool, smooth metal in his hands, feeling his tired eyes droop, it seemed best to leave the relic a mystery for now and try again tomorrow, armed with a good night's sleep. He was obviously not getting anywhere tonight. With one last look of defeat split between the rows of half-empty shelves and the piles of half-read books, he started towards the stairs.

But whether it was a change of light, or some kind of premonition, something caught Vyrion's eye.

An inky black tome, so dark as to be indistinguishable from the shadows, occupied a corner that Vyrion had previously thought empty. Just looking at it seemed wrong, like its very presence was a mistake. Vyrion's heart raced as he reached out to it. This one surely held the answers he was hunting for.

The moment he felt the slick, almost oily, cover, desperate whispers filled his mind. They came from everywhere at once, a storm of hasty breath and hurried words.

"*Immortality...*" some voice hissed, sultry and enticing.

"*Power...*" another said, guttural and rotten.

"*Lies!*" replied that familiar voice in Vyrion's head, booming out above all others.

The longer he held onto the cover, the louder their words became, leaving Vyrion barely able to decipher any more than a few words from what had become a deafening chorus of ghostly voices.

"*Unlock the secrets...*"

"*... Eternal damnation...*"

"*Blood and bone...*"

"*Flee...*"

Vyrion heeded that final word, finally managing to rip his hand away, only to stumble back and topple over a stack of papers in the process. The relic tumbled out of his fingers.

Without a roll or bounce, it plunged directly down onto its bottom face, landing with a single deep thunk that echoed across the library like the shutting of a monstrous door.

The symphony of whispers fell silent.

To say he was shocked was a massive understatement. Vyrion was nothing short of terrified. What in the Emperor's name had just happened? He still clutched the book, unnaturally slick as it was, in his trembling hands. Every part of him seemed to regard the thing as a danger, but Vyrion's curiosity outweighed his instincts; it was the only good lead he had found all night and he wasn't about to give it up this easily. So he pushed down his fear in the name of his investigation and reached out towards the relic once more.

Its metal facets watched with a silent menace as his hand inched towards it. Closer and closer he crept, until his fingers once again found the relic's cool embrace.

"*Power.*"

Vyrion's shot his hand back as if the metal pyramid had bitten him. The voices didn't follow.

"Right," Vyrion muttered to himself, as he looked to his hand for any kind of damage. "Holding both doesn't seem like the best idea."

Satisfied that he had suffered nothing but a scare, he left the small pyramid where it stood and turned his attention to the book itself.

Mouth dry and palms sweaty, Vyrion shakily opened the inky black cover.

Inside was an ocean of unrecognizable scrawl. Page after page, brutish runes forced themselves across the page without the slightest uniformity. Vyrion continued flipping pages, hoping for some sort of insight, but all he could understand were the illustrations. And that was horror enough.

One picture was of a man, slowly decaying each page that he appeared until he was a pile of bones and rotten flesh. In another, a woman looked to be draining the life out of a screaming child, who crumbled to dust. A laughing skull wreathed in flame, a man burning to death, a horde of demons slumbering in the depths of the earth; with each turn, another grisly image crawled out of its pages.

Hoping that he could get a better sense of the book in proper lighting, Vyrion moved closer to a bank of nearby candles.

Only then did he realize that it was written in blood.

He slammed the book shut.

A step creaked from the stairs just below.

Vyrion stopped mid breath, his ability to listen dampened by his heartbeat roaring through his ears.

Another stair shifted, no quieter than a bat's squeak. The sea of the Ruin around Vyrion shifted ever so slightly. Another Ruined was here.

Vyrion tossed the book away and jumped to his feet, runeblade in hand. He ignited it just in time.

The two runeblades collided with a crackling hiss. Bright sparks of green lit up one half of the room, while Vyrion's coiled runeblade flooded his side with its crimson glow. The two Ruined struggled to gain an advantage, but their weapons held firm, the blades scraping across each other in a near-perfect stalemate.

Halfway blinded, and desperate to create some distance, Vyrion spun away. His opponent did the same, only then allowing Vyrion to catch a glimpse of his attacker.

Armed with a messy mop of hair and kind eyes that echoed the deep emerald of his weapon, the man hardly seemed the assassin type. This was further confirmed when his next move was to stare blankly at Vyrion, as if he had accidentally walked into the wrong room.

He suddenly retracted his runeblade, laughing as he did. "Apologies, you must be Vyrion!"

Vyrion stayed where he was, vigilant, but more confused than threatened. "And who in the Emperor's name are you meant to be?"

"I'm Jarek," he said, looking more embarrassed than anything else, like he had only spilled Vyrion's drink rather than nearly lopped his head off. "I was out for an evening stroll and heard some commotion in the library. I thought someone had broken in. Though I probably should have asked who it was first, then we might have avoided this little misunderstanding."

"Misunderstanding?" Vyrion bristled, "You could have killed me if I hadn't heard you."

Jarek flashed a grin that made Vyrion want to hit him. "I highly doubt our master would put that relic in your hands if you were that incompetent."

Vyrion should have guessed, he'd heard quite a bit about the senior apprentice from their master. "Your insight isn't as valuable as you think it is, considering you weren't invited to Lord Victus' briefing this morning."

Jarek shrugged. "Oh I was, I just chose not to go. Victus entrusts me with far more delicate tasks, the kind that should not be shared in a briefing."

Vyrion elected to ignore the obvious jab at his research assignment and retracted his runeblade, confident that Jarek was not a threat, just an overconfident idiot. But he could feel Jarek's gaze on him.

"Anything else?" Vyrion asked, raising his eyebrows at the senior apprentice. "Or are you simply going to stare at me with that dumb grin on your face?"

"Bold in your assumptions," Jarek said, still maintaining said dumb grin before pointing at the floor just across from Vyrion, "But I'm looking at *that*. I've read nearly everything in this library over the last few years, but I've never seen anything that ... ominous."

Vyrion looked down. The black book was sat between them, open to a page displaying yet another grisly diagram, this time featuring what seemed like some ghastly spirit being ripped from someone's body by some metal contraption. If Vyrion looked hard enough at it, it might have looked a bit like the relic he was charged with, but without any knowledge of the strange runes lining the page he couldn't be sure.

"Your guess is as good as mine," Vyrion said, "I have no idea how to decipher it."

Jarek came closer, "I've seen similar runes at some of our master's previous dig sites, but nothing this complete before."

"So Victus could know their origins?" Vyrion asked. That would be a good place to start.

"More likely than anyone else, at least. The old man is surprisingly well read for someone who spent half his life on the battlefield," Jarek said.

Happy his night of investigating had gotten somewhere after all, Vyrion leaned down and picked up the black book. For whatever reason, suspicion, irritation, perhaps even curiosity, he looked up at Jarek as he did. Jarek's emerald eyes remained fixed to the open page, but noticing Vyrion's gaze, Jarek looked up too. His face was only a few inches away.

Jarek flashing that infuriating grin again, with those annoyingly perfect teeth and stupid freckled nose. "Who's staring now, Vyrion?"

Vyrion felt his cheeks flush as a wave of heat emanated off his face. He slammed the black book shut. "I was waiting for you to finish gawking at this so I could bring the damn thing to Victus, that's all. I would like to sleep at some point tonight, you know."

"Sorry for holding you up then," Jarek laughed, holding his hands up in mock surrender and stepping away.

Vyrion, fuming, wasted no time in speeding towards the stairs, desperate to put an end to the whole thing. He couldn't decide whether to describe the senior apprentice as an arrogant fool or an overconfident idiot, both seemed equally fitting.

"Vyrion?"

He stopped mid-step, "What?"

"Didn't you forget something, or was this meant as a gift?" Jarek said, pointing at the relic, still on the floor where Vyrion had left it.

Overconfident idiot, Vyrion decided.

He looked at the unassuming metal object biding its time on the floor. Recalling the effect it had when holding the black book at the same time, Vyrion decided on a different course of action.

"It *is* a gift, it means you're now coming to see Victus with me," Vyrion said, reaching out with the Ruin to levitate the relic into Jarek's hand.

Jarek rolled his eyes as he snatched the artifact out of the air, but made no protest. Vyrion was sure they could stomach each other's presence for a bit longer.

The pair of them made their way out of the library before navigating their way through the compound corridors to Lord Victus' chambers. Vyrion wouldn't admit it, but he appreciated Jarek's presence in the dark, it did not seem nearly as intimidating as it had been on his own.

The chamber doors were made of metal thick enough to stop a skyship crashing through them. But only moments after Vyrion knocked, a symphony of muffled clunks rose up from within, and the doors swung inwards.

Lord Victus hobbled into view, wrapped in the embrace of some night robes, breathing heavy enough that he could have just escaped the grasp of some furious predator.

"I sensed you discovered something only moments ago. Tell me what you found," he rasped. The Ruin Lord did not look well, his skin was pale, with a light cake of sweat over his brow.

"Master, are you alright?" Vyrion asked, concerned. He had never seen him look like this, the Ruin Lord looked haggard, drained.

"I'm fine." Victus had a coughing fit into his hand.

"You look like shit, Victus," Jarek said bluntly.

Victus glared at him. As he did, Vyrion could see something lurking just beneath the hem of his master's night robes, a shadow of scarring across his chest where the flesh had been blackened and twisted.

Catching Vyrion's eye, Victus drew the robes closer, concealing his chest. "Do not insult me with another word of this nonsense. Come in and explain what you discovered immediately."

The two apprentices dutifully followed him into his chambers. To Vyrion's surprise, they weren't much larger than his own. A worn bookshelf oversaw a simple cot, covered in ragged blankets, while Lord Victus' battle armor was proudly displayed on a rack in the center of the room, the interlocked set of godrium plating covered in a myriad of scars. A small kitchen was huddled into the corner almost as an afterthought.

Lord Victus limped over to a metal container hidden just behind his bed, on top of which was his hip flask. As expected, he went to take a swig, but despite him craning his head all the way back, and even shaking the flask for good measure, not a single drop came to wet his thirst. Swearing under his breath, Victus quickly leaned down to fill it up via a tap on one side of the container, his hands trembling, his motions panicked.

"Master, are you sure-" Vyrion started.

"I said not another word!" the Ruin Lord shouted suddenly, swiping his free hand at them. A wave of Ruinous power crashed into Vyrion and Jarek, tossing them into the air with ease.

Jarek, somehow half expecting it, managed to use the Ruin himself to quickly return to solid ground.

Vyrion, caught by surprise, flew into the nearby wall.

Clutching the now-throbbing back of his head, Vyrion could see Victus furiously gulping at his flask the moment he had refilled it.

Groaning, Vyrion looked up at Jarek for some kind of explanation. The senior apprentice, finally acting serious, only responded with a jabbed finger, telling him to stay put.

Vyrion, head pounding and back aching, did not object.

"Master, we mean no disrespect, we simply wish to convey our discovery, as you requested," Jarek said, voice even and tone calm.

Lord Victus ran a scarred hand through his retreating hairline and set the flask down, looking up at the ceiling as if it held the answers to life's mysteries. Whether he had heard Jarek or not, he said nothing.

Jarek persisted, holding the relic out to him. "Master, do you wish to hear what we have discovered?"

Vyrion held his breath. But just as soon as the storm had come, the clouds parted and Victus let out a deep breath, his tired eyes turning back from above and looking to his apprentices.

"Both of you, I apologize. I did not sleep well."

"The dream again?" Jarek asked.

Lord Victus looked at Vyrion for a moment before answering, as if he had briefly forgotten he were there, but nodded nonetheless. "My mind enjoys poking at old wounds."

"In that case, let's have some tea," Jarek interjected suddenly, outmaneuvering any potential silence. He quickly moved over to the kitchen, pulling out cups and implements with a practiced familiarity. There were no objections.

Before long, all three of them sat at the table with warm cups of tea in their hands and the black book and relic placed, the world's strangest table ornaments, in the center of them. Vyrion had explained everything, only omitting anything that would draw his sanity into question, such as hearing voices that were clearly not your own in your head.

"This book has remained in my library for over two decades," Victus said, barely touching his tea, "But I was never able to pry it open. Some kind of sorcery protected it, kept its secrets locked within its cover.

Now, it seems, that relic has somehow unlocked the contents within."

"If it has been here that long, why have I never seen it before?" Jarek asked.

Victus ran one calloused finger over the inky black cover. "Because it moves."

"Moves?" Vyrion asked. He hadn't seen it do that.

"It places itself in the library seemingly at random. Sometimes it disappears entirely, only for me to find it in my chambers, or in the guardhouse, or sitting in the courtyard," Victus explained, frowning at the book as if he expected it to teleport away at that very moment.

Vyrion and Jarek too, looked at the black book, curiously sipping away at their tea.

"Where did you find it originally?" Jarek pressed.

Victus waved a dismissive hand. "Unimportant. What matters now is this diagram you have discovered and the runes it is written in. You have both done well for uncovering this."

Vyrion was ecstatic. He had done *well*. Sure, Jarek was being lumped in with his glory, but that didn't matter, Vyrion was happy to share if it meant he was becoming a Ruined his master could rely on.

But Jarek spoke up. "Apologies, master, but I had no hand in this, it was all Vyrion's doing. I just happened to run into him."

Lord Victus gulped down the remainder of his tea all in one go. "Excellent work then, Vyrion. Clearly this task was all too easy for one with a mind like yours."

If Vyrion had been happy before, he was positively ecstatic now, the cursed voices that normally held him in such low regard had fallen completely silent. He was all smiles, finding himself looking at Jarek, who grinned right back. The senior apprentice might have been an overconfident idiot, but he was growing on him.

"Seeing as you have recently become available, Vyrion, I have a new task for you," Victus said, pushing himself to his feet suddenly. "One that you will find far more challenging."

Vyrion nodded, eager to please.

"But first," Lord Victus began, turning to his other apprentice.

"Jarek, I do not want you awake at this hour with such important duties in the coming weeks, return to your chambers and get some rest."

Jarek seemed surprised at the sudden dismissal, but honored his master's request nonetheless. He bowed to Lord to Victus before he left, only acknowledging Vyrion with some kind of mock salute when he was halfway out the room. Why Jarek was chosen as an apprentice was a mystery Vyrion still couldn't comprehend, but he still had to stifle a laugh at his antics, though he was absolutely sure they weren't funny.

Victus only started speaking once the thick metal doors to his chambers slammed shut once more.

"Lord Callida will be sending her newest apprentice out of the city soon. I want you to accompany him."

"Krothus?" Vyrion asked, "How do you know?"

"Because it's what I would do," the one-legged Ruin Lord said simply. "Highlord Malus has a powerful ally, but she is isolated, making it easier to corner her in relative secrecy. Callida will target her first if she is truly committed to her new path. And Krothus, despite being an arrogant ass, has her eye at the moment, so she will try to test him."

Vyrion nodded, noting his master's dislike of Krothus but not exactly disagreeing. "Who is this ally?"

"Lord Fira. She dwells in the jungles outside of Thanaton, and hardly involves herself in Imperial politics any longer. Unless Highlord Malus calls on her, of course. But that is rare. So naturally, if something were to happen to her, no one would know for quite a while."

Vyrion was following, but still didn't understand one aspect, "So is Lord Callida sending Krothus to kill her?"

Even with both of them, Vyrion doubted they could take on a Ruin Lord. Did Victus think they could? Was this a test he knew Vyrion would fail?

Lord Victus shrugged and took a swig from his flask, "Possibly. Though, knowing her, it is more likely one of her whisperers figured out some way to tame Fira, keep her in line. But that is irrelevant. I need time to decipher this book and confirm this relic's true purpose. This will delay my contribution towards Callida's little power play, which she will not appreciate. So, sending you is a clear indication of my support, which will hopefully be a suitable gesture. Enough to keep her happy at least."

It made sense, though Vyrion could only imagine what kind of debt Victus must owe Callida to warrant such concern.

Lord Victus hobbled over to his suit of armor, running a single finger down a long gouge down one side of the armored plates. The Ruin twisted and swirled around him.

"But regardless of what her apprentice is there to do," Victus said quietly, "I want you to make sure Fira suffers."

"I ... will try, master," Vyrion said hesitantly, not sure how he felt about the request but feeling it unwise to argue. "May I ask why?"

Lord Victus turned away from his armor to look back at Vyrion. His eyes carried with them a craze, a hatred, that made Vyrion want to simply run away. But despite every instinct he possessed screaming at him to flee, Vyrion stayed put.

Victus drew his lips back a feral snarl. "That witch took my fucking leg."

Chapter 7
The Drop

Mumbled morning conversations, accentuated by screeching cargo trolleys and the dull roar of skyships, composed an infuriating symphony that rang through the skyport, an unrequested encore going again and again. Krothus hated it, gripping his belt so tightly that he threatened to crumble the metal to dust. If he had to wait another minute in this hellpit, he was going to kill someone.

"You're in danger of rupturing a vein, gray one. Relax, they'll be here soon," said Captain Fareese, leaning against one of her ship's landing legs as if she hadn't a care in the world. She lit up another smokestick as Krothus considered whether her death would make him feel any better.

"If I wanted to hear your input, I would have asked you for it," he snapped, resisting the urge for just a little longer.

Fareese shrugged and took a drag of her smokestick.

Krothus turned back to stare at the port entrance. As frustrating as it was, he couldn't simply stroll out of Thanaton to wherever Lord Fira's jungle compound was, nor could he use a bloodstone to teleport there. It was too obvious. If his mission were to succeed, which it obviously would, it would need to be through deception, not bravado. So here he was with their only option: a skyship captain who happily would look the other way for the right incentive.

"That Ruined better have my money when he does show up. I don't fly unofficial flights for fun you know," Captain Fareese said, clearly wishing to annoy Krothus further. She exhaled a puff of smoke up towards his face.

Krothus had already realized his attempts to silence her were completely ineffective, but he couldn't resist.

"If you keep talking about your damned payment, you won't get it. So cease with your endless whinging."

Fareese scoffed. "Oh? Then I'll make sure you never see the inside of the *Donovan* and you'll have to *walk* through the jungle. Does that sound fun?"

Had she been talking to anyone else, Krothus would have laughed. The nonchalant defiance of a mere Imperial Captain in the face of someone very clearly her superior in both rank and strength was admirable. But she was talking to Krothus, a man who's destiny far outstripped anyone she had ever spoken to. This demanded consequences.

Still facing the port entryway, Krothus waved two fingers. Like it had suddenly gained a life of its own, the smokestick flew out of Fareese's fingers, floating freely off the edge of the dock and out of sight.

Fareese fixed Krothus with a stare of raw fury, before rummaging through a box at her waist for another. Krothus nearly cracked a smile. But as amusing it may have been, it was quickly diminished as he was once again nearly deafened by a skyship roaring into a nearby dock, heralding an onslaught of screeching trolleys which would follow soon after. And then his torment began anew.

So when Vyrion finally entered the dock shortly after, it felt akin to watching an uplifting sunbeam finally power its way through Thanaton's dreary clouds, if the sunbeam was also escorted by a contingent of soldiers bearing Lord Victus' symbol on their tabards.

"Ah, you're here already, Krothus," Vyrion said, as the soldiers and their gaunt-faced officer marched to the skyship's loading ramp.

"Unfortunately," Krothus grunted, "Let's waste no more time."

Captain Fareese blocked their way. She presented a hand.

"Payment first."

The officer next to Vyrion spoke up. "Forgive me, Captain, but I believe you meant Payment first, *my lord.*' "

"Don't start with this today, Lorren," Fareese snapped.

"Lord Victus sends his regards, and thanks you for your discretion on yet another personal errand," Vyrion said, tossing a hefty pouch to her.

Fareese, apparently satisfied, let them pass.

Unsurprisingly, much of the *Donovan*'s interior was taken up by the cargo hold, a cavernous metal maw packed to bursting with boxes. The next floor was the crew quarters, dark, cramped, and caked in a permanent layer of dust.

"I'm not much of a tour guide, so I won't bother," Fareese said, climbing up one more set of stairs.

"This is the crew quarters, my lords. Those ladders lead to the bolt-thrower turrets and those doors lead to the interior firing deck," Lorren explained, the words spilling out as if they were fleeing Fareese's retribution.

"Thank you, Sergeant Lorren. Now shut up," Captain Fareese said.

"Yes, Captain."

"And wait with your men in the crew quarters, it's cramped enough as it is up here."

Seeming to take his command to shut up quite seriously, Lorren followed her directive without a word.

Soon, Krothus found himself in the *Donovan*'s cockpit, a claustrophobic dome of metal and glass, with just enough room for a trio of seats blockaded in by panels of buttons and switches. Captain Fareese sat in the center chair, flicking switches seemingly at random, before a wheel slowly rose up out of the floor in front of her. The *Donovan* began to shudder and emit a low hum.

"Your crew?" Vyrion asked, gesturing to the empty chairs.

"Last I checked, still as dead as they were next week," she said with a shrug. "My commanding officer says she'll be putting in an order for some autos for next time. Third living crew I've lost, replacements are getting too costly."

"Autos?" Vyrion asked.

"Automatons. You know, clankers? Metal and stupid."

Krothus, as he often did when lesser beings were talking nearby, completely ignored them. The innards of the ship interested him far more. An aura had enveloped the vessel, a presence within the Ruin, almost like the *Donovan* were a Ruined itself. But the ship's aura was muddled, unrecognizable, a cocktail with far too many ingredients all shook together.

The two half-orbs on either of the skyship expelled streams of blue fire as the *Donovan* began to hesitantly rise off the ground. Krothus felt an emptiness appear in his stomach that he was very much opposed to, and found himself involuntarily gripping the nearest wall.

"You two may want to grab a seat," the Captain said, before pushing a heavy throttle forward.

The skyship rocketed out of the port, the force of the sudden acceleration nearly knocking Krothus and Vyrion over. They quickly pulled themselves into the two empty seats.

A spectacular view of Thanaton beamed through the cockpit windows; buildings, roads and Ruin Lord fortresses looked no larger than children's playthings from such a dizzying height. Only the Dark Pyramid still remained impressive, somehow appearing even larger when its full size was apparent.

As soon as the seemingly endless jungle filled their view and the *Donovan* began to smoothly cut through the skies, the two Ruined attempted to explain their plan to Fareese.

"So we *aren't* going to the Rylak Desert? Or are we?" Fareese asked, leaning back in her seat, clearly not understanding. Either that, or as Krothus suspected, she was surely trying to swindle some extra payment out of them.

"You and Victus' men will be, but we have another destination in mind," Krothus said, "We need for any outside observer to believe this is nothing more than a routine retrieval of expedition findings. No different than usual."

Fareese shook her head, "I don't have enough fuel to land at two destinations. If I have to refuel somewhere that will cost-"

"There won't be two destinations," Vyrion interrupted, "We can't afford any record of this ship landing anywhere but Rylak, so we will need to be dropped off mid-journey."

Fareese started laughing, "How? What are you two planning on doing, jumping?"

Krothus looked to Vyrion, who gave him a grin.

The Captain's laughter caught in her throat. "You've got to be joking."

"I'm sure I'm well known for my jokes," Krothus responded, "But this is not one of them."

"We only need you hover above where we direct you. We can manage the rest."

Fareese stared at the two of them as if they were insane. Krothus assumed that to a non-Ruined, their plan would seem as such. But the judgment of an Imperial regarding the jump was irrelevant - the Ruin had burdened them with great power and purpose, so they would succeed.

"I suppose I can adjust altitude and speed enough for something as stupid as this," Captain Fareese said finally. "But that still leaves the question of how you are supposed to get back onboard."

"After you've refueled and picked up whatever decoy cargo we've sent for, stay low and at a reasonable speed, we'll do the rest," Vyrion said.

Fareese shrugged. "Promising, I'm sure. But I won't be waiting around if you miss that window."

"As you should. We will make our way through the jungle if required," Krothus said.

The Captain seemed just as surprised by this as the declaration that they would be jumping out of her ship, and Krothus could understand why. The jungles were untamed and wild, filled with a wide manner of creatures he didn't bother to study, knowing Vyrion would instead. Thanaton's walls were testament enough to their danger. The suggested journey through those tropical trees were their last resort, but such a plan was pointless when there was a perfect point to return to the skyship.

Fareese sighed and flipped some switch above them, "I've heard better plans. Where will I be letting you off?"

"The Decrepit Temple," said Krothus.

For the third time in just as many minutes, Captain Fareese looked at the two Ruined as if they had lost their minds. "You two really know how to find the worst option. Jumping out of skyships was bad enough, but provoking ancient evils? I'll drop you off to your deaths if you insist."

"We do insist, Captain. Let us know when we're close," Vyrion said politely, turning back down the stairs to the crew quarters.

"This is why I ask for pay up front," Fareese muttered.

Krothus ignored her and followed Vyrion below.

He had never been afraid of such haunted tales. His journeys into the Ascendancy's catacombs had taught him a valuable lesson, the dead were silent and knowledgeable. But mostly silent. If the Imperials wanted to be superstitious and avoid the only suitable landing point for miles around, then so be it.

Vyrion had stopped midway down the stairs. "That went as well as could be expected."

"I can see why you insisted on paying her first, she would have increased her price significantly had she known the details," Krothus said. Of course, had it been him, he would have forced Fareese's involvement without the need for such things - but Vyrion had wanted to play it her way.

Vyrion nodded. "Now we wait. Let's find Lorren."

It wasn't hard to do so within the constricted confines of the crew quarters. The Sergeant sat at a table with one of his soldiers, leading a hushed conversation while the rest of his troops had already settled into passing the time via cards or napping.

Whatever Lorren was discussing with his subordinate had both of them concerned, with snippets of their agitated conversation barely audible.

"-not fit for his position-" the woman hissed.

"-out of my hands-"

But the moment they saw the Ruined approach they drew silent.

Vyrion drew up a chair and sat next to the wiry Sergeant. Krothus took one at the far end of the table.

"Too stuffy in the cockpit, my lords?" Sergeant asked, giving them a forced smile.

"Something like that," Vyrion said, returning the gesture. "Mind if we have a word in private?"

"Of course, my lord," Lorren said. The woman he'd been talking to quickly went to join the card game across the room as the gentle hum of the skyship droned on in the background.

Once the guard had retreated, Vyrion continued. "Captain Fareese has now been informed of our plan, so we will be departing soon. Do you still understand your assignment?"

Sergeant Lorren nodded and lowered his voice, which seemed quite unnecessary due to the card-players' ever increasing volume.

"Yes, my lord, though I fail to understand the bigger picture, as it were."

"You don't have to," Krothus said bluntly. "You need only to complete the cargo run and record the journey ship manifest. The bigger picture is for us to know alone."

Lorren gently cleared his throat. "Of course. Apologies, my lord."

Vyrion sighed, finding some reason to be offended by Krothus' truth. "Krothus does not command you, I do. Please speak freely, Sergeant."

"I would like to request a favor, if possible, my lord," Lorren said hesitantly, "For when we return."

Krothus rolled his eyes. The audacity of Imperials constantly surprised him.

But despite all logic, Vyrion seemed interested. "It depends on its nature, but I will certainly consider it."

Krothus couldn't help but object. "Come, Vyrion, do you not debase yourself with -"

"He is my master's soldier, not yours. I will hear him out," Vyrion interrupted, motioning for Lorren to continue.

The Sergeant swallowed and continued, clearly uncomfortable with the exchange. "My commanding officer, Lieutenant Farke, is not fit for his position. His blunders and corruption are obvious, his latest example being his refusal to assign more than a skeleton crew to retrieve the Lord Victus' relic, which resulted in another officer being reprimanded in his stead. I kept my position only because he would not be able to run his section without me."

"And what has Lord Victus said?" Vyrion asked, "I'm sure he would want to hear of this."

In Krothus's correct, but unasked for, opinion this Farke should simply be killed. If this were a Ruined matter, Krothus would have had no qualms about killing a superior who was only such in name alone. If they did not have the strength to defend their position, then they had no right to possess it.

But Sergeant Lorren did not suggest such an action and only shook his head. "Lord Victus would never grant an audience for such a trivial thing, nor should he be burdened with it. So the only avenue I have is Imperial military procedure. I would take Farke to trial, present evidence of incompetence to a superior, who would judge and sentence him, if found guilty. The favour I request is for you to be this judge."

Krothus watched Vyrion closely as he ran his fingers through his neatly combed hair, a sign that he was considering the prospect very thoroughly.

"Why not ask Captain Fareese?" Krothus asked, in part allowing Vyrion time to think, but also seeking an honest answer. "She is your superior as well."

That got a nervous laugh out of Lorren. "Well, my lord, she is superior in rank, yes. But most likely, she would decide the verdict purely based on whoever paid her the most. And I am far from a rich man."

Krothus could not disagree with that assessment.

"Then I will judge this case for you when we return," Vyrion said finally.

Upon hearing Vyrion's answer, Sergeant Lorren began nodding furiously. "That is fantastic news, my lord. I will begin building my case immediately."

And with that, the Lorren quickly vacated the table, signaling the woman he'd been speaking with to join him. She slammed down a hand of cards before getting up, much to the dismay of everyone else playing. Expletives were shouted, and a week's worth of wagered pay changed hands.

"One day, you won't be able to help every poor soul who comes your way," Krothus said.

Vyrion gave him a sad smile. "I have to make up for the both of us."

The remainder of Krothus and Vyrion's wait passed by quickly, and before long they heard a shout from above.

"Ruined, up here, now!"

Krothus could feel The *Donovan* decelerating at a rapid pace, fast enough that his stomach felt like it were a skyship itself. And the moment they got up the stairs, they were assailed by a powerful whirlwind, courtesy of a now-open hatch that led out onto the deck.

Fareese was there in the cockpit, her hair and jacket flitting violently as if fighting to escape, motioning the Ruined outside. With difficulty, Krothus waded out into the gale, Vyrion behind him. Then he slammed the hatch shut.

Despite the *Donovan* continuing to slow, the force of the winds on the deck was overwhelming, Krothus had to channel the Ruin downwards onto himself just to keep from flying off into the jungles below. Worst still, any words either he or Vyrion spoke were instantly carried away.

Vyrion turned to him, gesturing near one of the bolt-thrower turrets across the deck. As good a spot as any to jump off a skyship, Krothus supposed.

The *Donovan* rocked and bucked as the jungle grew closer, but not close enough. How low could Fareese manage to take them? The thrust-orbs were barely visible, their jets of blue now only a trickle.

Krothus felt a tug on his gauntleted hand. Vyrion pointed forwards.

A terraced pyramid, all decayed stone and overgrown vines, towered above the wilds like the corpse of a once-great sentinel. The Decrepit

Temple. The jungle trees seemed to shy away, even the clouds themselves passed it by. It sat alone and unchallenged.

With every passing second, the Temple rose up further to meet them. Krothus could feel the bite of the wind lessen. They were getting close.

Krothus put his hand on Vyrion's shoulder and the partners shared a brief glance. There would only be one chance for this to work; if they missed the temple, if they landed wrong, if the Ruin didn't slow their descent as they commanded it to, then their mission would meet a quick, grisly end. But Krothus knew he would one day die in a blaze of righteous glory, not by willingly jumping to his doom, so he was not afraid. Though his racing heart and somersaulting stomach would hardly agree.

The temple was nearly underneath them now. It looked closer than it had ever been, but while thirty meters was an improvement over three thousand, such a jump would still surely kill most mortals.

Thankfully, Krothus and Vyrion weren't just mere mortals, they were Ruined. A smile crept onto Krothus' wind-battered face he channelled the Ruin's presence further, feeling it pump through his legs, flood through his veins and seep into his muscles like liquid fire. He could feel the raw power flowing through him, more than enough to bring him to the temple's surface.

But as Krothus prepared to jump, a sudden sense of dread rose up within him. The hairs on the back of his neck stood on end, terrified adrenaline washed through his body.

A quick look at Vyrion confirmed he had felt it too.

Something was watching them from the jungle.

The top of the Decrepit Temple moved, a dark shadow rising up out of it.

A horde of bats, thousands of them, erupted from somewhere inside the structure, rising up into the skies like a plume of smoke. The endless chittering of the living cloud merged into a high pitched roar as the hurricane of winged creatures enveloped the *Donovan*.

Krothus could feel the rush of wings all around him. Vyrion, and everything else, disappeared from his view.

For a moment, the deck was as black as night, only pierced by the pricks of light from the skyship's plumes of thrust. But then the *Donovan* shuddered. Its half-orbs flickered, the flames within them sputtering before their blue energy completely disappeared.

The skyship's steady descent became an uncontrolled dive.

Krothus began to slide across the deck. He slammed his feet down, raw fury powering him. The Ruin rushed through his veins, holding him to the deck as he drew his runeblade.

Krothus had only one thought: that he would not be killed by *bats*.

A pillar of flame cut through the living haze. But despite the dozens of burnt creatures that dropped with each swing of his weapon, Krothus knew that it was doing nothing but feeding his rage. He needed to jump, and quickly, or he would meet his end in the fireball of a skyship crash. Vyrion's presence was absent, no doubt already jumped himself

Krothus took a deep breath, focusing the Ruin at his feet, trying to ignore the cries of the winged demons all around him. As he exhaled, he pushed with all his might and the Ruin erupted underneath him, sending him sailing into the air. The blackness around Krothus disappeared.

He was flying. The wind rushed over him as his gut performed great feats of acrobatics with every pulse of his heart.

No - he was falling.

Krothus looked down.

The top of the temple filled his view. He was hurtling towards it, too fast, too close.

Fear - no, *panic*, set in. What was he supposed to do? A voice whispered in the back of his mind. Perhaps he should just let the end come to him. Endless peace, pleasant darkness, an inviting-

No. Krothus refused to give way to the emotions of weakness. He would *not* be killed today. Not by bats, not by skyships, not by any Ruin-damned thing that Krothus had not given *permission* to kill him.

The temple was seconds away. He could see the individual leaves growing off the vines that covered it.

Krothus' rage filled every fiber of his being. The power of the Ruin flooded his body.

He could make out the cracks between the stones.

Krothus roared. The Ruin blasted downwards, slowing his descent, the force of which sent shudders up his spine and pressed his organs up against his back. The temple was right there.

The last thing he saw was a single beetle crawling below him. The last thing he heard was a crunch.

Then some presence, some dark embrace enveloped him. And his worries melted away.

Chapter 8
Nightshadow

The cloud of bats continued to swarm above, obscuring the *Donovan* as it plummeted downwards. Vyrion, having safely slowed his fall to a graceful landing on the upper steps of the temple, could do nothing but watch.

He had felt the flow of the Ruin energy coursing through the ship stall just before they had started dropping, like some outside source had suddenly shut it off. And as soon as the creatures, wherever they came from, had enveloped the skyship, Vyrion had jumped, with the last he had seen of Krothus being his partner's foolish attempts to fight on the deck of the doomed vessel. But now the blaze of Krothus' runeblade was nowhere to be seen.

The dark cloud was nearly at the trees now. Vyrion braced for a crash, but Captain Fareese apparently had one more trick up her sleeve.

Two jets of blue flame exploded through the haze of winged assailants, roasting scores of them instantly as the skyship halted its fall just above the jungle canopy. Then one of the thrust-orbs cut out, while the other doubled its output, sending the *Donovan* spinning into a deadly barrel roll. The stream of blue energy vaporised all that came in contact with it, each of the ship's spins taking out large swathes of the bats until the skyship's full form gradually emerged from the shapeless cloud.

The creatures, whether called off by some unseen master or themselves admitting defeat, scattered.

Vyrion let out a sigh of relief as the thrust-orbs equalised and the skyship began to climb high into the air once more. Their alibi, their troops, and their route home were still intact, at least for now. He had no idea what had caused the sudden chaos, and he didn't have the time to think too deeply about it. He needed to find Krothus.

Quickly climbing the mossy, crumbling steps of the temple, Vyrion reached out through the Ruin for any sign of his partner. A faint trace pulled at him from above.

Yet as quickly as Vyrion had felt it, Krothus' aura was quickly overpowered by another, a presence that permeated every pebble of the Decrepit Temple. A dark pit of despair filled Vyrion, pure fear crawled across his skin in a sinister caress. He could feel something watching him.

Vyrion ignited his runeblade and pressed forward. He was starting to understand why the Imperials avoided this place.

The top of the temple was flat, with a simple doorway that led downwards into an impossible blackness, partially sealed off by thick, spiked vines. Something told Vyrion that they should be left alone. More importantly, he could see Krothus just ahead, down on one knee but very much alive.

"Krothus!" Vyrion shouted, rushing to his side.

The grey-skinned Ruined was knelt in a crater of his own making, shattered stone and rubble at his feet. Upon hearing Vyrion's voice, he slowly stood up.

The presence within the temple was watching.

"Are you alright?" Vyrion asked. But he already knew something was wrong. Krothus was moving oddly, as if being held on strings, and worse still, his presence within the Ruin was warped, unnatural.

Krothus still said nothing. Instead, he slowly turned around to face him. His eyes carried a sickly emerald glow, his face twisted into a mask of animalistic anger as he looked not at Vyrion, but through him.

"Krothus?" Vyrion whispered.

"You should never have come here," a voice that was definitely not Krothus' rasped. Whatever had taken over Krothus urged him forward while the Temple itself seemed to rumble with murderous glee.

Vyrion started slowly backing away, towards the temple stairs, with a cautionary hand in front of him. If he could lead them away from that veiled doorway, away from that wrongness within, then there might be something he could do.

"Krothus, if you can hear me - resist whatever has taken hold of you. Remember who you are, why you are here."

But despite Vyrion's pleas. Krothus continued to jankily walk towards him with that frightening expression plastered to his face. Occasionally there would be some sort of spasm, a jerk in one direction or another where the emerald glow would flicker and Krothus' aura would briefly flash into being, before disappearing once more. He wasn't lost, not yet.

Vyrion took each step one at a time, feeling the crumbled stone under his heel as he slowly backed up. Slowly, very slowly. All he needed to do was stay on his feet.

"Your death approaches," the thing inside Krothus hissed, before his shaved skull thrashed wildly and the green glow briefly faded, "- how *dare* you, demon! I will-"

There was another thrash, and Krothus disappeared within himself once more. His body continued its slow shamble forwards. Whatever it was, the thing was clearly struggling to maintain its hold, which, considering Vyrion's own experiences with his hot-headed partner, was hardly surprising.

"Keep fighting, Krothus." Vyrion felt the temple stairs come up behind him as he continued to back up. A loose stone skittered down off his first step, nearly causing Vyrion to tumble down. It would have been fitting end to the least noteworthy Ruined in the Empire, killed by falling down the only set of stairs for miles around, but he managed to right himself just in time.

They followed the steps through the dense canopy. So dense in fact, that the moment they passed beneath the tightly interwoven treeline, the daylight disappeared, and the crimson energy of Vyrion's own runeblade became his only guiding light in the jungle. The air was humid, rich with the smell of damp soil, and alien sounds assailed him from every direction at once; the chittering of birds, the buzzing of insects, some strange faraway screeching.

And amidst all of this, the battle for Krothus' body continued, twisting and writhing its way down to the jungle floor right behind Vyrion.

Then Krothus let loose some bestial roar, and his runeblade flew into his hand. The cry echoed through the jungle, his warped face stretched wide to accommodate it. The symphony of jungle sounds ceased. Flames burst forth from his weapon.

"Krothus, you need to fight this," Vyrion said, eyeing the runeblade, "Remember all that we-"

"He's mine, worm," the thing inside Krothus hissed, swinging at Vyrion.

Vyrion parried the blow, sending sparks cascading through the clearing, "I think you have vastly underestimated who you're dealing with."

Krothus thrashed again, yelling as he emerged from his mental prison, *"My destiny is my own!"*

He swept his runeblade at a nearby tree, sending a flock of birds fleeing as it crashed to the ground in two smoldering pieces. Krothus' body tried to move left, only to be ripped to the right, his muscles straining so much it looked like they would burst.

Vyrion could only watch, desperate to find some way to help. Any specifics on how to do so remained elusive.

"Agh-" with another jerk of his head, Krothus was overtaken by his invader, that emerald radiance returned to his eyes, "I will have my vessel, and you will die for trying to interfere."

Vyrion saw the runeblade fly at him again and caught it with his own, locked them into a tight embrace as the fire enveloping Krothus' weapon began to surge, growing in strength as the warped presence within its wielder took control. Soon, the flames were singeing Krothus' armor, licking at his very flesh.

"He is mine," the thing gloated.

Its head jerked to the side, "You are weak, demon. Weak, pathetic and cowardly - my body is *mine!*"

Krothus was suddenly wracked by intense spasms, as though every part of his body were trying to pull itself into a different direction. A low growl rose up from within him, rumbling louder and louder until it swelled into a mighty roar. He called out to the sky, neck muscles bulging. His runeblade was a towering inferno.

"Krothus!" Vyrion cried. He had to take a step back to avoid getting burnt.

Then it stopped. The Ruined's eyes rolled back and he dropped as if struck by some invisible blow to the head. His runeblade fell out of his grip and the flames died out.

"Emperor above," Vyrion rushed to his partner, checking for any signs of life.

Only when he heard faint, calm breaths, did Vyrion let out a deep breath of his own, one he felt like he'd been holding since he'd jumped off the *Donovan*.

All of this was yet another thing the Ascendancy had completely failed to prepare him for. Demon spirits, swarms of bats, mystery relics - it was these types of things that made Vyrion wonder if every other Ruined was just faking it, pretending they were well acquainted with the chaos of the world when in reality they were mere passengers, desperately trying to keep afloat as waves crashed over them again and again. There was no way anyone could walk into it all with any kind of certainty, least of all Vyrion.

He watched Krothus slumber beneath him, surprisingly peaceful for a man so comfortable with violence. Krothus had certainty in spades. Even when he was wrong, he was so utterly convinced he was right that he would move heaven and earth to demonstrate it to everyone else, to prove himself worthy, to show himself strong. And that trait seemed to have made all the difference.

Krothus was a picture perfect Ruined, while Vyrion felt every day more like an imposter.

And now, imposter or not, things were left to him.

The sounds of the jungle gradually returned, nearby creatures deeming it safe to resume their cries. Once he had levitated an unconscious Krothus onto a flat stone, Vyrion waited. Waited for Krothus to wake, waited for his anxiety to give him a well-deserved break; but an hour went by with no success for either of them.

Krothus had surely been loud enough to disturb everything around them for miles, so Vyrion was hyper-vigilant; he'd read what creatures lurked here. It was best to be prepared. So it was no surprise when he began to pick out something moving in the undergrowth.

First it was to his left, then his right. Above, in the trees, and in the brush behind him. Vyrion held his runeblade close as sparks of Ruin energy twisted and crackled in his free hand. The Ruin was truly enjoying testing him today.

"Show yourself!" Vyrion shouted, sending a warning blast of lightning into the air. Why he thought any jungle predators would understand his words was anyone's guess, but he felt better doing it.

But whatever it was did not seem phased by Vyrion's demonstration. Instead, they took it as a signal to finally emerge from the undergrowth.

They came from behind snapped branches, dew-laden ferns, decayed stumps. Crimson skin, marked by black tattoos, stretched over heavily muscled frames, while predatory yellow eyes glittered in the shadows. Vyrion's first thoughts were a party of crazed men in warpaint, but the closer they came, the less he believed it.

They looked like creatures formed of nightmare itself. Instead of hair, they boasted tentacles tied down with golden trinkets, while boney ridges and plates emerged from foreheads. A pair of stubby tusks rose up from their bottom jaw.

Bizarre appearance aside, the creatures hardly seemed to be there for diplomacy; they all carried savage axes or bows, wearing armor of bone or hide. But they did not attack.

Vyrion stood there, runeblade hilt in his hand.

They too stood there, staring at him. Then, one stepped forward.

She carried a gnarled staff topped by a red crystal, and golden jewelry adorned the bone ridges on her forehead. The rest of the warriors respectfully moved aside as she approached.

"Who trespasses in the territory of the Nightshadow tribe?" she growled. Her voice was deep and guttural, her accent harsh and blunt, as if the soft sounds of the common tongue had been whipped into submission before being spoken.

The name sounded familiar, and Vyrion was suddenly thankful for his readings in Lord Victus's library. He knew what these creatures were - orkathi.

Vyrion cleared his throat and spoke loudly, "I am Vyrion, a Ruined of the Ruined Empire. I did not intend to trespass here, but myself and my companion fell from our skyship into your territory."

The orkathi woman narrowed her yellow eyes at him, "We saw, yes. Worse still, we saw where you landed."

Many of the orkathi shifted nervously, looking up at the temple looming behind Vyrion.

"We did not know of the strange force that lurks within that place," Vyrion said, "But I felt it, saw it invade my companion's mind and try to bend it to his will."

The orkathi stepped forward, the long tentacles hanging down from her skull writhing. She stared at Krothus, slumbering on his bed of stone.

"He was able to resist the touch of Pestus?" Intrigue seemed to overshadow her previous suspicion. That statement ignited a wave of murmurs across the assembled Nightshadow.

Vyrion could sense a trace of the Ruin within the orkathi woman herself. Not as much as a Ruined, but there was something there, that much was certain.

"Pestus?" he asked.

"The Nightmare Lord. An ancient, wicked force bound to the temple," the tribeswoman rasped, looking up at the stone steps. "He wishes to escape his prison. But to gain enough power to break his bonds, he requires souls, feeding on those who feel his pull."

She walked closer to the slumbering form of Krothus. Vyrion raised his runeblade ever so slightly, but sensed no malice in her actions.

"He must have a strong will," she continued, leaning over her staff to inspect Krothus. "When Pestus whispers, the souls he has ensnared seek death, bring it upon themselves and others. But this gray one's mind is whole, no longer tainted with the Nightmare Lord's touch. I sense it."

Looking at Krothus' body, burnt and battered, Vyrion could only wonder what would have happened if this Nightmare Lord had chosen him instead. His will was no match for Krothus. If this orkathi was to be believed, then Vyrion would have surely been lost. Just another example of what he already knew; he was the inferior Ruined.

Another orkathi shoved his way through the Nightshadow onlookers. The intruder was larger than any other, a gigantic double bladed axe carried easily in one hand and intricate black tattoos over his chest and arms.

"Soultotem, you dare speak to Imperials without your chieftain present?"

Soultotem sighed. "It is a shaman's duty to speak when the Chieftain is absent, and I have -"

"Silence!" he said with a wave of his crimson hand. The shaman stopped mid sentence, as if the wave had slapped her across the face.

The chieftain then approached Vyrion, leering at him from just beyond the reach of his runeblade, the distance between them some seemingly impossible barrier. His crimson lips parted to reveal a horrid smile that Vyrion silently vowed never to look at again.

"You speak with Lokk Headcleaver of the Nightshadow tribe. I've told Lord Fira before, if she wishes to expand her fortress further, she must come to me *in person*, I don't deal with her *dogs*," the chieftain snarled, saliva spraying at his final word.

Vyrion wasn't sure what to say. His first thought was at the amusing simplicity of calling yourself 'Headcleaver'. He couldn't decide whether it was a self-fulfilling prophecy decreed at birth, or a title earned through separating many heads from their bodies. Looking at Headcleaver's massive axe, there was a clear preference for Vyrion to leave that bit of knowledge a mystery.

More importantly, judging by what the chieftain had just said, the Nightshadow weren't just Lord Fira's jungle neighbors, they seemed like her allies.

"Well?" Headcleaver grumbled, adjusting his axe in his hands, "Speak, Ruined. Or I will end this conversation quickly."

Looking at the several dozen bulky warriors surrounding him, Vyrion didn't rate his own chances very highly. He wouldn't be able to fight through the Nightshadow, nor could he risk being handed over to the very Ruin Lord who's compound they were intending to break into. So he did the only thing he could think of - he confessed. At least partially.

"We were not sent by Lord Fira, nor do we serve her. We are merely trying to pass through your territory to enter her fortress."

Lokk Headcleaver's yellow eyes narrowed at this revelation, but his shaman shaman spoke first.

"My young Chieftain, they braved the temple to get here. They-"

Headcleaver snorted. "So I should trust the Nightmare Lord's agents now? If they came from the temple then they are already tainted."

"Normally perhaps, but the grey one survived his touch." Soultotem insisted.

The Nightshadow Chieftain briefly looked at Krothus, before giving only a dismissive grunt. "They will not be the saviours you wish them to be, Soultotem, and I will not lower myself to seek help from Imperials, especially those who are likely spies."

He then turned to Vyrion. "Tell me, Ruined, if you do not serve Lord Fira, then why are you here? My shaman pleads with me to consider your worth to the Nightshadow, but I will not jeopardise my tribe purely on her words."

Vyrion, committing to his path of talking his way out of the situation, retracted his runeblade. If he could demonstrate to their bone-headed Chieftain that he and Krothus had no hostile intentions, then perhaps Headcleaver would consider simply leaving them to their mission, not notifying Fira and not involving them with this Nightmare Lord.

"We only wish to enter Lord Fira's fortress. Nothing more."

"Yet you risk the temple simply for a visit?" Headcleaver scoffed.

"Only fools would do this if their intentions were pure. You are lying."

For all his bravado, the Nightshadow chieftain was not stupid.

"Like I said, we simply fell from our skyship," Vyrion started, "If you would let us continue to-"

"So you would want to be brought to Lord Fira inside her fortress?" Lokk interrupted with a knowing smile. He held his muscled arms open as he spoke, as if inviting Vyrion to immediately begin this journey.

Vyrion did not answer.

Lokk's yellow eyes studied Vyrion. "Remind me, Soultotem. What has Lord Fira told us to do if we discover intruders near her fortress?"

"Kill them," Soultotem said quietly.

Vyrion's grip tightened on his runeblade.

"And if we refuse to do so?"

Soultotem seemed reluctant to answer, but did so anyways. "Her abomination will kill the intruders, and us."

"And yet you wish for us to risk our destruction simply because the grey one barely survived an encounter with the Nightmare Lord. This somehow means he can also defeat Pestus's vessel."

"We have no quarrel with the Nightshadow," Vyrion interjected, trying one last peaceful gesture, "If you would simply leave us be, then nothing will come of this. We could -"

"Pestus has already seen you. His whispers to Lord Fira will inform her of this eventually," Headcleaver said, "Letting you go and pretending our encounter never happened will doom my people. So I will not."

"Lokk, please," Soultotem insisted, on the verge of begging, "Listen to me. We need them. The freedom I speak of is not just for our people, but for your father. This can only be done if Pestus is cast out. For the first time, we have been given a tool to fight back, don't let it pass by so easily."

Headcleaver did not meet the shaman's gaze, he still watched Vyrion, as if waiting for him to change his tune.

Vyrion thought of what Krothus would have done were he conscious. Intimidate.

"Killing me will not be easy, Headcleaver," he warned, forcing the Ruin to crackle around his hand once more. "Consider your options *very* carefully. If you choose unwisely, and try to hand us over to Fira, or worse still, try to take us on yourself, I will end a dozen of your warriors in a single instant."

A dozen might be a slight exaggeration, but Vyrion was certain Krothus would have said an even higher number.

Chieftain Lokk Headcleaver, for all his bluster, seemed unsure. He first looked at the energy discharging from Vyrion's hand, to Krothus, deep in slumber, then up to the temple behind them. The huge axe passed back and forth in his hands. He suddenly looked much younger than Vyrion had assumed, his tentacled hair was short, the tendrilled beard on his face nearly absent, and his eyes carried an uncertainty that wouldn't look out of place were Vyrion looking in the mirror.

As this happened, Soultotem was staring the Chieftain down, leaning on her gnarled staff. The Nightshadow warriors looked to both their Chief and their shaman, waiting for a decision to be made.

"Nightshadow!" Headcleaver suddenly shouted, raising his axe into the air, "Our future has been decided. If the spirits have told our shaman correctly, we have been given the tools to break free of our chains. And if not, then we will die warrior's deaths!"

Soultotem's face split into a tusked smile as the Nightshadow roared and raised their weapons as well. Vyrion relaxed, letting the Ruin energy circling his hands fade away.

Headcleaver quickly leaned in close to Vyrion as the orkathi continued cheering.

"Regardless of what happens next, the Nightshadow are committed to slaying this abomination. I do not care what your intentions are with Lord Fira, but we will get you entry into her fortress solely for our cause, not yours. If you try to kill her somehow, I do not care. If you wish to take her fortress somehow, I do not care. If you have lied, or try to betray us, you will die, whether by my hand or Fira's."

And without a further word, Chieftain Headcleaver stomped off into the jungle, his warriors following behind. Vyrion had no doubt the threats held merit, and could only hope that slaying this abomination was fully within Krothus' grasp.

Soultotem waved him along. "Come, Ruined. Take your companion and we will gather our forces. Entry into Lord Fira's fortress is not easy, especially if uninvited."

Especially if there were a Ruin Lord's daughter to kidnap, Vyrion added silently.

Chapter 9

The Grotto

Krothus dreamt. Some formless shadow would approach, offering him strength and power beyond his wildest imagination. But time and time again, Krothus would refuse, scoff even. Power given, not earned, was charity for the weak and the foolish, and an insult to someone with such great potential as himself.

When he was eventually dragged back into the waking world, Krothus found himself in yet another nightmare. He was in some damp cave, surrounded by crimson-skinned, tentacle-haired monsters. One of these creatures was attempting to feed him some liquid with a wooden spoon, a mistake Krothus would ensure was its last.

He smacked the spoon out of his face and attempted to ignite his runeblade - only to discover it was no longer in his hand. He stared at his palm stupidly for a moment. The creature who had been wielding the spoon sighed and moved to retrieve it, but Krothus was already on his feet.

He charged out of the cave and into the light beyond.

Blinking through the brightness as the warm sun caressed his face, Krothus tried to get a sense of his surroundings. Trees and stone loomed overhead, blocking his view, while the creaky wooden walkway he stood on quickly gave way to a sheer drop, beyond which the near-hidden sound of running water lurked. Curious, Krothus leaned forward, slowly edging over the side of the walkway as if he were trying to catch a glimpse of hell itself. But as he got a better view, hell was far from what came to mind.

Like some crater cast by the footfall of some impossibly massive giant, a deep crevice carved its way through the jungle. Grey stone and perfect, clear water emerged from the greenery; the bone and blood of the earth itself. The water cascading down waterfalls and gulleys into a mirror-like pool at the crater's center.

Had Krothus stumbled upon the place in different circumstances, he might have thought it a paradise. But the walkways spiraling down the crater and the half-hidden wooden structures growing out of every nook and crevice told him that he was far from the first to come here. Worse still, the crimson creatures, the very things he was trying to escape from, lurked everywhere.

He would have to use all his training, all his wisdom, to find his weapon and his partner and escape from this place. It would be difficult, yes, but Krothus lived for such challenges, they were the kind that let him prove his strength above all others, the kind that he knew he was destined for. His weapon and his partner may be lost, but when they were found, the creatures that plagued this crater would look upon him and despair, because -

"Ah, Krothus - you're awake. Here's your runeblade."

Krothus blinked. Vyrion was right next to him, holding out the hilt to a familiar weapon.

"I - what?" Krothus said, thoroughly confused, "Where are we?

Vyrion looked at him with concern, like Krothus were some idiot child who had said something absurd. Krothus swallowed down the urge to hit him.

"It must have been worse than I thought. What do you last remember?"

Now that was a good question, a question Krothus had been too preoccupied to consider. Images flashed through his mind; a horde of bats, him falling through the sky, then nothing.

"Tell me everything," Krothus demanded.

And Vyrion did. Ancient ghosts, a tribe desperate for help, and some threat only Krothus could defeat; it all sounded to be some nonsense story he imagined Imperial parents would tell their children. But, seeing as Krothus would undeniably be the hero of such a tale, he wasn't entirely dismissive of it.

"Does this Headcleaver know anything about Fira's daughter?" Krothus asked once he was up to speed.

"I didn't ask. Though I can't imagine the Nightshadow would carry any information regarding Lord Fira's family, they aren't exactly familiar."

Families, from what little Krothus had seen of them, seemed a complicated mess. They were allegiances and obligations that were decided for you from birth, regardless of your own say in the matter. Family made you weak, preying on your sentimentality to circumvent your own strength, weighing you down with burdens you never asked for. He took solace in the fact that he did not have one.

For as long as Krothus could remember, he had been on his own. Only when he deemed it beneficial had he and Vyrion become partners, and, unlike family, developing such a relationship had brought nothing but strength. At least, when Vyrion didn't rope him into helping whatever downtrodden fool came across their path. Much like he was now.

"If they have no information to provide, then why bother helping them at all?"

"Because it's the right thing to do," Vyrion predictably snapped, "Not to mention that it grants us allies and access to Fira's fortress."

Krothus scoffed. "I'm sure a handful of savages will make all the difference."

A pebble clattered to the ground nearby as something shifted above them. He looked up.

Dozens of orkathi, some of them children no taller than Krothus's waist, stared down from walkways of damp wood above, their wide eyes and open mouths treating him as if he were some foreign king. Krothus couldn't help but stand a little taller.

Vyrion smiled up at their observers. "There might be more than a handful. And you would do well to change your tune. They know the jungle better than we do, and if they see us as worthy of their help, then we should do our best to pay it in kind."

"All this time I should have been looking for some barbaric jungle-dwellers for the recognition I deserve. How quaint," Krothus grunted. Thanaton would one day kneel to him, that much he knew, but that day seemed further than ever.

"You have a very high opinion of yourself for someone who used to be no greater than a slave mere months ago," Vyrion said, "They too, are Imperial subjects, even if you refuse to treat them as such."

"Subjects they may be, but keeping them outside the city walls speaks volumes towards their true status," Krothus muttered.

One of the creatures walked up to them. A wall of muscle armed with a golden axe and a head of tied-back, tendrilled hair, the warrior growled and pointed one clawed hand down to the base of the grotto. "Soultotem waits for you in the Chieftain's tent."

Before Krothus could make his displeasure at the warrior's tone known, Vyrion interjected. "Of course - we were just headed down there now."

The warrior grunted as he moved aside to allow them passage. Krothus wasn't a fan of the thing's foul breath assaulting his nostrils as he squeezed past, but he had to acknowledge that an army of such warriors would surely be a mighty force indeed.

As they creaked down the spiral walkway further into the grotto, Vyrion turned back to Krothus. "Please do your best to act restrained, the last thing we need is to fight our way out of here."

Krothus snorted with as much disdain as he could muster, "I have no quarrel with their witch, I haven't even met her yet."

Vyrion looked unconvinced.

At the foot of the grotto was a structure built into the skeletal rib cage of some once mighty creature, a new skin of thick hide drawn across the bones, with a lazy stream of smoke wafting out above. But for a repurposed corpse, the chieftain's tent was far from quiet - a steady chorus of muffled shouts could be heard from inside.

"Their witch is not who I was worried about," Vyrion said.

He drew back a flap of hide to enter, only for a crude wooden stool to rocket out, smashing itself to splinters against the grotto wall. Harsh, unfamiliar words came from inside.

Krothus raised an eyebrow, Vyrion just shrugged, like it were as natural as the weather. They went inside.

An orkathi bigger than any Krothus had yet seen was clutching a massive axe in one hand and the broken shard of a wooden stool leg in the other. He had the look of barely contained violence about him, directing a hateful glare at a broad warrior with an eyepatch stretched over one side of her face. The feeling seemed mutual.

"Chieftain, calm yourself, I'm sure Drahka meant no disrespect," another orkathi huffed, switching to the Imperial tongue when the Ruined entered. She was trying to hold the young Chieftain back with her staff, but for all her effort it still looked like Headcleaver could have tossed her aside like a leaf in the wind.

"I meant *every* disrespect, Soultotem," Drahka hissed, "And you both know it's true. Lokk commands the tribe because Headcleaver the elder did, not because you earned it."

If Headcleaver had looked angry before, he was now positively furious. But even as his grip on his weapon tightened, and the fire in his eyes flared, he stayed silent.

The one-eyed orkathi then turned her grievances to Vyrion and Krothus, still spitting at her Chieftain but now with an accusatory claw pointed their way, "Worse still, you ally with Ruined when they enslaved our people. When they took our true Chieftain from us. It is a spit in the face of every warrior who-"

"Drahka, stop," Soultotem interrupted, almost pleading, "Now, more than ever, we need to be unified, not-"

Drahka heeded Soultotem's advice like Krothus heeded warnings from Vyrion - she didn't. In fact, she only grew louder.

"No. I have held my tongue for too long, thinking you could guide him away from his foolish tendencies. Now, Lokk has tarnished his father's legacy beyond repair; he stood by as Fira corrupted his Chieftain's mind, he watched as our warriors were slaughtered, he did nothing but bend his knee when Fira asked him to. He is *weak*."

Chieftain Headcleaver pushed Soultotem out of his path with a surprising gentleness. He was demonstrating far more restraint than Krothus would have, that much was clear. Such words said to him would have resulted in a swift end.

"Drahka," Lokk spat, his voice icy cold, "If you really think I am unfit to lead this tribe, then feel free to challenge me, instead of spouting shit from your coward mouth."

That did earn a moment's hesitation from the defiant warrior, but she continued along her mutinous path. "I meant every word. I challenge you, Lokk, and after I put you in the dirt, my first act as the new Chieftain will be putting these Ruined down after you."

Krothus scoffed, the thought of such a ridiculous challenge was amusing at the very least. He could snap her neck with a wave of his hand, dismember her with a single strike from his runeblade, the delusion of this orkathi woman was on full display.

Headcleaver rolled his eyes, sharing a look with Krothus for the first time. The bemusement seemed mutual.

Without another word, Drahka rushed forward, handaxe swinging in wildly from one side.

But Headcleaver hardly seemed concerned. The crude blade whistled through the air above his head as he ducked below it with ease. Drahka, to her credit, didn't fall off balance - twisting and shifting for her return strike almost immediately. But Headcleaver dodged that one too, leaping to one side, surprisingly agile for such a brute.

"Come now, Drahka. When I strike, you know I won't miss."

She hissed at him through her tusks before unleashing a flurry of blows, a painter trying to fill a canvas with red. But the canvas was not cooperating. Worse still, the canvas began fighting back.

Headcleaver pierced through the wall of strikes with a single sharp butt of his axe handle. It was only halfway between a slap and a smack, a good deal less lethal than the other side of his axe would have been, but enough to send Drahka teetering to one side, her balance lost.

Then Headcleaver pounced. Wailing through the air with a haunting screech, his axe came down with tremendous force, Drahka's eyes wide in a sudden fear as the inevitability of what was about to happen dawned on her.

The Chieftain was right, he didn't miss.

"Clear out this mess and toss it outside. Make it an example," said Headcleaver, pointing to his guards.

He pulled his axe out of his grim work with a squelch, not at all worrying about the gore dripping off the blade, pattering away like a particularly gruesome summer shower. The guards wasted no time in enacting his orders.

Now that was a proper display of leadership. Cutting down those who questioned you, using the result as an example for those who dared to follow in such traitorous footsteps. Perhaps these creatures were not as lost as Krothus originally thought.

Headcleaver grinned at them with a horridly ugly smile. "Now, Ruined, you can see why I am Chieftain, and why you should not seek to make me an enemy."

"Enough Lokk," Soultotem said, not at all happy, "You should not celebrate our tribe growing restless and defiant."

Headcleaver bristled at the chiding, but the shaman quickly turned to Krothus, "So you are awake, grey one. It pleases me to see you are still uncorrupted."

Krothus smiled. "My will is my own, as it always will be." He would like to see the day someone truly believed they could take that from him.

"Don't give him an opportunity to brag about such things, we will be here all day otherwise," said Vyrion, wiping the smile off of Krothus' face as quickly as it had appeared, "Now - what is the plan for Lord Fira?

The aged shaman casted one last glance at Headcleaver, almost daring him to interrupt her, before responding.

"We will help you into Lord Fira's fortress, as promised, provided the grey one understands what he must do to uphold his part of this bargain. Then we can save our people."

"I've already been told I alone am able to slay the abomination you fear so greatly, witch," Krothus said, "If you get us to our destination, I will consider it."

"I am a shaman, not a witch, Ruined," she hissed, "If I were a witch, then perhaps I could understand the dark magic at play. It is not something the ancestors understand."

Chieftain Headcleaver, uncharacteristically silent, shifted his massive axe from hand to hand like an agitated child.

"Dark magic?" Vyrion asked, always eager to hear the plight of lesser creatures.

Krothus already wanted to be rid of this place. But his desires, as always, were overlooked.

"Lord Fira is a powerful sorceress, able to corrupt minds with a whisper," said Soultotem, "She ensnared Lokk's father the moment she appeared to build her fortress."

Headcleaver scowled. "He volunteered half our tribe as a workforce in exchange for meaningless platitudes and trinkets, assuring us that this was a motion merely to gain her initial trust, leverage he would use to push for favours further on." He spat on top of the pool of blood where Drahka had been killed. "They're still there."

"As his passion for this alliance grew, so too did my concern," Soultotem said, "I advised him time and time again for caution, to reconsider this festering relationship with Fira. He dismissed my counsel with ever greater resentment as he continued doing her bidding."

Krothus didn't understand. Someone should have challenged his commands, questioned his rule, taken over the tribe if need be. Strength of the mind was as key as strength of the body, and if either faltered, then the Ruined code dictated that they were no longer destined to rule.

"And you did nothing?" he blurted out.

"I fought my father on every illogical decision he made," Headcleaver growled, "I tried to make him see reason. But he was my Chieftain, and my father. It's not something I would expect a fatherless Ruined to understand."

Krothus blinked at the insult, and then shrugged. If fathers stopped you from seizing power when you should, he was glad he didn't have one.

"Is your father with Fira now? Could we not retrieve him as well?" asked Vyrion, clearly eager to sideline Krothus yet again.

Headcleaver shook his head. "Whatever is left is my father no longer. He led our warriors into the Decrepit Temple, paving his path with the blood of Nightshadow honorbound to follow him, all for some cursed relic. And once he delivered this prize to Fira …"

The chieftain fell silent.

Soultotem put a gnarled hand on the young orkathi's massive shoulder. "In short, Ruined, we need to retrieve those of our tribe still trapped within the fortress. We cannot do so with Fira's abomination lurking within."

Krothus looked over the crimson beasts in front of him. Could these orkathi be trusted? They could easily inform Lord Fira of their trespasses, use himself and Vyrion as bargaining chips in exchange for those hostages. But he sensed truth behind their words. As savage as they were, the Nightshadow seemed to value their honor above all else, underhanded betrayal was far more likely to be the Ruined way, not the orkathi. Besides, if they tried crossing him, Krothus would deal with it as Ruined always dealt with lesser beings, like a boot crushing an insect.

Of course, Krothus already knew his partner's view. Vyrion's own opinion had surely been made up the moment he'd heard of the Nightshadow's plight. His softness for the downtrodden was always present.

"So, if my companion and I were to agree to help you," Vyrion began, his tone confirming Krothus' thoughts, "When would we leave?"

"Now." Headcleaver hoisted his massive axe on his shoulder and stomped out of the tent, tentacled hair swinging behind him. Soultotem followed, giving the Ruined a polite nod of her head before shambling out of the tent flap.

Krothus and Vyrion, left in the dim tent of bones, fresh gore at their feet, shared a look.

"Shall we?" Vyrion asked.

Someone grunted something just ahead, only to be met by a horde of shushing, as if every sound would somehow alert Lord Fira to their plan.

Vyrion had spent much of this march near the Chieftain and his shaman - at least he thought he had, there was hardly any way for him to tell. He could just barely guess the shaman's presence within the Ruin, some small trickle of power just ahead, a puddle compared to the vast reserves of power Vyrion's master emanated, but a noticeable presence nonetheless. Krothus, on the other hand, was much easier to locate, his aura as familiar as Vyrion's own, some vague feeling of superiority and impatience.

It was hardly surprising that Krothus was unhappy about their current situation. Vyrion had never known him to help another person unless it furthered his own goals, but the premise of a creature only Krothus could defeat seemed to be just enough to get him to cooperate.

If only Vyrion knew what was going on in that gray skull, what his worries were, his plans. Krothus had always kept his thoughts to himself, but serving different masters had resulted in yet another wall being drawn up between them, one Vyrion could very much do without.

The warband slowed, and then halted. The trees had thinned, the night sky peeking through all around.

"We're here," grunted Headcleaver from somewhere ahead.

Vyrion pushed his way to the front of the throng, standing side by side with Krothus.

"Lorfang," said Headcleaver, pointing at a sinewy orkathi with a long scar wrapped round his neck, "Take a group up the walls, find out where our people are being held. Silence is key."

"My pleasure, chief," Lorfang said, smiling with a jaw full of crooked, pointed teeth. He set off through the warband, hissing and snarling and grabbing whichever warriors he saw fit for such a task.

Though from Vyrion's perspective, neck craned up towards the sky, climbing seemed like a terrible idea.

A desolate field of charred tree stumps gave way to walls that seemed to stretch up and touch the stars themselves, towers springing out of angles and corners like nails holding the place together. Great beams of light prowled the ground below in wide arcs, and in the middle of it all sat a heavy metal slab that looked more armor than gate.

"This looks expensive," Krothus said, in the understatement of the century.

"It was a heavy price, paid in blood," rasped Soultotem, glaring at the walls as if they were killing Nightshadow warriors at that very moment.

"And you are planning to put it to siege?" Krothus scoffed. "Vyrion and I might as well have tried to knock the walls down ourselves."

Headcleaver bared his tusks. "Any wall built can be scaled."

Krothus frowned, unconvinced.

Vyrion too, was hardly optimistic. He was watching Lorfang, growling at his gang of conscripts and anointing them in blessings of dark mud like some jungle priest. Someone else was handing them hooked spears and long spindles of vine. Was this really what they were putting their faith in?

A beam of light crossed just in front of them. Vyrion thought he just could make out the silhouette of some guard above, hidden in the glint of the moving mirrors. Lord Fira was far from any reinforcements, but judging by just the size of the place, and the moving shapes up on the walls, her garrison was more than enough to outnumber any force the Nightshadow could assemble.

As the search beam moved along, leaving Vyrion musing about troop numbers, Lorfang and his mud-caked warriors charged out of the trees.

In the starlight and shadows, covered in jungle soil, they were nothing more than dark shapes. Even those pairs of yellow eyes that Vyrion disliked so much seemed to disappear. If he hadn't known they were there already, Vyrion doubted he would have been able to see them at all, and if they stayed out of those searchlights, neither would anyone else.

Another beam of light swung around. The group halted as one, the beam crossing in front of them, just out of reach. As it passed, the shadows charged forward yet again. The deadly dance continued each time the lights would near, and it wasn't long before the group reached the walls.

"Your warriors seem experienced," Vyrion said, trying to relieve the nervous tightness in his chest.

Headcleaver grunted in agreement. "They are. We have attempted to find our people before. The guards are lazy, predictable, always following the same simple paths."

It should have been encouraging, but Vyrion still found himself having to force a smile.

The shadows fanned out at the base of one of the towers. Then, in one fluid motion, they hurled their spears. Up and up they went, dark and near invisible things that sailed high into the air, the opposite of shooting stars. The walls were high, but not high enough.

Vyrion watched the wild strings sail up and over. One of them failed to make the distance, but it was caught before hitting the ground and thrown back up. The hooks must have found something to grasp, because the vines remained, slowly swaying as though the long tails of some giant jungle cat. A very thin cat, at that.

"Will the vines hold their weight?" he asked, trying to assure himself.

"Some might," Headcleaver shrugged, with as little care as he could muster. Krothus tried his worst to hide his smirk, while Soultotem frowned on like she'd just tasted something sour.

Some of the orkathi climbers latched onto their vines with their arms and legs, coiled snakes shimmying upwards, others planted their feet on the wall, trying to walk up it as they hoisted themselves along the vine. Whatever the method, luck seemed to be far more important. They were only halfway up when their vines started to give way.

The first orkathi plummeted to the ground like a silent boulder, a distant thump carried away on the evening breeze. Another dashed her head on the wall as she fell, painting the grey stone with a streak of red. Others followed in their stead, but the rest climbed on, not one making a sound as they plummeted to their demise - Headcleaver had demanded silence. They delivered it no matter the cost.

Some eventually reached the top, hoisting themselves up and

disappearing onto the battlements. Vyrion could have sworn he heard some distant shouts, maybe the clash of metal, so he braced himself for all those circling lights to converge, revealing the warband and shattering the fragile peace. But despite his fears, there were no alarms, no rallying bells. The night was silent, bar the jungle's ambience of leaves rustling, insects chirping.

One of the searchlights in the near tower halted its circling, then another. Someone leaned down and gave a wave.

"It's done, then," said Headcleaver, before turning to Vyrion and Krothus, "Ruined, you're next."

Vyrion swallowed. He had thought he would have calmed down, seeing that the wall could be climbed. But now it was worse, he could only think of those who had fallen. If he was quick, and the Ruin saw fit, he would surely be able to slow his fall enough to save himself were the worst to happen - but what if he went the way of the second faller, brains splattered over the wall midway down? The Ruin was only as fast as he was.

"And what about you, Headcleaver?" Krothus said, "Not planning on risking your own neck?"

Headcleaver gave him an ugly tusked grin. "As my name might suggest, I am not a warrior fit for stealth. When Lorfang finds our people and opens the gate, and you two have completed your business, whatever it may be, then you will see what I will risk for my people." He then drew himself up to his full imposing height. "Or, if you truly think I am trying to betray you, we can settle this right here."

Vyrion rolled his eyes, was this really the time? Some really couldn't help themselves.

Krothus just chuckled. "As entertaining, and one-sided, as that would be, I have business with Lord Fira. Perhaps another time."

"One-sided was what I was thinking as well," the young chieftain said.

"For the Ruin's sake, let's get this over with," Vyrion huffed, dragging Krothus away. Why did big men always need to prove themselves big?

The two Ruined left the jungle and strode across the wasteland towards the walls. Vyrion kept expecting the lights to suddenly move once more, to see piercer bolts rain from above as the trap was finally sprung, but they made their way to the base of the wall without any disturbance. Several more muddy Nightshadow warriors sped past them.

Krothus stopped at one particularly thick vine, looking up at the orkathi scrambling up the wall above, then down at the broken limbs and twisted bodies all around.

"You aren't afraid of heights are you?" Vyrion asked, grabbing onto a vine himself and pretending he wasn't terrified. He had to resist yanking his hand back immediately, the thing was covered in a layer of thick, sticky slime that made his skin crawl.

"I'm not afraid of anything," Krothus declared with a knowing smile. Then he wrapped part of the vine round his hand and started the long climb.

Vyrion sighed. He was sure Krothus took some perverse pleasure in making him look bad. Vyrion wasn't even afraid, he was *concerned*. Yes, that sounded much better. Concerned.

He wrapped his other hand up in the uncomfortable stickiness of the vine. One arm ahead of the other, that's all it would need. First it was his right; straining, struggling as it pulled up the rest of him. Then his left; elbow wobbling as it did its part to hoist up everything else. Right. Left. Right. Left. Soon enough, he was off the ground, legs wrapped around the vine, trying to keep it steady.

Right. Left. Right. Left. The winds picked up as he climbed, whipping through his previously neat hair. Right. Left. Right. Left. A quick glance down was enough to send Vyrion's head spinning. Right. Left. A gust of air rippled against him as some orkathi plummeted past. He heard a crunch below.

"One in front of the other, ignore everything else," he said to himself, not surprised to hear the wobble in his voice. His arms burned, his hands were numb, and it felt any second his vine would snap. Krothus as nowhere to be seen, no doubt already finished. Still Vyrion climbed.

For a moment, he was back at the Ascendancy. He felt the dry winds blowing over the dunes, the harsh sun beating down on his neck, and as he struggled, he could almost hear the acolytes laughing at him, always ready to make a bad day worse.

But Vyrion was no longer the hopeless boy he had once been, even if the darker recesses of his mind would tend to disagree. He reached out into the Ruin, drawing from it, letting it wash over his tired limbs and fingers rubbed raw. It was like drinking water to quench his thirst, like eating to satisfy his hunger; it just felt right. The moment he did, his aches disappeared, his pain vanished - his pace doubled, like he was being pushed from behind and pulled from above.

In no time at all, he was letting a gray hand yank him up over the wall.

The moment he got his footing, Vyrion's hands were on his knees, heaving great breaths of air into his lungs as if he had just nearly drowned.

"Are you alright?" Krothus loomed over him.

"Fine - I'm fine," Vyrion gasped. All that soreness started seeping back in.

"Good. Watch your step, it's slippery."

The stone beneath their feet was already slicked in blood. The source was evident enough; a squad of Imperial guards, their armor ravaged and their throats cut, piled atop a lone orkathi, leaking via a dozen piercer bolts. Describing the grisly scene as slippery was certainly missing out some details.

"They work fast," Vyrion muttered. He pulled the hem of his robe up, out of reach of all that work.

"They aren't done, either," Krothus said, nodding over to one side.

Lorfang looked like he'd just burst out of something's belly, covered head to toe in gore and mud, holding a crooked, dirty blade against a man's neck. The rest of the Nightshadow warriors who'd made it up the wall were watching as if it were a performance of the finest quality.

"I don't know. I don't, I swear," the guard sputtered, in a voice so high he might as well have been singing. He looked young, younger than Vyrion even, with bushy unkempt hair and watery eyes that never once strayed from the dagger shoved in his face.

But Lorfang just smiled through his tusks. "Slavers always know where slaves are kept. I am going to ask again, where are they?"

"... don't know ... I just don't," the guard whispered, his voice a barely audible squeak. He briefly glanced at Vyrion, his eyes carrying desperate pleas for help, but Vyrion said and did nothing, feeling sick to his stomach for it too.

Some of the surrounding orkathi growled, or hissed, clearly unhappy with the lack of progress, but Lorfang hushed them with one hand. "Now, now. He might be telling the truth."

The guard nodded furiously.

"Or he might not."

The guard stopped immediately.

"You have a family?" Lorfang grunted, tapping the side of the man's head with his dagger, leaving a bloody stain.

"A-a wife. And a boy," the man breathed.

Lorfang frowned. "And you think you're the only one? Every one of us here is searching for our family. Our wives, our boys."

That dagger was drifting very close to the man's right eye, the brutal tip a hair's breadth away.

"But they were *taken*. By you."

"I didn't, it was -"

"Then *tell* us," Lorfang hissed through his crooked, pointed teeth, "Where are they?"

The dagger started to draw a thin red line across the man's cheek.

Krothus was standing there with his arms crossed, unreadable. The guard was perfectly still, shivering as beads of blood started to bubble up on his cheek.

Vyrion had to do something.

"Soldier, just tell the orkathi where their people are. That's all they want."

Vyrion was surprised as everyone else to hear those words, least of all from himself. But he didn't want to watch this man be tortured, and even if the Nightshadow were their allies, he was not required to agree with their every decision.

The guard let out a deep shuddering breath, like a great weight had been lifted from his shoulders, a silent thanks in his eyes to the Ruined who had given him permission for such a betrayal. "The slave pens," he breathed, "They're in the slave pens. It's a wooden, one story building across the fortress, near the barracks."

"Good. Now was that so hard?" said Lorfang, gentle, but with all the warmth of a prison warden.

Vyrion watched the broken man let out a deep breath. He wasn't sure what they would do with such a prisoner, especially seeing as he had seen both himself and Krothus. Perhaps the Nightshadow would take him back to their grotto for now.

Lorfang seemed to have another idea.

"Now, slaver," he hissed, foul spittle spraying over the guard's face, "I will make sure you fully understand the *pain* you have put us through."

That dagger started to draw across the man's face again, considerably deeper this time.

"Every. Last. Bit."

"Wait-" Vyrion started, his hand going to his runeblade. He wouldn't just stand there and watch.

Then there was a horrid wet crack as the guard's head snapped to an unnatural angle.

Krothus held one clenched fist in front of him. As he released his hold and the surge of the Ruin faltered, the guard dropped to the floor. The orkathi stared at the man's broken neck, then at Krothus.

Lorfang whipped around. "What gives you the right?"

"I could ask the same of you, beast. He betrayed the trust of his superior, the punishment is death, not torture." Krothus said, every inch the proud, imposing Ruined Vyrion wished he was.

Eager to do his part, *any* part, Vyrion kept his hand on his runeblade hilt, eyeing the other Nightshadow warriors, who were just as unhappy with the turn of events as their leader.

Lorfang pointed his dagger at the broken-necked guard. "They deserve it, every one of them. My daughter-"

"I don't care," Krothus said bluntly.

Vyrion wanted to at least appear diplomatic. "I hope you find your daughter, Lorfang. But you have your mission and we have ours." But any attempt to bridge the gap was quickly dashed when Krothus already started walking off, leaving Vyrion surrounded by a very unhappy group of Nightshadow warriors.

"Good luck," Vyrion said meekly, jogging after Krothus.

"Ruined," Lorfang growled, and spat on the floor.

Vyrion followed Krothus down a staircase cascading down the back of the outer walls. The interior of the fortress was dim and cramped, a maze of narrow stone paths and blocky concrete, with the occasional stubborn jungle tree forcing its way out of the grey.

Krothus, as usual, was pounding the ground like it had personally wronged him, maintaining a pace that Vyrion had to half-jog to keep up with.

"Thank you for intervening, Krothus. That man should not have been left there to be toyed with. He was just doing his duty to his master." Hardly felt much better, saying it aloud. A master who was enslaving innocents.

"And we are doing ours," Krothus responded, keeping his eyes forward. "I only intervened because I saw you about to get involved. Your sentimentality continues to get the better of you, remember that we can't spare every person we come across."

"But that doesn't mean we should simply resign everyone to death."

Krothus snorted. "If they had the power to end our lives, our foes would hardly think twice. It's the Ruined Code, Vyrion. It's not personal."

Vyrion hated it when Krothus acted all high and mighty. "And when will you be pushed to the limit, Krothus? One day you are going to be presented with a choice that even you can't handwave away."

Krothus seemed like he was going to say something else, but stayed silent. There was something on his mind, but just as Vyrion had come to expect in recent times, he declined to share it. The pair fell quiet, sneaking through the fortress without much more to say.

It wasn't the first time the pair had argued, nor would it be the last. If he was being honest with himself, Vyrion envied Krothus in his commitment to the Code. Krothus was liberated; no responsibility for his actions, his choices already decided for him, his conscience crystal clear as a result. A mentality forged out of confidence, like Krothus, was not burdened by the anxiety and lack of logic that would so often leave Vyrion crippled and indecisive. Meanwhile, even for sparing that guard from a far more gruesome fate, Vyrion was saddled with guilt and regret at not doing more, doing better. It was a wonder he was a Ruined at all.

Vyrion and Krothus ducked into alleys and hopped over walls, sticking to the shadows to avoid any patrols. They could have easily taken the tired guards meandering back and forth, with their stifled yawns and heavy feet, but there was no need to risk Lord Fira's wrath.

An extravagant estate sat on a fenced hill in the middle of the fortress, a lone gem on an otherwise drab crown, outside of which was a gatehouse that Krothus had particular interest in.

The moment they drew near, Vyrion could sense someone inside, someone separate from the small army of patrols all over the estate.

"We aren't the only Ruined here."

"I know," Krothus said, "My master has an agent within Fira's compound, one that I have been told to check in with for further information on my task."

Vyrion felt an instant anger. "And you kept this from me? Why?"

Krothus shrugged. "It makes no difference. I will get the information we need, it changes nothing further than that."

"And what if this apprentice wants to complete Fira's task for themselves, killing you for her favor instead? What if they get alerted by my presence and raise the alarm, expecting betrayal on your part?"

They were partners, even if Krothus seemed to forget. Making the right choices for the both of them was impossible without the necessary information being provided, and worse still, Krothus forging ahead with his most incautious attitude was something Vyrion knew would only get them into trouble. At their best, Vyrion used to see himself and Krothus as two bickering halves of the same whole, their knowledge a shared pool that both contributed and drew from. But now, it seemed like a wall was being slowly built up, brick by brick.

Krothus looked at him as if he could sense exactly what Vyrion was thinking. "We serve different masters, Vyrion. We have different lives now. We will work together, yes, but we must each look out for ourselves as well, keep certain information close."

"Since when has that been your attitude?" Vyrion said, not understanding, "Only recently has-"

"Since my master can read my mind like an open book, that's when," Krothus said, a rare hint of shame in his tone, "I keep information from you because I must, not because I want to."

"Then speak plainly, Krothus. I'm sure whatever it is-"

"Little time, Vyrion. I will meet you back here shortly." Then Krothus entered the gatehouse.

Vyrion swore under his breath. Had Krothus always been this difficult? The fact that he wasn't beating Vyrion into the dirt at the first sign of argument pointed towards a successful rehabilitation, but there was still quite a ways to go. He seemed to bottle up any complications, hoping they would resolve themselves. And such things rarely did.

That was how Vyrion decided waiting outside in the dark, humid air for something to happen was a poor idea. It seemed far better to try and glean whatever slivers of information he could from this meeting instead.

So, managing to find a hold to hoist himself up on top of the gatehouse, Vyrion crept across the roof. Lucky for him, a ventilation grate wasn't too far off. Removing the grate with care, Vyrion carefully climbed down into a cramped shaft, metal slats delivering a partial view of the interior. He masked his presence in the Ruin as best he could and stayed very still.

Krothus had strode in, confidently placing his dark-armored frame in the center of the depressingly bare room. Another figure, half hidden in the caress of shadows across from him, sported a tattoo across her face and strange, bat-like ears.

"Nara, make this quick," Krothus demanded.

"I was expecting a Ruined. I don't recall my Master saying she would send some mindless brute," the woman said, each word coated in poison.

"Say that again. See what happens." Krothus' hand moved to his runeblade.

Vyrion was glad that Lord Victus did not foster the same level of competition between his own. Though with only four apprentices, the crippled Ruin Lord likely had too little to pit them against one another even if he wanted to. Vyrion much preferred being friendly with Jarek to being rivals.

"Silence, brute. After two years under our Master's guidance, I have maneuvered myself into an influential position as an apprentice within Lord Fira's power base, thinking me a double agent. I have earned her trust, and in turn, have learned a great deal for our Master."

"And?"

"Lord Fira has an army within these walls, her paranoia convincing her an imminent siege, some oncoming bloodbath, is on the horizon. She conducts experiments on forces she doesn't understand, trying to bolster these with demons from ancient times. If Highlord Malus ever catches wind of our Master's plans, Fira and her power base will be set loose on the capital, causing catastrophe and destruction, with the potential to rip apart everything Lord Callida has worked so hard to create."

"Meanwhile, you've sat here doing nothing," Krothus sneered, "How noble."

"I doubt you could understand the intricacies of subterfuge, you hulking oaf, or you would know the scale of the discovery I've made," Nara barked back, with an accusatory finger pointed Krothus' way. "Fira's daughter is the key to everything, she adores her above all else."

"And so your genius strategy is to get rid of her teenage daughter?" Krothus laughed. "What is to stop her from simply running amok with her primary attachment gone?"

Vyrion didn't like the way Krothus was describing what he had been told was a kidnapping. He felt sick to his stomach at the thought. Surely not even Lord Callida would be so bold.

"These are the directions of our Master, so hold your tongue," Nara snarled, "By placing the blame on Highlord Malus himself, he will not only lose an important ally, but gain an enemy."

Leaving his harsh retorts shelved, Krothus only nodded.

"I have arranged the patrols to avoid a sector between this house and the estate. You need only make your way to her daughter's room on the third floor, with a south-facing balcony. Once there, you need to leave this marker inside." Nara handed over a small scrap of colored cloth.

"What's this?" Krothus grunted, snatching the cloth from her hands.

"A scrap from a tabard bearing Highlord Malus' sigil, it will be enough to let Lord Fira's paranoid mind weave the tapestry of deception our master requires."

"Fine. And where will you be?"

Nara smiled, the serpent tattooed across her face baring its fangs. "I will be here, ensuring my position in Lord Fira's court is secure."

"So you will do nothing. What a surprise."

Cloth in hand, he began to walk back to the doorway without waiting for any further instructions. Vyrion, in turn, prepared to climb back up to the roof.

"And you know what to do when you're there don't you, brute?" Nara said, an edge in her voice making Vyrion's blood run cold.

Krothus stopped just before the doorway. "I do."

"Good, slit that brat's throat so she doesn't scream."

Krothus said nothing and walked out.

Vyrion felt his world crumble around him.

Chapter 11
Breaking Chains

The Ruined Code outlined a simple truth - the strong ruled the weak. The weak could be anyone, anything, their only purpose to test the strong, make them prove they were truly worthy to rule above them. Krothus had always found the code comforting. It painted reality in clear black and white, it let him understand that his destiny was to climb his way to the top, to prove to everyone in the Empire; Vyrion, Callida, and even the Emperor himself, that he was worthy.

But just like any great man, Krothus knew he wouldn't get there without doing terrible things. Things that he wasn't entirely comfortable with. Krothus really had no choice. He did them because he had to, not because he wanted to. He did them because he knew that when he got the recognition he deserved, he would be able to remake the world in his image, do away with all the evil men he'd met, repent for all the grim choices he'd made. It would all be worth it.

Until then, Krothus would be harried. Both by his own doubts, and by Vyrion.

"A child, Krothus?"

Krothus had been shoved against the gatehouse wall the moment he went outside. Despite doing the shoving, Vyrion seemed surprised, saddened even, more than angry. Like he was pitying him.

Krothus was not one to be pitied lightly. He easily pushed Vyrion's weak grip away and started walking towards the estate gate. "I do what must be done. I wasn't going to tell you to spare your conscience."

"*My* conscience? You seem to be the one with no qualms about killing children."

Krothus wheeled around. "Whether I take issue with it changes *nothing*. I can't simply refuse to do it, can I?"

Krothus vaulted over the fence and into the estate grounds, a feat easily done with the Ruin assisting him. Time and time again, Vyrion would insist on having these pointless discussions, as if he was some paragon of virtue that the Ruined code didn't apply to, but he always saw the right course of action when push came to shove.

"Of course you can refuse!" Vyrion was close behind, continuing to argue, as if his entire reason for being here was to challenge Krothus at every turn.

"And then what? Callida would kill me for disobeying her, and just send someone else to do the deed in my stead. The only thing that would accomplish would be my death and the girl's temporary safety." Krothus quickly dashed into the shadow under the grand estate building, seeing a patrol at the edge of his periphery. Vyrion was a split second behind.

"Defect, come serve Lord Victus with me, then. You don't have to do this," Vyrion pleaded. Fiery indignation was quickly turning into desperate suggestions.

"I do." He still didn't get it, did he? "Even if I did defect, Callida's new target would be Victus, his apprentices included. The girl would still die, and we would both be next. There is no way out of this."

Krothus found a suitable spot to begin climbing up to the third floor, some drainage pipe half clogged with moss, but before he could, Vyrion grabbed his shoulder.

"Don't do this, I know you don't want to."

Krothus looked down at his partner, who was wearing that same distraught expression carried over from his days of weakness at the Ascendancy. The same one he would wear when pleading for mercy from anyone who would listen.

Krothus slapped his hand away. "Of course I don't want to, But that girl was dead the moment Lord Calida gave the order. If I don't do it, someone else will. Nara, once my Master deems her cover's use spent, could make this same trip on any evening, and no doubt she would torture the poor girl before she finished."

"But Krothus, you don't -"

"I do. And as dishonorable and foul as it is to end the life of a weak child instead of challenging her mother, it will be done, by my hand or another. My Master will know if I haven't, and I dread to think of the consequences."

Vyrion just looked at him, shocked and speechless. Weakness had no place in the Empire, he knew this, yet still Vyrion objected. Krothus had hoped he would have hardened himself since the Ascendancy, but it seemed he still had yet to grow up, yet to see the reality of the world they lived in. But Krothus was done trying to educate him tonight.

"Come, Vyrion," Krothus grunted as he started climbing, "The sooner we get this over with, the sooner we can stop thinking about it."

"No," Vyrion said simply, "I can't watch you do this."

Krothus glared down at him. Vyrion always conceded, always fell in line. But not now.

"Fine. I'll do it myself."

Krothus kept climbing, dragging himself up the outside of the pipe. Each time he felt that cold metal against his hand, he expected to hear Vyrion struggling up behind him, sputtering and gasping like he always did when it came to such physical challenges. But Krothus arrived at the third floor alone.

He had to actively suppress the feeling of shame bubbling up within him. He was doing the right thing, the Ruined Code required it. His destiny required it.

"Just do this quickly," he muttered to himself. He slipped through a half-open window and into the house.

Inside was a hostile prison of cold metal. Strange statues of shadowy creatures and expensive, gaudy decor crowded the walls, while dozens of identical doors stretched down the corridor, lined up like soldiers on a parade ground. In between each sat great tapestries featuring a mask of black, the same featured on the tabards of Lord Fira's soldiers.

A room with a south-facing balcony, what a helpful tip that was.

What his master saw in Nara he couldn't possibly comprehend. Krothus started down the corridor.

Subterfuge was key. Alerting the fortress could be a disaster, Ruin only knew how many soldiers lurked within these walls. Worse still would be Krothus running into Lord Fira directly. He was proud, but not stupid; he wasn't strong enough to defeat a fully fledged Ruin Lord on his own. At least, not yet. Perhaps if Vyrion were with him -

But he wasn't. Krothus knew he was doing the right thing. Certain of it. Vyrion was just too soft to understand. Fira's daughter would surely grow up just to be as oppressive and deranged as her mother, and by ending her life before that happened, Krothus might as well be saving her from a worse fate.

He wasn't too far along the corridor when Krothus heard someone approaching. He tucked himself into the wall, right behind a statue of some terrible spiked creature eating its own young.

"It's not that bad," one guard said, his voice audible over the steady beat of their armored footfalls

"I'm telling you, it's unnatural. I won't go anywhere near it."

"Well you don't have to, that's why you're on patrol with me instead."

"And that's better?"

Krothus could feel how close they were, no more than a few feet away. They must have come around the corner. He reached down for his runeblade, but stopped himself. He didn't want to do anything that could potentially result in him being discovered. Leaving two singed corpses on the floor for example. Perhaps there was another way.

With a wave of his hand, Krothus ripped the window at the end of the hall open with the Ruin, filling the hallway with an echoing slam and a rush of evening air.

"What was that?"

The guards ran right past Krothus, towards the seemingly autonomous window.

Krothus wasted no time, slipping out of his hiding place and darting around the corner to the south side of the estate. This hallway was nearly identical to the previous one, except the rows of entryways ended at a single metal door at the end of the hall. A single guard stood in front of it, shoulders slouched and head wandering, clearly bored.

This complicated things. Krothus needed to be quick. Shifting his face into a scowl, an expression he had mastered through extensive practice, he strode down the corridor towards the lone guard, every inch the proud Ruined he knew he was.

The guard spotted him immediately, hesitantly moving his piercer into a readied position. "Halt. Lord Fira made no mention of any Ruined coming by this shift."

Krothus had to resist smirking, his gamble was so simple, so easy. He just hoped this exchange would be quiet enough to avoid attracting the other guards.

"How dare you ignore my title, wretch. I am an apprentice to Lord Fira, a Ruined, and I demand to be treated as such," Krothus spat, pointing a finger like it were a judge's gavel imposing a sentence. He was nearly at the door.

The guard was confused, Krothus could sense it, could see it. His piercer had dipped towards the floor already. "Apologies, my lord. I have strict orders not to open this door except for Lord Fira and a few others. Did you obtain written permission?"

"Of course," Krothus lied, briefly putting a gauntleted hand into one of his pockets. The guard was an arm's length away. His expression was unreadable under the dark helmet, but it didn't matter whether he truly believed Krothus or not. There could be no witnesses.

Lightning fast, Krothus lunged forward and grabbed either side of the guard's helmet. There was a bit of a surprised struggle, but nothing Krothus couldn't handle. With a mighty twist he snapped the helmet fully round. He waved a hand at the guard's body and his weapon, the Ruin carefully and silently laying them down.

Krothus let out a relieved breath. He was still unseen, but time was of the essence.

He inspected the heavy door the guard had been stationed at. Forged out of some dark metal, it was faceless, no markings or handles anywhere to be seen. Krothus frowned, not exactly certain where to start.

He leaned in closer, carefully scanning the door's metal face. He ran his hands over every facet, every groove, looking for any impurity, anything amiss. Something eventually caught his eye, one panel that looked worn down, a slightly different color then the rest of the door. Krothus pushed his hand against it, and another small panel slid to the side, revealing a keyhole underneath. He smiled - success.

Those footfalls started up again, heralding the return of the two guards that he'd passed earlier. A key, he needed a key. Krothus quickly searched the body of the man he'd killed, emptying pockets and turning out pouches. It didn't take long before he found what he wanted, a heavy key of iron.

The guards were nearly on him now. Krothus pushed his hand into the panel again, fumbling the key into its socket, and the door clicked open.

Krothus grabbed the slain guard and his weapon and slipped inside.

Any second, he expected some shouts of alarm, the clatter of armor down the hallway, a horde of reinforcements converging on his position. But the now-muffled footfalls passed right by. A quick breath of relief was all Krothus allowed himself. Now the difficult part began.

It was dark, with only a whisper of light peeking in from behind drawn curtains. The dim room was nothing like Krothus would have expected the chambers of a Ruin Lord's daughter to look. It was almost completely bare; nothing on the walls, no bed, only small bundles of crystals left on the floor, all of them oozing a sickly emerald aura. It was obvious something was amiss, Krothus could feel the sense of wrongness seeping into his bones. Had he been led into a trap?

In the far corner, facing the wall, was a chair, its metal frame twisted and warped. Not only was it bolted to the floor, but chains held it in place, as if the furniture itself was at risk of escape.

The Ruin pulsed from whatever sat within, Krothus could feel it.

A far off whisper, a phantom touch on his arm. It knew he was there.

What in the Ruin's name had Lord Fira been doing here? The mad

Ruin Lord's reputation left the possibilities endless. No path was too dark for her.

Krothus crept closer, his runeblade raised, as he rationed just enough Ruin energy through the runes to warm them, bathing the room in a soft orange glow. A pit grew in his stomach. Was it from the terrible task he was burdened with? Or was it from the hauntingly familiar presence emanating from the corner of the room? Krothus focused himself, trying to purge his body of anything but his mission. Fear was for the weak, but it was stubbornly refusing to surrender its hold on him.

Carefully, Krothus placed one hand on the top of the chair. He took a deep breath, then wrenched it around.

A teenage girl stared up at him. Stick thin, with ragged, raven hair. Her eyes were bone white, her pupils absent.

Krothus felt a chill run over his body. As her lips drew back over her teeth in a demented, predatory smile, every sense he had screamed at him to run, to flee. He tried to step back, but the girl grabbed his arm, straining against the restraints on her chair to hold him close. No amount of struggling could free him, her bony fingers were unbreakable, her grip iron.

A tiny crystal seated in her forehead, a dark and sickly emerald, began to glow.

And then she spoke.

"*Kyr'akyyqzz rilakz'bor ni fassh Gn'agh,*" groaned a deep voice, not at all her own. What little light was in the room seemed to fade into absolute blackness, all except the crystal. Krothus felt an icy cold crept up his arm where the girl, the creature, was holding him. Fear swallowed up any clear thought in his head.

It began to laugh, a horrible choking symphony in an ocean of shadow.

"*Dai'hsh Gulza'ka athraxus?*"

Krothus somehow understood. It was an offer, an offer to submit and spare himself. To keep his mind from being broken, his soul from being devoured.

The suggestion itself made him furious. His anger was what he needed, a warmth that burned in his belly and flowed outwards.

"Do I want your power, demon? I *am* power."

The Ruin rushed through Krothus and into his runeblade. It burst into flame. The demon shrieked as warmth and light overwhelmed it, sending any shadows scurrying for cover.

It was now or never. This creature must be slain, whatever it was. But Krothus hesitated, just for a second. The girl must already be dead, he told himself. There is nothing left but an empty husk, possessed by a demon, served on a platter. A single blow is all it would take to put it out of this world and succeed in his mission, prove Vyrion his cause was just.

Just do it, damn it.

The girl looked up at him mid-shriek, her eyes appearing normal, her pupils flickering into being for just a fraction of a second. Her eyes were a vibrant blue.

Do it.

Krothus roared and swung his runeblade.

The flames went out as his target fell to the ground in pieces. It was done.

The crystal's glow dissipated as its shattered remnants skated across the floor. A shallow horizontal gash across the girl's pale forehead was all of what remained of that wretched thing. The wound may not have been deep, but as a slow trickle of blood seeped down her forehead, the girl passed out. Whether from shock or relief, the result was the same.

Krothus furiously clenched his jaw. She lived. He had failed.

He had every opportunity to complete his task, the girl was even possessed by a demon for Ruin's sake, and still he couldn't do it. He could already hear Vyrion's insufferable preaching now, a lot of smug talk about 'doing the right thing' and 'being a better man'. For being such a better man, Vyrion never let an opportunity for some convoluted, condescending lesson pass him by.

Still, Krothus couldn't help but wish he were there. Vyrion would have at least filled the silence. For a moment, Krothus just stood there, looking at the girl and the crystal and the chair, wondering whether his destiny had already been shattered. He took out the scrap of cloth meant to signify his allegiance to Highlord Malus and let it slowly flutter to the floor. This plan seemed more pointless by the second.

Then he heard a series of clunks, and the door to the room opened, light pouring in from the torches in the hallway outside. Krothus expected to see his partner stride in, hair neatly combed, relieved smile on his face. Instead, all he got was a bat-eared woman with an ugly serpent tattooed on her face.

"She's dead then. Good," said Nara, a gloating smile wrapped round her face.

The amount of blood on the girl's face did paint a gruesome picture. But Krothus knew that she lived, that he had failed, something he was not keen on revealing.

"What are you doing here?" He didn't like this surprise intrusion at all. Something was not right.

Nara held her arms out wide, like she didn't know either. "I heard some commotion from inside. As a loyal servant of Lord Fira, I went to investigate and protect her most valuable prize, only to discover I was too late! Highlord Malus' assassin had already killed the vessel and shattered the phylactery shard."

She ignited her runeblade, the crackling green energy of her power runes dazzling in the half dim light. "The least I could do is ensure the assassin doesn't escape."

Krothus cursed himself for being so stupid. "You really think our master won't realize you've betrayed me? She'll hear of it, that much is certain."

"You think she'll care? The strong rule the weak, oaf, she'll do nothing but thank me for ridding her of such a weak prospect. The result will be the same, and her plans will continue."

Krothus knew she was right, this task was as much a test for him as anything else. Whether he failed it by a lack of conviction or by betrayal, the result was the same, he would be a failed apprentice who Callida would be more than happy to cut loose. In fact, she had probably expected Nara to pull this move, even encouraged it.

But Krothus was not about to roll over and simply let fate take its course. He reignited his runeblade, feeling its warmth rising up his arm. "If you think I will go down easily, think again."

"Not a thought I had, but it does remind me," Nara said, holding up a finger, "Never forgo an advantage."

She pulled a lever next to the door. The moment she did, a bell started ringing above them, deep gongs that shook the room and resonated out into the night. Shortly after, a disharmony of tolls answered, every type of tone and pitch ringing out all over the fortress. Shouts followed and all those identical doors along the hallway swung open, sending guards flooding into the corridor.

That wasn't good. Krothus felt it was dishonorable to rely on the strength of others over yourself, though he would have loved some soldiers of his own to make a sudden appearance. Instead, all he could manage was a scowl.

"Highlord Malus sent this assassin - kill him!" Nara called out, urging her troops forward.

A small army of swords and piercers were brought to bear as the wave of black armor rushed towards Krothus. Far too many to take on with only a runeblade. But the Ruin would always be a far more powerful weapon, so Krothus called on it, fueled by his biting anger at his failure, at Nara's predictable betrayal, at Vyrion's absence. From all around it flew into him, aided him. Krothus willed the raw power into barely-restrained submission in his palm.

Nara led the charge, her runeblade crackling with emerald light. She was only a stride away when Krothus released the power he held. With a thrust of his palm, he unleashed a bone-rattling wave of power across the room and down the corridor.

As if caught in the winds of an impossibly heavy storm, Nara and the guards were ripped off their feet. They slammed into walls, the ceiling, each other; filling the air with the crunch of armor and screams of pain. A fair amount didn't get back up again.

Krothus wasted no time in pressing the attack. Nara had managed to stay unscathed, bar a split lip, but was now sheltered behind the front line of her troops. So Krothus brought the front line to her.

Piercer bolts rained down on him. Swords slashed in from every angle. With the Ruin's blessing, Krothus continued his deadly dance, weaving past blows, carving through bodies, relentlessly staying alive. He ducked under a sword that nearly took his head off, carving a gulley in its wielder for his trouble, before tossing another into a hail of boltfire. He crushed a third inside his armor with the Ruin, the metal crumpling inwards like it had a mind of its own.

The thrill of battle rushed through Krothus' veins, washing away all his fears, all his doubts. He felt alive. But regardless of his enjoyment, it was not something he could keep up forever - for every guard that was slain, another appeared moments later, with no end in sight. To make matters worse, there was a Ruined to contend with.

Nara met every blow Krothus delivered with her own. She blocked an overhead slash and twisted away to open Krothus up to her troops. She intercepted a Ruin blast, allowing a bolt to graze his arm. Every time Krothus would thin the herd around him, she would slide in with a quick cut through his defenses.

Krothus had no doubt that, had this been a fair fight, he would have had her in two blazing pieces already. But Nara was no fool, she was always just close enough to harry him, never enough to truly be threatened. And worse, Krothus could soon feel the beginnings of exhaustion setting in.

He bled from a dozen cuts, the blaze of his runeblade dwindling, but every swing of his weapon delayed the end. Nara had begun creeping closer and closer, a predator sensing weakness, an end to Krothus' seemingly futile struggles.

"Time to die, brute," she snarled, "You can't keep this up much longer."

Krothus said nothing, too focused on survival, though he would have liked to think he could have come back with some biting retorts had there been no other distractions.

The guards kept coming. Krothus prepared for his imminent

destruction.

Then a glimmer of hope in the chaos. Krothus thought he sensed someone nearby, someone who was most certainly not Nara's ally.

Nara held her runeblade, crackling and pulsing, to Krothus' neck, clearly too preoccupied to sense anything amiss. "This has been fun, but I'm afraid we have to end it here. Your master will be informed of your death, assassin, but I doubt they will care. You were simply too weak to succeed."

Krothus looked over at her, trying and failing to conceal a smile. "You really do talk too much, don't you?"

Nara frowned. "What do you have to smile about, you-"

A deafening crash drowned her out, followed by a blinding surge of power. An arc of crimson lightning erupted into the hallway. It jumped from armor to armor, guard to guard, leaving the smell of burning flesh in its wake, setting Krothus' hairs on end. Only when the overwhelming luminescence faded did Krothus realize he was now surrounded by smoking husks and melted armor.

Nara, one side blackened and burnt, looked decidedly less confident. Especially when Krothus' saviour strode in.

"Vyrion," Krothus said. He was happy to see him, but not so much that he needed to embarrass himself.

Vyrion nodded back. "Krothus."

"What the hell is this?" Nara snarled, clutching her side, badly burnt and smoking.

"It's the end." Krothus wasted no time. He kicked her leg, sending her to her knees, then swung his runeblade down at her. One final strike was all it was going to take.

"No," she whimpered, struggling to hold Krothus' weapon at bay with her own. "It wasn't meant to happen like this."

"I guess I'm just lucky," Krothus spat, pushing down further.

Nara was breathing hard as she struggled. But the burning blade continued downwards. Like the inevitable tick of a clock, bit by bit, the flames licked at her face and arm, scorching through cloth and skin. Tears briefly welled in Nara's eyes as her arms wavered.

"Tell our master that-"

Her grip broke. The runeblade plunged down.

Then the moment it was over. Krothus fell to his knees, exhausted. Vyrion was already there. "What happened, then?"

"I failed," Krothus said simply, not able to meet Vyrion's gaze.

Vyrion said nothing at first, only walked past to the twisted chair. He looked over the girl with care, carefully examining where the crystal had been, now that bloody gouge across her forehead. The light shining in from the hallway let Krothus have a proper look. She was frighteningly lean and deathly pale, draped in that cloak of dark hair.

"You didn't fail, Krothus," Vyrion said softly, "Though you seemed very close to succeeding. Thank the Ruin you did not."

Vyrion's pity was something Krothus did not want or need, so he elected to ignore it. "She was possessed by some demon. It spoke through her, controlled her, all through that crystal in her skull."

Vyrion started fiddling with the girl's restraints. "Not unlike the presence that sought to gain a hold over you. I can only hope that Lord Fira's interest in the Nightmare Lord's domain came from her daughter's state, rather than the other way around."

One of the girl's chains clattered to the floor, Vyrion quickly moved to the other.

"What are you doing?" Krothus asked, pushing himself to his feet with a pained grunt. "We aren't taking her with us."

"She's seen you, hasn't she? So we must take her if we are to keep this mission intact," Vyrion said. "Unless you are planning on finishing her off?"

Krothus scowled at him, while Vyrion gave him a sad smile. The other chain hit the floor.

"After the skyport, this makes us even," he said, picking up the unconscious girl and handing her to Krothus.

Krothus effortlessly slung her over his shoulder. She smelled like sweat and stale fear, but that very well could have been Krothus himself.

The faint disharmony of bells continued to echo across the fortress. Vyrion was crouching down now, his palm on the charred armor of a nearby guard, like the fool was mourning a man he'd killed himself.

Krothus felt rage bubble up within him. He had failed. He couldn't kill someone that was very nearly dead already, whereas Vyrion had pushed past his own quandaries to save him. He had wanted Vyrion to harden himself, but not like this, not off of his failures.

The room violently shook as a monstrous roar erupted from somewhere outside. The clatter of armor wasn't far off.

"We need to go," Vyrion said, stating the obvious.

"Then we will." With a swipe of his hand, Krothus blasted open a nearby window, the clash of metal and glass barely heard over the bells. They jumped down out of the opening, using the Ruin to land softly on the grass outside.

Where the Lord Fira's compound had been eerily quiet before, it was now pure chaos. The walls' searchlights had been turned inwards, flooding paths with blinding light, while shouts and bells came from every direction. Krothus and Vyrion jumped over the fence around the estate once more, then ducked into the first alley they saw.

"The Nightshadow aren't going to be happy with this," Vyrion said, "Their struggle has just become a great deal more difficult."

"And ours, if you are still planning on aiding them," Krothus added, adjusting the living reminder of his failure on his shoulder. "We still need our own way out of here."

"We are not leaving them to their fate. Our escape can wait."

Krothus laughed. "How utterly predictable you are, Vyrion." It came out far more bitter than he expected it to.

"As are you, Krothus. You would only help them if it benefits you, same as anything else."

Krothus just shrugged, it was hardly something he cared about. "Does it make a difference? For their freedom or my glory, if I do decide to kill the beast they fear, the motivation is irrelevant. The result is the same."

Vyrion just shook his head, what he always did when Krothus had made a valid point. "Regardless, we need to get back to Lorfang and the others. I'm not sure if he's found those that he came for, but the only way to escape safely would be through the gate."

He pointed out at the huge portal of metal up on the walls just ahead of them. The tower they'd arrived at was just nearby, the lights still facing out to the jungle, the steps and wall filled with small figures.

"Even if they found the rest of their tribe, they won't be alive for much longer," Krothus said. "The moment Fira appears, its all over."

"Then we'd better hurry."

The pair mirrored their previous route at double speed, avoiding any open areas or lights; the last thing they needed was an ambush to slow them down. But with each step, Krothus felt some hostile presence watching them from the shadows. Something was reaching out through the Ruin; a faint whisper that tickled his ear, a light touch on his arm, some presence in the corner of his eye. It could only mean one thing, Lord Fira knew they were there.

Krothus sped up.

When they got to the stairs they had used to get down from the walls, they found them blocked. A sea of bodies clogged the stairs, Imperial guards and Nightshadow warriors engaged in a brutal melee over a landscape of shattered armor, severed limbs, and broken bodies. It heaved like a rough sea, each side crashing against one another but moving nowhere.

Wordlessly, Krothus and Vyrion ignited their runeblades. Then they dived in.

The addition of two Ruined quickly tipped the scales in the Nightshadow's favor. Pressed on both sides now, the guards were swiftly overwhelmed, dispatched either by runeblade or an orkathi axe. Krothus was careful to not let any harm to the girl on his shoulder. She was a sign of his failure, yes, but if someone did what he could not, it would only make him appear weaker.

When the final guard met his end, his helmet caved in with a spiked mace, the surviving Nightshadow let out a tired cheer. There were maybe half a dozen warriors left of those who had climbed the wall, the rest lay around them, unmoving.

"Where is Lorfang?" Krothus asked. The creatures could mourn when they escaped this place.

One of the warriors, a white hand painted into her face, stepped forward. "He is returning with our kin. We were told to open the gate when we returned."

Krothus shook his head, if they waited that long it would be too late. "Open it now."

She narrowed her eyes, "We were told to-"

"Do you think I care?" Krothus snarled, taking a step towards her. "Open it. *Now.*"

The warrior looked to those around her, but they offered no support.

"Fine," she said, and the warriors started towards the gatehouse.

Krothus could feel something unnatural in the air. A frigid wrongness that grew stronger with each passing moment, a frozen finger that scratched all along his back and sent shivers down his arms.

"Something terrible approaches," Vyrion whispered.

The orkathi were blind to it. Some malevolent being had turned its gaze onto them, malice and hatred seeping into their very being, and yet the Nightshadow still shambled along as if nothing were amiss.

"Faster, damn you!" Krothus bellowed, shoving the closest warrior forward.

To their credit, the Nightshadow picked up the pace. They found the wheel up on top of the gatehouse, and after a series of snarls and grunts in their foul tongue, they started turning it. Their crimson muscles bulged as the wheel of heavy iron began to slowly tremble around.

Krothus leaned over the wall as the gate started to tremble open.

With the searchlights unmoving, it took him a while before he could see them. The entire warband stood, eerily motionless and silent, in the shadows outside. Not a single torch in their midst, Krothus was reminded of the legions of corpse-soldiers in the tombs underneath the Ascendancy, who had watched over him while he trained in the night. Perhaps, if things went poorly, the warband wouldn't be too far away from corpse soldiers. A morbid thought, but if the full might of Fira was brought upon them, it would be the inevitable conclusion.

The unsettling presence around them only grew stronger. He was nearly trembling.

"Krothus," Vyrion said, tapping him, "They're here."

He wheeled around. A wide courtyard stood just inside the gate, the maze of concrete just beyond. Distant fires pulsed in the far corner of the fortress. First it was a mere trickle, a handful of orkathi shuffling into view, but it quickly became a flood. A horde of crimson crowded towards the gate. They were large and small, old and young, ragged and beaten down, but still very much alive. At least for now.

The gate continued to creak open.

But the soon-to-be rescued Nightshadow weren't exactly celebrating - they were fleeing. Pushing, crushing, screaming, all fuelled by looks of terror casted behind.

There was another monstrous roar, this time much closer.

The warriors turning the gate wheel were struggling, pouring all of their formidable strength into twisting that heavy wheel, sputtering and grunting. It was working, the gate was rising, but it was too slow, the gap still too narrow. Even if it was open, Krothus was sure that the mass of fleeing Nightshadow would be blocking the warband from entering, pinning them in place for the slaughter.

Screams came from the back of the crowd. A line of Lord Fira's troops pressed into them from behind, cutting their way through whoever they caught up with. Some of the recently freed Nightshadow held them back with a mismatch of salvaged weapons, along with what looked like Lorfang himself, his gangly form waving around that knife of his as he tried to urge the group on.

But Lord Fira's troops suddenly stopped their butchery. The air was growing colder with every passing second, some invisible blizzard howling over Krothus' skin. He saw the soldiers pull to the sides, making a gap in the middle of their formation.

Then, a screech pierced the air, a thousand needles scraping across rusty metal. It drove nearly everyone to their knees.

Krothus refused to move. His head felt like it was about to explode, but he knelt for no one, least of all now. Vyrion was doubled over next to him with his hands over his ears.

This was it. Krothus carefully set down the girl, somehow still asleep. Krothus briefly wondered what she dreamt, her face a mask of peace, a stark contrast to the chaos and death around them.

He drew his runeblade, felt its warmth flow through him, a welcome barrier against the frozen air. Then it came.

The creature burst into view, crushing a handful of Imperial soldiers underfoot as if mere blades of grass. It might have been an orkathi, once. Crimson skin stretched over an impossible volume of muscle, its massive arms ended in claws the size of swords, and within its chest sat a glowing emerald crystal, pulsing with unholy power.

Lorfang stepped in front of the beast, his weapon nothing more than a tiny twig in comparison. What he was trying to do, Krothus had no idea. He was ripped in twain instantly, and the slaughter continued.

Krothus, exhausted and wounded, was doubtless the only person smiling.

Finally, a worthy challenge.

Chapter 12

Awake

Vyrion watched as Krothus leapt from the battlements and into the chaos below, his blazing weapon like some comet tumbling down from the sky.

He couldn't help but wonder if he had just watched an insane man leap his last as that spark disappeared within the crowd. All because Krothus didn't take failure well. At the Ascendancy, losing a bout would send Krothus on a righteous crusade of brutal training and self-destructive revenge; this time, having a shred of empathy had sent him on a suicidal charge against the most terrifying creature Vyrion had ever seen.

Painted in blood and gore like some kind of brutal warpaint, the thing stopped its rampage for a brief moment, scanning the crowd of fleeing orkathi. Vyrion wasn't sure what had piqued its interest, but the moment Krothus' fiery torch emerged amidst the Nightshadow tide, the abomination was on the move. The crystal in its chest flared brightly. Vyrion's own chest was so tight that it felt like he was being strangled.

Suddenly a great gasp erupted from nearby. The poor girl was finally awake, her limbs flailing, chest heaving as if she were somehow drowning amidst an absence of water. Vyrion knelt down and gently held her arms to her sides.

"It's okay, young one. I won't hurt you." Vyrion hardly knew what to do with teenagers, or children in general for that matter, but the best he could do was try and keep her calm.

Her eyes narrowed; confused, suspicious. Her hand slipped out of his grasp to run along her forehead, bony fingers clawing at the fresh wound, pawing, searching.

"What did you do?" She reminded Vyrion of so many acolytes - that hunger in her eyes, those almost animalistic survival instincts kicking in.

The abomination roared its terrible roar once more, its cry leaving Vyrion's ears pulsing in agony. The girl didn't even flinch, only turning her head towards it, then the lone figure pushing his way towards it through a sea of fleeing bodies. Krothus.

"I didn't do anything. He did," Vyrion said.

"The flames ...," she muttered, reaching up to rub her forehead once more, then her face hardened. "The Nightmare Lord's beast will leave him maimed or turned, as it's done to everyone before."

"Krothus has resisted this Nightmare Lord before, hopefully he can again," Vyrion said, trying to convince himself as well as her. "I have found it helpful in the past to hope for the best and prepare for the worst."

The girl grunted in agreement. "I like that. I'm Inissa."

"Vyrion."

The wall underneath their feet rumbled. The fortress gate finally finished its slow crawl upwards and locked open. The Nightshadow warriors who had been clambering over the opening mechanism collapsed, utterly exhausted.

Vyrion briefly wondered if the Nightshadow would simply use Krothus as a distraction for Fira's abomination and melt back into the jungle. Their main priority had always been to retrieve their imprisoned people, but such a betrayal seemed out of character for their young chieftain. And, as much as Krothus and his imminent duel with the creature seemed like it would give the fleeing orkathi the time they needed, Fira's troops weren't about to let them leave.

Regrouped at the flanks of the square away from the abomination, Fira's Imperial guards had resumed their work. The dull thuds of piercers filled the air with death as they crashed waves of the projectiles into the rear of the fleeing Nightshadow. Some maintained a line of crude shields, but with every second more of them fell.

"When my mother arrives, she will destroy all of these creatures, and you," Inissa said quietly.

"Then where is she? Her fortress is assaulted and she is nowhere to be seen," Vyrion asked, not doubting the girl's words. He had seen a Ruin Lord's power already; Lord Victus might have only one leg but he could have easily swept away Fira's entire garrison with a wave of his hand. Fira herself would be worse than her abomination.

"In her lab no doubt, she hardly ever leaves it," she said, bitterness clear, "No doubt she finds this wonderfully entertaining."

Lord Fira must have been very confident in the outcome of the current engagement to be satisfied with simply hiding away. Vyrion wasn't exactly happy about their chances either.

"Is that where she was keeping that creature?"

"Yes," Inissa said, rubbing at the gash in her forehead again, "She believes her research, this creature, it's part of a prophecy, all to bring the Nightmare Lord back from whatever realm he's been banished to."

"She really is mad," Vyrion muttered.

"Handing her daughter over to a demon isn't enough to give it away?"

Vyrion didn't have a response to that. He was hardly an expert on mothers.

Inissa pushed herself to her feet, skinny arms wobbling, to gaze into the courtyard below. The Ruin swirled around her, around Vyrion too, whipped into a frenzy by the death, the fear, the terror.

Most of the fleeing Nightshadow survivors had made it through the gate. Bolts were still raining down, but the warband had pushed through and formed up, shielding their people as best as they could. Krothus, just ahead of them, stood alone, staring down the abomination, which had spread its massive arms wide, turning its claws up to the heavens.

"*Klr'zksz Zsrastohk nariss?*" it asked in some alien tongue.

It was unlike any language Vyrion had ever heard, every syllable was an assault on his ears, like it were some unnatural sound forbidden to be uttered long ago. The creature's voice seemed both far away and inside Vyrion's head itself, carried along the chilled air.

"It is taunting him," Inissa said quietly.

"You can understand that?" He couldn't make rhyme or reason of it.

But the girl went silent, her arms wrapped tightly across her chest, trembling.

Krothus, a small figure from Vyrion's vantage point, and further dwarfed by his otherworldly opponent, stood defiant. He raised his flaming runeblade into the air. The Ruin swelled with power.

In an instant, the volleys of piercer bolts directed at the Nightshadow halted. The projectiles froze in the air, a dark cloud of halted death. The soldiers continued to fire, the bolts swelling the cloud with every passing moment.

Then, as a general commanding his troops forward, Krothus levelled his runeblade.

The haze of bolts became a wave, rushing towards the abomination, an answer to his demonic challenge. If Vyrion didn't know any better, Krothus looked about to strike down Fira's pet in a single blow.

But whatever this creature was, it was not so easily removed.

With an earsplitting roar, it leapt into action. For all the show of the wall of projectiles, the abomination simply barrelled right through it as if it were a cloud of bothersome flies. Hundreds of bolts stuck in its hide as it rushed towards its prey. In only a few mighty strides, the experiment had closed the gap to Krothus.

It smashed a huge arm downwards. Vyrion braced for the worst.

Krothus only just managed to sidestep the blow, leaving a crater where he once stood. As the beast retracted its hand, he chopped at it with his fiery runeblade, sending a clawed finger flying into the air.

The beast roared. But whether in rage or pain, Vyrion couldn't tell.

Its horrid voice once again filled Vyrion's head.

"*Khj'ri harujsh, kiroskz'jkhu rah gorndoxxi.*"

"You think you are clever, insect, you *will* be made to serve," the girl translated quietly.

Vyrion stomach was doing flip after flip.

The abomination sprung forward again and again. Each blow demolished swathes of the courtyard, each swipe threatened to tear Krothus in two. All the while the crystal glowed ever brighter. Krothus was moving faster than Vyrion had ever seen him, channeling the Ruin through his limbs, his rolls and side steps only just barely quick enough to keep him alive.

After narrowly dodging a claw that would have torn his arm off, Krothus jumped at his opponent, swinging his weapon at the crystal pitted in its chest. For the briefest of moments, the end looked in sight, the crystal would be shattered and whatever sorcery was present would cease.

But the abomination had other ideas. It swatted Krothus down, sending him bouncing across the pavement. The gray Ruined barely managed to get to his feet, the ground cracked and his armor dented, before his opponent's relentless assault was upon him once more.

Vyrion knew Krothus needed help. Sooner or later his use of the Ruin would exhaust him, as it always did, and it would be all over. He might have been a heartless, egotistical, blunt bastard, but Vyrion wasn't about to let him be reduced to paste, not after today. Not after Krothus had proved he wasn't as lost as he liked to present himself. So Vyrion started down to the courtyard, trying to keep calm as he did.

But the girl grabbed his arm. "Don't. Once you get too close, you'll just be ensnared in his grasp. We should flee while we still can."

Vyrion stopped, slowly removing her hand from his arm. "I appreciate the advice, Inissa, but I can't stand by and do nothing."

"Don't say I didn't warn you. Everyone serves the Nightmare Lord eventually, you'll see."

A brief image of Krothus, a crystal embedded in his gray skull, filled Vyrion's mind. He saw Krothus cutting down Jarek, cutting down Lord Victus, his eyes blank and emotionless. He wasn't about to let that happen.

And he wasn't the only one. The Nightshadow battle lines opened, and Chieftain Headcleaver burst into the courtyard, charging towards the abomination.

"For Ruin's sake", Vyrion swore, "If Headcleaver gets anywhere near that thing he'll get crushed, he has no idea what he's getting into."

Hearing this, the Nightshadow warriors who had opened the gate were at his side at an instant.

"Is he truly in danger?" one asked.

"If he is, then we must warn him," another said. The rest nodded in agreement.

"Wait, we can't get-" the girl started.

"Stay here, Inissa. The rest of you, follow me," Vyrion said, ignoring her warnings and running down the stairs towards the gate. The group of warriors followed behind him.

"Father!" Headcleaver's voice rang out, "I have come to put an end to your torture."

Vyrion looked at the creature, then at the Chieftain. That image of Krothus flashed into his head again, ripping through those he cared about. Only now did Vyrion understand Headcleaver's insistence, his drive to end this creature, and his burning hatred for Lord Fira.

Fira's troops moved to intercept the Nightshadow Chief, but Headcleaver's warband were at his side. They retaliated with spears and arrows of their own, while shield-bearers flanked their Chieftain, keeping him safe as he continued forwards.

The abomination paid the Nightshadow no heed, focusing on the tiny gnat with its flaming poker.

Vyrion and his contingent of warriors from the wall were thrown into the melee the moment they entered the courtyard. He pushed and shoved and chopped at anyone he could with his runeblade, trying to get to Krothus.

A roar ripped across the courtyard as Vyrion saw another monstrously clawed finger fly through the air, billowing smoke. A retaliatory blow sent Krothus careening into the crowd.

Trying his best to maneuver his way through it all, Vyrion was just able to glimpse his partner smash into the courtyard ahead of Headcleaver. The beast started to emit some ghastly noise, halfway between choking and retching, which Vyrion could only assume was laughter.

A nearby Nightshadow warrior caught a bolt through her eye. Vyrion grit his teeth as he blasted the shooter with a bolt of Ruin lightning. Lord Fira must be enjoying this - he, Krothus, and the entire Nightshadow tribe were giving this fight their all while she seemed content to sit back and watch as this nightmarish creature toyed with them.

Vyrion was close now, close enough to see Headcleaver clasp Krothus' forearm and drag him to his feet. He looked terrible. The grey Ruined's chestpiece was half caved-in, his arms cut and bloody, his scarred face scraped all over, but strangest of all, Krothus still maintained a smile fit for a drunkard. What he had to smile about at a time like this, Vyrion had no idea.

Headcleaver chopped through a lone guard and tossed him aside like a broken toy, then turned to the abomination.

"It is time, demon," he shouted, raising his mighty axe in the air with one muscled arm, "The ancestors have promised me your death."

Vyrion barely registered his words. Being so near to the Nightmare Lord's creature, he felt sluggish, frigid, like he had been plunged into an icy cold lake. Vyrion heard whispers, somehow drowning out the noise of battle, soothing and calming.

Give up, they said.

None of this is real, they said.

Let us take you away, they said.

While this was happening, his vision blurred. The crystal in the creature's chest didn't just draw Vyrion's attention, it demanded it. It's emerald glow was warm, inviting, full of pulsing power. If only Vyrion could touch it, then he could claim it. Yes, claim it, that's what he wanted.

Krothus's bruised, bloodied arm appeared, slamming into him. Vyrion blinked and stopped. He had already managed half a dozen steps towards the creature without even noticing.

"Careful now," Krothus grunted, "I know you have a stronger will than that, Vyrion."

Vyrion shook his head, trying in vain to remove the aura that sapped his senses, "I know, I just - I thought-"

The creature croaked it's terrible laugh once more as the crystal in its chest grew blindingly bright. Ghastly emerald flames began to burn across its back, a cloak of fire and brimstone, while dark energy began to pulse into its muscles, turning faint crimson to an unnatural green. Then it spoke. It spoke in perfect common, with the voice of a crumbling mountain, contempt and hatred dripping off every syllable.

"You will *die.*"

Its voice came from everywhere at once, it echoed in Vyrion's mind just as it shook his bones.

"I will drink your blood and grind your bones to dust. I will wash over the world, mind by mind, city by city, only to watch it burn." Its rows of fangs drew into a smile. "I had been promised a suitable vessel before, but now I have found one more suitable, one with a pride that I wish to *break.*"

Its crazed eyes fixated on Krothus, who stood defiantly next to Vyrion and Headcleaver.

"Many have tried to break me, demon. All have failed," Krothus said.

"Its plans won't matter when it's dead," spat Headcleaver, "*Now!*"

The line of Nightshadow shield-bearers parted, unveiling a line of crude bolt-throwers fashioned out wood. The abomination roared in defiance. With a dull series of thunks, they let loose their payload, sending savage barbs hurtling towards the creature.

It took them head on. The first was smashed through with a flick of its hand. The second glanced off its hide and careened away, while the third splintered on contact with the crystal. But the fourth found its mark. The abomination hissed as the bolt sunk deep into its left shoulder.

Warriors rushed forward, Headcleaver leading them.

Vyrion had a bad feeling about this.

"Don't!" Krothus said, trying to stop them from drawing any closer. But he was too late.

The bolt in the creature's shoulder crumbled, demonic flames burning it to ash in seconds. With a terrible screech, the abomination struck. It ripped heavily muscled orkathi to pieces in the blink of an eye. One warrior barely managed a scream as his body was flattened under a massive fist. Limbs cascaded in all directions, blood painting the courtyard.

Headcleaver blocked a blow that would have meant certain death with his axe, the blade pushing deep into the beast's monstrous knuckle.

All the while it continued to laugh.

"Vyrion," Krothus said, his voice desperate, "Hit it with everything you have."

"But-"

"*Do it!*"

Vyrion channelled all the Ruinous energy he could muster, his heartbeat pounding in his ears. He doubted this would work, but he had no other alternative. Those focus runes ignited along his runeblade as power flooded through it, each one sending waves of energy cascading through him.

Heacleaver was still stuck, struggling with that fist bearing down on him. He held his axe with two hands, arms trembling, one leg bent badly. The creature's other arm swung around.

But Krothus was there. His runeblade, now the center of a vast inferno, crunched into the abomination's oncoming strike. Orange flames intertwined with demonic green as Krothus held its claw in place.

Break his chains, whispered a familiar voice, very different to the demon's. *Do it.*

Power flooded into him, and more runes ignited along his runeblade.

Then, with a crash louder than the strongest storm, Vyrion unleashed his channeled power. The crimson bolt followed a jagged maze through the air, crackling, burning the air itself, before slamming into his foe. The bolt ripped through layers of hide, flesh, and bone. It poured into the abomination's chest, into the crystal, carving a blackened crater all around it. Each beat of Vyrion's heart fed more and more energy into his attack.

"Break, damn you," Vyrion yelled, giving all he could, "*Break!*"

But his own strength gave way before the crystal did, and the attack faded out. The crystal was now as bright as the sun, sending sparks of energy cascading across the abomination's ruined chest.

It still wore its horrid fanged smile.

For a moment, nothing happened. Headcleaver struggled to keep upright, Krothus grunting as his blade wavered, and Vyrion gasped for breath, exhausted. Then the world turned upside down.

A huge shockwave erupted from the crystal, expanding out across the entirety of the courtyard. The expelled energy sent every being within its radius flying.

Vyrion skidded and flailed, only stopping when he collided with the metal armor of some slain guardsman. His head spun, he felt the iron taste of blood across his tongue. The beast couldn't be stopped. He shakily lifted his head, trying to gauge how much time he had left before it came to crush his skull.

In the center of a now blown over courtyard, the abomination stood victorious, a living force of nature. It was burnt, stabbed, mutilated; but still it reigned supreme.

Krothus and Headcleaver had somehow managed to stay relatively near, perhaps being stuck into the creature lessening the blowback from the shockwave. Vyrion tried to struggle to his feet, but he was exhausted, barely able to keep his head up to watch.

The two turned to each other and clasped their hands. An orkathi and a man, a Chieftain and a Ruined. Two warriors, seeking a warrior's death. Vyrion would have smiled if they weren't about to be ripped apart.

He may have opposed Vyrion at every turn, but Krothus never gave up, and it was always something Vyrion admired. Whether he was made an example of by the Ascendancy overseers, or beaten down by some senior acolyte looking for trouble, Krothus always fought to the end. Vyrion had always found it easier to submit, to plan for whatever came next instead.

But it didn't seem like there would be much coming after this at this rate.

The abomination rushed forward, no doubt eager to end those that had irritated it for so long. But Krothus and Headcleaver stood their ground. Vyrion thought he saw the slightest hint of a crack on one of the crystal's perfect faces. Had that been there before?

Krothus' fiery runeblade lit up once more, not much more than dwindled embers at this point. Headcleaver flourished his massive axe to one side, then the other. The creature drew closer and closer.

It lunged for Krothus, who lunged right back. Their flames collided in an explosion of heat and smoke. His runeblade, barely visible in the resulting smog, only just kept the abomination's claws at bay.

Something burst through the haze.

Headcleaver, flying through the air like some intervening God, flung his heavy frame at what had once been his father. Rippling orkathi muscles parted vapour and flame as they carried their devastating payload. The axe of Headcleaver, gleaming gold and thirsty for justice, crunched into the crystal. Then, with a high-pitched wail, it shattered.

There was a great flash, then a rush of air. The now smoking corpse of the abomination fell to the earth.

The chill that had permeated the air evaporated, and Vyrion breathed for the first time in what seemed like hours.

It was done.

Chapter 13

Return

Krothus stared at the girl. The girl stared right back. A Nightshadow shaman ignored them both and continued applying whatever strange lotion their wounds had been prescribed.

Krothus grunted as the shaman began gently rubbing it into the tear on his side, the mixture leaving his skin warm and tingly, like being comforted by a roaring hearth. If it hadn't been for his armor, that demon would have surely caved in his chest.

The girl whimpered as the same mixture was applied to her forehead. If it hadn't been for Krothus' weakness, she surely wouldn't have been there.

Still she remained silent, just staring at him with those sunken eyes.

Since the warband's hasty retreat back into the jungle, she had not spoken a single word to anyone except Vyrion, which Krothus preferred. The less talking the better. Though Krothus could have laughed at describing their exit as a retreat; it had been nothing more than an undisciplined rout. The moment that that crystal had shattered, Lord Fira's wrath filled the air, an irresistible rage, an impending doom that signaled her emergence from whatever pit she had been hiding in. So they fled, nothing more than rats scattering at the first sign of light. Krothus was not one for retreats, but even now he was so exhausted that he could barely stay awake, it was a wonder he had even made it back at all.

So, tired and aching, he sat there in that damp cave. Being stared at. And staring back. At least he could appreciate the silence.

"You tried to kill me, didn't you?" the girl asked.

Krothus frowned. So much for that silence.

"Yes."

"But you didn't."

She wanted to rub his failure in his face, clearly. But Krothus was not one to admit anything of the sort.

"I was interrupted."

"And then after that?"

If Krothus was going to frown any harder, his jaw would break. "Watch your mouth, girl. Who says I won't do it now?"

Now she was smiling. Why did he always have to be so charming?

"He was so very interested in you, nearly obsessed. I have never seen him try so hard to turn someone. Yet still he failed."

"Who?"

"The Nightmare Lord."

Krothus scoffed. "The demon? Yes, he was very insistent. He promised me much."

Those unholy words still echoed in his mind. Their exact meaning unclear, but their message crystal - limitless power for endless servitude. Never had Krothus felt such an overwhelming presence, such a temptation. He had seen images of himself crowned the new Emperor, Lord Callida bound at his feet. Mountains of gold. Endless feasts. The entire world; all had envied and worshiped him.

But he knew all of it was a lie.

Accepting such a 'gift' meant groveling at this demon's feet, begging for scraps of power like a worthless dog. He never had any doubt that those dreams would waft away, nothing more than meaningless platitudes that would never come to light, not to be included in the damning contract he was being presented with. Krothus already had a glorious destiny, he would not throw it away.

The girl shifted closer. "I know him better than most. He seeks a vessel, a body for him to reclaim his long-dead kingdom."

"Seeks? The demon is slain."

She shook her head. "For now. He eternally lingers, trapped in his prison. The crystals are a focus, tethering him to this world."

Krothus hissed, though far more due to the shaman's firm grip on his heavily bruised leg than the news that he had made an enemy of some immortal demon. "Then I will destroy all of these devices and you can stop pestering me about it."

The girl's expression hardened. "My mother will create more. Then she will force you to be his vessel and take me back."

"And what a great mother she was," Krothus sneered, not enjoying the threat, "I am glad I never gave mine the opportunity to shove a demonic focus into my skull."

If looks could kill, the girl would have ended Krothus where he sat.

They fell back into silence, only occasionally pierced by a distant drip of water somewhere in the cave.

But as much as Krothus was pained to admit it, he felt for the girl. He remembered being her age, his life had been nothing but struggles and trials, a constant fight for survival. At least then he had Vyrion, the girl seemed to have no one. He had also just kidnapped her. Or rescued her. The distinction was irrelevant.

"What is your name, girl?"

"Inissa."

"Tell me, Inissa, what was your mad mother thinking, giving you over to a demon?"

"She told me that he wanted to experience the mortal world through my eyes. That it was a gift, and I should be honored," she said quietly, "But Nara told me it was because I was a waste of space, so unwanted that my mother made a deal with a demon just to take me off her hands."

Krothus snorted, "It may please you to know that Nara is dead then."

Inissa glared at the ground, as if it had said some word in Nara's defense. "Good."

Krothus chuckled. This girl wasn't all bad.

The shaman gave them both a nod and headed out of the cave, her bowl empty and her job, whatever it was, finished.

"Our savior departs," Krothus muttered, his body finally forced into movement, despite its protests, as he grabbed his gear.

Inissa, having nothing to her name but her name itself, stood right next to him.

Krothus stared at her. She stared right back.

"Where do you think you're going?" he asked.

"With you," she replied.

Krothus' frown returned with a vengeance. "You can follow me all you want, but you won't get far. You aren't coming with us."

He was already on his way out the door, limping all the way. Perhaps if he moved fast enough his problem would just disappear.

The morning sun glared down at him as he wound his way up those spiraling paths through the Nightshadow Grotto. Inissa's footfalls were close behind, but Krothus ignored them and continued.

The air was filled with the steady beat of drums, cheers carried along on the wind. The Nightshadow were celebrating. And whenever Krothus passed, he was treated like the hero he rightfully was. Conversations were interrupted, dancing paused, and meals put on hold; all to give him the respect he deserved. Each time someone bowed to him, each time he was given a salute of respect, Krothus' mood soared. He had gained a valuable resource here. After only a few months of being a Ruined, he had already begun rallying forces to his banner, the first step towards many more.

Now, all he had to do was stay alive long enough to use them.

His ascent ended at a stout wooden gate built into stone, an open portal from the safety of the grotto into the uncertainty of the jungle beyond. Sentries stood guard amidst the celebrations, while the gnarled figure of Soultotem, leaning on her staff, talked to the runted form of Vyrion nearby.

The shaman swung around to face Krothus as he approached, her gilded tentacles swaying. "The ancestors are pleased this day, gray one. Our people are united once more and the abomination has been slain."

"As they should be, I won you a great victory." It was *his* victory.

Vyrion ignored the clarification. "I have just been discussing with Soultotem our current predicament, getting back to the *Donovan*. We may have found a solution, but you aren't going to like it."

"And why would that be?"

"Yes, what is it?" Inissa said, appearing at Krothus' side, an annoying gnat he couldn't seem to shake. He was certainly rethinking sparing her life.

But Vyrion was hardly able to open his mouth before he was interrupted. Chieftain Headcleaver limped up the path out the Grotto, flanked by a group of warriors that seemed to have been selected based on both tremendous size and explicit ugliness. His leg was tied to boards of wood and he was wielding his large axe as the world's deadliest walking stick.

"What a fight that was, Ruined!" Headcleaver yelled. "Songs will be sung of this day, that I can assure you."

It seemed like the young Chieftain's animosity had evaporated, which Krothus wasn't surprised by. Only an idiot would still doubt their sincerity, though Headcleaver wasn't far off from one.

"It was an honor to fight with you at my side," Krothus said, swallowing down the urge to publicly take all the glory for himself. If he wanted their assistance in the future he had to play nice, though Headcleaver wasn't about to make it easy for him.

Headcleaver had no such qualms. "Yes, it was. With your help I was able to strike a blow that freed my father and our tribe from damnation."

Then he reached out a muscled crimson arm, which Krothus clasped in turn.

"A blow that was only enabled due to my intervention," Krothus declared, gripping Headcleaver's forearm tightly and forcing his smile wider. Headcleaver too clamped down on Krothus' own forearm with his tremendous strength.

For a moment, both of them continued wrangling each other, as if their arms were treacherous snakes seeking to bite the other. The effort was considerable; false smiles were strained, veins bulged and muscles rippled. Krothus thought his arm was going to explode.

Vyrion softly cleared his throat.

Krothus and Headcleaver released their death grips and stepped back, grinning as they did.

Vyrion clearly just didn't understand. Having an underling with such ambition was amusing, especially one who thought himself Krothus' equal in such a way. Krothus couldn't help but wonder if Headcleaver, in his delusion, thought of him the same manner.

The Nightshadow Chieftain spoke once more. "If you Ruined have need of our tribe in the future, we stand ready to answer the call. We owe you a great service, and we never leave a debt unpaid."

It was Vyrion, ever the diplomat, who spoke first, "Thank you Chieftain Headcleaver, we will always keep you in mind."

Headcleaver then gestured to one of the warriors accompanying him, a big brute with a skull fashioned into a shoulder plate. He held a metal box in his clawed grip, looking absolutely terrified of it.

It was easy to see why, it carried with it a familiar sense of wrongness, a slight chill in the air.

"A parting gift," Soultotem croaked.

"A curse," Headcleaver muttered.

"One of my shamans had the foresight to take the shattered remnants of the crystal into her care just before we retreated," Soultotem said, watching the warrior place the box on the ground in front of Krothus like something were about to jump out at any moment. "We have sealed the container as best as we can, with every spell and blessing I know of. Please take it far away from here."

"We will," Krothus said, picking it up. It was ice cold to the touch, and harbored the faintest hint of whispers carried along the breeze.

Vyrion looked at it with concern, but moved on swiftly. "It is best we make arrangements for our departure."

"Yes, *our* departure" Krothus emphasized, stepping away from Inissa as best he could.

She scowled at him. Vyrion sighed and pulled Krothus aside.

"Come, Krothus, she-"

"Vyrion, we can't take her."

Vyrion pinched the bridge of his nose. "Why can't you just give her to Callida? That was the plan before."

Before you *lied to me* was no doubt how Vyrion wanted to end that sentence, but he had evidently held his tongue.

"If my master sees the result of my failure, she will think me weak. She would quickly dispose of me as her apprentice, and no doubt the girl too."

"You're lying to yourself, Krothus," Vyrion stated simply. "Callida would find a use for Inissa, whether it be as another apprentice, a spy, or even some pet. She is hardly one for looking the other way when an opportunity presents itself, and any of those options would be better than Inissa's previous fate."

Krothus snorted, as always Vyrion was refusing to let an opportunity to do good pass him by. "I will not be handing her over to my master, not when it would potentially result in disaster for myself."

Were everything in a vacuum, Krothus might have helped Inissa, but not when her survival itself was a potential threat to him.

"Then why not take her as an apprentice yourself? She is strong in the Ruin, and adding an apprentice to your power-base is an important step for any Ruined."

That stopped Krothus in his tracks. Of course, he knew he was being manipulated, Vyrion was trying to appeal to his ambitions to help Inissa and bring Krothus to his side. The softer side. But the thought did intrigue Krothus. Every Ruin Lord needed apprentices, they were the foundation of a power base, the footsoldiers and agents that carried out their Lord's will, just as Krothus and Vyrion were now. Sure, each apprentice would try to usurp their master one day, but that was simply the cost of doing business with the Ruined Code.

"Even if I wanted her as my apprentice," Krothus said, thinking aloud, "Lord Calida would know, just as she will know about all that has transpired here. She can see into my mind as easily as if it were an open book."

Vyrion smiled at him, putting a hand on his shoulder. "Then we will just have to ensure we show her only what we want her to see."

Without elaborating further, Vyrion turned back to those waiting for them.

"Shall we, Soultotem?"

"We shall," she said curtly.

They left Headcleaver, who limped back down the spiralled path, no doubt set to enjoy the celebrations, and followed Soultotem.

She led them to some ancient jungle tree, perched perilously on the upper reaches of the grotto, like it had only decided against jumping down at the last minute. A tightly carved pathway curved up to the top of the tree, so tight, in fact, that none of the beefier orkathi warriors were able to fit up it, leaving them stood at the trees base. Soultotem too, gave the Ruined a nod as they climbed, before disappearing the way they came.

Once at the top, Krothus realized a watchtower had been cut into the tree itself. Several spindly orkathi lookouts stood guard around a crude bolt thrower, the bolt loaded into it tied around a thick spindle of vine. In the distance, the Decrepit Temple watched them from its high perch.

Krothus immediately understood what Vyrion had planned.

"What is this plan?" Inissa asked.

"The *Donovan* is the skyship that we will be returning by. It will be flying slowly over the treeline nearby, waiting for us," Krothus began, hardly believing at how stupid his words were going to sound, "And In what I can only assume is a sign of madness, Vyrion has determined the best course of action is to shoot a ballista at said skyship, with us attached."

Inissa reacted with a mixture of disbelief and laughter, as if Krothus had explained his reasoning for why he was actually, in fact, a dog.

"If I could offer a correction," Vyrion said, raising an interjecting finger, "We are shooting it first, then using the length of vine behind it to climb up to the skyship."

"This is a stupid idea," Inissa said, as if she was the only sane person present. Krothus couldn't have agreed more.

"I know," Vyrion said, "But unless you have anything better to suggest, then we have no other choice."

The girl thought for only a moment before simply shaking her head.

Krothus too, could think of nothing else. It may have been stupid, but there really was no other option that didn't involve scaling the Decrepit Temple again, which he did not want to repeat.

So they waited. Krothus watched a lone cloud slowly crawl across the blue, taking a casual stroll towards the morning sun. It wouldn't have been too bad, had they only waited a few minutes. But when minutes turned to hours, Krothus was soon wishing he had simply started walking back to Thanaton instead.

But eventually, the ambience of the jungle was offset by low hum of something in the distance, followed closely by the first glimpse of a rapidly growing speck on the horizon.

"Wake up," Krothus said, delivering two swift kicks. One, gently tapping Vyrion out of his meditation, the other bowling over a formerly napping Inissa to her dismay and Krothus' amusement.

"Thanks," they both said, with vastly different meanings.

The team of orkathi who had been lounging about the bolt thrower began to wheel it around, the wooden contraption creaking in protest.

It was such a stupid idea. But stupid as it was, Krothus was going to do it anyways.

The speck had steadily evolved into a familiar silhouette; stocky hull with two orbs on either side. The *Donovan* cruised low over the treetops, meandering slowly over the jungle like it were a bird looking to roost. The bolt thrower slowly turned to face it.

Krothus looked down at vines attached to the crudely loaded bolt. They weren't much thicker than those used on Fira's fortress, and he had seen how those had fared.

The skyship was nearly on top of them now, rustling leaves off their branches and sending gusts through the treeline.

One of the orkathi crew hit the back of the ballista with his fist. The cord snapped forward and the bolt flew into the air. Krothus was fairly sure he saw a chunk of the device itself fly off into the jungle for good measure too.

Krothus sighed. It really was stupid.

But considering all of the things that could have possibly gone wrong, the trip wound up being slightly better than Krothus had anticipated.

Sure, the bolt had lodged quite deep into the hull of the skyship, but the *Donovan* had stayed airborne. And of course, the wind had whipped them back and forth like it had a personal vendetta, trying desperately to fling them from their lifeline, but they had stayed firm. Even more surprising was the fact that the *Donovan* itself had not simply whisked off when an unknown projectile had pierced its metal skin. It had stubbornly maintained its low, steady course as if nothing had happened at all.

Only once the three Ruined had managed to plant themselves on the top deck of the skyship, the consequences of their method of return became very apparent.

"What did you bastards do to my ship?"

Captain Fareese, loose jacket rippling as great waves of air assailed her, shrieked equal parts obscenities and curses as she peered out of cockpit doors, her gaze fixed to the bolt dangling off the otherwise spotless skyship.

Krothus, who would have normally taken swift retribution against such insults, instead trudged through the invisible forces buffeting him, seeking the shelter of the cramped cockpit. The others followed. His ears instantly thankful for the quiet, Krothus' face began to regain its feeling the moment he was away from the biting wind.

Captain Fareese, after spending a few more moments shouting her frustrations out into the sky, eventually bolted the cockpit doors closed and slid into what little space was left in the cockpit.

"This room isn't meant to hold four, let alone six," she grumbled, squeezing her way through a gap under Krothus' arm.

"Six?" Krothus asked, not that he could see anything forced into a small corner of the cockpit. Only when Inissa managed to scramble down the steps, did Krothus have just enough room to garner a proper view.

Two metal beings sat in the copilot chairs, unperturbed by their new guests, minutely adjusting levers or turning dials. They looked like a child's interpretation of a man, a bizarre mockery of a face instilled on what served as their head, their metal innards a whir of clanking and clicking. Krothus didn't know why, but he had a sudden urge to smash them to bits.

"I bought these clankers at the Tartoiine skyport," Fareese said, lounged across her chair and tying up her hair up from where the wind had its way with it, "Got tired of having to pilot this ship all by myself." It looked to Krothus like she had gotten tired of doing anything at all.

Vyrion ignored the statement entirely. "Did you do as we asked at your destination?"

Captain Fareese shrugged, "We were logged in the ship manifest when we landed, and we made a big show about our cargo and our Ruined passengers. Someone might suspect something, but it's out of my hands if they do."

Krothus couldn't help but feel that it was all futile. While the rest of Thanaton may not think anything amiss, his master would find out about his failure in her own ways soon enough, and that's all that mattered.

"And who, or what, is this?" muttered Fareese, gesturing at the scrawny teenage girl poking out of the stairway.

Inissa glared at her.

"None of your concern," Krothus snarled, pushing his way past Fareese's metal copilots and motioning Inissa down the stairs, with Vyrion just behind. The less people who knew about the girl the better.

"Well done on doing the impossible, boys. I might even feel bad asking for payment this time," the captain called down after them.

Krothus wondered how easy it would be to replace Fareese with one of those metal contraptions. It would certainly talk less.

The crew quarters was exactly as they had left it, dreary and confined, with Sergeant Lorren's detachment of guards looking just as bored as when Krothus had last seen them. Only Lorren himself perked up at their return, rising and saluting instantly.

"My lords. Anything I can do?

"There is," Vyrion said, gesturing to the sergeant to sit back down, which he did. But even despite Lorren's utmost professionalism, it was obvious that he was staring at the same complication Krothus was struggling to accept, Inissa.

Lorren cleared his throat and forced himself to look at Vyrion, "Does it involve-"

"Yes, it involves Inissa," Vyrion said, "And more importantly, it involves your utmost secrecy."

"Of course, my lord."

While Vyrion and his pet soldier began their hushed conversation, Krothus dragged his new apprentice to the side for a conversation of their own.

"Listen up, whelp. You listen to every word I say, every command I give you, or more likely than not, you will wind up dead. Whether that is by another's hand or my own, that is up to you."

"Okay," Inissa said, not exactly sounding enthusiastic.

Krothus frowned, "The correct response is 'Yes, master'."

The girl sighed. "Yes ... master."

"Good. Now your first task is to get some rest. Don't talk to anyone."

Inissa didn't have to be told twice. She crawled into one of the cots, and without a moment's hesitation, went to sleep.

Vyrion appeared by Krothus' side soon after. "Arrangements have been made for her, she will be safe for now."

"Good," Krothus said, still unsure about the whole thing.

"Now, to the more important matter - we need to stop your master being able to find out about this by reading your thoughts."

"How long do we have until we land?"

"A few hours, I hope," said Vyrion, glancing at Inissa, snoring away.

Krothus scratched the back of his shaved skull, as if feeling around for the gap Callida used to enter it. "Do you have any ideas?"

"Just the one," Vyrion said, grinning.

*

"*Where is my master?*"

Krothus was already shouting. It was a poor habit to have, raising his voice when nerves were getting the best of him, but he always felt it gave him a bit more authority when he would be doubting himself most.

The subject of his verbal assault, a guard who seemed to be flip flopping between terrified and surprised, gave him a shaky salute.

"Lord Callida is in the gardens, my Lord."

Krothus didn't dignify the weakling with a response, he just strode through the front doors of his master's compound, a man on a mission. Or a man finishing one, at least. His back ached from the skyship ride, and the rest of his body ached from everything else, but he was glad to once again be in a place where his authority was recognised. He allowed himself the satisfaction of seeing servants and soldiers scurry from his path. Nothing more than roaches fleeing a boot.

His actual boots, formerly squelching through the jungle mud, now pounded into the pavement below with satisfying cracks. It was good to be back.

With each step, Krothus cleared his mind. He and Vyrion had discussed this first step, he was only to think about the here and the now, anything else was unnecessary, deadly even. He would not allow himself to fall victim to his Master's tricks.

After one final turn, Krothus' footfalls fell silent over a bed of neatly trimmed grass. Rows upon rows of neatly arranged flowers, bushes, and trees spread across to a far wall, separating the rainbow of colors from the extensive view of the rest of the city's grey drab. Pleasant citrus smells swept through the air, and cobbled walkways arranged the leafy soldiers into ranks so neat a general might have wept. It was eerily silent, except for the occasional snip of something from the far wall.

At that end of the garden there lay a wicked looking plant; a dark twist of branches, leaves and thorns. Behind it lay an impressive view of the Dark Pyramid, and beneath was who Krothus sought. Lord Callida, with unparalleled care, wound her way around the plant's defenses, its small fruits in a basket at her feet.

"Ah, my young apprentice," she purred, not bothering to turn, "You have returned."

"I have," Krothus said lamely. His mouth felt very dry.

His master frowned as she snipped another fruit into her basket. "And?"

"Nara is dead," he blurted out.

That got her to turn around, her dignified face not betraying a single thought. She waited for a moment before responding, staring at Krothus as if waiting for him to confess to any other crimes. "I see. A shame, she was most useful to me, dedicated apprentices and tactful spies are so hard to come by these days."

She fixed him with her dark eyes. Krothus felt that familiar tingling at the back of his head.

He started speaking, staying ahead of her probe. "Her ambition got the best of her. Nobody betrays me and lives."

He briefly thought about Nara's face, moments before his runeblade had made its mark; displaying nothing but desperation and fear. She had no business being a Ruined if that was how she met her end.

"So it seems," Lord Callida mused, sounding completely unconcerned at the death of her longtime apprentice. "I had a feeling she would attempt something along those lines. But well done, Krothus, you passed a test I had not even set out for you. By killing her, you have proved you deserved her place at my side more than she did."

Krothus was sure she would have been just as happy had he been killed. It would have cemented Nara's position, and he would have been nothing but a footnote. An unintended test? More lies.

"Despite Nara's intervention, Malus should still be the one Lord Fira thinks is responsible," he confirmed.

"And the girl?" she asked expectantly.

"Dead," Krothus mumbled. He knew her foray into his mind had started the moment she had asked, so just as he and Vyrion had discussed, he gave her exactly what she wanted. Images flashed by his mind. The abomination. Killing Nara. The girl, strapped to her chair, nothing but the whites of her eyes. Demonic promises. Finally, the runeblade striking through her head, blood everywhere.

"*Dead*," he said again, louder this time. Get out of my head, Krothus demanded silently, you've seen what you wanted. But she stayed. Other images came and went. Headcleaver shattering the crystal. Krothus jumping out of the skyship. What was she looking for?

It was only then that Krothus decided to enact Vyrion's plan. Instead of setting up feeble barricades across his mind, only for his master to burst through with ease, he let her in completely. All his defenses evaporated as her probes marched through his head unimpeded. Krothus started offering up specific frames of his memories as tribute, desperate to keep her attention as he carefully kept only the most inner recesses of his mind locked away. The memories flew past; arguments with Vyrion, shaking Headcleavers hand, the terrible force of the Nightmare lord.

As he did, Krothus felt a strange sensation tickle his skull, like his brain were a book that was being quickly flipped through. A moment in his mind was thrown to the forefront, so clear that he could paint a picture. Krothus stood, a lone defiant figure, against the abomination, its back alight with green flame.

"My, my," Callida whispered, suddenly next to him, her hands dancing over his shoulders, "You have done so much more than I had hoped."

Krothus had never been this close to her before, her smell was overpowering, intoxicating. Her finger was under his chin now, her face just across from his. "You destroyed Fira's work, harried Malus' plans far more than I could have anticipated. I am so very grateful."

"I ... " Krothus started, his voice hoarse.

But she suddenly twisted away. Krothus frowned.

"With Lord Fira believing Highlord Malus had sent you to slay her apprentice, her daughter, and her experiment, she will be seeking vengeance on a mighty scale," Callida said, leaning against the wall, gazing up at the bloodred pyramid towering above, "I must capitalise on his newfound weakness immediately. There are only a few more pieces to topple before the game is won."

She practically sang those final words.

"I look forward to toppling them for you, my master," Krothus said.

Perhaps now she sees his worth, late was still better than never.

Lord Callida turned, a glint in her eye. "And I look forward to giving you the opportunity, young Krothus. Though I must ask, what did your companion get in exchange for his assistance? No doubt his master pressed him for something in return, knowing I only cared about the political fallout of this little expedition."

"The remnants of the demon crystal that Lord Fira had communed with. Vyrion claimed that Lord Victus would be very interested in it."

"Oh yes, Victus does love his relics, doesn't he?" she laughed, the first time Krothus had ever had the pleasure of experiencing its musical tones. "I suspect he may have a use for it in whichever ancient ritual he wants to poorly recreate."

"Ritual?" Krothus asked.

And, as quickly as Lord Callida's good spirits had appeared, they began to retreat. "None of your concern. And even if Lord Victus stays alive long enough to complete it, then it will be my worry, not yours."

"Of course, master," he conceded, not sure what she had meant.

"Now, get some rest and prepare yourself, I have an important task for you in the coming weeks. A conflict that has been a persistent thorn in my side requires personal attention." Calida said, shooing him away with a hand and turning back to her twisted plant.

"I await your command, master," Krothus said, giving a respectful nod of his head and turning back around.

He could hear the snips of her shears even as he made his way to the exit of the garden.

One by one, Lord Callida was going to work her way through Highlord Malus' power base. All Krothus had to do was stay safely in her good graces, and keep Vyrion out of her way. If he didn't, she would cut both of them down, no more than fruits off a plant that never got to grow to its full potential. That was not his destiny.

But despite his confidence, that doubt was always there, watching, waiting for something to go wrong.

Chapter 14
Errands

Something was always watching. Sometimes Vyrion could see it in the corner of his eye, some shapeless form lurking just out of sight, a shadow that never fully revealed itself. Other times it was that blasted voice in his head, speaking some cryptic riddle, some basic command. It was always a strange feeling, like someone stood just behind him, breathing down his neck, waiting for just the right moment to whisper into his ear.

Though after so many weeks of this unwelcome presence following his every step, Vyrion's attitude towards it had slipped more towards annoyed than unnerved. Why him? He had enough to worry about as it was.

Lord Victus had been stretching him thin, his neverending list of tasks leaving Vyrion exhausted and frustrated. He was hardly the Empire's most competent apprentice, but he felt his time was wasted an errand boy; countless hours lost fetching reagents from dealers in less than savory areas of the city, pulling favors for dusty tomes from whichever Ruin Lords still held Victus in high esteem, not to mention taking notes from what seemed like every book in the Empire. It scarcely left him enough time for sleep.

But today was different. Today he had his own errands to run.

Making his way through the packed streets, those endless canyons of grey, Vyrion finally spotted his destination. The headquarters of Thanaton's Imperial Guards couldn't decide whether it wanted to look impressive or functional, so it had attempted both and succeeded with none. It was nothing but overambitious columns, dull right angles, and a stubborn coating of Imperial crests, like the architects had given up on exterior design and slapped the only symbol they knew everywhere they could.

Just outside the main entrance was Sergeant Lorren, standing at such rigid attention that Vyrion nearly mistook him for a statue.

"Thank you for coming, my Lord," the thin man said, giving a picture perfect salute.

But Vyrion shooed it down, feeling uncomfortable with the admiration in the man's eyes. "It was nothing, a favor for a favor is simply good business."

"If you say so, my Lord."

The near fanatical dedication Lorren tended to display to Lord Victus and his apprentices was something that Vyrion appreciated, but not something he wanted. It was not something he'd earned. If Lorren knew how Vyrion truly was; the anxiety, the self-doubt, the weakness he held in his heart, then Lorren would know there was nothing to admire.

But Vyrion pushed all that down, trying to focus instead on doing his duty. "Shall we?"

"Of course, my Lord," Sergeant Lorren said, doling out yet another salute before leading Vyrion inside.

The Imperial Guard Headquarters was halfway between a courthouse and a barracks. every room Vyrion passed contained either a bureaucratic mob of paper pushing or disciplined ranks of officers being lectured. Lorren was powering ahead, his steps so rehearsed that it seemed his gaunt form was gliding across the floor's smooth stone.

"In normal circumstances I would have loved to provide a full tour of the facilities, but we are ever so slightly late, my Lord," Lorren said, sounding as if he was admitting to murder.

"Are we?" Vyrion was sure he had showed up on time.

"I'm afraid so."

They weaved from hallway to hallway, around a corner, then up several staircases, the speed of which left Vyrion's head spinning, before finally stopping at an elaborate set of wooden doors.

Lorren brushed down his uniform, frowning at a rebellious crease on an otherwise meticulous jacket, before flashing a nervous smile. "As my dear father used to tell me: If you're early, you're on time. If you're on time, you're late. After you, my Lord."

Vyrion, not sure what else to say, gave a polite nod and pushed the doors open. A high podium dominated the room, towering over two desks that faced off with each other, while a blackboard loomed over on one side, battle-scarred by countless chalk assaults.

Lorren leveled a thin hand at the podium. "You are the adjudicator for this trial, my Lord."

Adjudicator, now that was a title Vyrion could appreciate. He climbed the steps to the prominent position at the head of the room. Lorren, meanwhile, had procured a tower of loose papers out of what seemed like thin air, arranging them into a near-perfect stack. Only when the papers sat triumphantly still did Lorren finally relax, returning to his statuesque posture.

They waited in silence for a moment. Then a moment more. Then several.

"How early are we exactly?"

"Twenty minutes," Lorren said proudly.

Vyrion was beginning to regret this. But Lorren had done him a service, so he would have to follow through. Hopefully their final attendee would show up sooner rather than later, and in the meantime, Vyrion could at least make himself comfortable. He sank into the chair at the podium, which was surprisingly pleasant.

In fact, it was so pleasant, and Vyrion so tired, that he managed to drift off to sleep. For the briefest of moments, he was finally calm, content.

Then the doors slammed open, rocketing Vyrion awake.

Lorren, the gargoyle he was, had not moved a muscle. The only moment from his desk was a single paper slowly drifting down off the stack, disturbed by the newcomer pushing past.

The man plopped down at the other desk, throwing up a poor salute at Vyrion before running a comb through the few scraggly hairs he still possessed. His uniform was tight around the waist and his chin nonexistent, held so far upwards that Vyrion was very surprised he had not snapped his own neck, allowing him to look down at everyone present, even Vyrion, sat far above.

So this was Captain Farke.

"Let's begin, then," Vyrion said, looming over the podium, hoping it made him look like he knew what he was doing.

Farke almost looked like he rolled his eyes.

"Thank you my Lord, I will make my opening statement," Lorren said, his long tenure as a statue coming to an abrupt end. "I aim to prove Captain Farke is unfit for his position, a danger to everyone under his command, and most of all, a hindrance to Lord Victus. He has caused disasters wherever he has served, with far reaching consequences for everyone involved, a fact I can and will prove."

And with that, Lorren sat back down.

Captain Farke pushed his chair back with a screech, and, in a tone so flat you could lie down on it, so too began his own opening statement.

"My lord, this accusation is nothing more than a baseless slur against my professional reputation. It is absolute nonsense and a waste of your valuable time and Imperial resources. Sergeant Lorren is stretching the truth, if not outright lying, in an effort to further his career, and I fully object to any and all statements that he has made."

Then he sat back down, his comb appearing in his hand instantly.

Vyrion frowned, there was something about the man he didn't like, a slimy coating more fit for some street swindler than an Imperial Captain. But as the adjudicator he was sure he was meant to remain neutral, so he dismissed these thoughts, and, unsure of what to do next, simply motioned for Lorren to continue.

In a flash, the Sergeant was on his feet and on the attack, the blackboard a sudden helpless victim of a thousand chalk strokes, the air filled with their frantic staccato. Casting just a cursory glance at his papers, he kept up the assault until the board was more white than black. Only then was his withered piece of chalk substituted for a thin metal pointer.

"Firstly, my Lord, we look at a key engagement in the Second War, the battle of Icebron Pass."

The pointer smacked against the blackboard, just under a diagram of some valley.

"Captain Farke ignored scouting reports concerning the Republic forces flanking assault on Lord Victus and Lord Gorn. The flanking force *here*. Instead, Farke refused to act, leaving the entire division's left flank exposed. The Republic capitalised on this to devastating effect."

The pointer tapped a lone rectangle on the diagram, like it were wiping out the division itself.

Vyrion raised an eyebrow at the accused, whose face had turned a violent red.

"Untrue!" Farke spat. "Bold-faced, utter lies, my Lord. I was following orders to hold our position. The Republic bastards slipped past us without our knowledge."

Lorren hardly seemed concerned at this objection and continued immediately, tapping another diagram of a circular fortification. "While involved with the Boraxxus Offensive, Captain Farke was tasked by his commanding officer to lead a scouting patrol into the surrounding area. The objective: look for possible Republic ambushers before setting up camp. Captain Farke ignored these orders, fabricating this patrol and advising that the division camp be set up regardless. The subsequent ambush resulted in a premature end to the offensive, heavy casualties to the Imperial forces, and Lieutenant Opro subsequently handed the blame and court-martialed."

Vyrion again turned to the accused, expecting a similar rebuttal.

But this time, Farke only leaned back in his chair with a smug smile. "The subsequent investigation found Opro at fault, and I stand by the court's decision, as I will here."

It was the kind of response Vyrion would have expected of a man only just acquitted, not one on his second accusation of what turned out to be many, many more.

Again and again, an incident was named, the pointer would swing down, and the consequences revealed. Kybel Bridge. Alder. The Qorx

Expedition. The alleged failures continued to file up, and so too did the associated body count.

By the time Lorren was finished, his arms were wobbling and he was nearly out of breath. "These incidents are only those related to Captain Farke's leadership failures during combat scenarios. I could discuss the rumours of bribery, nepotism, and complete disregard for confidentiality, but I do not have the evidence needed to formally accuse him of such."

"This a joke," Captain Farke retorted, "It is not like you have any evidence for your accusations to begin with, Lorren. It's all hearsay, you have given credence to nothing more than barracks gossip. I will be submitting a formal injunction into your time-wasting and baseless slander, as I have for every other sham trial that has come my way over this."

Lorren looked confused. "Sir, these papers contain sworn statements from eyewitnesses, troops under your command who were present during each of the events I mentioned. There are at least three for every incident I brought to the court."

The Captain's chinless jaw hung open, seeming to notice the hefty stack of paper on Lorren's desk for the very first time.

"Did you not read them? I left a copy in your office last week along with the summons to the hearing. My Lord, I assume you read your copy?"

Vyrion sharply inhaled. He knew he had forgotten something.

"It doesn't matter," Farke said, waving a dismissive hand. "They are most certainly works of fiction, bound in forged signatures. I'm sure my good friend, General Paras, would confirm that this is the case." He dropped the name of the far superior officer with a practiced deliberateness, an avenue frequently utilised.

Lorren had no response, he only looked up at Vyrion, his frustration cracking through his rigid shell of discipline.

Had anyone else been presiding, Vyrion was sure that they would have already acquitted Farke and moved on, their career very clearly threatened. But Vyrion was a Ruined, far outside the bounds of any

Imperial soldier.

But Farke didn't seem to care. He cleared his throat and pressed on. "My lord, we should end this here. My sergeant seems to have done nothing but repeat tales any drunk private would tell at the bar. It has hardly been the first time one of the troops under my command has gone this route, and I suggest-"

"You do not get to *suggest* anything," Vyrion said. Even if he were a poor Ruined, he was not to be spoken down to.

"Of course, my Lord, I was merely providing-"

"No. You were just accused of directly causing hundreds of deaths, those of your own men who looked to you for guidance," Vyrion pushed, "Do you take responsibility for any of it? Not even a single mistake?"

Farke's comb was nowhere to be seen, and his chinless head began to shrink into the collar of his uniform as if it instead belonged to a scared tortoise. "I deeply regret the circumstances, of course, my Lord. But none of those events were my fault, I can assure-"

Vyrion found himself leaving the podium, some righteous anger burning in his belly. He still thought of the men and women he and Sergeant Lorren had lost in the hanger bay. He still had nightmares about the man on the walls of Lord Fira's compound more than once, his head twisted round in some sick gesture of mercy. Not only would Vyrion immediately take responsibility for these deaths had anyone asked, they were within his hearts and mind all the time.

"Not a single death has ever been your fault?"

"Well, no, if you look at the records-"

Farke's words withered into a squeak as he sunk his chair, Vyrion suddenly an arm's length from him.

"Do you seriously expect me to believe that you, Captain, have never made a mistake?"

"Perhaps if you spoke to General Paras, my lord, then he would be able to clear this up," Farke said, half suggesting, half pleading, "I *obviously* regret *any* death under my command, but I have never been found-"

"No," Vyrion said, "I have reached a verdict."

The chinless Captain gulped, his neck bobbing up and down like he had just swallowed any hope of an easy resolution. Lorren's eyebrows raised an inch, as much of a reaction as he could muster.

Vyrion, for the first time in a long while, felt powerful, in control. He let a smile slowly crawl across his face as he watched Farke squirm.

"Guilty. Of all charges."

Farke's mouth hung open.

"Normally, I would discharge you immediately, or perhaps execute you just because I feel like it," Vyrion lied, thinking of what Krothus would say, or do, depending on his mood.

"But?" Farke whispered, a glimmer of hope in his watery eyes.

"But I am merciful," Vyrion said, recognising an opportunity, "And instead of such a harsh punishment, you are now indebted to me. Your life is in my hands until further notice. Do you understand?

Farke nodded with such force that his head nearly fell off.

Vyrion smiled at him, "And of course, I will see to it that you are demoted to ... let's say a Corporal."

The former Captain sunk so far into his chair that Vyrion could barely see him.

"Excellent, my Lord. I will get the paperwork for you to sign immediately," Lorren said, sounding very happy indeed,

"Good. Now, I have urgent business with Lord Victus," Vyrion declared, moving towards the door. "Farewell Sergeant."

"Thank you for your wisdom today, my Lord," Sergeant Lorren said, responding with his twentieth salute that afternoon.

"Farewell Corporal Farke," Vyrion added.

The folded mass of limbs stuffed in the chair released a sound halfway between a moan and a grunt.

Then Vyrion was out of the building and onto the street, heading back to his master's compound.

That was one favor paid, and a new one acquired. He did not yet have a function in mind for the now disgraced Corporal Farke, but Vyrion had learned that a good Ruined should never let an opportunity for leverage pass by. The amount of favors, debts, and blackmail he had seen Lord Victus utilize in the last few weeks was enough evidence of that, it seemed like half the city had once been in his pocket.

Would Vyrion one day have that level of influence? Would he be marching through the streets with a column of soldiers and his own apprentices? He chuckled to himself, drawing the eyes of several concerned Imperials as he passed by.

No, he didn't think he would ever get that far. He lacked the skills, the knowledge, and most of all, the cutthroat attitude that was necessary to fight your way to a position like that. In the meantime, he was happy exercising his very limited influence where he could, such as using Sergeant Lorren's connections to Lord Victus' compound staff to his benefit.

Once he was through the doors of the compound, Vyrion sat down at a bench in the gardens at the predetermined spot.

Someone sat down next to him, dressed in the dark, prim uniform of the kitchen staff. To anyone else, she had struck up an ambitious, if not outright dangerous, conversation with someone far above her station, but to Vyrion, she was just early.

"Your position here is secured, for now," he said.

"Great," she muttered, "My mother would be so proud to see me working in the kitchens like some common slave."

"Until Krothus and I find a more permanent home for you, this is the safest place we could find."

A token of gratitude would have been appreciated, but Vyrion didn't think he would have been particularly happy working in the kitchens either, though perhaps he would be better at it than he was at being a Ruined. The bar wasn't very high, at least.

"Mhmm," Inissa grunted, her mouth full, already turning her attention to the bundle of food in her lap.

"At least you seem well," Vyrion said. Where Inissa had been not much more than a skeleton when they had found her, that was starting to seem like a distant memory; gone were the bones poking through her skin like they were trying to escape, and even her coloring had left its unnatural paleness behind.

"I need to be," she said in between mouthfuls, "Master Krothus' training has shown me how weak I was, how much I still have to learn."

"*Master* Krothus?" Vyrion laughed. He really did let it get to his head.

Inissa stared daggers at him. "I am his apprentice, and he is my master. One day I will surpass him, but first I will learn everything I can."

"I have no doubts about that," Vyrion said, doing his best to suppress his smile. "And has anyone harbored any suspicions about your arrival?"

Inissa glanced around the courtyard, like she were expecting Lord Victus to hobble out of the bushes, or descend from the open sky above. "Not yet. They-"

She stopped. Someone entered the courtyard, someone Vyrion most certainly did not want to introduce Inissa to.

Vyrion quickly straightened his clothes and stood up. "You should go."

Inissa quickly slipped away, muffin in hand.

Now alone, Vyrion took a deep breath and moved to greet the newcomer, his stomach doing flips against his will as he did, far more excitement than his usual anxiety.

"Where's my red carpet? My honor guard? I was expecting a grand display for my return," Jarek said, swaggering up to Vyrion, eyes twinkling.

"I was all Victus could afford," Vyrion laughed.

The two gripped each other in a tight embrace before drawing apart. Vyrion's stomach increased the frequency of its acrobatics.

"Have I missed anything while I've been gone? Victus grown his leg back?" Jarek asked, laughing like he hadn't made the joke himself.

Vyrion couldn't help but smile, even if it wasn't funny. "If he managed to regrow his leg over the last couple weeks I would be surprised."

"Where is the old man anyways?"

Vyrion shrugged. "Likely in his chambers. He's been sending me on quite the scavenger hunt lately, gathering materials and reagents. This ritual is all he can talk about."

"So it seems."

Jarek's good humor quickly vanished, and he was suddenly pulling Vyrion into a nearby corridor.

"What are you-"

They stopped in the shadows of one of the walkways, the air cool and dry, a gentle breeze whispering over them and back out to the garden.

"I need your help," Jarek said quietly.

"With what?" Vyrion asked, sounding far too eager than he would have liked. They were very close now, tucked into the corridor like it were the only shelter in a storm.

"I've been in Randor, checking in on some contacts, the kind that lost the privilege of walking down the streets of Thanaton long ago. It didn't go well."

Vyrion had heard of the place, of its reputation. "And? Are you in danger?"

"No, no, nothing like that," Jarek said, "The old man sent me to find out who hired that thug to take his expedition findings. That red-haired woman."

"Jayn Reed?" Vyrion asked. It was a hard name for him to forget.

Jarek didn't seem to share that same issue. He snapped his fingers, as if he had only just remembered, "That's the one! Anyways ... she's dead. I took-"

Vyrion stared at him. "What? Wasn't she being held-"

Jarek gave an impatient sigh. "In the holding cells, yes, she was. I took her with me, hoping it would make my job easier. It didn't. Those contacts weren't happy, Jayn wasn't happy, I wasn't happy either, obviously. Things got complicated, and she wound up dead. So-"

"Is that what you needed help with?" Vyrion asked, confused.

For a second, Jarek just looked at him. Then it was like a switch had been flicked, like Jarek had been replaced with someone else. Someone worse.

"If you would shut your mouth and let me speak instead of interrupting me again and again, I would tell you, wouldn't I?"

Vyrion's stopped in his tracks. His stomach wasn't flipping anymore, he wasn't even sure it was there, replaced with that familiar deep pit, all anxiety and doubt. Had he really been interrupting that much?

Rage poisoned Jarek's handsome face. It was an unnatural look on him, like a mask had slipped to reveal someone unfamiliar underneath. But as quickly as it appeared, the anger evaporated.

"I'm sorry, Vyrion. I shouldn't have said that," he said, his usual smile returning in force, "It's been a long day."

"No, I'm sorry," Vyrion said, all too eager to keep that anger quelled, "I didn't mean to interrupt you so much, I just wanted to know how to help."

Jarek put a hand on his shoulder. "Well all that you need to know is that I failed. I learned nothing new, and our only source of information is dead. But what I need your help with is keeping this quiet, on backing up any claim I make to Victus, even if it's a lie. He'll have my hide for this otherwise."

Vyrion swallowed, all too familiar with their master's temper. "I can do that."

"Thank you, Vyrion. You're a good man, a man I can trust."

Vyrion felt his cheeks turn a bit red, that maw in his belly close up. He hated it. He hated how easy it was for him to forgive, to roll over. But he loved it too, loved the excitement, the little spark from the one thing in his life that he might deserve.

As if reading his thoughts, Jarek gave him a wink. "Come then, let's find the old man."

They found Lord Victus in the drillyard, as he often was, fencing with a handful of guards who had clearly drawn the short lot for that day's duties. The guards, lined up with practice blades in their hands, were obviously exhausted, while Victus only had a hint of sweat beading on the remnants of his hairline as he hungrily suckled away at his flask.

"Pathetic footwork!" the Ruin Lord snapped, hobbling back and forth and adjusting each of their stances with a savage whack of his own wooden weapon. "Do not lean too hard into any one direction, you must always be *centered*."

"The irony of a man with one leg preaching about balance," Jarek muttered. Vyrion snorted.

With one last smack, Victus limped back into position ahead of the four guards.

"Now, again!"

They swung into action. Two came at him head on, while the others flanked on either side. Lord Victus flourished his practice blade left, then right, eyeing up his opponents as they surrounded him, his hip flask carefully secured on his belt. The first guard struck, but her blow was swiftly deflected, her weapon clattering to the ground. At the same time, the two guards behind Victus tried their own luck, one going for his legs, the other for his head. A swift shoulder bash knocked one of them into the path of his comrade's strike, sending them both sprawling.

The final guard held back, looking very unsure of herself. Vyrion could very much understand her position, his own lessons with Victus had not gone much better.

"Balance, this is what I was just saying," Victus barked, "Garen, you deserved that if an old man can knock you over."

Garen, a young man with a particularly crooked nose, wisely kept his angry muttering unintelligible.

"Sawna, come now," Victus said, gesturing to approach with his practice blade, "You have to at least give it a try."

The guard still hesitated. She looked to Vyrion and Jarek, though she didn't get much assistance. Vyrion gifted her a shrug, Jarek unveiled a smile.

Victus started laughing. "Here is an incentive: I won't use my hands. You can't possibly object to fighting me unarmed, can you?"

He placed his weapon on the floor. His opponent, finally approving of her odds, shuffled forward.

"I remember when I fell for that too," Jarek said.

Lord Victus, as promised, held his hands behind his back. His weapon, not mentioned in his enticement, slowly floated into the air.

Vyrion could feel the flow of Ruin energy between Victus and the wooden blade as clearly as he could feel the ground underneath his feet. Sawna, surely not able to feel anything of the sort, hesitantly pressed on, committed to her lapse in judgement. Vyrion would have done the same, he always found it was better to get it over with.

She didn't get far, the practice blade fought as well as Victus wanted it to, and the bout ended with several brutal whacks into her side, the last of which let out a crack that left Vyrion guessing which one had given out first, the weapon or her ribs. Lord Victus was unconcerned, and left her groaning on the floor.

"No better way to ensure strong troops than to beat them into shape yourself. Right, my boys?"

"If you say so," Vyrion said, watching the bruised guards limp off the drillyard.

Lord Victus took a swig out of his flask, swishing it around in his mouth before swallowing with a mighty gulp, "So - did you find out any information in Randor? The ritual approaches, I can't have any meddlers getting in my way."

Jarek looked briefly to Vyrion, then back to Victus, "I did. There was a collector of ancient antiquities who had taken an interest in your findings, someone with enough influence and power to cause trouble."

Vyrion felt his breath catch in his throat, he hated lying, but Jarek seemed to have mastered it. Each word of the lie oozed confidence, like he were saying it under oath.

"And what did you do about it, boy?"

"It won't be a problem."

Victus nodded. "Good. I can always rely on you, Jarek."

"Thank you, master. One last thing," Jarek said, effortlessly continuing his deception, "Jayn Reed continues to remain unhelpful, and my contacts didn't seem to think she would give us anything to go off of. Shall I dispose of her?"

Lord Victus waved a dismissive hand. "I don't care, do what you will with the wretch."

"Of course, master," Jarek said with a bow.

Vyrion couldn't help but feel guilty. He had been lying to Victus too, by omission at least, by keeping Inissa there, but at least he hadn't done it to his face. He hadn't forced Jarek to become involved either.

Victus cleared his throat, "Now, let's-"

Seemingly out of nowhere, a brutal bout of coughing descended upon him. Convulsions wracked his body, sent him to his knees. Vyrion briefly wondered if he had simply drank something from his flask poorly, but the wet racket emanating from his chest was far too serious for that.

He and Jarek tried the best they could. Jarek hoisted Victus back to his feet, holding him upright, while Vyrion tried to get him to drink down some water in the wild hope it might cure him. But Victus, still in the midst of his hacking fit, slapped the water aside and shakily raised his flask to his lips instead. He barely managed to slip a gulp in between coughs, spilling some of the foul black liquid across his greying stubble as he did. Only then did the retching slowly subside.

It wasn't long before Victus' breathing returned to normal, but by then a throng of concerned guards and servants had got quite an eyeful. That wasn't good. Whispers were sometimes all it took to leave a Ruin Lord's reputation in tatters, and with Victus' reputation in a precarious enough position already, moving him out of sight was a necessity.

Vyrion and Jarek each held an arm as they carried their master to his chambers. Lord Victus was by no means fat, but he was certainly getting there, and regardless of whether it was his weight, the metal leg, or Vyrion's own weakness, the journey was a struggle, and Vyrion's body was screaming in protest.

With a synchronized grunt, they managed to drop their master into his bed in as graceful of a manner as they would muster. Victus didn't object, consciousness having left him already. The room was a whirlwind of books, papers and reagents, which Vyrion recognised as ones he had recently acquired himself. Good to know they wound up on his master's chamber floor.

Vyrion just watched him, that graying face lying almost perfectly still, sucking in breaths that might very well be his last. His master, a Ruin Lord, one of the most powerful beings in the Empire, now looked no different than a decrepit old man. It was far from the first time his health had been called into question. But each time it seemed to be getting worse, each time Vyrion was drawn to the same question.

"What's to stop us from killing him?"

"Vyrion!" Jarek gasped, clutching at his chest feigned outrage.

"I'm being serious," Vyrion said, smacking his arm. "We're meant to, aren't we? Eventually."

The thought had crossed his mind, in a purely hypothetical way. Vyrion doubted he would ever be able to do it, but it had always seemed a long way off, some distant dream he pushed away to deal with at another time. But now it seemed closer than ever.

"We need him, at least for now," Jarek said, watching Victus with a hard look. "His knowledge, his experience, it's too much to waste, and he knows it. He drip feeds his lessons, rationing them, keeping us wanting for as long as possible. I've been here for years and have barely scratched the surface." Then he smiled, like it was all a big joke. "And if we killed him right now, right after his whole compound saw us taking him in here ... we wouldn't survive the day. Allies, enemies, power bases, none of them take kindly to blatant power grabs. Either be powerful enough that nobody questions your takeover, or clever enough that nobody notices it even happened. We still have a while to go until it's safe to do either."

They both stood there for a bit. Listening to those ragged breaths, waiting.

"And what happens to us if he doesn't make it?" Vyrion asked. Worst case scenarios were the only thing his mind considered.

Jarek shrugged. "You don't see many Ruined running around without a master, except maybe the Emperor himself."

"I don't think I would do well under another Ruin Lord," Vyrion said, "Victus may be odd, but I've seen worse." Lord Fira. Lord Callida. Victus wasn't all bad.

"Optimistic to even think you'd get a choice. Nobody likes taking scraps. At that point it's just survival, you do everything you can to avoid being brought down with him." He paused, looked at Victus before continuing. "But I have been thinking about where to go. I can help if you-"

Lord Victus' snoring stopped. He suddenly erupted out of the bed, flask in one hand, runeblade in the other. He looked like some drunk, roused from his stupor and ready to jump into the nearest bar brawl.

Vyrion and Jarek stared at him.

"Damn it," Victus muttered, deflating into the edge of his bed,

"It's getting worse you know," Jarek said, all the tone of a scolding parent.

"Don't you think I know?" Victus snapped, mustering enough anger to send Jarek back a step.

Ruin energy still ebbed and flowed all around the Ruin Lord, reminding Vyrion of the last time he'd been in these chambers, how effortlessly a furious Victus had thrown them aside. He just wanted to know what was happening, whether it made Victus angry or not.

He needed to know. It was his right to know.

"What is going on? This ritual, the artifacts, your sickness, what in the *Emperor's name* is this?"

Vyrion's agitation had caused his volume to rise far beyond what he had intended. The tension thick in the air, the sparks of anger, the unstable ocean of the Ruin around them; he knew it was a recipe for disaster.

Lord Victus narrowed his eyes, the usual storm brewing behind them.

But then with a long, drawn out sigh, it all drifted away. He seemed to sag downwards, defeated.

"I have not been myself as of late, it's true," he grumbled, massaging the left side of his chest. "The reason for this is ..."

He looked to Jarek, then back to Vyrion.

"Complicated."

"Then keep it simple," Vyrion suggested quietly, any fire that had possessed him earlier now snuffed out.

"Fine. You want it put simply?" Victus snarled, "I am cursed. Cursed with a rapidly approaching demise, cursed with a desperate desire to survive, and cursed with the knowledge that all this was entirely my doing."

Vyrion felt that tightness in his chest again. If Victus was going to die, Vyrion could be cast out, some loose end to be tied up. Nobody liked taking scraps.

"I do hope you're going to give him more than that," Jarek interjected.

"Shut up, boy. I hadn't even started."

Victus took a big swig from his flask before continuing. "I used to command legions in the Emperor's name as one of the Council's most favored generals. But in the final days of the Third War, a lifetime ago now, I was ambushed. Not by Republic troops, but my own. A group had grown jealous of my power, my imminent ascent to Highlord, and so tried to end my path to glory prematurely."

His metal leg creaked as he tapped it with one calloused hand.

"They didn't kill me. Not quite. But my leg wasn't all that they took. My legions tore each other apart, for their own ambitions or mine. Lords from all corners of the Empire smelled blood, an opportunity to further their own ambitions, and jumped to the aid of whichever side they deemed strongest. My reputation became one of weakness, for the crime of not foreseeing such a rebellion, and for ending a campaign that could have seen the Republic in tatters. It took direct intervention from the Council themselves to stop what was quickly turning into a civil war."

He swallowed with great difficulty, and gestured to the battlefield of books, papers, and parchment.

"This became my legacy. A fool's quest to regain the fruits of the past, restore my body and reputation."

"And the curse?" Vyrion pressed, not able to make the connection just yet.

Lord Victus barked out a laugh that quickly turned into a trio of coughs. Another gulp from his flask followed.

"Some slain Ruin Lord, locked away in an ancient tomb, was said to have the ability to use the Ruin to alter time itself. In my desperation, I ignored every warning and attempted to contact his spirit, learn the secrets she held. But it all went wrong."

"You got off the lightest, I would say," Jarek muttered.

Victus frowned at him, but continued, "The spirit was not as expected."

"The demon," Jarek corrected, glaring.

Victus waved a hand at him, "Shut *up,* boy."

The elder apprentice stayed silent, but something lurked beyond his gaze. Something that Vyrion didn't like.

"The spirit was hostile, furious even. I entered the tomb with three apprentices and the hope of fixing the past. I left with only Jarek and this damned curse."

He pulled down part of his shirt, exposing the skin beneath. Blackened, withered, dead; it was like he'd been burned by some unholy flame. Vyrion had seen glimpses of it before, but it had crept across the older man's chest, across his shoulders, ending just below his neckline. Victus moved his clothing back into place, as if the very admittance of his own mortality was some embarrassment.

"How long do you have?" Vyrion asked.

Lord Victus shrugged and took another swig of his flask. "Until it reaches my throat. Then I will die, choked to death by my own ambitions, just like that blasted spirit wanted."

The trio sat in silence for a few moments, the rattling of Victus' ragged breaths marking each passing second. Vyrion felt useless. He thought knowing the nature of his master's affliction would help him to feel better, to feel like he could do something, but it had only made him feel worse. Powerless. Maybe if he had studied more, been more vigilant in his readings, he would know what to do. A wave of guilt washed over him. If he had only stayed awake in the library more nights, slept a little bit less, then maybe-

"So what are you going to do?" Jarek asked, his calming voice briefly ripping Vyrion out of his own self-destructive thoughts.

"The only thing I can," Victus said, heaving himself up off the bed to stare at the arrangement of drawings and runes on the far wall.

In the center of all of it was a familiar inky black book. The air around it seemed warped, a hazy barrier swirling around the mysterious pages within, like it were trying to shield them from its terrible secrets. Vyrion already knew that nothing good had ever come out of reading that blasted tome, and he dreaded to think what Victus had in store for it.

"How do you know it will work?" he asked.

"Because now I know that it's been done before," Victus said, almost giddy.

Vyrion frowned, unsure of what he meant. But then he followed his master's gaze, to the area just below the black book, where two objects caught his eye. The first was the small pyramid Vyrion had retrieved months ago. The second was a smooth metal box, the faintest hint of whispers emanating from within, a chill in the air.

Vyrion had a bad feeling about this.

Chapter 15

Expendition

Krothus hated many things; weakness, the laughter of fools, the way the sun shined into his face in the morning. But if there was one thing he hated above all, it was cowards. Not just those who fled at the first sign of danger, but those who avoided danger entirely, staying so far beyond it that the very thought of death became numbers on paper.

And right now, Krothus was exactly that kind of coward.

Below, hundreds clashed. Battle lines were a distant memory, replaced by a muddy chaos. The swamp muck stuck to everything. It painted bodies, both dead and alive, his side and theirs, into indistinguishable silhouettes, rendering his vantage point useless.

"I'm going down there," he declared, runeblade already in hand.

"If you do, you'll be declared a traitor and shot," snarled Agent Dedri, her tone forged in frustration.

This had hardly been the first discussion they'd had on the subject. Her position never changed. The aging Imperial agent was like her neat bun of grey; uncompromising, not a single strand unconsidered.

Her squad of fellow agents, each sporting the same smart ashen uniform, casually slid their fingers towards their piercers' triggers. They were confident for Imperials, Krothus had to give them that. The Imperial Intelligence Bureau were no strangers to defying Ruined, or the Republic, or anyone bar the Emperor himself for that matter.

Perhaps in changed circumstances, then Krothus would have slain them the spot for such a threat, but, in doing so, he would be directly disobeying his master in spectacular fashion, as well as actively sabotaging the current political interests of the Ruined Council. In short, if the agents didn't kill him, his failure soon would.

"Shall I dispose of her, lord?" Spinebreaker rumbled, the musclebound orkathi pointing at her with that absurd bone spear of his.

Krothus frowned, his bodyguard, far from doing anything useful, was getting increasingly annoying. He made a mental note to refuse any of Headcleaver's 'gifts' in the future.

"No. If I wanted to do such a thing I would do it myself." He hooked his runeblade back onto his belt. Emperor above, he was done with this blasted swamp.

Dedri smiled. "Wise move, Ruined. That brute might intimidate some, but I have more important things to worry about."

"Like the fact that the militia you have been training is now retreating?" Krothus said.

The Imperial Agent hissed, pressing her spyglass to one eye.

The skirmish was gradually slowing now, both sides either exhausted or their bloodlust sated. A collection of mud-bound shapes began to slowly return to their position.

"Looks like that got nowhere," Dedri sighed, "At least Harden is still alive."

"Lucky us."

The local militia leader was as incredibly eager to please as he was incredibly stupid. The short, stocky shape leading the mud coated survivors back seemed like him, but was only confirmed when Krothus could hear the man's strangely twangy voice.

"That didn't work," Harden said, spitting out some mud in the process, "I guess you were right, Dedri."

Agent Dedri gave him a smile so severe that her lips seemed to have jumped into the swamp and disappeared, "That is why we are here, Harden, To advise, and to train. One stalemate doesn't mean the end of the campaign does it?"

Her tone suggested that the end sounded very near indeed.

Harden looked at her with a blank expression, as if his brain had given up halfway through Dedri's sentence. It took a few moments before he said anything at all.

"I get it."

Krothus extremely doubted that was the case.

But Harden wasn't finished, "Why we can't just have a few Empire skyships come in and just blow 'em up? Seems like it would be easier, right boys?"

Harden's troops, if the motley crew of uneducated farmers, criminals, and frontiersmen could be called that, gave a murmur of agreement. A few hearty spits puttered onto the muddy ground, though whether this was done in agreement or opposition to their leader's statement was unclear.

Dedri managed to smoothly convert a groan into a quick cough before answering in the poorest attempt at a pleasant voice Krothus had ever heard, "As we've said Harden, we are not able to engage directly with Republic backed forces, or we will break the twenty years of ceasefire that our two nations have maintained."

Krothus couldn't help but imagine them as a strict headmistress trying to explain something to her slowest pupil. Harden may have been a bit old for the role, but Dedri had the look of experience and impatience spot on, even her laugh lines were frowning.

Harden just stared at her, taking careful moments to comprehend her words, his stocky shoulders coddling his mud caked head between them. After a short while, he gave a nod.

"Sure. Don't want to get you into trouble, 'specially after all the weapons you've given to us. We'll give it another try tomorrow."

And without another word, the mob of mudmen dispersed back to their equally muddy town, just a bit back from the ridge.

Dedri sighed, then, with a angry growl, she attempted to break her spyglass in half. The sight of it set Krothus chuckling.

"Think failure is funny, Ruined?" she snapped, straining with her spyglass over one knee. One of her squad tried to help, but was rapidly shooed away.

"Are you talking about Muckbron's continual lack of progress, or you and that spyglass?" Krothus asked.

"You think you're funny, do you?" Dedri said, still struggling.

"He is very funny," said Spinebreaker.

"Shut up," Krothus demanded.

"Yes, lord."

The spyglass, still in one piece, flew off the ridge. Krothus heard a distant plop from the swamp below. One of Dedri's squad procured a new spyglass instantly.

But far from appreciative, Dedri wheeled around to Krothus instead. "You won't find it funny when you have to tell Lord Callida yet another one of her proxy war ventures has run into trouble. I may be performing the ground work here, but you are the one who is ultimately responsible should we fail, not me. I'm sure she'll be especially furious knowing who Cresslog's Republic advisor is."

Krothus frowned, knowing full well that she was right. "This isn't over yet."

"One more failed attack and it will be."

"Then perhaps you should listen to me," Krothus said, "I am sick of others fighting for us, we need to get involved."

Agent Dedri looked at him as if he was the world's biggest cockroach, before signaling for the rest of her squad to leave them. They followed her order immediately, melting into the shadows in the blink of an eye.

She cleared her throat. "I am not going to bother pretending your brute is even a person, so for all intents and purposes, we are alone. Let's speak plainly."

"I always do." He braced himself for a barrage of bitter complaints.

"You do understand that engaging with the Republic directly will cause a grand conflict the Empire is not likely to win? Or can you not resist prattling on with your useless bravado?

"I-"

"Do you prefer to sit and complain about your assignment like a petulant child?"

Krothus felt his face burn hot. He did not like being spoken to this way.

"Perhaps I should go fetch your Master and inform her of how useless you have been this entire-"

"*Silence,*" Krothus boomed, seconds away from calling upon the Ruin to snap her neck.

It was enough for Dedri to hold her tongue, ending her onslaught.

"Shall I slay her, lord?" Spinebreaker said, brandishing his bonespear once again.

"No!" hissed Krothus, feeling a strong urge to hurt something, anything. "Get out of my sight."

The orkathi bodyguard walked roughly ten steps away and stepped behind a tree.

"If you don't explain that outburst I will make sure he doesn't have anyone to slay," Krothus continued, looming over the Imperial agent as best he could. But she hardly expressed any fear at all, if anything she was looking up at him with - was that pity? It only made Krothus want to hurt her more.

"You are hardly the first ambitious young apprentice I've worked with, Krothus," she finally said, "And all of you are so predictable. It's always a mad rush to prove yourself worthy of the position you find yourself in, and it never really dawns on you, the reality of it all."

"The reality of what?"

"The slimmest possibility you have of getting what you want."

What he wanted? Krothus knew his desires to an exact degree. Recognised, powerful, feared; these were all things he would be, and to some degree already was. He had a grand destiny, one that would lead him to the highest points of the Empire. To think of the possibility as slim was absurd.

"I'm not like any other apprentice," he said, "I will be so much more."

Dedri sighed. "Do you know how many others believe the same thing? I have seen more of life, and death for that matter, than you have. Ruined may rule this Empire, but only the lucky few. The rest die senseless deaths along the way, killed by each other more often than not.

Krothus laughed. "Senseless? Harden's mongrels died senseless deaths today. The swamp is littered with bodies, they lay there because we goaded two settlements into a war that only benefits us."

"And who benefits from our actions along the way? We are all pieces in someone else's game, Ruined. The sooner you recognise that your will is irrelevant, the sooner you will adapt to playing the part you are told to."

Krothus had run out of patience, he just scoffed and walked to the edge of the ridge that overlooked the swamp, where the dying rays of the sun battled with countless specks of lightbugs dancing across the dusky air.

He knew that Dedri had already slunk off. Rightfully so, seeing as he had made it very clear that he no longer wished to speak with her - the aged Agent had been getting under his skin recently, there was no denying that. But the question was whether she was right or not, whether he knew what he was doing there.

He knew his role. Ensure that the residents of Muckbron succeed in their campaign against Cresslog, not because it was important, but because Cresslog had been backed by the Republic. A war within a war.

It was the politics, this conflict by proxy, that bothered him. Perhaps it was because just by its nature, that he could recognise so easily that he was playing some game, gambling on a grand scale under the direction of others. But Dedri's words echoed in his mind. Who benefited from this? Muckbron winning the conflict would result in them eventually being added into the Empire's fold, Krothus already understood that. It was a settlement of a decent size and Agent Dedri and her squad had already been here for some time, arming and training Harden and his goons for this very purpose. So why send him?

His master had taken a specific interest in one conflict out of countless others, that much was obvious. A longtime thorn in her side she had said. Though, the more Krothus thought about it, the more it seemed out of place, Lord Callida rarely admitted any difficulties or failures. Appearances meant everything, especially in Thanaton. So if whoever was on the Republic side of the swamp had truly been able to complicate her plans, then that reflected poorly on her, damaged her reputation in the eyes of the Council and any other Ruin Lord who was furthering the Empire's goals after the ceasefire.

"So I'm here to clean up her mess," Krothus muttered to no one, "Improve her image ahead of her play for power."

That was his role in the game, to supervise a conflict that didn't benefit those who fought in it, or even himself. Is this what being a Ruined truly meant? Pathetic.

He sighed and turned around, half expecting to see Dedri still standing there. Instead, he saw a wide crimson frame poorly hidden behind the nearest tree.

"Spinebreaker, come here."

The hulking Nightshadow warrior approached immediately, tentacled beard swaying with every step.

"Tell me, when you receive orders, do you question their purpose?"

"No, lord."

"And why not?"

Spinebreaker shrugged. "Good warriors follow orders."

"And if you disagree with orders?"

He shrugged those mountains of muscle again. "Good warriors follow orders."

"Bah," Krothus hissed. This was going nowhere. It wasn't like he expected the orkathi to have the same towering ambitions as he did, but he could never live such a simple life. He was destined for more.

This brought him back to that which plagued him: his master's orders were incompatible with who he was and what he wanted. Dedri may be right about why he was there, but she could keep her depressing tales of failed ambition and regret to herself. Krothus was better than them, better than her, better than anyone present in this damn swamp.

And with that in mind, Krothus could already think of a solution to his problem, at least his most immediate one.

"Come, Spinebreaker, we're going back to the city," he declared, knowing full well that describing Muckbron as a city was a gross oversimplification. At best, he would describe the ramshackle frontier settlement as nothing more than a cesspit, filled with ten thousand degenerates. But unfortunately for both him and his bodyguard, two of those degenerates themselves, they had a room in the inn that awaited them.

The brutish pair swept through the muddy streets, any denizens wisely giving them a wide berth. Krothus spoke to no one, and Spinebreaker only spoke when commanded. They ate the disgusting swamp fish they were provided in silence, and after an uneventful sleep, filled with angry dreams of violence, Krothus and his bonespear-wielding companion returned to the ridge.

The Imperial agents and Harden joined them once the sun made its first appearance, the swamp standing ever vigilant, emitting a symphony of calls and croaks from those hidden amongst its muddy expanse.

One call in particular stood out to Krothus, that being Agent Dedri tearing his plan to shreds.

"Do you not see how risky this is?" she scolded. "One mistake, one slip-up, and we could start a war that would leave millions dead and the Empire in tatters."

Krothus couldn't keep the sneer out of his voice. "I don't make mistakes. Another war is coming whether you like it or not, but it won't start today. Not if you follow my lead."

The rest of Dedri's Agents seemed very agitated indeed, plans being altered didn't seem to sit well with them whatsoever. They were huddled together, a circle of plotters with their voices so quiet the slight breeze swept away every word.

Harden and his boys seemed to have a completely different outlook.

"Well I think it's a swell plan," the militia leader said slowly, a full several minutes after he had heard it.

Those of his mob nearby gave a grunt of approval, several spit in the affirmative. The rest of Harden's troops had mustered near the edge of the swamp, a loose collection of ragged men and women holding piercers that were likely worth more than their own homes.

"I'm not authorizing this operation," Dedri insisted, completely ignoring Harden, "Even if we succeed, my superiors would have me court-martialed for this."

Krothus shrugged, "Then blame me. I am the superior in rank here, regardless of your experience, Dedri. But this will be done."

"What's to lose?" Harden asked, apparently not listening to the possible consequences when they were laid out for him moments ago.

Agent Dedri didn't say anything, she just looked at Krothus, tight-lipped and frustrated. Krothus could have laughed. For all of her bluster last night, surely she must have expected him to find his own way of fixing this situation, he didn't present himself as the type to sit down meekly and take what life had dealt him. Perhaps she needed a final push?

"I'm changing the game, just like you said. I will not be a name forgotten to history, a piece for others to toss away as they see fit. I will forge my own path from what is given to me."

First she was angry, as if she thought he was blaming her for his sudden madness. But then Dedri seemed to deflate, to understand that this was entirely her doing. If she hadn't urged Krothus to think more thoroughly about his role, then he would still be complaining atop this very ridge.

"Now," Krothus continued, turning to the motley crew assembled around them, "Who else wants to kill some Cressloggers?"

He was answered with a hearty cheer, Harden's own yell coming moments after everyone had quieted down.

Krothus raised an eyebrow to Dedri. It was much too late to protest now, the attack would go ahead regardless.

She sighed, and motioned her squad forward, none of whom seemed happy about this turn of events but marched down the ridge towards the swamp regardless. They were followed closely by the remainder of Harden's militia.

"We'll do it your way," Dedri said as she passed, "But there can't be any survivors. I don't want the slightest chance of this getting back to the Republic."

Krothus had no problems with that. "You heard her, Harden."

The stout militiaman's face steadily split into a savage grin, but Krothus knew that if they were going to wait for him to say something, the war would already be over. And his ambitions did not wait.

The Agents, Krothus and Spinebreaker joined the rest of Muckbron's forces, loosely arrayed at the edge of the swamp. The stench drifting out of the muck was far worse up close, and already Krothus was struggling not to wretch. The things he did for power.

Harden had busied himself trying to organize ranks, but whether it was his agonizingly slow speed or the simple inability of his ragged mob to follow orders, the result was the same: a motley band of society's worst, armed to the teeth with weapons that they, despite the Imperial Agent's best efforts, barely knew how to use.

The mob limped onwards, the first rank steadily sloshing into the thick mud. Many of them wore thick boots, tall enough to nearly reach the top of their legs, but the swamp didn't seem to notice, filling them up to the brim with muck regardless.

"Thanks for this," Agent Dedri muttered, looking mournfully at her pristine uniform before taking her first step.

Krothus grunted and did the same, making sure his runeblade hilt was securely attached to his belt before doing so. He couldn't use it of course, far too obvious a Ruined was engaging directly with the battle, but losing it was not a possibility he was willing to entertain. So he now needed a weapon, and he wasn't nearly barbaric enough to use one of those blasted pierces.

One of Harden's troops, a rotund man who looked entirely unfamiliar with the concept of bathing, was struggling with his initial foray into the swamp. Krothus couldn't have cared less about his fate, but stuffed in one swollen hand was a simple axe, worn down but still useful.

"I'll take that," Krothus declared.

"Hey!" the man blubbered, his weapon swiped from his grip. He took a swing at Krothus with one swollen fist, but his attention was quickly diverted towards the swamps current attempts to swallow him up.

"Thank you for your service," Krothus said, leaving the man to his fate. The sounds of battle up ahead drowned out the panic of the sinking man as he pressed on.

Now for the first stage of his plan. With only the smallest hesitation, Krothus began heaping mud and slime onto himself, steadily covering every bare facet of armor, every glimpse of grey skin, until he felt the lukewarm muck all but seep into his very bones.

The squad of Imperial agents was doing the same, none too happy about their ordeal. But after they too lost their distinguishing features into the mud, the group blended seamlessly into the mob of Harden's men pushing past.

Dedri, or at least a grimey silhouette that bore resemblance to her, approached.

"Why is he so lucky?" she growled, pointing at Spinebreaker and his bare crimson torso.

Krothus shrugged. "Orkathi can live wherever they like, perhaps even Muckbron."

The large Nightshadow warrior said nothing, far too busy staring longingly towards the battle lines.

"Fine," snapped Dedri, "Let's go then."

"One last thing," Krothus said, his heart's rhythm beginning to steadily climb, "Stay behind me, watch my back."

Dedri's ill-temper receded just slightly.

"Don't get yourself killed, kid."

That got a laugh out of Krothus. He couldn't imagine a single scenario where that was the result.

"Onwards!" he shouted, urging those around him forward as he pressed on through the swamp's mire. To his satisfaction, several Muckbron soldiers, no doubt recognising actual leadership from someone who wasn't a dim witted fool, began to trudge through the muck close behind.

It wasn't long before Krothus found the front line. One minute he was trudging through the chaos of mudmen, then the pack of muddy bodies suddenly parted, exposing a narrow strip of space in between the two forces. Any battle had lulls, though instead of complex maneuvers taking up the time, the ceasefire's source was the same as it had been every day before that.

Fatigue.

Both sides were undisciplined and untrained, tiring easily in the mud and the fighting, the only difference possibly being Cresslog's ability to properly form into a line. Each day Krothus had observed, he had seen the skirmishes gradually peter out, only to ramp up again when Harden finally caught wind of the situation. But whoever had been commanding the Cresslog forces was smart enough to know that all they had to do was wait. The Empire may have armed Muckbron to the teeth, but once they used up all of their ammunition firing wildly into their enemies' vague direction, they would need to retreat for the day, same as always.

But while all of these combatants were unfamiliar with combat, Krothus was intimately acquainted with it. Like a great fist, he smashed through the first layer of Cresslog soldiers, sending bodies and limbs plunging into the murky water. He may not have had his runeblade in his palm, but he could still command the Ruin, feel it flowing through his veins, empowering every blow. One swing of his axe caved a rusty helmet in, the next carved a red gulley through a woman's shoulder.

Spinebreaker was at his side, a faithful bringer of death to anyone unfortunate enough to catch his eye. His bonespear pierced right through a worn breastplate, punching out the back with a screech.

In moments, a crack had opened in the Cresslog battleline, with a few of the Muckbron troops hesitantly following the path of red ruin just behind. Piercer bolts flew everywhere and in all directions, impossible to tell where they were from and where they were going.

An oasis of discipline, the Imperial Agents advanced in a tight group, steadily unloading their weapons with every step. Every bolt found its mark, slamming through skulls, weaving through armored plates, soldiers all around Krothus dropping like flies. Harden's forces didn't take long to notice the effectiveness of their fellow mudbound troops, and quickly began handing them extra ammunition.

The crack in the lines quickly widened into a gaping hole, and Krothus could feel the sweet taste of victory's arrival. The Cresslog soldiers began to retreat, steadily backpedaling away from a seemingly unstoppable force, while Harden pressed his troops forward, the dull roar of his voice ringing out from somewhere down the line.

This was it.

But just as the swings of his axe slowed, and he looked towards Dedri to gloat about his expert leadership, a frown forced its way onto Krothus' face. He could sense something.

Someone was approaching, the Ruin itself loudly heralding this new arrival. They too, had a presence in the Ruin's ocean of energy, but whoever they were, they felt different. A quiet calm descended upon him, a heavy blanket of comfort enveloping every facet of his being.

The sounds of fighting suddenly halted. Everyone must have felt it. Troops on both sides were reduced to staring blankly at one another, like they had wandered into a room and forgotten why. Even Spinebreaker had given pause to his relentless slaughter.

Krothus initially resisted this unseen power, his chest still burning hot with the thrill of battle. But as that too began to fade, he was left only with his own confusion.

He could hear a bit of commotion from just behind the line, troops slowly moving aside to allow someone through despite their haze. Krothus' hand involuntarily drifted towards his runeblade hilt at his belt.

Eventually, the few troops in front of Krothus parted. Moments ago, they had been terrified, facing him with all the resolve of a newborn kitten, but now they shuffled to either side, faces blank.

Two people made their way forward. One was every inch a soldier, battle-scarred white armor covered his body like the carapace of some heavy set beetle, bushy brows drawn into such a severe grimace that his worn face threatened to collapse in on itself. The other was grace and calm given form, a woman wrapped in simple tan robes that held herself as some queen, a crown of golden hair atop her head.

Krothus had to admit, his first glimpse of the Republic didn't disappoint. But that also meant he may have started something he was not prepared to finish, a war that neither side was prepared for so soon after the last.

He had to show strength, show that he was the one in control.

"Come to surrender?" he demanded, sounding far more confident that he was.

The armored man barked out a laugh. "Not quite."

"Not at all, I would say," the woman added, her voice surprisingly soft for someone with such presence.

"To die then." Krothus felt for his runeblade. If the Republic knew who he was already, there was nothing stopping him from tapping into the bloodlust he had been suppressing so diligently.

But a glint drew his attention to another hilt, pristine and golden, in the hand of the robed woman.

"You are not the only one with a runeblade, young one," she said, still calm, "But if you wish to throw your life away, I suggest you reevaluate your decision."

With a hiss, a white beam extended out of her runeblade, flanked on either side by neat, simple blades.

Krothus channelled the Ruin into his own weapon, the flames erupting along the hooked blades, the warmth piercing through the cool layer of mud over the arm that held it.

But his opponent held her ground. She made no move of aggression towards him, but did not retreat either. Her armored companion only crossed his arms, the gentle breeze rustling through his bushy hair, the eerie stillness brought about by the newcomers staying in place.

Krothus remained where he was, not sure what their plans were.

"You're Krothus, right?" the man asked, jabbing a gauntleted finger at him, "Lord Callida's apprentice?"

"Perhaps."

The man jabbed a stubby thumb at himself. "Commander Oar. And this is Deus Master Seefa."

Krothus snorted. "I didn't realize I'd walked into a social occasion."

"You haven't," Seefa said, the slightest hint of sourness entering her voice, "You have entered a negotiation, one where you stand to profit a great deal."

"It really is my lucky day then," Krothus said, forcing himself to laugh. "The Republic wants to make me a rich man."

"Riches? No, you don't strike me as a man interested in money," Oar said, "You seem like a man who wants power, and can recognise an opportunity when he sees it."

"Every Ruined wants power. Why should I care what you have to say?"

"Because we have a solution to both of our problems," Seefa said, before angling her white runeblade towards him, "Or you risk starting another war that the Empire will lose."

"Nobody starts a war thinking they'll lose. That's how wars work. I think the Republic would lose, so why don't we get this war started here and now?"

Krothus was hoping his bluster would put them off guard. It did not.

"Perhaps you should learn your history, Ruined," Oar growled, "Your people have a habit of turning on one another with far more frequency than they do winning campaigns. The Third War ended with an Empire on the brink of breaking apart, facing a united Republic."

Krothus' frown returned in force. "If you are so certain, then why has the Republic not finished us off with the Fourth War?"

The low hum of Seefa's runeblade was cut off as it drew back into its hilt. She calmly tucked a loose strand of hair back behind her ear.

"Because we don't want to. We never have. We may be confident in our chances, but the Senate, the Deus Masters, and the Arch Minister himself do not want any more bloodshed."

"And neither does your Imperial Intelligence, from what we've heard," Oar added, nodding to the mud-covered forms of Dedri's incapacitated squad.

"Then speak plainly. If you don't want war, then why are we talking?" Krothus snapped. His patience for their dancing around the subject was rapidly dwindling.

"To stop it while we can," Oar said.

"And to do that, we need to stop your master," Seefa added, "Stability is the foundation of peace. But her ambition will only be sated when those foundations are ripped up and fashioned into a form of her own design, one she will use to reignite old fires. She and I are well-acquainted, and I understand her many faults just as well as she does."

So Seefa was Callida's longtime foe. But Krothus was still not convinced. "Do you think I would betray my master so easily? Her success is my own."

"For now, perhaps. But what will happen when your flame begins to rival hers?"

He had no response to that, it was a point he had considered many times himself. But this was not something he would discuss with those loyal to the Republic. They were the natural foe of Ruined, of the Ruined Empire, and he would never stoop as low as to be labelled a traitor to the Emperor.

"We have learned a great deal about you, Krothus," Seefa continued. "We know that you will not let your flame get snuffed out so easily. And sometimes, all you need is the right fuel to add into the mix just to make it all burn just a tiny bit brighter. Bright enough to threaten your master's own."

"I tire of this conversation," Krothus hissed, "And I tire of this sorcery. It's time for this to end."

He had noticed the moment Seefa had adjusted her hair, a cluster of sweat droplets had run down her otherwise pristine face, betraying the true cost of her spell. This power she was wielding, the dampening of all the minds in the swamp, it was not something she could keep up forever. Even now, Krothus could see the slight tremble of her hands. How much energy did it take to cloud the minds of this many people? Deus Master or not, if Krothus could catch her unawares, he would put a swift end to this pointless exchange.

"Good," Oar said, sharing a look with his companion through his bushy brows, "Then we surrender."

Krothus blinked several times, completely bewildered.

"What?" he asked, not sure if he had heard correctly.

"We will take our troops and evacuate the residents of Cresslog immediately," Seefa said, smiling her irritatingly pristine smile.

The two stared at Krothus, waiting for an answer. It felt like a trap, a completely unnatural one at that. But such a swift victory was enticing. If they tried anything, surely he would get the honorable fight he wanted regardless.

"Fine," he managed to grunt, with the intention of amending their terms.

Though as soon as the word left his lips, a fog descended upon his mind. The murk enveloped his senses just as the swamp muck had enveloped his body, in what could only have been the Deus Master's aura washing over him once more. He had managed to shake it off before, but this time it was nothing short of overwhelming. It dulled every touch, blurred his vision, slowed his thoughts.

He was not one to be toyed with. Ruin-fueled rage slowly boiled over the forced serenity, breaking Krothus free.

The moment his clarity returned, his runeblade sizzling by his side, he scanned his field of view for someone, anyone, to fight.

A lone frog looked at Krothus and croaked.

It was too late, they were gone. Not just Commander Oar and his Deus Master companion, but the entirety of their forces seemed to have vanished into thin air. The Muckbron side of the swamp remained, the rapidly growing wave of grunts and moans heralded the return of Harden's troops to the conscious world.

Krothus now realized his new acquaintances could have easily slain everyone in the midst of their mental prison. But they hadn't. They surrendered instead. What in the Ruin's name was happening?

Agent Dedri appeared at his side, trying to paw off the mud from her uniform, each scrape of her hand revealing what used to be pristine grey cloth underneath.

"How did you do that?" she asked.

Krothus frowned, "Do what?"

She paused for a moment, detaching a frog from her arm before continuing. "How did you intimidate a full blown Deus Master? I've never seen one retreat like that before."

Krothus felt his frown deepen. "Is that what you think happened?"

All around him, the weary, mud covered Muckbron soldiers were shaking hands and cheering, realising their victory was finally at hand. Many of them gifted Krothus with the worst salutes he had ever seen, others clapped for him, or gave a spit of appreciation.

Harden wobbled his way through the swamp water to appear at Krothus' side as well. He stood in silence for a good period of time before finally, slowly, getting his words out.

"Well done, Ruined. We've won thanks to you."

The stout man gave him a pat on the back.

Spinebreaker joined the rest of the huddle, the large brute's tentacled expression unreadable as always. He merely delivered a single nod, the small gesture bundled with whatever recognition he saw fit.

"Let's finish the job!" Harden shouted, pointing towards the hazy image of Cresslog in the distance. His men gave a rousing cheer and rushed off, no doubt trying to be the first in line for the best loot.

Krothus simply stood there in the swamp's mire, stuck in the mud, stuck in his thoughts. The Muckbron troops continued to pass by him, each slosh of their push through the swamp disturbing the surface of the murky water.

If Seefa was powerful enough to suspend an entire battlefield, including himself, she could have easily won the day. But they had taken the whole of Cresslog's forces and disappeared. It didn't make any sense.

"I doubt the Republic will escalate tensions over this," Dedri said, as much to herself as to him. "They don't want a war, neither do we. They'll chalk it off as a necessary sacrifice to keep the peace, while we take what we deserve."

"I suppose," Krothus mumbled, still trying to rack his brain for an answer.

"But still, earning a victory over a Deus Master, that's one way to get a name for yourself," Dedri said, clapping him on the back, "You will be earning quite the reputation, Krothus."

Then it dawned on him. His victory, if you could call it that, was a curse. With his help, Muckbron, and by extension, the Empire, had won the swamp and the surrounding territory owned by Cresslog. But it was a small price to pay for the Republic, in fact, it could have even turned them a profit. The area controlled a nearby mountain pass, sure, but building over the swamp would be exceedingly expensive, and the would be relatively useless until then. No, by giving up Cresslog the Republic had won a smaller, far more subtle, victory.

Had Krothus only overseen this campaign as he had been instructed, this would not concern him. Harden and his soldiers would have been the heroes of the day. But now that he had inadvertently tied his victory so closely to his own prowess, he had been thrust into a dangerous situation.

To any outside viewer, Krothus had humiliated his master, not only by being hailed as the sole victor, but by sending one of her biggest foes fleeing like some beaten puppy. It made Lord Callida look weak. A target was now painted on his back, a set of alleged achievements that would happily cause others to prove themselves against him, and, more importantly, his master to now perceive him as a threat to her own position.

This was the scenario that the Republic was betting on, the conflict between master and apprentice being disruptive enough to topple her careful schemes and keep the status quo of the Empire, and by extension, the ceasefire, intact. Quite the compliment to him if that were the case.

As Krothus stood up to his knees in mud, pondering how long he had to live, he couldn't help but smile. Had he been any other apprentice, being caught up in such a convoluted scheme would result in a quick death, a swift end to a book that never got past the first chapters. But he was Krothus. If the Republic wanted to keep his master's plans from succeeding, fine. If they wanted to do so by boosting his own reputation, allowing him to swiftly climb the savage rungs of the Ruin Lord ladder, even better.

"Something amuses you, lord?" Spinebreaker grumbled.

"Yes," Krothus said, "I've just realized I have an impossible battle to win."

"Will this battle bring us glory, lord?"

Krothus' smile stretched across his face, "I'm certain of it."

Chapter 16

The Depths

"Do you think Victus could have picked a place any more grim than this?" Jarek asked.

A wave of his torch sent several scarabs scurrying into the darkness.

Vyrion didn't want to think about how many more there were, hidden amongst the crevices and cobwebs. But that was expected in the catacombs - the twisted set of dark corridors were wrapped in wrongness and filled with all manner of things best left unseen. The best he could do was focus on their mission and nothing else.

"How grim it is doesn't matter. You feel it as well as I do, this place has power," Vyrion said, feeling the Ruin's presence so strongly that it was as if they were wading through it.

Jarek laughed. "Well it's certainly what you would expect, burying every dead Ruin Lord in history here. Though I can't say they've kept it up very well."

Everything was covered in a thick layer of dust and grime. Rusted braziers crackling with unnatural emerald flame flanked the corridor, each pair marking the crumbling, gilded doors to some ancient tomb. The braziers seemed to stretch and warp the shadows with every dance of their fiery payload, enough for Vyrion to believe that the corridor would actually be lighter without them at all.

As they came to yet another intersection, Vyrion looked down at the map Victus had drawn for them. Left here, and only a bit to go now, provided the scale was right.

Jarek was busy staring at the cracked, rotten bones of some unlucky skeleton, sprawled across the entrance to the right hand passageway. A horde of ants continued their macabre march from one eye socket to another. "I don't think it's wise to disturb whatever lurks here."

"Then hopefully we'll be quiet enough." Vyrion grabbed his shoulder and gently nudged him in the right direction.

Vyrion had no idea what stalked these halls, and he didn't care to find out. His only immediate concern was Lord Victus. His master needed this ritual to succeed or he could very well end up in a tomb of his own.

"Won't matter how quiet we are when half of Thanaton will be buried here soon," Jarek said quietly, "The city is reaching a boiling point, I can feel it."

For someone concerned about how much noise they were making, Jarek was making a concentrated effort to talk as much as possible. He always did that when he was nervous.

"It's not something I think about," Vyrion lied. Between Victus' imminent demise, and the continued chaos spun by Krothus' master, it was all that was on his mind. Krothus had been keeping him updated on her plans, all of which were advancing at a breakneck pace towards her final goal, the Ruined Council. Vyrion had no idea how she even kept track of it all, the amount of people she had caught up in her web of ambition was enough to make his head spin.

"Well if you do eventually think about it, you might want to consider which Lord you would appeal to if Victus doesn't make it. I'd want to throw my lot in with the person as close to the top of the pyramid as I can."

"You don't think Victus will survive the ritual?" Vyrion asked, "He seemed confident it would work. I trust his judgment."

"Why do you think we're doing this first? He's too weak to even set it up himself. If he was truly confident, he would come along with us, bring Lash and Partha too. Hell, I'd even throw in that brute friend of yours."

"Krothus isn't a brute."

Jarek shrugged. "He is a man whose ambition is so naked and visible that he is a liability to just be associated with. Everyone knows about his attempts to humiliate his master, which is stupid enough on its own, but that's not even mentioning this supposed apprentice of his. What is he thinking?"

Vyrion already regretted sharing that last tidbit of information with Jarek, but it was hard to keep secrets when he and Jarek drank plum wine late into the night.

"Keep your opinions to yourself," he said, "Krothus knows what he's doing."

"He'd better not, or Lord Callida will make sure he doesn't make it to the end of the week."

Vyrion had nothing to add to that. They kept walking.

Jarek's torch carved a bright arc through a giant cobweb blocking their path. Vyrion didn't even have to look for the displeased scarabs to make their presence known, he could hear their clattering across the stone walls.

"This looks promising," Jarek said, peering into the corridor beyond.

The passage seemed in a slightly better state than those they had been traveling through, the carvings on the stone walls were still visible, the floor's neatly paved stones weren't covered in centuries of grime. In fact, Vyrion thought that there was a line where the years had stopped, as if an invisible wall had kept the decay from seeping through after all this time. A quick glance showed that even the ever-present scarabs were keeping clear.

"This is it," he said.

Jarek turned and gestured Vyrion forward, complete with an obnoxious bow. "After you."

"What a gentleman," Vyrion said with a roll of his eyes, but stepped forward nonetheless. He cautiously inched his hand forward, anticipating some resistance, an indication of some sorcery at work. But his hand passed the boundary without any notable effect, followed swiftly by the rest of his body.

"How odd." It was not what Vyrion had expected.

Jarek stuck a foot through the nonexistent barrier, joining him soon after. His torch flickered just for the briefest of moments as it too crossed the threshold.

"Can you feel it?" Jarek said, looking around them quickly.

"I can."

Power. It was all around them. Not just the ancient marks of the Ruin that had populated the catacombs as a whole, but a distinct aura, a presence that emanated through the hall. Just like Lord Victus had said it would.

"We had better hurry then," Jarek said, "She may be dead, but I don't want to join her."

And off he went, Vyrion in close pursuit. The engravings on the walls seemed to move as the torch's shadow danced over them, legions of soldiers, shattered runeblades, a mountain of corpses; the storied past of a renowned Ruin Lord long since gone.

They didn't have to travel far, this seemed to be the one corridor in the catacombs with an ending; a formidable stone door flanked by two of those cursed braziers. An inscription had been scrawled along the top of the archway.

Jarek raised his torch to the writings, and began reading aloud. "The Ruin honors Lord Qora, Conqueror of Keero City, Destroyer of Lord Razush, 45th Member of the Ruined Council, Master to Lord Wrun..." He fell silent as his eyes danced across the text carved into the stone for several more moments. "Let's just say it goes on for a while."

Vyrion was only interested in the final line, which he read quietly, "Any who enter will face her wrath."

Jarek gave a nervous chuckle. "No tomb is complete without a dramatic warning to potential intruders. I'm sure it's nothing."

"I hope so," Vyrion said, "Let's get this over with."

The two of them each took up a side of the tomb's door, bracing themselves against the cool stone before giving a coordinated push. But for all their effort they might as well have asked it nicely. Only after blasting the door with waves of the Ruin did they get any results. Each shockwave sent the door scraping and rumbling back a step, far louder than Vyrion wanted, but eventually, they broke through.

The moment the seal was broken and the stone slab crumbled away, they got a glimpse into the blackness that lay beyond. Jarek's torch faltered in the face of shadow so pure, its feeble light seemed to shrink at the challenge. The torch's wielder didn't seem much better.

"Damn Victus to hell, why does he need this ritual done *here*," Jarek muttered.

"I don't know," Vyrion said, "Perhaps it's the only place with enough power to supply it."

"So he sends us to set it up," Jarek continued, "Sends his two most accomplished apprentices to some haunted crypt miles underground while he continues to waste away."

"So it seems," Vyrion said quietly. Jarek had called him accomplished, that was something at the very least.

After thinking for a moment, staring at the inky blank portal, Vyrion swiped a small pebble off of the floor. With careful precision he tossed it underhand through the doorway. The shadow swallowed it up instantly, he never even heard the stone hit the floor.

"I think this is another barrier," Vyrion suggested, "Like the one we just went through, only stronger, blocking out more than just the rot of this place."

"Your guess is as good as mine. How do you propose we get past it, then?"

Vyrion shrugged and flashed him a smile. "I'll see you on the other side."

"You have got to be-"

Vyrion walked through it. The moment he passed through the shadowy barrier, all sound and light side ceased completely, as if he had teleported somewhere else entirely. He could feel a smoothness pass over his skin, like oil had been rubbed across it. And then he was through.

The room's brightness briefly assaulted his senses before he was able to get a hold of himself. The chamber was covered in golden reliefs, all arranged around a single staircase that ascended up to an elaborate stone altar. Upon it lay a golden sarcophagus, a queen on her throne.

But despite the finery, and the presence of proper lighting, Vyrion felt that something was horribly wrong. It screamed at him from his very bones.

It didn't take long for Jarek to stumble through the dark barrier moments later, fast enough that he must have got a running start, nearly colliding with one of the four columns that spiraled up to the ceiling. His torch didn't survive the journey, and was now nothing more than a once bright, now smoky, stick. Jarek quickly tossed it aside.

"This place is even worse, somehow." His runeblade hilt was in his hand already.

Vyrion was in full agreement. The room felt outright hostile. "Then let's make this as fast as possible," he said, sounding far more confident than he was, "Get everything ready."

Jarek gave him a mocking grin. "Since when did you get so assertive? I like it."

Vyrion rolled his eyes. "Just hurry up."

Still grinning, Jarek started unloading reagents out of his pack as fast as he could. Vyrion, for his own contribution, pulled out a scroll covered in Lord Victus' frantic scrawl. His Master had recommended against bringing the Black Book to the Catacombs, he had said it was sure to attract unnecessary attention. Attention from what, Vyrion hadn't asked, but the scroll seemed a suitable alternative.

He wasted no time, directing Jarek in strict adherence to their Master's instructions. The rune-engraved skulls were lain in a circle around the altar, four emerald crystals placed on each side. Several vials of blood, their sources unknown, were used to paint focusing runes on each of the pillars and to form macabre rings on the floor, where various objects of power were placed; a helmet from an ancient Ruin Lord, a runeblade hilt from ages past, even a single bone, said to be from a Grandmaster of the Deus Order. Soon, all that was left was the centerpiece, the key to the entire ritual.

The metal pyramid's icy touch crept across Vyrion's clammy hands as he drew it out of his own pack. Strange, to think how long ago he had first come in contact with the relic, how simple his tasks had been then. Things had accelerated since then at a breakneck pace.

"That should be everything, right?" Jarek asked, his voice wobbling.

Vyrion was glad to see he wasn't the only one deathly frightened of whatever would come next. "Let's hope so." He was peering through the chaos that was Victus' directions to find the next stage of setting up the ritual. He could only see one further note.

"Well?" Jarek pressed, "What's next?"

Vyrion turned the parchment over and back again, and then another time just for good measure, trying to be absolutely sure there was nothing else to decipher. But that was it.

"It just says to place the pyramid on the altar."

"That's all?" Jarek asked, peering over at the parchment himself.

"And then to wait until she takes notice."

"Leave it to Victus to sound as cryptic as possible," Jarek muttered, "What does he expect this Lord Qora to do? She's dead."

Vyrion couldn't shake the feeling of dread that had burrowed into him, but pushed it down regardless. "Let's find out."

He cautiously climbed the mountain of stairs towards the altar, the golden sarcophagus glittering at its peak. Every part of his being was begging him to flee, but he pressed on, his trembling hand slowly bringing the pyramid to its destination.

Beware, that voice in his head hissed. *Prepare.*

The pyramid emitted a dull thud as it made contact. Vyrion took a step back, waiting for something to happen. All was still.

Jarek popped out from behind one of the pillars, "Well? Where is she?"

"Let's give it a moment."

They did.

"Vyrion, are you sure you set it-"

The four facets of the pyramid sprung open. A high pitched screech filled the air, sending Vyrion to his knees, clutching his ears. His pulse pounding into his forehead like a drum, each beat threatening to split it open.

A blue light appeared above him, a blur without form, the pyramid's screech growing in volume as the shape slowly gained clarity. Vyrion's eyes began to droop, his legs buckled. He could feel consciousness slowly slipping out of reach.

But then it all stopped, leaving him gasping, sweating, sprawled across the stone floor. He only just managed to gather enough strength to push himself up and see the result of their preparations.

A shape, a woman clad in ornate armor, hovered above the sarcophagus and the relic appended to it. Her presence was tenuous at best, Vyrion could see right through her spectral form in some places, but the blue spirit was unmistakably the incorporeal presence of a Ruin Lord, a Ruin Lord that could be none other than the denizen of this crypt - Lord Qora.

"Who dares disturb my eternal rest?" she hissed, the echoes of each raspy word coming from everywhere at once, rattling Vyrion's sore head.

A chill gripped the room. Vyrion had no idea how to respond.

The specter hovered closer to him.

"You have come a long way just to die."

Vyrion gulped, his mind still blank.

"My Lord!" Jarek said suddenly, popping out from behind his pillar, "We are humbled by your presence, your reputation is known to all in the Empire."

His flattery seemed to improve her mood ever so slightly. She didn't say anything, but her translucent form drifted back to the altar as she watched him.

"I am Jarek, and this is Vyrion," Jarek continued, "We have been sent here by our master, Lord Victus, to speak with you."

"You disturbed my rest for a *conversation*?"

Vyrion wasn't even sure they were there to speak with her. The ritual surely wasn't meant to just summon her spirit, how was that meant to help Lord Victus restore his body? But they were working with essentially nothing, so the best they could do was try to keep Lord Qora calm.

"Not at all, we seek your wise council," Vyrion lied, "Only you can help us save the life of our Master."

"The Ruined Code would have you slay your master if he is too weak to continue," she said, baring her spectral teeth, "The strong rule the weak, and if you two fools have a master on the verge of death, then he should not be saved."

"It's hard to argue with that," Jarek whispered to Vyrion, earning a disapproving glance.

"What he meant to say," Vyrion said, pointing at Jarek, "Is that our master has not taught us all that-"

"What is that?" the spirit hissed, pointing a spectral finger at Vyrion's outstretched arm.

Vyrion realized he had been pointing at Jarek with the diagram of the ritual.

Lord Quora's spirit began to comb the room, glancing down at the ritual skulls and crystals, taking in the bloody runes scrawled around her. She slowly turned back to the two intruders.

"The brazen delusion you have displayed will be your last. I will not be used as some puppet for this sorcery. To wake me from my eternal slumber for such blasphemy is a grave insult, one I will never forgive."

The chill in the room was now enough for the very air to hurt Vyrion's skin. Still, he tried to salvage the situation. "Truthfully, we don't know what the ritual's purpose is. We meant no insult."

"Your intent matters not," the specter hissed, "I only need your bodies. I will perform this ritual myself and walk the world once more."

One of her hands shot forward, and a shockwave of Ruin energy sent Vyrion and Jarek tumbling down the steps. She began to laugh, a shrill, grating shriek, as the entire room seemed to attack them.

Vyrion barely rolled out of the way of a Ruin shockwave which crushed the floor next to him, only for a chunk of the ceiling to slam into his shoulder. Stones flew at them from almost every direction. Jarek had his runeblade out, the crackling emerald energy of its power runes cutting through any projectile he could reach, but there was so much flying at them that made almost no difference. The pair hid behind one of the stone pillars.

"This can't be what Victus wanted!" shouted Jarek, struggling to be heard over the din of flying rock and ghastly laughter.

Vyrion was furiously reading through Victus' instructions, looking for something, anything, that could help them. Was he really going to die here? In a tomb, destroyed by an ancient spirit he himself had summoned - it was hardly his first choice.

The relic, that voice in his head whispered.

Vyrion felt his head turn to where Lord Qora was directing her assault from, almost as if he wasn't in control of his own body, as if someone was forcing him to look. The pyramid lay where he had placed it, its facets pointing up in the air like a spider's corpse. And inside those facets lay a single bright point, a singularity at the center of the chaos.

Vyrion could sense some sort of energy tethering this point to the specter that was currently trying to murder them, not enough to know exactly what, but perhaps enough to formulate a plan. All of which he wouldn't have noticed without that nudge. Whatever presence enjoyed stalking him was trying its best to ensure he would survive this, perhaps Vyrion would thank it one day.

But to that, he needed to survive. Vyrion ignited his own runeblade as debris crashed all around him, the crimson focus runes covering the area in a dull red glow, and as he did, he shouted to Jarek.

"Get her attention!"

Jarek initially looked as if he was going to refuse, but he eventually jumped out from behind the pillar as requested. The moment he did, the storm of rock and Ruin turned towards him, unleashing its relentless bombardment.

Vyrion knew he didn't have long. He reached out through the Ruin, focusing on the relic that had begun all of this, sitting atop the sarcophagus that hosted that angry, vengeful spirit.

Lord Quora had started drifting towards Jarek the moment he had left cover. A weapon started appeared in her hands.

"Hurry up!" Jarek was still trying to hold back the barrage of debris being flung his way. His arms were raised out in front of him, creating some invisible wall to hold it all in place, but his elbows were wobbling, that wall cracking.

Vyrion could feel each facet of the pyramid, he could feel the power of the singularity within, the smooth panels, the mechanism inside holding it open. He just needed to give it a little push, just enough to sever that connection it held.

Lord Qora was just in front of Jarek. A hiss erupted from her hand as a spectral runeblade finally materialized.

Jarek could do nothing but stare up at her, frozen as he held his barrier up against the onslaught of falling rock.

Vyrion's hands were trembling as he tried again and again to sift through the storm of Ruin energy. It was like trying to catch a loose page in the wind, pluck a fish out of a raging river. He could feel it just on the tips of his fingers.

Lord Qora's runeblade began its arc downwards. "Die, ingrate. Your soul will fuel my terrible vengeance."

Then Vyrion got it. The pyramid's facets snapped back into place with a clunk.

Lord Qora's runeblade halted, inches from Jarek's head. She whipped around.

For a second nothing happened. Then Qora's spectral mouth stretched into what would have no doubt been a furious scream, but all that she managed was a quiet hiss, as if she had forgotten to draw a breath. Some invisible force started dragging her back to the relic, her form shimmering and fading as she passed over the circle of runed skulls and emerald crystals.

As the spirit's presence dwindled, the crystals grew brighter, feasting on her essence like famished infants, suckling away.

Then, with a final great flash of light, Lord Qora's specter was torn apart. The smell of ozone filled the air as the crystals pulsed, painting the room a dark azure blue. Then all was still.

Vyrion nearly collapsed, exhausted. They'd done it. His master desperately needed to improve the clarity of his instructions for any future such adventures.

Jarek walked over and put a hand on Vyrion's shoulder. "You just saved my life."

Vyrion smiled at him, feeling like the most accomplished Ruined in the city. "And Lord Victus as well, if that was what was supposed to happen."

"That remains to be seen," Jarek said, smirking, "But we can at least return home and celebrate conquering death before he gives it a try."

"That we can," Vyrion said, his heart racing.

And they did.

Chapter 17

The Ritual

"Again."

Inissa crept forward, practice blades held tight in each of her hands. Spinebreaker, towering over her, held his lazily at his side, the dull metal looking no more than a twig in his crimson claws. The leaky roof of the abandoned warehouse provided a steady beat as water dripped down.

Krothus watched her intently, scouring her form for weaknesses. Her stance was fine, if a bit sloppy, and her focus razor sharp, but it was her grip that drew his eye. Held too tightly, too high. And even then, it was still a marked improvement - she used to be too weak to pick up the blades at all.

She danced into striking distance, feinting with her left blade and swinging around with her right. A smart initial attack. But Spinebreaker barely moved, he completely ignored the feint and thrashed the true strike aside with no effort at all. He may have been a being of few words, but he was strong and experienced, something Inissa needed to learn to deal with, or she would be useless against anything except fellow teenagers.

Inissa continued to probe for openings, as Krothus had taught her. The next few attacks had similar results, like a bothersome fly being shooed away, but one return slash caught Spinebreaker on his shoulder, slamming into the wall of muscle with a quiet thud. The first successful strike she'd made all morning.

Spinebreaker didn't like that.

In a flash, he was on the offensive, pressing forward in an unrelenting wave. His blade was everywhere at once, the skill and strength of the Nightshadow warrior turning the blunted practice tool into a deadly weapon, one that would have very easily killed an Imperial. But Inissa was still a Ruined.

She whirled past Spinebreaker's strikes, narrowly ducking each savage arc, wisely electing to avoid a parry that would just send her flying. Krothus could sense the Ruin flowing through her, empowering her senses, lending her its strength.

She was doing well.

Spinebreaker stopped a blow mid-air, suddenly changing his grip. Inissa, already leaping to the other way, careened off-balance and toppled over. The warrior's practice blade swung around, finding its mark and leaving her in a mewling heap.

Doing well or not, it was still not good enough.

"What happened to holding back?" Inissa muttered, clutching her side.

"That *was* holding back," Krothus said, giving a nod to Spinebreaker. "He could have easily ended your life if he wished to."

Spinebreaker shrugged, not a bead of sweat on him, while Inissa sat up, her grunt of pain hardly carrying any appreciation towards the mercy she had been shown.

Krothus made no move to help her up. Pain and injury needed to be savored for a lesson to truly sink in.

"You have improved, using the Ruin to heighten your senses, improve your reflexes - but it will not be enough. You cannot be reactive, it only lets your opponent dictate the flow of battle, you must anticipate their actions, be ready to catch them off guard, lay traps of your own."

Given even the slightest crumb of praise, Inissa's full cheeks turned bright red and a wide smile crept across her face. "Thank you, master. I will make sure to train with that in mind."

"Good," Krothus said, feeling a strange urge to smile back, which he vigilantly suppressed, "Because I don't know when our next session will be, it's becoming too dangerous to meet here."

"I wonder who's fault that is."

Krothus frowned, "I've told you, I had no hand in what happened at Cresslog."

"I believe you, lord," Spinebreaker said.

"And a burden is lifted off of my shoulders," Krothus snapped, before turning back to Inissa, "Regardless, Callida's eyes are too focused on me for this to continue in the short term, so I need you to continue on your own, or with Vyrion's direction, provided Lord Victus does not catch wind of it."

"Yes master."

Krothus caught a glimpse of the sun's position through a crack in the warehouse's crumbled roof. "Speaking of Victus, we must end here, as he has requested my presence at his compound. My master has told me it is of utmost importance that I attend."

"Is there something wrong?" Inissa asked.

"Of course not," Krothus lied, knowing full well that it was surely nothing good. "But I can't refuse. I have to continue playing Lord Callida's game, have her think I am nothing more than a willing pawn in her plans. If she suspects I am anything less, then things will turn sour very quickly."

Inissa nodded, suddenly looking much younger than Krothus had remembered. The age between them sometimes felt like a gaping chasm, filled with all the struggles, all the brutalities he had to endure and inflict to make it out of the Ascendancy. It had made him strong, yes, as all conflict did, but he had never known a family, unable to remember even what it was like to be held by his parents. Though in Inissa's case that had hardly seemed to help her.

In a different life perhaps, he could have been a dutiful son, on his way to being a proud father. But for now, Krothus was an unruly apprentice to a power-hungry Ruin Lord, and a master to a fugitive teenager given to a demon by her own mother. So really, he was halfway there.

Though ironically, Krothus was in far more danger than Inissa was these days, fugitive or not. Callida's displeasure at his success was obvious, and his position was tenuous one, entirely reliant on her valuing him more alive than dead. The moment he had returned from his expedition and rumours of him besting her Republic rival came pouring in, Callida had gone cold, treating him more like a hostage than an apprentice. He knew she would end him the moment the prospect of doing so contributed to her plans. And if he was gone, he dreaded to think what his master would have in store for Inissa when she found her.

"Be careful."

Inissa blinked at him in surprise. Krothus frowned, not sure why he had said it at all.

The awkward silence hung for a moment before Inissa bowed. "I'll try, master. You know where to find me if things don't go your way."

Krothus let out a bark of laughter, amused at the thought of Inissa being his savior one day, before waving her off. She heeded his command, casting one more look back at him before slipping out a side door and disappearing.

Once she left, Spinebreaker and Krothus waited in silence. Leaving at the same time was foolish. So there they stood, counting the drips down from the roof. Four hundred seemed like a good number.

After the hundred ninety nine water droplets, Krothus pushed the creaky wooden door open and stepped out into the street.

Street was a generous word for the mess of cracked concrete and marshy mud that passed for roads out in Thanaton's boroughs, but he was there for privacy, not aesthetics. His main gripe was the smell; hundreds of poorly washed bodies packed together had a knack for emitting a stench halfway between a farm and a brothel, their foolish conversations a constant buzz in Krothus' ear.

A familiar beggar sat nearby, long mop of hair reaching down to his half-empty bowl of coins. For a beggar, he sure got around a lot, Krothus had seen the disheveled man nearly everywhere he went, no doubt a clear warning from Lord Callida that he was being watched.

Krothus frowned at him, the man smiled back with a rack of rotten teeth.

Someone was shouting nearby. "Unjustly imprisoned! Oppressed!"

It was some wild man stood atop a rotten box, burning flames crudely drawn across his clothes. "The Emperor, the Council, they are biding their time until they will drain us dry! Only the great prophet Yordu can save us, and he has been taken away!"

A small crowd had gathered, clutching pamphlets and listening intently. They were in Krothus' way.

Utilising Spinebreaker's wide frame as a plow through the field of Imperial citizenry, Krothus pushed his way past. Lord Victus' compound wasn't far from the boroughs, an insult to the old Ruin Lord and a boon to Krothus, who arrived there quickly.

The guards, with that ridiculous metal leg plastered across them, waved him through into the drab corridors.

Crossing one of the courtyards, Krothus spotted Lash and Partha, two of Victus' other apprentices, huddled together in the corner. They halted their conversation immediately when Krothus walked past them, staring daggers at him as though he had interrupted them on purpose. He wasn't sure what he had done to warrant their hatred, but could only assume they were jealous of his strength, his reputation. They were second-rate nobodies, stuck in their station with no hope of escape, their lack of ambition was a given, their lack of ability implied.

The pair would be stuck even longer if their master's ritual succeeded and Victus lived. Vyrion had told Krothus everything about Victus' delusional plan except why Krothus had been invited to witness it, which remained a mystery to them both. Perhaps Victus did not trust his own apprentices. Perhaps he was afraid of some outside intervention. But whatever the reason, Callida had told Krothus to attend, so there he was, fetching Vyrion and preparing for the unknown.

With Spinebreaker stood silently behind him, Krothus rapped Vyrion's door three times with a gauntleted fist. "Vyrion, let's get this over with."

"Just a minute," Vyrion's voice called out, sounding entirely unlike himself.

Krothus heard hurried movement on the other side of the door, felt some unfamiliar presence. Something was off, that much was clear.

So naturally, Krothus slammed the door open.

But the moment the door gave way, Krothus realized he had drastically misread the situation. And he was furious.

Vyrion was half dressed, staring at Krothus with eyes so wide they could have been mistaken for dinner plates. Next to him, sat on the bed in a similar state of undress, was a man with a mop of curly hair and an irritating smile.

"That was the fastest minute I've ever seen," Jarek said.

"Krothus, I told you-" Vyrion started.

But Krothus had already stormed out.

It was ridiculous. They had spent so much time, so much effort, trying to keep themselves free of Thanaton's web of plots, its landscape of complications and implications, and Vyrion had done the most dangerous thing he could. Getting *involved*. He was making himself vulnerable, and by extent, plaguing Krothus with that vulnerability too.

"Krothus, wait!" Vyrion called out, sprinting to catch up.

Krothus stopped, spun around. Vyrion was dressed, at least, but still missing his shoes.

"Why, Vyrion? So you can give whatever excuse you think justifies this brazen stupidity? One of your fellow apprentices - you barely thought about this at all, did you?"

Vyrion's own anger made a swift appearance too. "Why does it matter? It just happened. That's it, nothing will come of this."

"And how do you know that it wasn't part of his plan that something 'just happened'? Or someone else's plan? You know you can't trust him," Krothus snapped. Vyrion's naivety continued to amaze him.

Vyrion let out the world's least convincing laugh. "Please spare me your paranoia. You don't know Jarek at all, how can you possibly say that?"

"And is my lack of knowledge supposed to make me feel at ease? I doubt you know him half as well as you think you do."

"Do I have to know the intimate backstory to every person I share my bed with? You slept with several people at the Ascendancy, each of which you knew even less. So why does it matter?"

Normally Krothus would have struggled to diplomatically convey his next point, but anger had a nasty habit of making words far too easy to say.

"Because I'm not you."

That stopped Vyrion in his tracks. "What?"

"I may have had some arrangements in the Ascendancy, but I never got attached. You on the other hand ..."

Vyrion stared at him, disbelief instantly turning to indignant fury. "So because of a mistake I made when I was sixteen, I'm never allowed to touch anyone again?"

"You know what I meant."

"I'm not a child anymore, Krothus. I know what I'm doing."

But Krothus pressed on, hoping Vyrion would just concede the point they both surely knew was true. "We both know you struggle with your emotions getting the better of you. I really think-"

"Enough. I won't hear any more of this."

Krothus frowned. "But-"

"No. I will meet you outside Victus' chambers for the ritual, but we are not speaking."

And just like that, he was gone, leaving Krothus in the corridor.

Vyrion was blind to his own mistakes, that much was clear. Krothus could only hope that he had maintained the sense to keep mouth shut and his guard up; trusting someone else was a deadly risk, especially when you were as unwary as Vyrion. The poor fool had no idea what he was getting into. Worse, there were secrets he held that Krothus did not want getting out - his secret apprentice, for example.

"Do you want me to kill him, lord?" Spinebreaker asked.

"Shut up," Krothus hissed. He stormed off.

He did manage to calm himself by the time he arrived outside the heavy door to the one-legged Ruin Lord's chambers. Directly across from him were Lash and Partha, still maintaining their tradition of staring him down like some mongrel. Krothus didn't care, though he did find it soothing to imagine cutting them down; wiping that grimace off Lash's idiot lopsided face, ensuring Partha's head was bashed in with that foolish circlet she wore like a poor man's crown.

They didn't have to wait long for Vyrion and Jarek to appear. Had Krothus not known better, nothing seemed amiss, though Vyrion was making a concentrated effort to avoid Krothus' gaze.

Jarek gave Lash and Partha a nod, then rapped on the door, "Master, we're ready."

When Lord Victus eventually emerged, Krothus almost didn't recognise him. Where the old Ruin Lord had once carried himself with the aged power and dignity of a once-great hero, Victus now could barely walk, hobbling along with his metal leg and a cane as if he were on death's very door. His face was sunken and pale, and some black rash had crawled up his body, emerging out of his collar to strike up at his throat. Strangest of all, his hip flask was nowhere in sight.

"Ah, you're here," Victus rasped, speaking to them all but staring only on Krothus.

Krothus was getting very tired of people staring at him, apprentices and Ruin Lords alike.

"We're ready, and the ritual site is prepared as you requested," Jarek said, "Though I'm not sure whether you want all of us to come along."

All of Victus' apprentices, except for Vyrion, turned to Krothus and Spinebreaker. Krothus was half expecting someone to spit in his direction.

"Nonsense," Victus said with a wave of a blackened hand, "The more who are here to ensure this ritual goes smoothly, the better. Besides, our friend Krothus will play a key part."

Jarek shared a look with Lash and Partha before turning back to Victus. "Surely you don't want that orkathi brute coming along as well? He won't-"

Lord Victus' face darkened. "Did I stutter, boy? I don't care how many mindless savages are in attendance. Time is vital, forget this nonsense and get going before I lose my temper."

Jarek scowled but remained silent. Spinebreaker remained a mute wall.

Lord Victus did not wait for anything further, hobbling off to what very well may be his final destination, his stride with cane and leg a chaotic metronome. The rest of the Ruined fell in behind him and the guards saw them off, closing and barring the compound gate as they departed. Best to keep the place under lock and key if the only Ruined left inside was one hidden in the kitchens.

Krothus was certain their little band was doomed to fail. If this sorcery turned out successful and Lord Victus returned to his full strength, then Thanaton's power balance would begin a violent reshuffle. No longer would Victus spend his days searching for lost relics, no longer would his combat prowess and reputation be marred by a permanent reminder of his failures. Krothus knew the extent of influence and honour Victus had once held, it was not too far of a stretch to think that many prominent Ruin Lords would not enjoy such a rival, least of all his master. Lord Callida would never let her plans be derailed in such a way, especially when Lord Victus' current state was no more than a faithfully useless curiosity.

The group carried on, weaving their way to the Old City, a district Krothus had never visited, constructed in and around the ancient remnants of Thanaton's past. Vyrion and Jarek stood at the front next to Lord Victus, shambling along, while Krothus drew the short straw, sandwiched in between the other two at the rear.

"What reason could Callida possibly have to send her dog with us?" Lash said, talking as if Krothus wasn't there.

"Perhaps she is finally cutting him loose after his attempts to upstage her," Partha suggested, adjusting her idiotic circlet.

Krothus remained silent, imagining their horrible deaths. Lash's lopsided face crushed. Partha's circlet shoved up her-

"I wouldn't be surprised," Lash said, "Lord Callida will be Highlord soon, and she'll want to make sure her power base doesn't have any delusional upstarts trying to fracture it."

Krothus was reaching levels of frowning he never thought possible.

Partha was nodding now. "Her campaign is nearly at an end. I heard

Lord Zorin's estate went up in flames last week, and no one has heard from him nor any of his apprentices. So now Highlord Malus is refusing to leave the Dark Pyramid's vicinity, surrounded by what is left of his power base, hoping he will be safe there."

"You two seem very well informed," Krothus said. Even he hadn't heard about that.

Lash gave him her best wonky smile. "Thanaton has no secrets. But even as rumors swirl, the Ruined Council knows who is truly behind it, and they are not happy about its blatant nature."

Krothus shrugged. He just wanted them to shut up.

A mash of modern concrete built into half-ruined stone rose up on either side of their silent band as Victus led them further down into the Old City.

"Your master only gets away with this because she is impossible to pin down as the perpetrator," Lash said bitterly.

"Impossible," Partha echoed.

Lash smiled like her companion had uttered some grand philosophic statement. "Exactly. During Lord Olar's disappearance last month, she was at the theater, seen in attendance by hundreds. Everyone knows she gave the order, but there is no way to prove it."

Krothus was barely managing to keep a smile from his face. The weak always struggled to understand the actions of the strong, and even if he was far from his master's good graces, her political maneuvers were admirable. She was taking the Ruined Code into her own hands.

"Nothing to say?" Partha prodded, "What about her other schemes? That skirmish outside of the Crebin Corridor? The gang wars in the lower levels?"

Lash piled on. "Each time Lord Callida made sure she was in public attendance, with all of her apprentices on missions elsewhere. I'm sure you know nothing about that."

Krothus just shook his head. "What do you want me to say? If you fools want to believe your conspiracy theories, fine. But you should know that my master's power is beyond your pathetic understanding."

Lash instantly had her hand on her slightly askew runeblade hilt.

"You won't be saying that for long, you gray freak. We'll make sure you-"

"Behave. We're here," Lord Victus croaked, wedging himself in between them.

Lash seemed to seriously consider ignoring her master's command, but both she and Partha came to heel eventually. Only then did Spinebreaker move his bonespear back into place.

They were at the foot of a huge doorway, cut into the side of the mountains that surrounded one side of Thanaton. The entryway, covered in skulls, carried with it an aura of dread into the air, seeming to blot out the sun and drive the surrounding area into a dense fog. Krothus felt like he was staring into the underworld itself.

"The catacombs," Lord Victus mused, "Home to generations of Ruin Lords who have shaped the Empire in ways we can scarcely imagine. Today, they will pave the way for a new age."

"We're going to need these," Jarek added, handing out torches.

Vyrion gave one to Krothus, still not properly acknowledging him, which Krothus had to admit was starting to get on his nerves. He would have continued their previous debate and made him see reason, but the presence of the others prevented it.

With their torches lit, the group passed through the threshold and into the mountain, each step closer into the catacomb's chill embrace, each twist and turn further from the world above.

After only a few minutes, Krothus was hopelessly lost. He was forced to follow Lord Victus, hobbling down the endless corridors with a grand sense of purpose and the only knowledge of their route. If Victus happened to keel over right then and there, they would never make it out of this place.

The power of the catacombs enveloped them as they walked; it seeped in through the walls, filled the very air, enough Ruin energy to reforge the whole of the Empire, lying dormant and untouched. Why had this well of energy been left to its own devices? Krothus would have thought some Ruin Lord would have tried to use it to pave a new path for the Empire, but clearly it was not a popular idea; a thick layer of dust and grime covered every surface, and scarabs marched through their subterranean empire with impunity.

Something ahead caused Victus and his apprentices to tuck close to the left side of the corridor. Lash stepped in whatever it was and swore loudly.

Only when he was closer could Krothus see the body. It seemed like it had once been someone's least favored apprentice, clad in a shabby coat and broken armor.

Lash wiped the gore off of her foot and onto the corpse's sleeve. "Blasted graverobbers."

Krothus only gave the body a passing glance. The cause of death was unclear, the scarabs made sure of that. Perhaps they had come seeking power, and something in the catacombs had not taken kindly to this venture. He had read tales of spirits being tethered to the living world, their mastery of the Ruin keeping a presence behind, halfway between a memory and a curse. These tales had never given the impression that these specters were friendly.

Soon after, they came to some corridor that was less grim than the others. It was hardly in a pristine state, but from what little Krothus could discern through the torchlight, it looked like it had been abandoned for weeks, rather than centuries. There were even less scarabs lurking in the shadows.

"The barrier is gone," Vyrion said up ahead.

Lord Victus did not dignify him with a response, scrambling to the end of the hallway as best he could, half-dead and crippled. The rest of his apprentices followed. At the far end lay an elaborate tomb, endless titles carved above it. The other Ruined seemed hesitant to pass through.

"The living were never meant to come here," Spinebreaker rumbled, clutching his bonespear as if it were not made of bone itself.

Jarek wheeled around. "Wait outside then, brute. We don't need you here."

The warrior looked to Krothus. He gave him a nod, allowing him to remain outside, it was always good to have a rearguard, anyone could have followed them there. The area was perfect for an ambush; one way in, one way out, no other witnesses.

Lash and Partha smiled as Spinebreaker walked back down the corridor. Then they all went inside.

Krothus frowned. He didn't like it, but he liked the thought of standing outside and waiting for something to go wrong even less, so he left Spinebreaker outside and went into the tomb.

The heavy doors had been split open, leaving a faint haze in between, a light fog that shuddered away as the Ruined trundled through it. His torch flickered like it would if a wind had run through it, but it stayed alight.

The place certainly set up for a ritual; there were runes of blood spattered the wall, relics encased in focusing circles, and several crystals packed to the brim with Ruinous energy, all of which surrounded a golden sarcophagus up on an altar. A small metal pyramid triumphantly looked down upon the rest of the room atop the slain corpse of that sarcophagus, cracked and split in half down the middle.

Lord Victus struggling up the steps. "It's all set up perfectly, well done. Did she give you any trouble?"

"Some," Vyrion said, helping his master to stay steady. He cast a glance down to an unnatural crater crushed into the ground. In fact, there was debris scattered all around, as if some explosion had ripped through the tomb.

Krothus kept a close eye out.

Victus' other apprentices remained at the foot of the steps, all watching their sick master, meant to be a powerful mentor, a deadly teacher far beyond their capabilities, struggle to climb a simple set of stairs. None of them seemed happy about it.

Krothus understood their misgivings, the Ruined Code did not work well with shades of gray. A healthy Lord Victus was far above his apprentices, but struck with this mysterious illness, this relationship became blurred. Anyone in this room could strike him down, but they would lose his protection, his connections, his knowledge. Krothus doubted any of them would survive longer than a week trying to piece together their own power structures from the corpse of what Lord Victus once had. They would tear each other apart if another Ruin Lord didn't swoop in to pick up the scraps themselves.

And if this ritual didn't work, the end result wouldn't be much different. It would instantly be a free-for-all, a bloodbath, one that would start in this very chamber.

Krothus made sure he had a good view of the other apprentices. If they wanted to kill each other, he didn't want to miss out.

Vyrion finally managed to yank Lord Victus up to the last steps to the altar, his master wheezing but all smiles, like he was thankful for each and every one of those rattling breaths.

Once at the top, the Ruin Lord shooed his apprentice away. "Stand back, boy."

Vyrion hesitantly descended a few steps, only for Victus to double over in a coughing fit, each of his wretches echoed through the tomb. Only once it had subsided did Lord Victus speak again, his croak of a voice rough and hoarse. "Krothus, you must be up here with me."

Now that was surprising. Krothus glanced towards the other Ruined. Jarek leered at him with some secret smile, Lash and Partha looked moments away from ripping out his throat, which was not unusual, but Vyrion just looked worried. Krothus took a small satisfaction in seeing that his partner could not keep up his indignance towards him when push came to shove.

"Fine." He brushed past the others and climbed the steps.

As soon as he did, Lord Victus began chanting in some unknown tongue, staring down at that pyramid perched on the shattered sarcophagus. With each strange syllable, it began to rise further into the air.

Krothus definitely didn't like this.

A final word was spoken, sealing the ritual and Victus let out a long breath. "It is done."

Tendrils of spectral azure energy began to lazily twist out of the crystals surrounding the altar and flow into the tip of the pyramid.

Then Victus turned to him. "I must thank you, Krothus. First of all for getting that crystal phylactery out of the jungle and into my hands. Without it, I would not have found a method of retaining enough Ruin energy for this ritual."

Krothus frowned at the gemstones arranged around the altar. On closer inspection they looked almost identical to those he'd seen in the chest of Lord Fira's abomination, only blue instead of green.

"Does that mean -" he started.

"No, they are not the same," Victus rasped. "Each of these crystals is a focus, retaining whatever power that has flowed into them. The one you brought to me retained an element of the Nightmare Lord's spirit, these contain another."

What could very well have been a ghostly face slowly flowed out of one of the crystals, emitting a silent scream as it was funneled into the pyramid. A chunk of the broken sarcophagus crumbled to the floor.

That explained why they had come here, at least.

As the pyramid grew stronger, so too did the fanatic look in Victus' eye. He ran a hand over his neck and the black, withered pattern that had crept up it.

"It all passed so quickly. When did I become this old man, crippled and dying? I, like all of those gifted with youth, used to think time would never catch up with me. Such a fool."

Then he looked over at Krothus like he were an old friend.

"You know, you reminded me of myself. When we first spoke. I noticed it right away; the strength of will, the limitless ambition, the deep desire to become something more, something better. It was like looking in a mirror, staring down the same hungry man I once was. But power is like nothing else in this world. Once you get just a taste, you are trapped within its grasp, always desperate for more. For a moment, I was the most feared man in the Empire, second only to the Council. Just for a single, beautiful moment. And I have been chasing that high ever since. A waste of twenty years."

"This seems like a bad time for a life lesson." And an unwelcome one at that.

Victus ignored him, instead leaning close and clutching Krothus' shoulder in one gnarled hand. "Tell me, Krothus, have you lived your life with no regrets? Do you wish you could rewrite it all, start again?"

"I don't regret anything," Krothus said. He had no idea what the old man was talking about, perhaps he needed another swig from that flask of his, wherever it was. But one thing was certain, Krothus had never regretted anything in his life. Everything paved its way to his destiny in one way or the other.

Victus let out a deep breath, as if a great weight had been lifted off of his shoulders.

"I wish I could say the same. But it pleases me to know that you have made the most of your short time on this world."

The pyramid looked like it was about to burst; flickering, gorged on power, amplified by the various relics and runes arrayed across the room. A field of energy emanated out from it, impossibly bright. Victus reached out a blackened hand. The pyramid reached back. Then there was a flash.

The aged Ruin Lord let out a howl of triumphant laughter as he began to levitate just above the relic, its aura quickly forming a loving embrace around him. His cane and metal leg clattered to the floor like broken chains.

Krothus took a step backwards, disoriented by the light. Echoes of the words Victus spoke earlier began to repeat rhythmically, echoing across the room, rippling through Krothus' skull. There were powerful forces at work here.

But for all the ritual's power, Krothus felt something amiss. Something twinged at the back of his mind. Krothus glanced behind him, down the steps, just in time to see Lash and Partha pulling out their runeblade hilts. The intention seemed far from friendly.

Jarek, the grating fool, just watched them do it, doing nothing but resting his hand on his own weapon. Vyrion, too engrossed in his master floating through air, hadn't seen them at all.

Lash and Partha ignited their runeblades, one with yellow absorption runes, the other crimson focus runes, and rushed up the stairs.

"Vyrion!" Krothus shouted, barely audible over the vortex now brewing above them. He swiped his arm forward, sending a punch of Ruin energy barrelling down the stairs.

Vyrion turned just in time to see Partha send Krothus' strike crashing into one of the pillars. Lash swept her weapon at him with no hesitation.

"Have you gone mad?" yelled Vyrion, barely managing to get his runeblade out in time to block the strike.

Krothus ran to his aide, crashing into Partha and sending her stumbling backwards.

"It's over!" Lash hissed, "Victus is the one who's gone mad, he's pissed away his reputation, *our* reputation. Step aside."

Krothus blocked a poor overhead slash and, far from stepping aside, kicked Partha in the ribs. "What utter cowardice," he sneered, "Waiting until a dying old man is unable to defend himself before betraying him. Pathetic."

"And you'll have to get through us first," Vyrion said, sending a jagged bolt of crimson lightning down the steps.

Lash caught the lightning on her runeblade, giving her ugliest lopsided grimace. "Fine, die with him then."

Krothus had to admit he was glad they were stupid enough to attempt this - now he had an excuse to cut them to pieces. But Lash and Partha, to their credit, were matching them blow for blow, their experience keeping them on the front foot. Their swordwork was near-perfect, accompanied by a bag of tricks that Krothus had to struggle not to get caught out by; a double feinted slash nearly took his hand off, a kick to the side of the knee almost sent him tumbling down the stairs.

Jarek, meanwhile, had finally taken his own runeblade out, but he was just stood at the foot of the steps, green energy cracking off of his weapon. Krothus couldn't decide whether he was a coward or an opportunist.

Victus' voice filled the room. "I can feel it, the power flowing through me. *Limitless*. I will leave this broken body and fix the mistakes of the past, bring the Empire back from the brink."

If Krothus could have tuned out the racket the old Ruin Lord was making, he would, but he could hear it as clearly in his mind as clearly as his own thoughts.

The brutal stalemate continued on the steps. Only once he sent Partha reeling from a punch to the gut did Krothus risk a glance back to Lord Victus.

The Ruin Lord's body was hovering above, encased in a shell of azure energy. He didn't appear to be moving. In fact, he didn't appear to be alive at all. But still Krothus could hear the Ruin Lord, his disembodied words boomed through the room, audible even over the clash of combat and the wailing of the vortex spewing from the pyramid relic. "I will be reborn. I will once again wield a powerful body, a vessel powerful enough to contain my might."

Krothus' glance back had nearly cost him. He barely managed to parry away another blow from Partha, feeling her golden runes lap up a sliver of his Ruin energy as he did. An arm's length away, Lash and Vyrion were toe to toe, a dazzling display of crimson blades and crimson lightning.

Krothus saw an opening, a quick strike would leave Lash in two blazing pieces. He made ready to lunge for it.

But Krothus couldn't bring himself to do it. Not that he had suddenly developed a strong preference for pacifism, but his limbs suddenly felt like concrete, impossibly heavy, entirely unresponsive.

"We will be their savior, Krothus," Victus's voice declared, "Together, you and I will tear out the corruption eating at the heart of this Empire. We will cleanse the city of Lord Callida's misguided, foolish ambitions in the Emperor's name, finally allow our great nation to regain its security, its stability."

"What is this?" Krothus managed to grunt, his mouth barely able to move. He strained and struggled, but all his might was useless against this overwhelming force, an invisible hand dragging him away. He twisted his neck, his very tendons fighting their best just for the tiniest increment.

And then he saw it. A specter, hovering above Lord Victus' empty husk of a body, tethered to that cursed pyramid. A ghastly chain connected Krothus and the spirit, a lifeline tossed out in a storm, one that he was quite sure was not pulling him to safety.

"Krothus!" Vyrion shouted out.

But Krothus knew that for all his shouting, Vyrion would never be able to stop the ritual, not while Partha and Lash were both bearing down upon him. Each of them was more than a match for him on their own, and now he had to deal with both.

As the altar grew closer, the relic's grip grew tighter, and Krothus was finally granted an understanding of what was happening. The ethereal form was free from the shackles that had once plagued him; perfect skin, a full head of hair, even two legs. Lord Victus, shorn from his mortal form, hovered, splendid and triumphant, above his former shell.

"For what it's worth, Krothus, I am sorry," Victus said, a sad calmness in his voice, "The nature of the Ruined Code decrees that my apprentices take my place, and that you, one day, will rise far within the hierarchy of the Empire to where you rightfully belong. But this is not to be. It is selfish, I know that. I am taking all this from you, an opportunity that I have already squandered. But please know that it is for a noble cause, I must save the Empire from itself, prevent it from breaking apart at the seams. Do you understand?"

The pull halted, just for a brief moment. Every movement of Krothus' lips felt like a herculean task, but he would be heard.

"Fuck. You."

Victus looked at him with a mournful stare. "I see. An unfortunate misunderstanding, but you do not get a say in the matter."

"Vyrion won't forgive you," Krothus hissed.

The ghostly Victus shrugged. "He will in time, if he survives this at all."

"Partha, Lash-"

Now Victus was smiling. "They will die."

The spectral chain began to slowly pull Krothus back once more. All he could do was look down the steps towards Vyrion. He was no match for the others together; his power sapped by Partha's runeblade, and his shoulder bleeding from Lash's, it was only a matter of time before he fell.

Though Vyrion was never one to give up. He diverted a blow from Lash and sent Partha tumbling off the staircase with a push of the Ruin.

But Lash recovered quicker than he expected. Her runeblade swung back.

A sudden flash of green appeared behind her. Then a runeblade burst through her chest, the crackling energy filling the room with the scent of burnt flesh. Jarek.

Krothus would have smiled, if he could.

He could feel the air from the vortex at his back.

Partha, circlet askew, was now rushing up the steps in a desperate bid for vengeance. Vyrion caught her with a blast of energy, which she deflected, only to be intercepted by Jarek.

They pressed against each other, runeblades clashing in a flurry of sparks.

Partha started shrieking. "You were supposed to-"

She stopped, her hands clutching at her neck. Jarek was holding a fist to his side, trembling as if he were trying to crush an invisible insect. And then, with a flick of his wrist, he snapped her neck.

Partha collapsed, her circlet clattering to the floor.

"Help me stop this!" Vyrion shouted.

Krothus was unable to voice his growing concern.

Jarek was already moving.

Krothus' vision began to blur as he was pressed into the shell of power around Victus. He could feel a deathly calm wrap around his body. That was never a good sign.

"So close," Victus' voice cooed, "So close."

Krothus saw the flickering light of Jarek's runeblade slashing through one of the binding runes on the far side of the room. In an instant, the air was flooded with unrestrained Ruin energy, a storm of uncontrolled power.

"No!" Victus' voice called out, "Jarek don't - you'll ruin everything, all that we've worked for! Stop this, you idiot!"

But Jarek didn't stop. Deafening crashes ricocheted across the room as flashes of lightning pounded down, which could only be Victus lashing out in fury. Each ritual object shattered was accompanied by another scream of rage.

Krothus felt a cold touch crawl across his skin. His hairs stood on end as the icy touch passed into his spine. Was this it?

Vyrion was holding back Victus' rage, shielding both himself and Jarek. Another binding rune shattered and an earsplitting shriek rang out. The ritual, empowered by the crystals, by the fighting, and by Victus himself, became unbound and volatile.

The icy touch creeping across Krothus' paralysed form became a deathly cold, like someone was holding frozen fire to his skin. He wanted to shrink away, to scream, but he could not. A black curtain slowly descended over his vision.

"It matters not," Victus' voice whispered, now coming from within Krothus' head, "They can't stop us now. We will show our apprentices the error of their ways. They simply do not understand our glorious purpose."

They understand it perfectly well, you madman, Krothus thought. But even his own mental voice was practically a whisper. He could feel his mind being pushed aside, compressed into some small compartment of his being, like a package put away in a storage room. A new presence poured in.

Then Krothus heard something.

"Lord?" a familiar voice called. A crimson blur was all Krothus could make out, silhouetted against the emerald light from the corridor.

"Spinebreaker!" Vyrion shouted from somewhere, "You must-"

"Get back you *brute,*" Jarek interrupted, "You'll disrupt everything I'm trying to-"

But Spinebreaker either hadn't heard them, or didn't care. The crimson blur got larger and larger, the orkathi sprinting up the steps like a creature possessed, right through the hurricane of Ruinous energy.

"We are ready," Lord Victus said in Krothus' head, seemingly unaware of the living missile flying at them.

We are not, Krothus disagreed.

Spinebreaker, disregarding both of their thoughts, crashed into the vortex.

Chapter 18
Aftermath

It felt like a cruel joke. Vyrion had set out to help his master, to give him a second chance at life. Instead, Victus exploited that trust, and Vyrion had helped seal his fate, a punchline that he was still struggling to wrap his head around.

Now he and Jarek were in their master's former chambers, watching Krothus and Spinebreaker, sprawled across the bed like they were their ugly, slumbering children.

"We need to find a new master," Jarek said, repeating the same sentiment for the sixth time in just as many minutes. "We're vulnerable, it's only a matter of time before someone finds out and tries to take the compound. We don't even have any bargaining chips; Victus' relic is buried under ten tons of rubble and the old man made sure to hide the Black Book before he set out to meet his end."

"I know," Vyrion said weakly. That was the last thing he wanted to talk about. He could still see the tomb crumbling around him, feel the cracks that shook the earth as they sent the ceiling crashing down. The image of Victus' broken body crushed under a mountain of rock was still fresh in his mind.

Jarek was just staring at him, like he were expecting Vyrion to say something.

"What?" Vyrion snapped.

"We're running out of time. Every second that we can get ahead of this is invaluable, but we're wasting it waiting for *them*." He threw a dismissive gesture down at the bedridden duo like they were a hand of losing cards.

"What do you suggest we do? We aren't going to leave them."

"Why not? I mean-"

Vyrion cut him off immediately. "You've got to be joking, Jarek. What's wrong with you?"

"Look," Jarek said, gripping Vyrion's shoulder far too tight for his liking, "We can't be sure if Victus' ritual succeeded. Krothus could be already dead, his body some unwitting puppet. And, when Victus wakes in his new body, the first thing he will do is to punish the apprentices who so clearly defied him."

Vyrion shrugged his hand off. "Clearly defied him? All you did was stick a final dagger into his back, the man who trusted you most out of everyone. I was forced to do what I did to save Krothus, what was your excuse?"

Jarek held his hands up in mock surrender. "I understand tensions are running high, but I wasn't planning on doing what I did when I walked into that room. I did it to help you. I knew you weren't going to be able to do it on your own, so-"

"You only 'helped' once you found it convenient. We were fighting for our lives while you just stood there, waiting to kick whoever went down first."

And then, Vyrion had a sudden realization, one that sent rage pulsing through his heart. Cowardly was one thing, but conniving was another.

"Worse than that, Partha and Lash seemed completely unconcerned about your allegiance until the end. Did they tell you what was going to happen?"

"Of course not!" Jarek said, recoiling at the suggestion far too easily.

Liar, the voice in Vyrion's head whispered.

His face felt hot, his breath came hard and fast. He found himself balling up his hand.

Jarek's arms instantly folded into his sides as Vyrion slammed him up against the wall with a blast of the Ruin.

"Don't you *dare* lie to me." Vyrion could feel angry tears welling in his eyes. Jarek was struggling, but Vyrion only tightened his grip. What else had he lied about?

"Okay, okay-" Jarek squeaked, barely able to speak with the force constricting him. His legs flailed in protest.

Vyrion opened his hand and Jarek dropped to the floor, gasping for breath. Only once he recovered, blowing a few unruly curls out of his face, did he answer. "It wasn't like that. They had been talking about trying to take Victus down for years, but it was always just talk, no more than a few hushed complaints. I had an inkling they might try something, but I couldn't know for sure."

"Then why didn't you say anything? And why wait so late to pick a side?"

"Vyrion, you know them," Jarek muttered. "They are hardly the brightest pair of Ruined in the city, are they? I knew if they were going to attempt something, it wouldn't work. And, for the same reason, I knew that if I let them get on with it, I could catch them off guard. That's it."

Vyrion felt his anger slowly peter out, a flame with no fuel. It did make sense, and if Jarek hadn't intervened, then Krothus would not be here, none of them would. But as logical as Vyrion knew it was, it still didn't sit right with him. He would never be able to stand by and do nothing as Jarek fought for his life.

By the Ruin he was tired. He sat at the foot of the bed, head in his hands. So much was going to change. Vyrion had spent every day at the Ascendancy wishing for a home, and now that he had found one, it was being swept away. He looked over at Krothus, slumbering peacefully nearby, and hoped Jarek was wrong, that the ritual had failed. On top of everything else today, he couldn't stand to lose him too.

Jarek sat down next to him, snaking an arm around his shoulder. "It will be okay. I promise."

But Vyrion wasn't listening, there was too much to worry about. "What will happen to the guards, the compound staff?"

"Not our concern. Whichever Ruin Lord takes over the largest chunk of Victus' power base will decide."

"Perhaps it's best if we keep them in their positions then. None of them know about Victus' fate, and until we find a new master it would be best to keep up appearances," Vyrion suggested. He didn't want them to panic. They had done nothing wrong, nothing but serve the wrong Ruin Lord at the wrong time, a crime Vyrion could very much sympathize with.

"It entirely depends on what our new master would have us do. I doubt that she would be taking suggestions, we hardly have any chips to bargain with."

She. It sounded like Jarek already had someone in mind, and Vyrion had a distinct feeling he already knew who.

But Jarek didn't say anything more, his gaze was suddenly flanking Vyrion completely, looking back to the bed.

Vyrion slowly turned, expecting the worst.

The landscape of scars, the stone jawed frown, the hair relentlessly shaved down; nothing about Krothus looked out of place. He sat up, glaring at them. Alert. Suspicious.

Was this Victus? Krothus? Vyrion held his breath, waiting for something, anything, to point towards the truth.

But Jarek clearly had a very different idea. He sprung at Krothus, emerald runeblade ignited.

"Jarek, no!" Vyrion yelled. But he was too slow to react, surprise poisoning his reactions.

Krothus' runeblade met Jarek's in a flash of light, the heat of the fiery blade emanating out into the room.

"We'll put a swift end to your 'rebirth', Victus," Jarek hissed, struggling to break their stalemate. But Krothus held firm, the strength in those gray arms making it look easy.

Krothus didn't say anything at first, only baring his teeth in an animalistic snarl of defiance. Then, in the blink of an eye, he cut away from the clashing runeblades and away from them both.

The Ruin swirled around the room, supercharged off of the chaos and conflict, masking Vyrion's ability to sense the true nature of what lay underneath that gray flesh. Nothing was certain, Victus and

Krothus both seemed to have a presence there. He needed to make a decision. Vyrion, hand shaking, slowly took out his runeblade.

Krothus watched him do it, eyes narrowed in suspicion. "Are you really joining your lover's betrayal, Vyrion?"

"I'm just being cautious," Vyrion said, "Nothing more." Lovers. The childish insults certainly seemed like Krothus.

Krothus briefly looked down at himself, like he was checking for any wounds. Or inspecting a new body. Then he pointed his fiery weapon at Jarek.

"I'm surprised at the sudden hatred of your former master, Jarek. I didn't realize you were so attached to me after our brief conversation, enough to commit yourself to betraying him so quickly."

"Stop stalling. You'd better come up with something better than that, Victus, or we'll put you down," Jarek said.

Krothus laughed. "As amusing as that would be, you are wasting your energy. Let me speak with Vyrion privately, he is more than capable of seeing the truth."

If this was Victus, he had certainly adopted Krothus' arrogance. But Vyrion still wasn't convinced. "I'm sorry, Krothus, but we can talk here. I need to test you. We can speak freely, I trust Jarek."

"That makes one of us," Krothus said flatly. "So - what are these benign riddles you are suggesting?"

Vyrion had already thought of one only moments ago.

"Who was the first person you killed?"

Krothus smiled, like he were remembering a fond memory or a past love. "Yaryn, who tried to kill me in my sleep. I snapped his neck."

Vyrion nodded to Jarek, that was correct.

But Jarek remained undeterred. "I'm not convinced. What is the name of your apprentice?"

Vyrion's stomach sank, he was not supposed to know that.

Krothus frowned, eyes flicking to Vyrion. "Good to see that my secrets are being kept appropriately." Then he turned to Jarek. "You had better hope his trust is not misplaced, or you will wind up in pieces."

"Answer the question," Jarek snapped.

"Inissa."

"And?" Jarek pressed, "Come on now, I'll need more than that."

Krothus glared at Vyrion before answering, his growing fury plain as day. "She has long black hair, she adores black cherry pastries, and she is probably working in the kitchens in this compound as we speak. Are we done?"

"Nearly," Jarek said. Vyrion needed no further proof, but he figured Jarek knew Victus better than anyone, if there was anyone who could draw him out, it was him.

He walked over to the far wall decorated with ancient vases, filled with shelves of relics, then pointed towards an elaborate medal mounted above, all sharp corners and rich crimson. Vyrion knew it as Victus' most prized possession, a reward for his victories at the height of his power, whispered to have been bestowed by the Emperor himself.

"Of course, if you weren't Victus, you wouldn't care if something happens to this then?"

"I couldn't care less what you do, idiot," Krothus snarled back.

Jarek smiled at him, shadows cast from the light of his runeblade dancing across his face. Then he struck. He swept his runeblade through the wall again and again, leaving deep gouges in the concrete and sending molten rock spraying across the room. Only when the vases were in pieces, the shelf was nothing but charcoal, and the wall was a smoldering mess did Jarek stop, standing there gulping in furious breaths.

"It's a good thing objects don't fight back," Krothus sneered.

Vyrion couldn't help but laugh as the waves of anxiety that had been crushing his chest finally lifted. He practically jumped onto Krothus, struggling to wrap his arms around his huge frame, but trying anyways.

Krothus stiffened up initially, before awkwardly patting him on the shoulder. Vyrion knew when to take a hint, stepping away almost instantly.

"Sorry, I just thought ..." he said, not even sure how to put his fear into words. With all that had happened that day, fighting Victus within Krothus' body might have been the thing that finally broke him.

"I know. But things are as they should be," Krothus said, with the slightest hint of warmth underneath his tone, as much as Vyrion knew to expect if someone else was present.

"Well isn't this sweet," Jarek said, finally putting his weapon away.

"You need to learn when to shut your mouth," Krothus said.

"I can't really argue with you there," Jarek agreed, all smiles, "But there is one more thing we need to discuss."

Krothus wasn't listening, as Vyrion expected. Instead, he was busy checking over Spinebreaker, each careful touch carrying a surprising gentleness, each motion indicating a very deliberate ignorance of Jarek and anything he was trying to say.

The deliberate ignorance was a trick Krothus pulled often, something that usually drove Vyrion up the wall. But not this time. Vyrion highly doubted Krothus had forgotten the argument they had before the catacombs, and neither had he. Had things in that tomb gone as expected, perhaps they would still not be on speaking terms. But it all seemed so small now.

Still, they needed a plan.

"Krothus," Vyrion said, "This is serious,"

"And this isn't?" Krothus asked, pointing to a nasty gouge across Spinebreaker's arm, no doubt delivered by some falling debris. "Besides, I know what Jarek wants, and the answer is, perhaps. My master may find usefulness in you, she may not. All I know is that she will want me to bring you to her regardless, for it is her decision to make, not mine."

"Good. Then take us to her," Jarek said.

"What, just like that?" Vyrion asked, annoyed that the decision was being made for him, "There are plenty of other Ruin Lords we can go to."

Jarek laughed, a harsh singular bark. "Then who do you have in mind?"

Vyrion thought for a moment. There were hundreds, even thousands, of Ruin Lords in Thanaton, but there was no telling who would take them in. More than a few would happily end their lives for simplicity's sake. He racked his brain for any suitable options.

Two candidates came to mind. "What about Lord Krag? Or Lord Ovoros? They are both powerful, with vast power bases and a reputation for being level-headed. I'm sure they would take us in."

"That's true," Jarek said, "But given a choice between Highlord Malus and Lord Callida's ongoing crusade, they will pick the status quo every time, putting you directly at odds with a certain gray-skinned bundle of sunlight."

Krothus glared at him silently from across the room, but Jarek paid him no heed and continued.

"So that would leave us only picking from those Ruin Lords backing Lord Callida, so why not Callida herself?"

"I suppose so," Vyrion said quietly. But was it really that simple? It felt so rushed, so disrespectful, to move on so quickly.

"And, more importantly, she's least likely to kill us when we arrive at her compound with news of Lord Victus' unfortunate demise," Jarek tacked on far too cheerfully.

"And even more importantly," Krothus said, finally speaking up, "Both of you don't have a say in the matter. My master will make her own choice." He had his hand on his runeblade hilt, but the gesture was unneeded, the threat in his voice was clear as day.

"Glad we're all in agreement then," Vyrion muttered. It seemed the decision was already made - he'd been outvoted.

"Then let's get moving," Krothus said.

"Aren't you forgetting something?" Vyrion asked, pointing at the slumbering orkathl snoring away on the bed.

Krothus's face didn't even twitch. "He'll be taken care of. Now, go."

With no further arguments, Vyrion and Jarek left Victus's chambers, now no more than a sad, near empty room. Krothus followed right behind.

The moment they left, a shape appeared out of the shadows near the door, a round face with long black hair. Inissa must have been learning quickly, her presence within the Ruin had been nearly invisible. She gave Vyrion a nod of recognition.

"Don't let anyone in this room unless I'm with them. And no

questions." Krothus said to his apprentice.

Inissa was looking at the trio as if she were catching them in the act of some mischief. "Where is Lord Victus? And what happened to you? You look terrible."

"Do you listen to anything I say? No questions, no visitors."

Inissa nodded, saying nothing, but casting a very Krothus-like glare at Jarek. Then she was gone, the heavy chamber doors slamming shut behind her.

"She seems nice," Jarek said.

"Shut up and get moving," Krothus growled.

The trio quickly made their way to the exit of the compound, but were interrupted just at the doors as a familiar Imperial in an impeccably tidy uniform bumped into them, flanked by a patrol of guards.

"My Lords," Lorren said, giving a salute and a deep bow, "Good to see you."

"We were just on our way out, Sergeant," Vyrion said, trying to appear composed. Nobody could know what happened, at least not yet.

Lorren cleared his throat. "Apologies my lord, it is actually Lieutenant Lorren now. All thanks to your help at the tribunal."

That got a smile out of Vyrion despite everything that had happened that day.

"Congratulations!" he said, shaking his hand and leaning in close. "Lock down this compound, no one in or out. But do it quietly, don't make a show of it,"

Lorren swallowed, his stringy neck wobbling as he did, before saluting stiffly. "Good luck, my lords, I have some business to attend to." He then gathered up his patrol and quick-stepped towards the barracks.

Vyrion was sure he was leaving the compound in good hands. Once they were out of sight, he turned to Krothus. "That should make sure no word of this leaves this compound,"

"Fine," Krothus said, "Now hurry up."

Jarek just rolled his eyes.

Out on the streets, Vyrion's anxiety was battering him worse than ever before. It burrowed into his guts, eating away at his insides, his body's only solution to this invisible threat being a coat of sweat and an impossibly rapid pulse. Every step felt like his last.

With every person he passed, his mind would put him through the same tortuous cycle. They knew. They knew Lord Victus had met his end, betrayed by his own apprentices. They knew that they only had to say one word, then a gang of opportunistic Ruin Lords would stamp out everyone Vyrion cared about. They knew that he was panicking. That he was *guilty*.

And worst of all, that presence was there, in his head, watching his every move. Maybe it knew too, knew all that he had done.

Soon, it whispered. Vyrion tried his best to push it away, to clear his mind, but even as they drew up to Lord Callida's compound, it remained.

Krothus was suddenly in front of him. "Focus, Vyrion. We're here."

Vyrion nodded, swallowing down all his demons as best he could.

Callida's fortress was an elegant monstrosity, chaos given form. The walls engaged in a twisted dance of interlocking and overlapping, towers erupting out of them like the limbs of intertwined lovers. A dark forest of spiked ramparts loomed overhead, part of the wild expanse of fortifications that seemed to grow out of the ground, a parasite of metal and stone. The black sun banner of Lord Callida was everywhere.

"Krothus returns, open the gate!" called out some voice from above, heralding the screech of metal as the gatehouse slowly raised a girded steel portcullis. Only once the chains stopped their rattling and the gate locked into place did they enter.

"Your master seems to value her security," Vyrion said quietly. Guards crawled over the walls like bees patrolling a hive, not a single position unmanned, behind the gate lay a courtyard packed to the brim with even more.

"It is necessary when half of the city wishes you dead," Krothus said, "I doubt anyone would risk an attack so blatant, but it's best to deter even the most foolish of notions. Highlord Malus and his own now have no options outside of assassination attempts."

"And how have those turned out?" Jarek asked.

"What do you think? I'm not planning on bringing you to a corpse."

Jarek fell silent. Vyrion sighed, he had always hoped these two would get along, but that seemed like a true impossibility.

Another screech rang out as the portcullis fell back to the ground with all the grace of a blind drunkard. Then it was quiet.

Krothus was undeterred, stomping through the mob of guards, pushing them aside without a care in the world, Jarek close behind.

But Vyrion hesitated. All the guards, the walls; he was putting his life entirely within the hands of a woman he had never met, one with a reputation of being the most cutthroat, ambitious Ruin Lord in the Empire. If this went poorly and Lord Callida elected to finish wiping out all that remained of Lord Victus, then there was nothing anyone could do to stop her. But what other choice did he have? His only other option was to go out on his own, become some untethered Ruined more likely to meet death than anything else.

No, this was the only choice, one that had already been made for him despite his protests. So Vyrion followed Krothus and Jarek through the courtyard of guards and further into Lord Callida's domain.

The dim corridors were draped in so much crimson, be it furniture, rugs, or tapestries, that a splash of blood would have been nearly invisible, perhaps by design. And with every turn it got darker.

Krothus was leading them at a breakneck pace, with Vyrion on the cusp of having to jog just to keep up. But after yet another turn, Krothus suddenly stopped, staring down someone who had blocked their way. He was a tall man with long hair, standing in their path with a big toothy smile.

"The prodigal apprentice returns," the man said in a scornful baritone, before looking over Vyrion and Jarek like they were lost vagrants off the street, "And with friends."

Krothus did not looked pleased. "I don't have time for your nonsense, Amar. Get out of my way."

"Why the rush? Killed another one of our fellow apprentices? No? Perhaps you're off to publicly humiliate our master again."

"I'm in no mood for your meaningless dribble. Move."

Amar's smile disappeared. "A bit of courtesy goes a long way, especially when I am here on our master's business. Show some respect."

Krothus didn't say anything, which Vyrion figured was the most respect he could provide.

And just like that, Amar's off-putting teeth made a return. "I've been told to collect your guests. Lord Callida has been expecting them." He made a flourishing bow towards Vyrion and Jarek, in a way that was almost certainly meant to ridicule.

Vyrion shared a brief look with Krothus. Callida expecting them was a surprise, and not a pleasant one at that. Had she already heard what happened?

If Jarek was concerned, he didn't show it, he looked as though he were in the middle of a pleasant dream, a content grin on his face, halfway ready to drift off into the sky.

"If our master insists," Krothus managed to say through gritted teeth, "But we will follow you only because she has commanded it so."

Amar watched him carefully. "You know, you are profoundly unlikeable. Blunt, rude, arrogant; rivalries do not have to be unpleasant, yet you absolutely insist on it. It's no wonder you have blundered your way into unpopularity, it's just the natural course."

"I am truly glad you have thought so deeply about me," Krothus said, looking as far away from glad as he could.

"I doubt anyone else will. No one will be mourning your passing when you're gone," Amar returned. It was strongly implied that passing would be sometime soon. He looked again at Vyrion and Jarek, his nose wrinkled like he had caught a whiff of some unbearable odor. "Let's not keep her waiting."

With a dramatic twirl that sent his long cape of hair swaying, they were once again on the move, Amar gliding up twists of stairs and sweeping through crimson corridors. Krothus stomped behind, grumbling all the way.

"You're uncharacteristically quiet," Vyrion said, leaning in close to Jarek.

Jarek kept his eyes forward. "And you're characteristically worried. This will work."

"I hope so."

They wound up one final set of stairs, an ascent that seemed to change its mind and dip back down several times, before finally emerging into the groggy Thanaton murk. It must have been the top of Callida's fortress, the dim expanse of the city filling the horizon, the Dark Pyramid dominating the skyline. And they weren't alone.

Atop the platform, a dozen Ruined stood at rigid attention, a menagerie of the uncomfortably mutated and the disturbingly beautiful; horns and scales and teeth that Vyrion couldn't rip his gaze away from. Just behind were a handful of high-ranking Imperial officers, their chests awash with colors and shapes denoting increasingly elaborate titles and increasingly filled out uniforms. None of them moved a muscle when Amar slithered past, all eyes remained on the woman staring up at the Dark Pyramid.

Her presence in the Ruin was a swirling tempest of confidence and ambition, her physical form just as imposing as the power she emanated, draped in expertly tailored robes and standing so tall that even Amar had to stretch up mutter into her ear.

Only once Amar slipped into line did Lord Callida turn. Her face was unreadable, all sharp angles, masked in a practiced expression of regal indifference. Beautiful and frightening all the same.

"So here they are. My most *ambitious* apprentice brings me a gift."

Ambitious had not been meant as a complement. Krothus, wearing a rare nervousness, gave her a deep bow, before taking his place among the others, as if awaiting an imminent punishment. Callida's other apprentices gave him a wide berth.

Before Vyrion could respond, Jarek sprung forward, kneeling down so far that he might as well have thrown himself to the floor. "Lord Callida, we come to you wishing to serve. Our former master, Lord

Victus, is dead."

Vyrion felt sick. Victus's body was barely cold, and already Jarek was prostrating himself before another Ruin Lord like the man had never existed. It wasn't respectful.

Vyrion remained on his feet.

If she was surprised by this news, Callida didn't show it. She just looked at them, looked at Vyrion. He felt a tingling at the back of his head, a shiver across his scalp. He saw an image in his mind, all other thoughts pushed away as it pressed to the forefront, clear as day. He saw himself kneeling. That practiced expression on Callida's face slowly darkened. A different image, a grisly corpse that Vyrion quickly recognised as his own, began to materialise in his mind's eye. It was standing, yes, but only because it was spit with a stake. Its mouth hung open in a final silent scream of pain.

Vyrion swallowed and slowly got down on one knee. Callida smiled, and the images vanished.

She continued as if nothing were amiss. "If this is true, then a chapter has closed. Lord Victus was a crumbling relic of a time long gone, an artifact of an Empire burdened by its own failings. I will mourn him. We had a mutual respect, but for far too long he looked to the past for answers, when he should have been looking to the future."

She looked at her apprentices, in all their malformed glory, then back to the Dark Pyramid, gazing down like some multifaceted god. "The past has answers. The future poses questions. And there is one question that is asked above all else - who is truly worthy to rule? Highlord Malus and his followers, deluded as they may be, believe it to be him. I disagree.

"Make no mistake, he has been weakened by the past months. He has lost many key allies, cornerstones of his power base removed from under his very nose. I know nothing about this, of course, but have never been one to forgo an advantage."

There was a deliberate pause, during which all those assembled exchanged knowing looks and less than subtle chuckles. Vyrion was sure Imperial Intelligence had some very pressing questions for all of them.

Callida cleared her throat, and everyone fell silent instantly. Laughs died in throats as if the air had been sucked out of their lungs, while smiles soured and withered away. Her eyes flicked onto Krothus for half a second before she continued. "Make no mistake, these deaths will be investigated. If any foul play is suspected, if any element of the Code has been broken, the consequences will be severe."

Vyrion knew that if Lord Victus' death was treated as anything other than an accident, things would get complicated very quickly. Accusations would run rampant. He and Jarek, the only surviving apprentices to the late Ruin Lord, would no doubt be the number one suspects. But the Imperial authorities were not what was causing that knot in his stomach. The strong ruled the weak, and they had taken their master's position by force, as was permitted, so they would be safe, at least in theory. They might even be able to call themselves Ruin Lords in his stead. But this had no bearing on any of Victus' dwindled power base, who would be perfectly justified in seeking retribution, either for Victus' sake, or their own political gains. Nor did it consider opportunistic Ruin Lords who might just sweep in and take what they could. These were not fights Jarek and Vyrion could win.

But if Callida took them in, they might just survive.

Callida was watching Vyrion carefully. He felt that tingling at the back of his skull again.

"So it must be fate, that right after Victus' demise, his apprentices come to me. They come to me knowing that I alone can protect them. They come to me knowing that I could just as easily sentence them to death, and no one would bat an eye. That is true power, the kind that sees others risk life and limb just for a taste. The kind that Malus no longer possesses."

Jarek was looking up at her like she were some prophet, hanging on her every word, seeming to sink lower to the ground at every syllable. Vyrion couldn't understand his enthusiasm in the slightest, too busy trying to battle down all his guilt and anxiety, all the while both their lives remained in Callida's hands.

But if she were actually going to have them killed, she didn't seem to be in a rush to do so. Callida was nearly even smiling, the same half-hidden way the overseers would when a brutal lesson was lurking just around the corner.

"But now, you are mine. I believe I will have a use for you both."

Vyrion slowly let out the breath he had been holding.

There was a bizarre round of applause that came from the other apprentices, forced and brief, as if they were applauding a prison sentence being handed out. Krothus notably remained still, his arms remaining crossed over his chest as the awkward claps slowly faded.

"Thank you, master," Jarek said, finally getting up off the floor.

Vyrion followed suit, not keen to say anything. No matter what he said, he would only sound ungrateful next to Jarek's enthusiasm.

Callida ignored Jarek's comment and waved a dismissive hand. "You will have a room allocated for you both."

A single room? Vyrion looked at Jarek, starry-eyed and practically giddy with excitement at the recognition. He wasn't sure he wanted a single room between them, at least not for now. More than anything, Vyrion wanted to go back to his own room, go back to Victus' compound, and sleep for Ruin knows how long.

"And you are not permitted to return to Lord Victus' former holdings. Not until this situation is taken care of."

Now that was not what Vyrion wanted. Not the way she had said those final words. Not the way she had once again turned those all-knowing eyes back to him. Not the way Amar was baring that toothy grin.

But Callida was finished. "You are all dismissed. Leave me." And she faced back around, towards the view of the city she was very clearly intending to rule.

Vyrion sighed. What a terrible day it had all turned out to be.

He and Jarek stood at the foot of the stairs off the platform, waiting for Krothus to appear. Each of Callida's other Ruined filed past; a man with curled horns spiraling out his skull gave them a dismissive snort, another blinked at them with just a single large eye. Eventually, Krothus' grey-skinned form squeezed through the opening. He did not look happy.

"A great deal of theatrics for something that could have been done in a few moments," he grumbled, "But now it seems we all serve the same master."

"Thank the emperor for that," Jarek said, "No more clambering at the foot of the ladder, waiting for an opportunity to climb that never appears."

Krothus frowned. "Truly poetic."

Then he looked to Vyrion, seeming to already know where his worries lay. "There is no need to be concerned. The compound itself is no longer your responsibility."

Vyrion would have delivered quite the lecture if he had the emotional energy. Krothus was missing the point, as usual.

"But that is precisely why I am concerned," he said, "Who knows what Callida will do? We're not trusting her just with the compound, but everyone in it. I want to go back and check on things."

"She's our master now," Jarek said, "Stop worrying." He put a hand on Vyrion's shoulder.

Vyrion shrugged it off. "I will worry if I want to. And I want to go back."

"You can't," Jarek snapped, as if Vyrion hadn't heard it said moments ago. Vyrion wasn't enjoying Jarek's newfound attitude.

But Krothus extended an olive branch. "Tomorrow, I'll check the compound myself. I need to fetch what is left of my bodyguard, if he manages to wake up. If something is amiss I'll let you know."

Vyrion deflated. That was probably better than nothing.

"See? It's going to be fine," Jarek said, his hand once again appearing on Vyrion's shoulder. "Now let's get to our room, it's been a long day for all of us."

Vyrion involuntarily tensed up. What was wrong with him? He felt so on edge that even Jarek's normally comforting touch was twisting his stomach in knots.

Krothus was frowning with a frightening severity. "Vyrion can stay in my room tonight if he wishes. I have business to attend to so I have no need of it."

And just like that, the intensity of Jarek's grimace matched Krothus' own.

"Business to attend to the night after you were involved in slaying a Ruin Lord? You really aren't bright are you?"

"I'm sorry, did I ask for your opinion?" Krothus sneered.

"Come, Vyrion, let's leave this fool to his own devices."

Krothus just stood there, gray arms crossed.

Vyrion looked between both of them. Why did everything in his life have to be complicated? He wanted to turn back time, to return to yesterday, when he and Jarek were close, when Krothus had no idea about them, when Lord Victus was still alive. But now none of that was as it was.

He turned to Jarek, "I'm sorry, I think I need some space - just to meditate over today's events. It's nothing you should ... I hope you understand."

Jarek looked at him, his face molded into that inch-perfect mask he sometimes wore, like he was playing a character in the theatre. He didn't say anything at first. Only once he had taken a few deep breaths did he speak.

"Disappointing."

Then he left. Vyrion felt the back of his throat tremble. In the Emperor's name he needed to toughen up.

"Not a distraction you need," Krothus grumbled.

"Now is not the time," Vyrion said, "No more talk of this, or I might change my mind."

Krothus shrugged, clearly not willing to engage in yet another conflict. He marched off through the dim corridors, Vyrion close behind.

They eventually arrived at a nondescript door, which Krothus wasted no time in flinging open like it had personally insulted him. Inside was the most basic living space Vyrion had ever seen. It rivalled their Academy quarters in its bare state, the only furniture being a neatly kept bed, a folded pile of clothes, and a stack of books in one far corner.

"This looks ... nice," Vyrion said.

"Comfort is the enemy of activity," Krothus said.

"And the enemy of guests."

Krothus frowned.

"I'm joking. Thank you for letting me stay here."

The frown lessened. "It's no issue. Besides, I have some late night reading to attend to, something has been biting at the back of my mind all day."

Vyrion froze, mid-way through taking off one of his shoes. "What is it?"

"Lord Victus may not be entirely gone."

Chapter 19
Fight or Flight

Inissa took another bite of her muffin. The sugar let out a light crunch between her teeth as a gush of blueberries ran over her tongue.

Normally the treat would have calmed her, but she still felt nervous. Krothus and Vyrion should have been back by now. What if something terrible had happened?

On a different day, Inissa wouldn't mind some time to herself at the compound. A few hours without Cook harping in her ear to fetch this or bake that would have been nice. It could have been some time for a nap, or a snack, or even some training if she felt up for it. But this felt different.

They had certainly left in a hurry; no explanations, no answers. But Inissa hardly needed to be a full blown Ruined to know something was wrong. The bruises and cuts painted all over them had been enough of an indicator, and Lord Victus or his other apprentices were nowhere to be seen. She feared the worst, but, of course, Krothus still didn't trust her enough to fill her in. One day he would, one day he would realize that she was just as competent as he thought himself to be. But in the meantime, while she waited for that realization, Krothus had left her there, standing guard in the cool evening air without the slightest idea why.

"It's times like these that decide the future, I think."

"Wha-?" she asked, mouth still half full.

Lieutenant Lorren cleared his throat and stepped closer. "All of these clandestine errands, I mean. The secrecy, the hushed outings; I have no idea what they have truly accomplished, only that Lord Victus seems to be confident in their outcome. I haven't seen him this determined in years."

In all honesty, Inissa had nearly forgotten Lorren was there, the thin man stood at attention so rigidly that he could easily be mistaken for a statue. But she was glad for the company, even if he rarely spoke.

She swallowed her muffin. "The servants say that his obsession has driven him to near obscurity. And that he's gone a bit mad."

Lorren looked like he was going to object, but settled only into a long sigh. "One can't argue with that."

Inissa continued, hoping maybe the Lieutenant had some further explanation of their current situation. "Mad or not, I saw Lord Victus leave earlier today, but he hasn't come back. Neither did Lash or Partha. My master refuses to tell me anything more than that."

Lorren shifted his feet briefly, which Inissa knew was his subtle way of dealing with what he saw as improper behaviour without saying.

Of course he knew where she had come from, he had secured the job in the kitchens for her after all, but Lorren always stiffened up when protocol was broken. Secretive apprentices included. Though despite his objections, he had been nothing but kind to her since her arrival, it was not uncommon for him to drop by the kitchens to check up on her.

"I'm sure he's fine," Lorren finally said, "Regardless of the nature of his latest schemes, he always returns. He always comes back." He seemed like he was convincing himself as much as her.

"If you say so."

Lorren brushed off the slightest hint of dust off of his uniform with a thoughtful flick of his hand. "I have served Lord Victus for quite some time. Perhaps I am cursed to remember him In his prime; an unstoppable force of nature, the kind of man who inspired fear, awe, and pride in anyone he met. I would have followed that man to the ends of the earth. But he's lost more than a leg since then, and it is difficult to remind myself of that fact."

Trying to picture Victus as anything but the eccentric one-legged outcast proved impossible. "I can't imagine him like that."

He gave her a sad smile. "And I can't imagine him as anything different."

The kitchen staff usually had a few choice words about each and every person in the compound, from the foul smell of the lowest guardsman to the awkwardness Vyrion emitted when he entered a room. But they had only ever spoken well of the Sergeant turned Lieutenant. His long years of service may have blinded him to his Ruin Lord's condition, but it had not blunted his own reputation.

"Did he at least have hair back then?" Inissa asked.

"Oh yes, a wild mane of it."

"And both legs?"

Lorren laughed. "For a time."

Inissa grinned back at him, but shortly after their smiles faded. The cool night air was gradually starting to nip at Inissa's skin, each brief gust of wind seeming to carry the full moon higher into the starry sky.

"How long has it been since they left?" she asked.

"Nearly eight hours I would say. Any idea when they are meant to return?" Lorren tightened the buttons around his collar, as if an extra stitch of fabric over his neck was all he needed to stay warm.

Inissa shook her head.

"In that case, I will take another patrol around the compound," Lorren declared, "You are welcome to join me, especially if you are feeling the evening chill. My wife was correct, as usual, in saying that I would need a coat tonight, and this will be the last time I disagree with her."

"I would like to, but my master commanded me to stand guard," Inissa said. She was already feeling an army of bumps raising across her arms and a chill running down her back, but it would all pale in comparison to Krothus' wrath if he discovered that she had disobeyed him.

"Stay in Lord Victus' quarters then, look after your companion. It should be a bit warmer. I won't be far." He then gave her a quick salute and then disappeared around the next corner.

It only took a few more moments in the chill before Inissa finally admitted defeat. By the Emperor, she had a weak will. Krothus would have been disappointed.

The heavy doors to Victus' chambers seemed to hold firm in a silent punishment, only moving aside after Inissa heaved with all her strength, sending her stumbling inside.

The room was dim, scarcely lit bar the occasional defiant candle, the only sound the steady rumble of Spinebreaker's breathing in the corner. He was bundled in a bed far too small for him, muscular legs dangled over the side like some unused lures of a particularly ambitious fisherman. Seeing him, Inissa had to stifle the urge to laugh.

But even the slightest giggle was quickly suppressed. Endless pages of indecipherable scrawl and cryptic images plastered the walls, a forest of curses looming down. Watching her, judging her. They knew she wasn't meant to be there. She didn't belong; not in the compound, not in the city, not in the Empire. Her mother was waiting for her, waiting for her to return home.

As her hands trembled and her heartbeat roared in her ear, Inissa swept another pastry out of her pocket. She bit into the flakey crust, revealing the blueberry prize underneath, and all those thoughts drifted away.

Inissa's mother would never let her touch such treats as a child, even before she had locked her away. Healthy meals for a healthy successor, she had said. A healthy host, more like. And when that demonic parasite had crawled into Inissa's mind, she no longer had even the smallest say in what was given to her. She had refused as much as she could.

A mighty snore rattled out of Spinebreaker, sending his tentacles twisting round and round.

"Wake up you great brute," Inissa muttered. Her strongest poke bounced off his thick skull without the slightest acknowledgement.

The only result was another rumbling snore.

Inissa sighed. Spinebreaker was hardly a conversationalist at the best of times, but a friendly face, even one as monstrous as his, would have been better than nothing.

Bored and alone, she started wandering around the room.

A suit of elaborate armor was mounted on the far side, an impressive centerpiece of gilded black and gold. Papers covered the floor, and a half-melted pile of ash smoldered under a series of deep gouges in one of the walls, like someone picked a fight with the room itself.

But in one dark corner, she saw it. A smooth box of metal, one that heralded a chill that danced over her arms. An image of an emerald crystal filled her mind; she could hear the whispers, feel the cool facets of the gem as it was buried into her forehead. She ran her fingers over that scar above her eyes.

No, she was stronger now, she was not that girl any longer.

But before she could even think, Inissa had rushed over to the box. With a shrill battle cry, she thrust her leg forward, kicking with all her might.

Her yell of triumph quickly dwindled to a shocked squeak as her foot collided with solid metal. A ball of pain shot up her leg. The shock nearly caused her pastries to make a return appearance out of her stomach, but she held them in, hopping up and down on her intact foot, trying to bite back tears. That was hardly her smartest idea. Worst still, the lid of the metal box had fallen open, revealing nothing but an emptiness beneath.

"Kicking an empty box," she muttered, clutching her foot and settling down into a chair next to the bed, "Mother would be so proud."

Inissa doubted Fira had ever been proud of her. Her mother and Krothus had that in common.

She sat there, nursing her bruised foot and staring at Spinebreaker for what seemed like hours. It was certainly less than that, but only using an orkathi's snores as a time measurement was bound to have flaws.

Soon enough, Inissa's eyes began to slowly shut, only to be forced open whenever she caught wind of it. But the rhythmic nature of Spinebreaker's snores whittled away at her self-discipline. It wasn't long before they eventually cracked down her defenses, carrying her away into a deep sleep.

She dreamed of demons and shattered crystals and warm, blueberry pie. Time passed as it always did in dreams, both fast and slow.

Then she suddenly woke.

A loud creak dragged Inissa back to the conscious world. The kind of strained squeak that heralded a shifting of weight or a sudden movement.

Spinebreaker was no longer sleeping. In fact, he wasn't in the bed at all.

The orkathi warrior stood several strides away, peering into the mounted set of gilded armor like it held the secret to life's many mysteries. Inissa thought it immediately strange. He stood oddly, slightly off balance, his claws clasped behind his back. Still he stared into the armor's polished chestplate.

"Spinebreaker?" she asked, slowly getting up out of her chair. "How are you feeling?"

He did not answer. Instead, he slowly ran a claw down a gouge on one side of the armor, the bone quietly hissing as it scraped across the metal's past.

She took a hesitant step towards him. "Spinebreaker?"

He looked up, glaring at her with those yellow, predatory eyes. There was no welcome behind them, no recognition, as if she were interrupting him. Intruding, even.

She swallowed, feeling like a rock was stuck at the back of her throat. Keep him calm, that's what she needed to do. It was no secret that Spinebreaker could rip her apart if he chose to, all those training sessions had indicated that plainly enough. Keep him calm.

"Are you okay? Please just talk to me, Spinebreaker. Please."

But he remained silent. He just stood there, looking down at himself, looking at all those muscles, claws, and tentacles with an expression that was either a grimace or a smile. It was always difficult to tell with those tusks.

But Inissa wasn't about to take any chances. She quietly backed towards the door. If she could just fetch Lieutenant Lorren and his men, then maybe all of them together would be able to restrain

Spinebreaker until -

"Where are you going, girl?"

She froze.

"Step away from the door." His gravelly voice sounded strange, the words slurred, like his mouth was suddenly struggling to accommodate his tusks.

Inissa looked towards the doorway, only a few strides away. If she ran, she might be able to make it. But first she had to buy some time.

"Good to see you're awake, Spinebreaker," she said, putting on her best smile but making no moves away from the door. "You were giving me quite a scare." And still was.

But he wasn't having it. Spinebreaker only lumbered closer, "And why would that be?"

Inissa swallowed. "I thought you were hurt, that's all."

He was speaking now, but something was still wrong, that much was certain. In only a minute, she had heard him speak more words to her than usually would in weeks. And he kept coming closer - now he stood just in front of her, towering up nearly to the ceiling.

Then, he made it all worse. He did something that Inissa knew would never happen if Spinebreaker were in his right mind; he started smiling. Lips drew back over tusks and teeth, revealing those stubby, pointed fangs that were more beast than man. It was an action she had never seen him perform, and, deciding after only a short view, something she hoped to never see again.

"Your concern is noted. And in many ways, you are correct; I was very nearly destroyed."

He clenched those mighty claws, muscle and sinew rippling under crimson skin.

"But not quite."

Inissa's heart dropped. There was no way this was the orkathi she knew, even if he looked the part.

"You aren't Spinebreaker."

"I was," he said, his monstrous smile diminishing, "And I still am, in a way."

He snatched some scrawled diagram off the wall, glaring at it like it had just insulted him, "But this was not how it was supposed to go."

Inissa looked at him for a moment. *Really* looked. At that odd stance, at his familiarity with the room, how he spoke. And then all the pieces fell into place.

"Lord Victus?"

He looked up from the paper. "Yes, I suppose I still am, despite everything. And who are you?"

"Inissa," she said lamely, like that said everything.

"You are familiar, I must admit. Though I can't seem to recall why."

"What happened?" she blurted out, "I thought your ritual was supposed to-"

He waved a dismissive claw. "It was. It was supposed to be a new beginning, not just for me, but for the Empire. But now I am here, inhabiting the body of whatever this is."

"Spinebreaker," Inissa clarified. "Is he ...?"

"He is not dead, no," Victus answered looking down at himself again. "I am him, as he is me. We share this body, and our mind, but it seems he is a creature of very few words."

"He is." Tears of relief welled up at the edge of Inissa's eyes, which she quickly wiped away. Krothus would have berated her for showing such weakness, but frankly, she was overwhelmed. It was a lot to take in.

Victus didn't seem to notice, already sifting through the whirlwind of untidiness that was his chambers, lifting furniture and shifting papers, like he was looking for something.

After another minute of fruitless searching, he turned back to her. "Tell me, girl. How did you know of my ritual? Failed or not, it was being kept with the utmost secrecy. Did your master tell you?"

"Yes," she admitted, surprised. Victus certainly hadn't known about their arrangement before, at least not that she was aware of. But Spinebreaker had.

"Bah. Damn book," he grunted, tossing a stack of papers to the side as he gave up on his search and stood up. "Krothus should not have told you. Told anyone. Even if things had worked out the way they were meant to, he could have brought far too many interested parties after us."

"It doesn't matter now, does it?" she asked, not sure what he was talking about. "It hasn't been long, why don't we just let Lorren know that- "

A meaty crimson claw grabbed her shoulder, stopping her in her tracks instantly. She had nearly gotten to the door.

"No," Victus growled, "No one can know about this, not yet."

Inissa tried to shake out of his iron grip to no avail. "Why not? Everyone in the compound is nervous, nobody has heard from you or Lash or Partha and fears the worst."

"Those two traitorous wretches are dead," he snarled, "And if I can help it, so is Lord Victus. The last thing I need is someone coming to finish the job."

Inissa thrashed against his grip, but it proved futile. "Let me go!"

"Calm yourself. If I wanted you dead, you would be."

She stared in defiance at Spinebreaker, or Victus, whatever he was. He stared back. The stalemate continued for several moments until, to Inissa's surprise, she was released.

"I admire your persistence, girl. But do not test me any further."

He looked so tired. Spinebreaker's face, normally a mask of determined indifference, was now a weathered wax visage, sagging down like existence itself were a struggle. Sensing an opportunity, Inissa thought for a moment about fleeing back to the door, but as she looked at the Ruined-orkathi hybrid in front of her, she hesitated. She wasn't sure whether Krothus knew about this turn of events, but he was trusting her to maintain the security of the result at the very least. And she couldn't do that if she fled.

So she stepped back from the door. Victus looked thankful more than anything, watching her do it. But then his face drooped even further, Spinebreaker's tentacles sadly writhing below his jaw, as if that simple action had reminded him of some tragedy.

"Tell me - do you think of the day that you will seek to slay him?"

Inissa blinked, surprised. "What?"

"Your master, Krothus, the day you carry out your right as his apprentice and rise above him."

It was a thought she had not considered in the slightest. She had yet to even make her own runeblade, to overtake her master now seemed nothing more than a deluded fantasy, bordering on a nightmare.

"That day seems so far off that it may never happen," she said, "I have so much to learn."

"Heh," Victus grunted, "Master, apprentice; we all think in such a way, at first. But death is the same inevitable sentence, delivered onto souls without their knowledge or consent. Who is to say the difference between dying in your own bed or at the hand of another? Nobody thinks to plan for it, to expect it, but it comes all the same."

Inissa wasn't sure what to say. She had thought that sometime down the line, years and years, she hoped, she would begin to perhaps consider Krothus had taught her everything he could. Only then would anything about her situation change, so why consider it now?

"Why are you telling me this?" she asked.

"Because one day. You will have to bring death itself to your master, as I have, all those years ago."

His hands wrapped themselves into great crimson fists, and Spinebreaker's yellow eyes glared down at her. "And one day, your apprentices will make attempts on your life, as mine have."

Inissa took a step back.

"And then, you will look back and think - what would *my* master have done, if *my* attempt had failed?" Victus asked, now staring at his scarred suit of armor across the room. "Would she have killed me where I stood? Or would she have bided her time before having my world crumble around me, gloating in my despair?"

He let out a great breath, rattling through his chest.

"Perhaps she would have only felt guilt, for now understanding her own actions," the Ruin Lord growled, his anger fizzling down to a tone of utter defeat. "Perhaps she would eventually realize her dreams had dwindled to nothing, and she was utterly alone."

Inissa was stuck between reconsidering running out the door and comforting him. But suddenly Victus looked towards the door, tentacles twisting. "Do you hear that?"

"No," Inissa said, "But if you're now hearing voices, I'm not surprised."

"Nonsense, girl. Open the door," Victus insisted, looking deadly serious.

Inissa didn't have to be told twice, she ripped the door open, glad the target of her efforts for the last several minutes was finally within reach. But the moment she did, her heart sunk.

The evening rang out with the clash of metal and the screams of desperate men.

"Improved hearing is always a happy surprise," Victus remarked.

"I'm sure your ears will save us all," Inissa snapped, leaning out and looking round.

A squad of guards sprinted past, loaded piercers at the ready. They didn't notice them.

"Can you see anything?" Victus asked, trying to peer through the doorway himself, hampered by his now immense size.

"I don't need to see anything to know we're in trouble," she said, feeling adrenaline pump through her. Last time she had been this close to combat, she had at least had Krothus, Vyrion, and the entirety of the Nightshadow tribe nearby. Now, she was left only with an orkathi stuck in his Ruin Lord past, and Lieutenant Lorren, nowhere to be seen.

"Trouble?" Victus scoffed, "A mighty underestimation of our situation. This is an annexation. Few Ruin Lords would dare invade another's holdings while they yet lived, so someone has already heard of my apparent demise, seeing an opportunity to grow their own holdings in the process. And I can think of only one person who would know about my situation so quickly."

"If they think you are dead, why not just show yourself? Then they would surely have to stop," Inissa suggested, but it sounded stupid even to her.

"And give them the opportunity to correct their mistake? I think not."

They stood there for a moment, listening to the sounds of battle draw closer.

Inissa had no weapon, no experience, and no plan. All she could do was let out a frustrated sigh, feeling increasingly powerless. "So what do we do? What *can* we do?"

Another squad of guards ran past. But this time, someone dropped away from the group.

Lieutenant Lorren, prim uniform tarnished with cuts and tears, skidded to a halt in front of Victus' quarters, piercer pistol in one hand and a bloody sword in the other. He could scarcely breath, but forced as many words out as he could in between each deep breath.

"We're under attack - overwhelming force - defense impossible - must evacuate." He weakly gestured the way he came.

"Who's sent this force? Any indicators?" Victus asked in Spinebreaker's deep growl.

Lorren stared at the orkathi warrior, stood tall and mindful with his hands clasped behind his back, as though struggling to place him. But he seemed to give up quickly and continued once he had caught his breath. "I have no idea. The attackers are not bearing any tabard, which I might remind you is expressly against Code Three of the Thanaton Interior Conflict Act, concerning identifying yourself when in close proximity to-"

"Lorren, the evacuation?" Inissa interrupted.

The newly promoted Lieutenant stopped immediately, quickly righting himself. "Right, yes, the evacuation of the civilians must proceed. Inissa - where would the staff be hiding?"

"The servant's quarters," she responded instantly. That's where she would be, at least.

"Good," Lorren said, "That's not too far from-"

A nearby wall burst open with a crash. The broken body of one of Lorren's men skidded across the ground before thudding into a far wall as a squad of tabardless soldiers burst through, piercers at the ready.

"Go!" Lorren shouted, already on the move.

The soldiers opened fire, sending a horde of bolts their way. The sharp barbs glinted eagerly in the moonlight.

But Inissa wasn't about to flee, at least not without a few tricks. She focused her mind, clumsily handling the Ruin around them, trying to focus on what Krothus had told her. She couldn't just request the Ruin's help, she had to command it. Dominate it.

She reached out a hand, reaching out and demanding the invisible force to mold to her will. To her pleasant surprise, the Ruin heeded her call and a wave of power erupted out of her palm. But Inissa knew it wasn't enough.

She had wanted to send the bolts screaming back to those that had shot them. Instead, they wobbled and slowed, before clattering to the floor. Better than being skewered, at least.

Troops bearing Victus' metal leg across their chest rushed at the attackers.

"Hold the line!" Lorren shouted, being sure to grab Inissa's hand as they made their speedy retreat. "Hold the line for the civilians!"

"You have a lot to learn, girl," Victus grunted as he jogged alongside them, "But not bad."

Inissa briefly wondered why he hadn't helped with his own abilities, but that thought was quickly lost in their mad dash through the compound. Lorren was leading them at a full sprint, racing down corridors and skidding around corners, before eventually bursting through the rickety door to the staff quarters.

"Cook, we need-"

There was a loud clang as a pan smashed into Lorren's chest. A rolling pin followed immediately after, but before it could dent his skull, a gnarled hand reached out and grabbed it.

"Goodness Carlen, it's Lorren," a raspy voice snapped, "Don't kill the poor man."

Lorren pushed himself up, wincing and clutching his chest as he did. "I agree with Cook. Let's try to keep me alive, if possible."

A dozen familiar faces peered out from behind cupboards and under tables, each looking more relieved than the last. It seemed like every one of them was accounted for.

"You're alright, thank the Emperor," Cook rasped, hobbling over and wrapped Inissa in a tight embrace. "We were so worried, we had no idea where you'd gone last night."

The familiar scent of the kitchen pantry and Cook's warm touch drew out Inissa's emotions all too easily. She didn't want to leave, her time working at Victus' compound had been far and away the best months of her life. But she had to be strong, what would Krothus think of her if she started crying in the middle of all this? She squeezed Cook one final time before stepping back.

"We need to leave. Lieutenant Lorren is going to escort us to safety," she said, noting with pride that her voice didn't wobble, not even once.

"Hurry along, we must be swift if we are to make it out of here," Lorren said stiffly, staring down at the newest, pan-shaped stain to his uniform.

"What's that thing?" Carlen the dishboy squeaked, pointing out the door at Victus, peering in but unable to fit through .

Victus did not take kindly to this description, baring his teeth, "This *thing* deserves your respect, boy. I have fought in more-"

"He's a friend," Inissa interrupted, earning an angry glare from the possessed orkathi, "Now let's get moving."

The staff didn't need any further prodding, they quickly filed out of their hiding places and out into the corridor. Lorren did a quick head count before briskly jogging away, with Victus following just behind. As the group picked up speed, Cook reached out and took Inissa's hand with a gap toothed smile. Inissa returned the gesture, pulling her along to keep pace with everyone else, mindful of the danger lurking nearby.

Lorren led them further into the compound, his sword and piercer at the ready. Inissa could sense the aura of fear emanating from the rest of the staff, herself included. The sounds of battle had faded, with only the occasional outburst, a singular yell or loud crash, breaking the tension. The struggle for the compound seemed to be already over.

"The boldness required to attack Lord Victus' compound so brazenly," Lorren muttered, peering around a corner before motioning everyone else forward.

"He's dead, that's why," Victus growled, giving a very impressive Spinebreaker impression.

Lorren shot him an angry glare. "And what would you know of this, orkathi?"

"I saw the ritual fail, his body crushed underneath tons of rubble," he responded bluntly, whether speaking from Victus or Spinebreaker's perspective, Inissa couldn't tell.

The Lieutenant slowed for just a moment as his sword drooped down and his face fell. "Grim tidings. He was a great man. Lord Victus had his flaws, as all of us do, but I never regretted a moment of my career with him, both the highs and the lows. I would have liked to give him a proper farewell, though I doubt he would have cared too much."

Victus looked like he were about to say something, but Inissa cut in.

"We need to hurry, do you hear that?"

Heavy footfalls were echoed up the corridor behind them.

Lorren waved them forward. "I do. We're nearly there, search for the torch on the right hand side of the wall."

Inissa thought the instructions bizarre, they were going to a torch? But as the rest continued on, Lorren passed to the back of the group, pulling Inissa to the side quickly.

"If I don't return in one minute, pull the torch down and leave without me."

Inissa didn't like the sound of that. "You had better come back, there are more people than me who are counting on your return."

Lorren gave her a terse smile and readied his weapons. "I know, but my duty calls. Run along, I'll be back shortly. "

And just like that, Lorren walked back the way they had come, towards those ominous steps behind them.

Inissa kept going until they all stood in what looked like an ordinary corridor, a single torch lit on the right hand side. Was this really Lorren's escape route? Victus stood there with his monstrous arms crossed, while the staff looked on the verge of a panic. Worst of all, Inissa could hear yelling from somewhere nearby. Lorren might not be coming back after all.

"Right," she said, trying to stay as quiet as she could, "Lorren said this should work."

Inissa reached up to the torch above their heads and gave the warm metal a tug. Sure enough, it sunk down, ending in a click that heralded the whirring and clunking of some invisible machinery. A steady beat could be heard behind the wall, and soon the entire section of concrete began to rumble, steadily shifting to the side, inch by inch.

So this was their escape route.

"Carlen, you go first," Inissa directed. He was the smallest, could fit through before anyone else.

Carlen, trembling so much that he looked about to explode, bobbed his head up and down. As each steady clunk pulled the passage open a tiny bit more, the boy repeatedly tried to push his way through. Emperor above, that door opened slowly.

"Trouble," Victus grunted, pointing a claw down the other side of the corridor. A pair of shadows were stretching over the floor down the hall, the silhouettes of two people just about to round the corner.

"Keep trying, Carlen," Inissa hissed, then she ran to intercept. She wasn't even sure what she could do. It wasn't like she could defeat a fully armed soldier in close combat, at least not without a weapon.

But thankfully, Victus got there first.

As soon as the first soldier rounded the corner, a great crimson arm picked him up by the throat and slammed him into the far wall. A loud snap was the only sound the man's body could muster. He fell into a heap on the ground, his helmeted head lolling back. The man's shocked partner stood, slack jawed, before whipping her piercer up in a firing position.

The soldier pressed the trigger. There was a click, but nothing happened. She looked down at the weapon, and back up to Victus, who had taken up his victim's sword, nothing more than a large knife in his hands.

Click. Victus gave her a tusked grin. Click. Click.

"Shit," the soldier said.

"Indeed," Victus snarled. He plunged the sword through the soldier's chestplate.

Inissa let out a breath as she released the Ruin's hold on the piercer's trigger.

"Good thinking, girl."

"Keep lookout here, I'm going to check the other corridor," she said, taking the soldier's weapon for herself. Inissa had never fired one, but how difficult could it be? It was just pointing and shooting.

If he had any complaints, Victus didn't say, he just started dragging the soldier's bodies back around the corner and out of sight.

The hidden passage was wider now, enough that Carlen had managed to squeeze through. Inissa saw the others nervously pressed forward as she walked past, trying to push their way to the front, to their eventual salvation.

Fearing Lorren's continued absence to mean the worst, Inissa crept down to the end of the hallway, searching for some kind of clue towards his fate. She didn't even want to think about the possibilities. He had to be okay, he just had to.

But before she found him, he found her. Sporting a piercer bolt to the shoulder and a cut to his leg, Lorren hardly looked the man he was minutes prior, his once pristine grey uniform now a mess of blood, anyone's guess as to whether it was his or others.

"Emperor above. Lorren, are you okay?"

He hobbled past, clutching his shoulder and trying to stay off his cut leg, "I've been better. Is the passage open?"

Inissa tried her best to help him along. "Take a look for yourself."

Soon they were back with everyone else. The passage, formerly nothing more than a crack in the wall, was now a gaping hole, swallowing up the rest of the group as they pushed through into the darkness beyond. Their plan was working, Inissa was nearly relieved. They might make it out after all.

But it seemed like the invaders weren't giving up without a fight; the clatter of armor echoed down the hall in every direction.

"There's no time to lose," Lorren said, limping towards the passage himself.

"Hurry, hurry!" Cook was hissing, pushing everyone ahead as soon as there was room. Mura and Arlison and Ro-Yal; Inissa could name every person who went through, their friendly faces warped into anxious terror as certain death rapidly approached. Only a bit longer now.

"Cook, you too," Inissa said, shooing her into the tunnel. Cook gave her a frantic bob of her head and shambled into the darkness.

"We're leaving!" Inissa called out, trying to get Victus' attention.

He stopped trying to drag away his most recent victim, a soldier with their arm hacked off, and lumbered over. "Shall we?"

Lorren, Victus, Inissa; now it was their turn. Victus barely fit Spinebreaker's tremendous frame through the passage entryway, while Lorren limped over to one side of the tunnel and pulled down a lever tucked into the wall there. There was a click, and a rumble, but nothing else happened. Lorren frowned and pulled it again. Same result.

Inissa felt panic stab at her heart, "What are we waiting for?"

"The quick door release isn't working," Lorren said, sounding very matter of fact for the dire strait they were in, "We'll have to close it the slower way."

He stepped back into the corridor and began pushing the torch back up. Inissa swore. They needed to go. *Now.*

"Why are we closing it at all?" Inissa asked, "Can't we just run?"

"And be pursued by a Ruined and dozens of soldiers through nearly a mile of dimly light corridors?" Lorren asked, grunting as the torch clunked back into position and the machinery groaned to life once again, "I don't think so, that's a recipe for -"

Someone shouted out in the corridor. A volley of piercer bolts peppered the wall and Lorren fell back into the tunnel. Initially, Inissa thought he had managed a stroke of good fortune, it looked like all of the bolts had clattered against the stone and fallen to the ground. But then she saw it. It looked so small, so innocent, a bit of metal no bigger than her forearm. And it was sticking right out of Lorren's gut.

"Oh dear," Lorren breathed, looking down at the bolt in his torso. He dropped his sword and tried desperately to brush off the blood that was now sullying his already ruined uniform even further but it was fruitless. For each handful he cast off, another pulse of crimson liquid bubbled up from the wound, soaking the cloth more and more.

Inissa felt all the color drain from her face. She nearly dropped the stolen piercer she carried. She had seen death before, sure, Victus had gutted a soldier just a few steps away from them only moments ago, but it had never been someone she knew. All Inissa wanted was to help him, to tell him he was going to be alright, though they would all know it was a lie. She felt helpless.

The passage closing mechanism continued at a snail's pace. A helmet briefly peered into view, but Inissa found herself squeezing her piercer's trigger without thinking, dropping the soldier instantly with a neatly placed bolt. That might buy them a few moments.

"Go," Lorren said weakly, waving them down the tunnel.

"No, we aren't leaving you," Inissa said.

"I can hold them off for a time," he coughed, spitting a glob of blood off to one side, "I still have bolts left."

"We can stay too, and -" Inissa started, having to stop to wipe the tears already streaming down her face, "And we'll wait until the door closes, and then we'll get Krothus and Vyrion to-"

Another soldier moved into the gap, her piercer levelled. A shot whizzed an inch past Inissa's face, but two bolts from Lorren sent the soldier to the floor.

Inissa didn't know what to do. She felt rooted to the spot, stuck. What would her mother think of her, distraught over some Imperial?

Clawed hands pulled Inissa out of the way with a surprising gentleness. Victus placed her in the tunnel behind him.

"No need for tears, girl," he said, "We live to fight another day, while a soldier gets a mighty death, one many would envy."

There was some shuffling of armor outside and hushed voices, barely audible over the sound of machinery. The soldiers might be getting some second thoughts, Inissa hoped. The entryway could still easily allow them in, it seemed to taunt her as it scraped closed so slowly it might as well have not been moving at all.

"Kind words, orkathi," Lorren said, smiling as best he could with blood over his taut jaw.

Victus took the piercer out of Inissa's trembling grip and put it into Lorren's free hand. "A creature I might be, Lorren. But I remember you at Icebron, at Boraxxus, I never forget a good soldier, especially one who was there when everything went wrong. One who stayed despite it all."

Lorren's brows furrowed as he looked at the orkathi, then at the piercer in his hand, then back up to the tusked figure towering over him.

"We can only hope to be remembered," Victus said quietly, "That's what I told you then, and that's what I tell you now."

Lorren's eyes widened in recognition, then instantly filling with tears. He shakily raised his piercer to pistol to his brow in the best attempt at a salute he could muster. "It was an honor to serve, my lord. Through all of it."

"The honor was mine, Lieutenant," Victus said, returning the salute with a clawed hand.

"Goodbye, Lorren," Inissa croaked, "Thank you, thank you for everything."

"My pleasure." Then he coughed, giving her a weak smile before turning back to the doorway. "Now go, quickly!"

Inissa suddenly felt very heavy, like the world was trying to crush her to the floor. The Ruin around her ebbed and flowed as a new presence, a Ruined, drew closer. But still she couldn't muster the strength to move a single step.

Then she felt herself rise up into the air, scooped up into Victus' claws as if she were nothing, carried away into the darkness. Inissa watched the tunnel entrance slowly fade out of sight over his shoulder.

Shapes were briefly silhouetted against the entryway, only to collapse, the crash of bolts and armor resonating down the tunnel. More would appear, and still they fell.

The light from the corridor behind them gradually faded as the distant slit of the passage slowly narrowed. Inissa thought she heard one last bolt being fired before the light disappeared completely. Then the final boom of the passage closing roared down the tunnel, and Inissa let out a final shaky sob into Spinebreaker's shoulder.

They'd made it.

Chapter 20

Shadows

Krothus was furious. Not only had he not been informed of the attack on Victus' compound, but there was no sign of Inissa or Spinebreaker anywhere.

He stood, simmering with rage, in the courtyard outside Victus' heavy chamber doors, which had been ripped open like the ribs of some slain beast to expose the loot within. Bodies of soldiers and guards were everywhere, those that had served Callida collected in neat rows, with Victus' guards thrown into heaps or kept where they fell, casting macabre shadows across the courtyard with the help of the morning sun.

A sergeant walked briskly out of Vicus' chambers and delivered a salute. "He says you can enter, my lord."

"Oh wonderful, where would I be without his *permission*," Krothus sneered, brushing past the sergeant and entering the chambers.

If Krothus hadn't stumbled upon the aftermath, he doubted he would have known about this at all. It had been by pure chance that he had decided to return and check on Inissa early that morning. If Krothus had known that he would have been returning to a bloodbath, he would have been sure to bring Vyrion.

There was only one man inside Victus' chambers, his long hair pulled back as he hummed to himself.

"Ah, nice of you to drop by, Krothus," Amar said, his rich voice swelling with glee as he looked over a handful of glittering medals, "I didn't know our master had sent you as well."

"She didn't."

Amar stopped fiddling with his stolen trinkets. "Oh."

"What in the Emperor's name is all of this? Victus is already dead. His soldiers would have simply joined us had Vyrion and Jarek commanded them to."

His fellow apprentice smiled that toothy smile, which Krothus took as an insult, before setting the medals down onto a hefty pile of stolen goods. The whole of the room was ransacked; drawers opened, shelves smashed, papers burned. There was no sign of Inissa or Spinebreaker anywhere.

"They fought our efforts at a peaceful occupation, it was entirely their own doing," Amar said, sounding positively giddy at the suggestion of such resistance. "But I digress, if you aren't here due to Lord Calida's orders, then why have you come to bother me?"

Without waiting for an answer, Amar strode over to the impressive godrium armor displayed in the corner of the room, looking at it as though he were a prospector who had stumbled upon a grand vein of fine ore.

"I was coming to deliver the news of Victus' death, to offer a place under our master for those who wished to serve," Krothus lied. He might have, once he saw that Inissa was safe.

"And who would they serve?" Amar snapped, "You? Or our master? You have quite the reputation for trying to forge your own power base, blatantly disregarding our master's standing in the process."

Krothus had to resist rolling his eyes, "I would have to be a fool to do such a thing so openly, even if that were my intention. Which it isn't. Instead I come to find you looting the place after needlessly slaughtering what seems to be every soul that resided here."

Amar ran his fingers over the armor, before turning back to Krothus and smiling. "To the victor go the spoils."

Krothus just glared at him, imagining snapping the insufferable man's neck, perhaps taking Victus' exceedingly expensive set of armor for his own when he did.

"No need to dwell on it," Amar continued, "Callida merely did what any Ruin Lord in Thanaton would have done with the knowledge she had. We're fighting a war, with control over a Council seat in the balance. We need to act quickly with opportunities like this."

"We?" Krothus scoffed, "And what do we get out of it, Amar? Our master uses us in her grand game as a means to an end, but this end isn't about us, it's about her."

The other apprentice sighed, as though Krothus was complaining about lunch, not their lives. "My, I didn't realize I was talking with one of the brightest minds of the Empire," he said, enough sarcasm to paint the room, "Of course it's about her. But Callida's victories help our own standing as well. We are linked. To be an apprentice to a successful Ruin Lord is something countless people would kill for, even dear defected Jarek is much better off under our banner than *that* one."

Amar's neatly manicured finger pointed at the banner on the far wall, which no doubt used to display a metal leg, now torn up to a degree that it was nearly unrecognizable.

Krothus had already decided it was time to leave. There was no use dawdling on. "You are nothing more than a poorly trained dog, running off and wreaking havoc the moment your chain is loosened just a single link."

"I do enjoy our chats," Amar said as Krothus stomped out.

A pointless conversation. Krothus stood back in the courtyard watching Callida's soldiers mill about, carrying away anything that wasn't bolted down. A loop of the compound seemed wise, to see if he could pick up any clue as to Inissa and Spinebreaker's whereabouts.

Not only was their fate unknown, but now, so was that of Lord Victus. From what he had determined last night, poring over countless pages in Callida's library, a Ruin Lord who has had their spirit severed from their body can linger indefinitely unless destroyed. And judging by what Vyrion had told him about the setup for Victus' ritual, it had taken a tremendous amount of preparation and struggle to merely imprison such a disembodied spirit. Krothus strongly doubted that Spinebreaker's last minute blunder into the ritual would have been enough to truly destroy Victus.

He had no idea where Victus could be now, the crazed Ruin Lord could still be lingering within Krothus' own skull for all he knew. But if Krothus had any inkling of this, then there was no doubt that Callida did too, which meant that this excursion had a far more nefarious purpose than a simple pillaging.

Not much of note was found on his sweep. Vyrion and Jarek's rooms alone remained untouched; no broken lock or bashed in door, no dirty bootprints trailing in and out, an island of calm in the otherwise ransacked compound. Callida must have given strict orders for them to remain untouched.

When he returned to the courtyard empty handed, Krothus was back at square one, still with no idea of Inissa or Spinebreaker whereabouts, and no guess of where to start.

It wasn't long before he stormed out of the front gate and onto the street, frustrated at his lack of progress. He could only think of one other place that they could be, so he set off to the boroughs, to their training ground.

But as soon as he arrived at the warehouse, Krothus felt something amiss. He couldn't put his finger on what it was exactly, but the moment he put his hand on the creaky warehouse door, the Ruin screamed at him to remain alert. He knew when to recognise a warning sign when he felt one.

Krothus turned to scour the mess of a crowd around him, looking for anything out of the ordinary.

That damned cultist was still screaming about his prophet, imprisoned somewhere for something Krothus didn't care about, preaching about rising up in the streets. But in between the mass of Imperial citizens, past the fistfuls of flyers with a flaming skull on them, he could see the usual suspect, the old beggar man who he had deemed a spy, observing him as he normally did. But this time, he wasn't alone.

Krothus thought he could see at least four others, all of whom were making a poor effort at finding excuses to stand nearby. One woman had been browsing the same poorly-made jackets in a street-stall the entire time Krothus had been there, while a rugged looking man had developed a sudden interest in watching the foot traffic below his perch on a grimy wall.

Krothus swore silently. There was no telling how long they had been following him, or more importantly, who they worked for. It could be anyone; more of Callida's whisperers, a rival apprentice, even Highlord Malus himself, scoping out potential threats. The result was the same - he needed to get somewhere else. He would be able to see how many of the silent enemies he was dealing with if they had to give chase.

To the horror of any passerby in his path, Krothus suddenly started sprinting down the street. He cared little for how they felt. If they were too slow to get out of his way, then being thrown into the dirt would be a fitting punishment, as his destiny was greater than any of theirs.

Shouts rang out as he ran, but Krothus paid them no heed. Whether they were cries to follow him or curses for his disruption were irrelevant, he had already turned onto the next road and was rushing through the next crowd all over again.

Minutes later, his greaves splattered with mud and his lungs afire, Krothus skidded to a stop in the central square of Thanaton, the very beginning of his journey in the city. A fitting place to end it if it were to come to that. He marched up to the towering blood crystal that served as the centerpiece of the grand courtyard, a single blossom of red among the grey clouds and ornate buildings towering around the open space, and sat down on a bench nearby.

And then he waited.

Krothus wasn't alone here, far from it. In between the frequent Ruined passing through the crystal's invisible gateway, the square hosted a collection of Imperial citizens, walking and talking like their pitiful lives had meaning. There were enough for Krothus to feel at ease in a public space, but not too many that he couldn't scan those around him for signs of danger.

He wasn't sure what his next step was. His own master might have picked up her spying. Perhaps she finally decided he needed to be put down? Or it could have been Victus, his spirit in some new host, out for revenge.

Everything seemed calm for the moment. But Krothus knew better than to relax, who knew what could be lurking just seconds away? So he stayed vigilant.

This made it all the more surprising when someone appeared next to him.

He hadn't seen or heard them approach. Krothus immediately had his runeblade in hand. But before he could ignite it, the stranger's hand gently pressed down on his own.

She gave him a curt smile, her face struggling to accommodate the unfamiliar gesture.

"Let's wait a moment," Agent Dedri said, her tone completely calm, "There's no need to get so agitated."

Krothus frowned and kept his runeblade where it was. "What do you want, Dedri?"

"I'm here because you're being reckless," she said, tucking an unruly grey strand behind her ear, "And if you continue along this path, you'll be dead very quickly."

"What a noble cause," Krothus retorted. He didn't believe her motivations to be charitable. Imperial Intelligence always had some other angle, some other reason.

"I did tell you I was tired of seeing Ruined meeting their ends prematurely."

Krothus grunted out a laugh. "I am sat in the most public place in the city, I would hardly describe that as reckless. Nor am I intending on meeting my end anytime soon."

"It isn't that simple," Dedri snapped, old habits rising above her forced calmness, "Do you see that man?"

Krothus followed her finger to a familiar beggar, a figure who had scarcely left his side in weeks.

"Of course, I can recognise my master's spies perfectly well without the aid of any Imperial Agents," he said smugly.

Dedri shook her head. "He's not your master's agent. He's mine."

Krothus had to admit that caught him off guard, and his expression must have indicated as such, because Dedri continued.

"He and two others have been part of an ongoing counter-espionage initiative to track Lord Callida's spies, quite a selection of which seem to be following you at all times."

"I suppose the answer as to why is coming next."

"Why Imperial Intelligence has taken an interest in Callida is not important, nor a secret," Dedri said, "She represents instability, a sickness that we have been very carefully purging to keep this Empire afloat. No, what you *should* be concerned with is how every ill-advised move you've made is being used in a narrative, one that has quickly spun out of control."

"And what narrative would this be?" Krothus pressed, "If you've been following me for so long, you would know that I have done nothing to break the Emperor's laws."

"Unfortunately, what an Imperial agent knows is not the same as what a high-ranking Ruin Lord says," Dedri said, the bitterness in her voice obvious, "And in this case, you are being directly implicated in the death of Lord Victus."

Krothus had to bite down the urge to laugh. "That old fool's death was of his own making, he botched his ritual by gambling on the loyalty of his apprentices. And even if it wasn't, surely Lord Callida would take the blame, taking in her previous track record for such things and the fact that she took on his remaining apprentices."

But much to Krothus' surprise, this retort was met with another shake of Dedri's head.

"Your master is indeed known for her *boldness*, let's call it. And despite her and Victus' relatively close relationship, if you believe such things, she would still be blamed by the majority of the city. Hence why she has a scapegoat, a way to kill two bats with one stone."

Krothus was growing frustrated, he wasn't here for a political lecture.

"Is there a point to all this? Or do you enjoy boring me."

Dedri frowned at him, the lines on her face falling into their usual formation.

"I know about your apprentice," she started, "I know about your close relationship with Victus' apprentice Vyrion. And if I know this, then so does Callida. That's why she's been saying you did it. The narrative is that you used this friendship with Victus' apprentice to engineer a way to kill him, with the goal being to attempt to take Lord Victus' place for yourself. He is not your master to succeed, so this is against the law."

"That's absurd."

Only a fool would think that to be true. He hated to admit it, but had Victus been at full strength, he would have most certainly been able to take on both him and Vyrion, as well as every one of his other apprentices. They would have a chance, as any Ruined would, but it would be slim, barring on completely impossible. Though this itself perhaps played into the narrative itself, inferring he used some cowardly, sloppy poison scheme to do the deed. The thought of such a thing only made him angrier.

"It doesn't matter if it is, or isn't," Dedri said, sounding annoyed at the creation of subjectivity itself, "Being suspected of killing a Ruin Lord with no political backing to protect you is a dangerous position to be in. Especially if you were seen returning to his holdings the day after his demise on some sightseeing stroll. What were you thinking? You already knew that you were a single step away from disaster before, now you're blundering headlong into it like some witless pup."

Krothus would have liked to think that he would have had some witty retort on a normal day. But for now, he was silent. He wasn't Victus' apprentice, if Callida pinned Krothus for killing him, there was no convenient excuse. Others would believe he circumvented existing precedent in a greedy stab at power by any means necessary. Admirable, to some, suicidal to others. The strong ruled the weak, yes, but the Emperor's laws kept the Code within reason. And the Ruin Lords had a habit of correcting those that strayed from their determined path.

"Then what now?" Krothus asked quietly. "Or am I to be executed based on the hearsay of some woman who has put the stability of the entire city on a knife's edge?"

Dedri sat up a bit straighter on the bench. "No, there must be an investigation first. We would first need to ascertain whether this rumor is true before we can determine whether the method of death fits within the Council's interpretation of the Ruined Code. For that, you will be brought in for questioning."

"Brought in by who, exactly?" Krothus asked. He'd like to see them try.

"By me." Dedri didn't even blink.

Krothus snorted. "Do you really think I'll go willingly? Why bother?"

"Krothus, do you really think you are the first Ruined I've dealt with?" the older woman snapped, "I know you well enough to be lenient and ask you politely, but I won't ask again. I am trying to protect you."

"I can protect myself."

Dedri erupted. "I'd like to see you try when both Callida and Malus want you dead. Your master wants to end your jaunt of embarrassing her on the political stage, while Malus needs to retaliate for the death of his subordinate and prop up his rapidly deteriorating public image. The only safe place for you would be staying in our custody until your hearing with the Council."

Krothus pushed down his rage for long enough to reflect briefly on the offer. He still didn't know where Inissa or Spinebreaker were, and even if he were to find them, it seemed like they would only be brought into more danger if Dedri was being truthful. But that was a big if, Krothus felt that only fools would trust Imperial Agents to be charitable.

"And what do you get out of this then?" he asked, expecting some grand lie.

"The illusion of a clear conscience," Dedri said.

"That's it? No favors? No conspiracies or bribes?" Krothus pressed, reaching out through the Ruin as he did. That couldn't be it.

But Dedri didn't rise to the bait. "You'll understand when you get to my age, convincing yourself you've been doing the right thing is worth more than you can imagine."

Krothus felt nothing that would indicate she was lying, her heartbeat was steady, and her mind deathly calm. But Dedri was not the only person he could sense, and it became clear quite quickly that everyone nearby didn't seem to possess that same calmness. The Ruin swirled with anxiety and anticipation from all angles.

Krothus scanned the loose crowd nearby, all of whom seemed very interested in the result of this discussion. He felt his pulse quicken, felt that rush of adrenaline run up his spine. Bystanders who had previously been milling about their business now held nervous hands inside their jackets or down their pockets. He looked back to Dedri.

"What is this?"

"Assurance," Dedri said with a tight-lipped smile, "Now, are you going to let me help you, or is there going to be a problem?

Krothus clenched his jaw. He knew a threat when he heard one. And the threat seemed considerable indeed, he could sense that there were other Ruined nearby as well.

Krothus' hand drew closer to his runeblade.

Dedri raised an eyebrow at him. Those around them seemed to freeze.

But with a deep breath, Krothus moved his hand back to his side. As he did, he noticed Dedri doing the same, the handle of a compact piercer returning back into her boot. Then the Imperial Agent raised and circled her other hand into the air.

Nearly everyone in the square relaxed. Krothus could see that there must have been at least three dozen people, all of whom were now standing down and concealing any weapons they had once more, All the while a handful of Ruined stood at the ready nearby, all of whom were wearing the pure crimson tabard of the Emperor himself.

As Krothus watched Dedri procure a pair of restraints, he silently hoped that Vyrion would be able to make sense of all this. For the first time that he could recall, Krothus had been outplayed, utterly and completely. Now he could only trust in his partner to spring him out of this mess.

Vyrion was his only hope.

Chapter 21
Conspiracy

Vyrion woke up in Krothus' room feeling the opposite of well-rested. Like his sleep had drained him of energy, the kind of tired that only came from a slumber so restless and fragmented that it would have been better not to doze off at all. His eyelids seemed like they had weights pulling them down, his head stuck in a thick fog.

It had been this way all week, ever since he had pledged himself to his new master. Ever since Krothus had disappeared.

He forced himself up and out of bed.

Slipping on his robes, the pit of anxiety in Vyrion's stomach seemed to burn all the way through him. It wasn't like Krothus to leave without saying anything. And yet, days later, the last Vyrion saw or heard from him was the very first night he'd arrived at Lord Callida's fortress. Then he simply disappeared.

And things had only got worse when Vyrion finally received permission to collect his things from Lord Victus' compound. The first place he had considered home, scalded by flames, desecrated by the corpses of those he knew and recognised; it was all too much to bear. Lorren had a family, now he was gone. The best he could do was push it out of his mind, pretend it was only some horrible nightmare.

With his runeblade hooked onto his belt, Vyrion left Krothus' bare room. Another day of fruitless searching ahead of him, what a life he led. Not only was Krothus missing, but Inissa and Spinebreaker were gone as well. Though, seeing that Vyrion hadn't found them in the piles of corpses strewn about the place, he could only hope they had somehow escaped the slaughter. The thought of it all made him feel physically sick, but he forced himself to move past it. He would find out what happened to those he cared about, and that was that.

Arriving in the main courtyard of Callida's fortress was like stepping into the twisted jaw of some massive beast, the crooked towers looming down at its mouthful of guards. Vyrion quickly picked out Jarek, carelessly lounging across a set of steps with Amar and a heavily tattooed apprentice Vyrion didn't recognise. The trio were laughing at some joke, but all three of them fell silent when Vyrion approached, as if his mere presence somehow soured the punchline.

Jarek smiled at him. "Look who finally decided to come into the daylight."

Vyrion didn't respond, too busy glaring at Amar. He was wearing Lord Victus' godrium armor, crudely strapped down to fit his much leaner frame, like a gangly sibling wearing an older brother's clothes far too big for him. Like a sibling who had looted the corpse of a once-great man for his own amusement. Amar either didn't notice Vyrion's gaze or didn't care, only letting out an exaggerated yawn. Emperor above, Vyrion wished he could just chop him down where he stood.

"Vyrion?" Jarek said, waving a hand.

Vyrion cleared his throat. "Can I talk to you briefly?"

"Go ahead."

"Privately?"

"Fine," Jarek sighed, pushing himself back to his feet. "I'll be back soon."

"There is no conflict quite like that of quarreling lovers," Amar murmured, eliciting a laugh from the third apprentice. Jarek rolled his eyes but said nothing in response.

The moment they were far enough away, Vyrion snapped at Jarek.

"What is your problem?"

But Jarek didn't back down. "My problem? What about you? Ever since we arrived here you've been nothing but distant and cold. This is the first time you've talked to me in days."

Vyrion knew he was right. He had been avoiding Jarek, only speaking to him when absolutely necessary. Though he had been doing that with everyone.

"You know why."

Jarek huffed, like Vyrion had said something profoundly annoying. "I went back to the compound too, you know. I saw the bodies. But like I've said, you need to move on, there's no use dwelling on it. We're in a better place now. And avoiding me is not going to change what happened."

"She killed them, Jarek."

"Our *master* was annexing the compound. They knew that, but still they resisted. Anyone would know the consequences."

Vyrion felt tears biting at the back of his throat, but he choked them down. He would have loved to shout and yell, demand to know why Jarek didn't seem to care what happened. But what good would it do? The last thing he needed was losing Jarek too.

"I'm sorry," Vyrion said quietly, "With everything that happened ... it's been difficult."

"Understandably so. But things will get better, I promise."

"Have you heard any news?"

Jarek sighed. "No, nothing. But you will be the first person I tell if I do. And in the meantime, you need to stop worrying about Krothus so much. You look terrible. Have you been sleeping?"

"A little," lied Vyrion. His mind was still swimming through sludge, he was exhausted and tired of the uncertainty, the anxiety. Krothus was missing and nobody seemed to care.

"Look," Jarek said, taking a step forward and wrapping his arms around him, "Focus on yourself first. Everything else will fall into place. My room is no doubt more comfortable, come by tonight and you might sleep better."

Vyrion nodded, feeling ever so slightly better in his familiar embrace. But just as quickly as it came, Jarek awkwardly retracted his arms.

"I nearly forgot, Lord Callida was asking for you," he said.

Vyrion was surprised, he had hardly exchanged a single word with the woman since arriving there. Countless Ruin Lords came and went through the fortress gates, their business both known and unknown. Allegiances broken or forged, it didn't matter, they all played a part in whittling down Thanaton's fuse, bit by bit. All it would take was a stray spark to set it all blaze. None of this had involved Vyrion, at least not yet, but this could be his chance to gain some idea of what was to come.

"Asking about what?" he asked.

"I have no idea. She only said to look for her in the Upper Districts."

"I will," Vyrion said, eager to finally have something to do which could take his mind off its self-destructive spirals, at least temporarily. "And thank you, I feel a bit better."

Jarek flashed him a smile. "I'm always happy to help, you know that."

Vyrion smiled back, but something in him felt that Jarek was only saying the words, like they were some meaningless pleasantry, a shield to hide a more difficult conversation. He had no evidence of course, nothing but his anxiety laden gut continuing its habit of ringing every alarm it could. Figuring out which warning carried even the slightest grain of truth was the tricky part, they all rang through with equal urgency.

"I will go see Callida, then," Vyrion ended lamely. But Jarek was already off to his previous position, laughing away with the others like nothing had happened. Something about it rubbed Vyrion the wrong way. The speed that Jarek seemed to flip temperament was odd, to say the least. But who was he to judge? Jarek was ten times the Ruined Vyrion was anyways.

So off he went.

The Upper Districts grew up out of a low hill which slowly climbed towards the cliff edges that bound the city, never quite reaching, but just close enough to tower above the rest of Thanaton, an inherent superiority in the geography itself.

When Vyrion briefly stopped his march up the neatly paved streets to look back down at the view behind him, it was easy to see the appeal. Thanaton's concrete maze was visible in its entirety; stern walls, ambitious towers, and the Dark Pyramid, silently staring back at him.

But Vyrion's eye was drawn to something else.

Near the chaos of the boroughs rose a lazy plume of smoke, a grim reminder of the smoldering remnants of what used to be. The former compound of Lord Victus had been burning for days, not a single soul was brave enough to risk Callida's wrath in putting it out. It had been his home, once.

Vyrion turned back around and kept walking.

The further up the hill he got, the richer the materials became, the more gaudy the decor, the more obscene the scale of it all. He started to think the buildings were made with the express purpose of goading others to knock them down. One particular residence, vibrant green and with more columns than sense, was certainly tempting. But more importantly, Callida was nowhere to be found.

So why not ask for help? Vyrion was hardly alone here. The Imperials passing by were frequent and well-dressed, surprisingly calm when passing near him, at least compared to any others who spotted his runeblade elsewhere in the city.

Vyrion cleared his throat as he hailed down a young man sporting a thick pair of spectacles and a book-stuffed satchel. "Excuse me. Do you have a moment?"

The man froze instantly, like he had just been singled out for execution. Vyrion could even see his hands trembling as he quickly adjusted his glasses.

"O-of course, my lord," he stuttered.

Vyrion tried to give him his most genuine smile, intending to keep the man calm. "There's no need to worry, I only want to know if you have seen Lord Callida nearby."

But this seemed to have the opposite effect, at the mention of her name he went white as a sheet. "What? Is she here?"

"Yes, though I don't-"

But the man was already halfway down the hill, leaving a trail of flittering pages and papers as he ran.

Vyrion sighed. So much for that plan.

It was odd to think that in another life, Vyrion could have been the one sprinting away, fearing the mere mention of a Ruin Lord. If the Ruin had not made its mark on him, had it chosen another, he would be a different man. And he couldn't help but think that it would have been better. If he kept his head down and stayed out of the way, he would have it all; parents, friends, family. A calm, fulfilling existence. But at what price?

He looked down at his hand, at the scars over his palm. Each one carried a story, a lesson he learned, a struggle he somehow managed to survive. If he lost all that, if he lost the past that forged him into who he was today, could he even say he would be the same person? Maybe that's what he wanted to change in the first place. He wasn't good at being a Ruined, nor a person in general. A chance to do it all over again, that might be what he wanted. A chance to disappear.

Vyrion smiled at the thought. Disappearing sounded nice.

The further he trudged up the Upper District, the less people he saw, like the altitude simply made them disappear. So when the hill eventually leveled out, and the overindulgent buildings reached their pinnacle, it was practically deserted. Though it only took Vyrion a quick glance to determine it was far more than an aversion to height that had left the place empty; cafe tables were left with food half eaten, any window in sight locked down tight, and even the residence guards were nowhere to be seen.

No, the streets weren't just empty, they had been cleared.

He might not have been able to see anything, but Vyrion could feel it. It was like something in the corner of his mind's eye, an immense presence that drew his attention, sent the Ruin around him swirling and twisting. There were Ruin Lords nearby. Worse, the air was crackling with opposing waves of power, their auras all but smashing into one another.

As he followed the presences through a passage sandwiched between two manor complexes, Vyrion finally spotted their source.

A wall of Imperial guards had dammed up the passage. Their ranks gave way to the towering figure of Lord Callida, the centerpiece of this vessel of arms and armor, flanked on either side by two Ruined that Vyrion vaguely recognised. Some of her other apprentices perhaps. Across from her stood a lone Ruin Lord, accompanied by a mere two soldiers, hardly seeming confident about their chances.

The moment Vyrion appeared, Callida's lips twisted upwards, as if she had found it suddenly amusing that he had come, before she continued speaking to her outnumbered Ruin Lord counterpart.

"Sanata, I still need an answer."

Lord Sanata, as it must have been, was a small woman who could have been mistaken for a freakish bird, her skin covered in feathers, and her long nose not too far off a beak. She looked far from happy, the Ruin whispering her displeasure all around.

"I am bound to Malus, Callida. It is my duty to serve him, as it should be yours to respect the Emperor's hierarchy. Your games are doing nothing but destabilizing the Empire," said Lord Sanata, her voice ringing out strongly, though even Vyrion could hear the slightest whisper of uncertainty poisoning her position.

Callida did not seem bothered by the retort. "Honorable words, I never took you for being so old-fashioned. I'm sure Lord Victus would have appreciated them, were he still alive. He shared a similar nostalgia, the type of naivety that has kept the Empire from flourishing, but even he would advise that after a certain threshold, loyalty is no different than stubbornness."

"How easy it is to conjure up the words of the dead to support your position," Sanata snapped.

Callida laughed, a sickeningly sweet twinkle that couldn't have sounded more forced if she tried. "It is, isn't it? I certainly don't think he can object to it, not anymore."

Vyrion swallowed. He was trying to keep calm, but Callida was making it very difficult.

"But my question remains," she continued, "Malus cowers in the Dark Pyramid, his power base rapidly dwindling. Why should you be forced to remain in your seat on a sinking vessel? Join me, and a position will be waiting for you in the new Empire."

New Empire.

Her words echoed through Vyrion's head, rippling through his mind, like each syllable was a string pulling him ever closer to her. He tried to resist, pull back, but he was only drawn further in.

He saw images of burning compounds, massacred guards, the Dark Pyramid shorn in two. Above it all, Lord Callida in a golden throne, and with a wave of her hand and the fires ceased, the bodies disappeared, and vibrant sunlight beamed down on streets suddenly filled with crowds of adoring subjects.

New Empire.

Then she released him. And when Vyrion looked to her, for some sign of her invisible attack, she hadn't moved at all. Sanata, meanwhile, was watching him with her avian eyes. They shared a look, like she knew what had just transpired.

Vyrion wasn't sure what he would do, were he in Sanata's situation, Loyalty was a valuable trait in a Ruin Lord, a rare one at that, but at what point does it become a liability? He had been loyal to Victus, and it had only made him blind to what was happening under his very nose. Worse, despite everything, he still wasn't sure what to think of the man now that he was gone. But Highlord Malus wasn't Victus, Vyrion had no doubt that the Highlord would throw any member of his power base under his feet if it meant winning his struggle with Callida. Such was the nature of power.

"He won't give in to your shadow war, you know," Sanata said eventually, "Malus will never leave the protection of the pyramid while he knows you are waiting for him. He may well stay under the council's protection forever."

Callida's serenely neutral face darkened in an immediate storm of fury. "Then I'll come drag him out myself."

Sanata laughed, almost a birdlike squawk. "Then I can only wish you good luck. Not only would you be committing treason, putting the council members in harm's way, but you would have to raise an army to even try. An army that would crash against the Dark Pyramid with absolutely nothing to show for it."

For a moment they just stood there, their glares fighting a war all their own. Vyrion was half-sure they were about to come to blows. Then Lord Sanata let out a heavy sigh.

"I won't join you, Callida. I know how this scenario plays out; last to join up, first on the front lines. And no matter how much you whittle away at Malus' power base, his connections remain, both on the Council and across the Empire. They will ensure any attempt to enter the Dark Pyramid will cost you. Dearly. And I do not intend to risk the lives of my people just for your vanity."

"What you call vanity, I call progress," Callida snapped, "Your commitment to your cause will not end well for you."

"Perhaps. I suppose we will meet again when your vanity finally exceeds reason." And then, with a ruffle of feathers, she and her escort walked off.

Callida did nothing to stop her, only watched her go with nothing short of pure venom in her eyes. Vyrion could feel her rage pulsing all around them, like the beating of a monstrous heart, leaving him silently praying he would never earn her ire to the same extent. But then, as quickly as it came, Callida's anger evaporated.

"Ah, young Vyrion, I wasn't expecting you to come to me so soon. Walk with me."

Without waiting for him to follow, she strolled off, her heeled boots cracking against the pavement. Vyrion jogged to catch up to her as the rigid formation of her escort followed behind.

"What was that about, master?"

She waved a dismissive hand. "A temporary setback, nothing more. Malus's protections can dwindle via diplomacy or violence, and in some cases the preferred option may not be clear. Sanata's choice has made that decision for me."

Vyrion nodded. The power base of a Highlord was significant. Malus most likely had dozens of Ruin Lords under his command, working through all of them was a tremendous task, one Callida seemed quite keen to complete.

"But regardless, the campaign is proceeding more or less as planned, most Ruin Lords in the city recognise my claim," she continued, "It is only a matter of time before the Ruined Council will be forced to acknowledge my position, regardless of their personal views on the matter. They, like Sanata, know the end is near but have refused to admit it."

Vyrion did wonder how the Ruined Council could be forced into anything at all. They were the ultimate power in the Empire, second to only the Emperor himself. The thought of them bowing down to pressure from someone outside their coveted position raised many questions that Vyrion purposely chose not to think about. Instead, his mind could only focus on that which had troubled him all week.

"Where is Krothus?" he blurted out.

Callida stopped instantly.

"As my apprentice, you will address me with the proper titles. I will only tell you once."

Vyrion swallowed nervously. "Of course. Sorry, master." He would have given himself a good slap if he weren't in public, he was making a fool of himself.

"And no, I haven't seen him," Callida said, carefully eyeing Vyrion, "Not since I sent him away several days ago."

Krothus had not mentioned anything of the sort. And why would she send him away in the middle of the night?

"I only ask because no one has seen or heard from him," Vyrion continued, "And it is very much unlike him to disappear on such short notice, master."

She looked at him for a moment, her face betraying just a hint of sourness, like she had caught wind of food that had gone off. "Your concern is noted. But Krothus is an ambitious Ruined, the type that only pursues the advancement of his own position above all else. I would be careful, young Vyrion. Careful to avoid being caught up in the actions of someone who could so easily drag you down with him."

The threat was clear. And as she spoke, Vyrion felt an overwhelming force wash over his mind, a powerful wave crashing onto a rocky shore, finding every hidden nook and crevice. He tried to resist, but images flashed through his mind despite his efforts. He saw Lord Victus, his spirit severed from his body, the collapsing catacombs, Captain Lorren's brief farewell, and-

The slideshow of memories halted. Vyrion felt a familiar presence cast out her mental probes. That strange observer, always there, bolstered his defenses, its sudden surge of power slapping away Callida's next attempt as well.

She lies, it whispered.

Vyrion blinked and looked back up at his new master, expecting some kind of reaction, but if she were surprised, or angered, or felt anything at all regarding her sudden expulsion from his mind, Callida revealed nothing. Her face was blank, so expressionless that she might as well be made of stone, leaving Vyrion wondering if anything had really happened at all.

He cleared his throat, eager to move on before she probed him again. "You sent for me, master?"

That at least got a baring of teeth that might have been a smile, which only managed to frighten Vyrion more than anything else. "I did. I have a task for you, one that is critical to my plans ahead. Think of it as a test. A test that, if you fail, will ensure you will no longer be a Ruined in my employ."

"I see, master," Vyrion said, the knot in his stomach tighter than ever. She knew where Krothus was, but had lied about it, according to the permanent stowaway within his mind. He needed the truth, but she would hardly share this when she clearly didn't trust him. Perhaps this task was the key to that trust.

A light gust of wind blew through the street, sending loose paper flying, rattling some of the shuttered windows. There was no one else here, bar Lord Callida and her troops. And Vyrion. She could strike him down in the middle of the street, and not a single soul would lift a finger to stop her; it would be entirely within her right. She was strong, and Vyrion was weak, and that was that.

She was watching him, as if she were a chef thinking of ten different ways to slaughter a pig.

"You still think of Victus as your master."

Vyrion let out a nervous laugh, "Of course not, he betrayed my trust and got himself killed as a result."

She frowned at him.

"I mean - of course not, master."

Her frown lessened, but only slightly. "I am aware of what happened. And yet you still think of him as your master, despite his transgressions. Why?"

Vyrion wasn't sure himself. Was that even true? He could think of a dozen reasons why he would prefer a stable, pre-ritual Victus over Callida; the lack of threats, fewer enemies, better humor even played a factor. And yet, he was still not convinced of any of it. Was he just nostalgic for a simpler time?

"I ... don't know, master," he said eventually, feeling like he had answered incorrectly. Perhaps she expected him to refuse, to kneel down before her and reaffirm his loyalty to her and her alone.

But his assumption seemed incorrect. Callida even seemed pleased.

"Honesty. How refreshing," she purred, "Know that I understand your confusion. The Empire is a place built on it, built on the basis of misplaced loyalty and the forced dynamic of a master and their apprentice. The promise of power, of moving up in our society, is dangled in front of us from the moment we arrive here. If you follow your master, if you follow the Empire's rules, you will take their place, one day. That's the promise. That you will rise up to the place you deserve. But what happens if that illusion is shattered?"

With a wave of her hand, a loose paper sailed up into her hand.

"Victus is dead. The promise of succeeding him, of moving up and taking his place, is gone," she said, twisting the page round and round in front of her, "But I say that that promise was never there in the first place."

The page began to fold in on itself, to steadily crumple inwards.

"The Empire wants you to think small. To think only of petty rivals to your insignificant, incremental ambitions. You cannot change the status quo when you are focused on the shuffling of pointless titles and useless loyalties."

Vyrion watched the paper, mesmerized as it became smaller and smaller.

"That's why I aim to rip up this false promise. To start again. And to do that, to ensure an Empire where the strong truly do rise to the top, I need to tear down those who uphold this lie."

Now nothing more than a tiny dot, the paper suddenly blew itself out, shredded into a million tiny pieces.

Disaster, the voice in Vyrion's head whispered.

"I understand, master," Vyrion said, not sure what to think.

"I doubt you do," Callida said, "But you don't need to. You only need to do what I tell you."

She brushed her hair back and looked around, as if she were confirming the street was still empty before continuing.

"There is an item of great importance that I need you to deliver to an ally. Take Jarek with you, he knows its destination."

"Yes, master," he said. A new master, the same errands. "What is it?"

"You don't need to know. It is of absolute necessity that you do not open its container. To do so would jeopardize everything."

He didn't like the sound of that. "Yes, master."

Callida took a step closer. Her sweet scent filled his nostrils, her breath rang in his ears.

"Be careful, young Vyrion. Curiosity can be a great asset, but if you aren't careful, it will kill you."

Chapter 22

Running

Inissa could barely breathe. Pressed on all sides by the crowd, any desperately needed air was blocked as she shoved a half-stale roll of bread into her mouth, chewing it the ferocity of a starving animal. Was she actually starving? Perhaps not, but she was in no rush to return to the sorry state she had once been in.

"Thief! Thief!" a ragged voice rang out.

All heads turned towards Inissa, her mouth full, as a stout man shambled right at her, an accusatory finger pointed her way.

"It wadn't muh!" Inissa shouted, her explanation foiled by the bread stuffed into her cheeks. She tried to press through the crowd to continue her escape, but she might as well have been swimming upriver, through a horde of indifferent fish.

"Like hell it wasn't," the merchant growled. He was close enough now that Inissa could smell his foul breath, see the curved dagger at his side.

Inissa painfully swallowed her prize, finally welcoming a swell of air into her lungs. She wasn't about to die over a bread roll. So she focused the ever present force of the Ruin, demanding it into a wall in front of her, feeling it swell like a wave approaching the shoreline.

But as the merchant swiped his dagger around, someone bumped into her. Her balance lost, Inissa toppled to the floor, swearing a thousand curses as the reserve of Ruin power collapsed.

The knife had no such issues, and sailed through the air towards her, uninterrupted.

But just as Inissa could make out the individual chips of rust on the blade, a muscled crimson arm swung out from the crowd. It stopped the merchant's strike instantly. A crescendo of agitated murmuring rose up as a familiar orkathi warrior stepped forward, head and shoulders above anyone nearby.

The merchant struggled and writhed, a fish caught in a net, but the grip that held him was unbreakable.

"Where is the glory in killing over bread?" Spinebreaker said simply, plucking the rusted weapon out of the man's hands and dropping it to the floor. A quick shove sent its former wielder stumbling the other way.

The muttering spectators parted to allow the merchant to make his undignified retreat, but many still stood, staring.

"What are you looking at?" the orkathi snarled, swiping the air with a clawed hand.

Everyone nearby gained a sudden interest in continuing about their day, and the street quickly cleared out.

Inissa breathed a sigh of relief, but it wasn't long before shame quickly overtook her. She'd been caught like some common urchin, and defended herself like one too - had any of the bystanders been told she were actually a Ruined, the daughter of a Ruin Lord, they would have surely scoffed at such a blatant lie. She felt the bite of tears welling up, but she pushed them down.

"Reaching life's lowest points is the best motivation to never return there," Victus said in Spinebreaker's gravelly voice, reaching a clawed hand out to her.

Inissa clutched at the lifeline as she was effortlessly pulled to her feet.

"Thank you," she said, brushing dirt off her trousers, "But my lowest was considerably worse than a botched theft and a fall in the dirt."

"Good," Victus said bluntly, "The harshest of life's trials are the best of life's lessons."

"Wisely said," Spinebreaker agreed.

Inissa was still struggling to cope, watching them take turns speaking from the same mouth. It was unnerving, and looked closer to one insane person talking to themselves in different accents than two inhabiting one body.

"Now come along, girl," Victus said, "I know where to find someone to help us."

Not waiting for a response, he started plowing his way through the crowd in pursuit of this new goal. There was hardly any other option but to follow. So Inissa blew a black strand of hair off of her face, dusted her ragged clothes off, and followed behind him as he battered his way through the mob.

She and Victus had been laying low, spending several days in the grimiest streets in the city. Inissa, not used to the lack of needed amenities, notably good food, clean water, and basic shelter, had been struggling, her bread heist evidence enough of that. But Victus had seemed completely at home, both in his new union of body and soul with Spinebreaker, and with the hardships of their predicament as a whole.

Inissa understood, at least a little. If she had morphed from a crippled old man into the warrior Spinebreaker was, no problem would be too large for her, even if she had to share her skull with another.

Victus continued his journey through the sea of street merchants, off-duty laborers, and beggars, managing to only briefly hesitate in front of a rather sad-looking brothel as they passed by.

Inissa pushed him along. He was in a new body, sure, but she wasn't about to wait for him to try out all the bells and whistles. The older woman posted at the door wore an expression of undisguised relief as the hulking warrior elected to pass by.

Only a few doors down from the brothel was where Victus finally stopped. A half-broken sign swung limply above the entrance, hanging precariously from one corner. Inissa had to turn her head sideways to read the name: *The Grinning Bat,* complete with a crude drawing of an upside-down bat which was very clearly frowning.

"Follow me and stay quiet, this is no place for the curious," Victus said, holding a claw to his tusked lips.

"Fine," she grumbled. He sounded like he had decided he was her father. A frightening thought.

Two exceptionally wide bouncers flanked the doorway, their only acknowledgement of the mismatched duo's entry a pair of almost imperceptible nods. It left Inissa wondering who, if anyone, would be barred entry to the place if they were allowing grimey orkathi warriors and underage companions in off the street.

The temperature immediately dropped a few degrees as they passed into the dimness, a single turn bringing them to a stout room, halfway between a cave and a bunker, filled with some of the strangest people Inissa had ever seen. Groups of shady mercenaries quietly murmured in dark alcoves, with other colorful characters sat around the bar that dominated the center of the room, one that looked like it hadn't been cleaned since the Empire was founded. On the far end, a peculiarly out of tune band played an upbeat, alien melody on a lopsided platform, a glazed over look in their eyes.

Inissa sensed danger everywhere, but to her relief, not a single pair of eyes turned to look at the new arrivals as they made their way to the bar.

Victus casually gained the attention of the barkeep, an ancient woman who looked to be half made of dust.

"I'll have what he's having," Victus grunted at her, gesturing to another orkathi sat further down the bar. That earned a raised glass from the stranger, his tattooed skin closer to brown than red. Victus, or Spinebreaker, delivered a nod of recognition back their way.

The barkeep wordlessly poured some green substance, neither a solid nor a liquid, into an extraordinarily dirty cup and handed it over, barely acknowledging Victus at all. To his credit, the orkathi-Ruined hybrid didn't balk at his questionable purchase, and tossed a coin over the counter regardless. Inissa, who had been the one who earned that coin, if you could call pickpocketing earning, could think of a hundred things, mostly food, that she would have rather spent it on.

Victus leaned close to her just as he was stepping away from the bar.

"Stay here and out of trouble."

Then he and his drink disappeared into the darkness.

Inissa took a deep breath and sat at a high chair on the bar, crooked and creaky. All she needed to do was stay put without catching anyone's attention, which sounded easy enough. At first, she stared silently at her hands, hoping nobody was looking her way. But boredom soon got the best of her, and she started looking over those nearby.

Two people, encased head to toe in battle scarred armor, were having a conversation entirely through elaborate hand signals. Inissa was unsure how they were meant to drink with their heads covered.

She moved her gaze onto another pairing nearby, where a woman seemed to be berating an automaton that had piercers affixed to its metal arms. The source of the woman's frustration was a mystery, the band's tilted melody easily drowned it out, but the automaton seemed disinterested.

With no sign of Victus, Inissa turned her head to the disheveled man next her, staring off into his glass with his mind in a different time. He looked as though he'd been handsome, once, but now a portion of his face sagged, like wax held to a flame, some unnatural decay taken root.

An eye, an unnatural grey mass in the middle of this deformity, blinked back at her.

"What are you looking at?" he snarled.

"Nothing!" Inissa said quickly, immediately unsure of what to do. In a panic, she reached out to the first thing she saw, a bowl of some unidentifiable bar snacks, and stuffed a handful of them into her mouth, too stressed to come to terms with the possible hygiene issues associated with it.

This did nothing but enraged the scarred man, who quickly stood up, his barstool loudly screeching across the ground.

"Now you're stealing my food too?" he raged, "You picked the wrong day to fuck with me."

He smashed his glass onto the floor, sending shards skittering in all directions. The band's melody quickly petered out. So too did every conversation in the *Smiling Bat*.

"I'm sorry," Inissa said, roughly swallowing, "I didn't know. How about I buy you some more?"

But the man was not interested. "Do you think you can just buy my respect? I have the death sentence in twelve cities. Insulting me is worth more than a bowl of battered roaches."

Inissa couldn't resist gagging, now burdened with the cursed knowledge of why her ill-advised snack had been so crunchy.

The furious man threw himself at her.

A punch sailed in from her left, but Inissa sensed it, dodging out of the way just in time. The man followed up with with a swipe from his shattered glass. It whistled past her face, severing strands of her hair. Close.

But as he swung the glass again, Inissa acted on pure instinct. The Ruin swirled all around her, excited by her fear, eager to be unleashed. With a thrust of her palm, a wave of energy crashed into her foe, his attack halted instantly as he was blown back into the air.

The man crashed into a nearby wall and slumped to the ground.

As the brief surge of power faded away, Inissa could scarcely believe what had happened. She'd finally managed to control the Ruin in the way she wanted, and with no hesitation, too. It had been as easy as throwing a punch herself.

But the man wasn't beaten. He forced himself to one knee, even more furious than before.

"A Ruined? I'm going to enjoy-"

He suddenly fell back with a pained grunt, a piercer bolt stuck into his shoulder.

"Honestly, Sorog, can't you just let us drink in peace?" a voice called out from one of the alcoves. "I'll pay for your meal if you just shut up for once."

The man frowned. Then, as if it were nothing but an inconvenience, ripped the bolt out of his shoulder and got up. He started walking back to Inissa, completely indifferent to the resulting dribble of blood going down his arm.

Inissa froze up, ready for him to strike once again. But he simply dragged his chair back and signaled over the barkeep like nothing had happened. The band hesitantly started up its tune once more, followed by the low din of conversations resuming.

Struggling to make sense of it all, Inissa peered into the shadows where her savior had struck from. It wasn't long before Spinebreaker's wide frame emerged, a clawed hand beckoning her closer.

Inissa had scarcely made it a few steps towards him when he grabbed her arm and effortlessly tossed her into a chair hidden in the darkness.

"What part of staying out of trouble didn't you understand, girl?" Victus snarled, looming over the table like a giant red column.

"Now now, Victus, play nice. Sorog just gets self-conscious when people look at him." The woman who spoke looked familiar, her ashen officer's jacket unbuttoned and worn loose over her shoulders, a hint of a swindler's grin on her lips.

"Captain Fareese?"

"In the flesh," Fareese confirmed. She leaned back into her chair and a drink was casually handed to her by one of her two automaton crewmates, whirring and clanking as they continually watched the room.

"Everyone in this place will have noticed us now," Victus growled, still unhappy with the recent turn of events.

Fareese rolled her eyes. "In all your time shifting bodies, have you ever been a young woman sitting at a bar alone?"

"No, but-"

"Then you'd realize how impossible not being noticed truly is," Fareese scoffed, lighting up a smokestick, offering one to Inissa as well, who politely declined.

The automatons' heads seemed to follow whoever was speaking at the time, vaguely human-like, equipped with basic, wax-like faces. Inissa found them extraordinarily unsettling, they seemed like a pair of possessed toys.

"But, like I was saying before," Fareese said, stopping briefly to take a drag of her smokestick, "Your 'death' seems to have caught the imagination of the city. It's a popular gossip topic, but nobody knows who was behind it. Many suspect Callida, of course, but that goes for everything - she's the people's scapegoat for every problem in the city at this point, from burnt food to botched assassinations. Though speaking of scapegoats, she offered up a particularly convincing one."

"Who?" Victus pressed.

Fareese puffed out a cloud of smoke. "Her own apprentice, our good friend Krothus. He took the fall. She's replaced him with Vyrion and Jarek."

"What?" Inissa said, "That could never be true."

She caught Lord Victus' eye at the tail-end of her exclamation, expecting a similar disbelief, but for all the viciousness of his new outer flesh, he looked deflated and disappointed, though who with, she couldn't be sure.

"It's to be expected that Callida would throw her apprentice to the wolves," Victus said eventually, "He's already caused blows to her reputation with his antics, and it would be an easy way to get rid of him while saving face. Where is he now?"

Fareese took a deep swig of her drink. "I'm not too sure, my memory can be so very hazy these days."

Inissa initially didn't understand her meaning, but once Victus angrily slammed the rest of their stolen coins onto the table, she quickly caught up.

"Don't play us for fools, Fareese," he hissed, "I don't have time for your games today, there is so much more at stake than your petty greed."

"Oh?" the Imperial Captain asked, uncaring, already opening the bag and beginning to count the coins within.

"If Highlord Malus is indeed hunkering down within the Dark Pyramid, and Callida truly plans to force her way through, then we will be dealing with nothing short of a full-scale civil war" Victus ranted, angry spittle dripping off his tusks, "And if that doesn't destroy the city, you can be sure that the Republic will - they'll be knocking on our front door the moment they sniff weakness. It will be the end of the Empire's as we know it. Is that enough of a reason to care, *Captain*?"

Inissa felt a chill run over her. Were they really that close to the end? The Dark Pyramid was a sacred place, home to the Ruined Council and the Emperor himself. To attack it for your own political aims seemed insane.

Fareese initially said nothing. First, she stopped counting her prize and slugged back the remainder of her drink. "I heard the gray bastard was arrested by Imperial Intelligence."

Victus gave an unreadable frown, while Inissa was instantly angry, frustrated at how hopeless it all seemed.

"Great," she found herself saying, "Now what are we meant to do? Krothus is imprisoned, we're on the run, and Vyrion is right under Callida's nose."

Fareese took another drag of her smokestick. "There's nothing you *can* do. Regardless of what changes at the top, what kind of Ruin Lord schemes rock the boat, life plods on. I doubt you'll even see a difference."

This seemed to hit a nerve with Victus.

"You clearly haven't been paying attention," he declared, struggling to articulate his anger through his still unfamiliar mouth and tusks, "There is much happening behind the scenes that you could never understand, powder kegs that have sat untouched for decades. And whether you like it or not, the resulting explosion won't discriminate, right or wrong, Ruined or Imperial, we'll all suffer."

Inissa had not seen Victus so fired up, not since they'd left his compound. Though it did make sense - Ruin Lord scheming had cost him his leg, his reputation and now his whole power base, it wasn't something that she or Fareese would be likely to understand. But Inissa wanted to help.

Fareese, on the other hand, still didn't seem convinced, and her automaton companions even less so. She started counting her coins again. The lack of engagement only seemed to impassion Victus further.

"Everyone will be affected if the worst happens and the Republic uses the opportunity to take control, especially here," he said, gesturing all around the cantina as he tried to get through to the defiant Captain, "Republic rule will be a death sentence for the types of activities you're involved in."

Fareese finally had her interest piqued enough to stop her coin counting and look up to Victus as he continued.

"Make no mistake," he said, giving her a tusky smile, "Imperial Intelligence knows the ins and outs of this city's underbelly, and the whole of the Empire. But while there is the Republic to worry about, any potential clean-ups have been put on the back foot. If this changes, and the Republic move in with their less *understanding* policies regarding smuggling..."

"Fine, I understand what you're getting at," Fareese conceded, "But how in the Emperor's name do you propose we change anything about it?"

"We should -" Inissa tried to suggest.

"No," Victus interrupted, "We need to stop Callida before she sets things in motion, or we'll be too late. We don't have time for anything else. Fareese, we would need your piloting ability and your ship in order to ferry loyal supporters to key flashpoints."

Inissa tried to speak up again, "What about-"

"Time is a resource we cannot waste, I don't want to hear any more of this," Victus growled.

Inissa felt her cheeks burning. Spinebreaker would have never spoken to her in such a way. He would stay silent, like he currently was. Perhaps Krothus might have, though she would always know he didn't mean it.

"I would very much like to know what Inissa wants, old man," Fareese said, "Considering you haven't asked for my help, and I haven't accepted, I don't see why you are already ordering us around as if you're the one in charge. You're a Ruin Lord no longer."

Surprisingly, Victus said nothing, only crossed his massive orkathi arms, looking expectantly at Inissa.

She wasn't sure what else to say, or what Fareese expected her to come up with. Inissa wasn't even a full Ruined, she had no idea what political moves would be able to salvage their situation.

"I think ... " she started, but with Fareese and Victus both looking at her, she faltered. She briefly thought of what she wanted, what they could do, but concrete plans seemed to elude her as her heart sped up and her breath felt short.

Inissa's words edges out, slowly, painfully. "I think we should get Vyrion's help. And Jarek. They are close enough to Callida to be able to change things if they are truly her apprentices now."

Victus shook his head. "You hardly know the specifics, but Vyrion and Jarek would never work with me, even if it were a choice between that and death. Part of the reason for my current situation is their inability to see the big picture, and stopping my ritual before it was completed. They've made their choice."

"Vyrion would at least hear us out," Inissa said, still not understanding how their relationship could have changed so quickly. "Say what you will about him, but he's not one to react rashly. He would speak to me at the very least."

Fareese blew a puff of smoke off the side of the table. "What would be something you could do to bring him to the table? You can't exactly just stroll into Callida's compound."

"Then it's a good thing that my master is being held in prison, isn't it?" Inissa said, "So if we can get Krothus out, then Vyrion would be more than happy to help us, regardless of his new allegiances."

"I'm not sure if I'm interested in risking my neck and my ship for a prison break. We would need to even the odds," Fareese said, leaning back in her chair and taking another drink from one of her automaton's metal hands.

It swiveled its vaguely humanoid head to look at her, before returning back to its previous observations of the room. Inissa wasn't sure what need the auto would have for a drink, perhaps Fareese was using them as elaborate cupholders.

Victus stroked his tentacled beard. "We have allies elsewhere. Perhaps they could prove useful, if not for breaking Krothus out, then at least for stopping Callida if the worst happens. Vyrion could appreciate that."

Inissa wasn't sure what he meant.

"Fantastic," Fareese said, every syllable dripping in sarcasm, "I hope recruiting them is dangerous."

"Only in the worst case scenario," Victus said, smiling over his tusks.

It was then that Inissa finally realised his plan.

Nightshadow.

Chapter 23

Interrogation

Krothus, as usual, was furious. His anger stemmed from every crack and crevice in his damp cell, every disgusting mashed meal he was expecting to eat, every reminder of the foul stench emanating from the latrine pit in the cell's far corner. His rage only fanned further thinking of Dedri's betrayal, how she had left him in this cell for weeks without so much as a word, and more importantly, how she had made sure his cellmate was the most infuriating man alive.

"Shut up. You're breathing too loudly."

Krothus, resting against the wall he was chained to, opened an eye at the ragged man across from him, all greasy hair and dirty skin.

"And what are you going to do about it, Zlaterek?" Krothus sneered, "I could sing if I felt the need."

"You're just lucky I'm chained up," his fellow prisoner spat back.

"I could say the same, idiot."

Zlaterek huffed in frustration and looked up at the singular grate above their heads.

"I hope someone shoots you from up there."

Krothus rolled his eyes. "And I hope it kills me, so that I don't have to hear your constant drivel any longer."

"I'll be out of here any day now," Zlaterek insisted, "And when I do, I'll make sure you won't have to hope for that outcome."

"And how long will that be?" Krothus asked, "I'm not familiar with the sentence for being an insufferable blight on society."

"Lucky for you, being a blight carries no sentence," Zlaterek said,

"Though if this blighting includes murder of important individuals, vandalism, terrorism and such, then yes, that would carry a sentence."

"Delightful," Krothus said, "I'll be sure to keep that in mind when I decide to commit a terrorist attack."

"Which I was never convicted for!" Zlaterek shouted, aiming up at the grate above them.

"Has that ever worked?"

"Would I be here if it had?"

Krothus shrugged. "I don't care."

Zlaterek's gap-toothed grin disappeared. "You will when you've been trapped in this cell for as long as I have."

Krothus sighed. He did not want to think how long Zlaterek had been stuck in their cramped quarters, it only made him imagine how he could suffer from the same fate. How effortless it would be for his current sentence to continue from weeks into months, or, Emperor forbid, months into years.

He was meant to be out in the world, proving himself to the Empire, proving the truth behind his grand destiny. Instead he was chained to a wall, a few paces away from his own shit.

"It has been five years since I was tossed in here," Zlaterek declared, unprompted.

"In the Emperor's name ..." Krothus muttered. He had thought a week or two, maybe a month, would be the maximum amount he could withstand, but five years? He wished Zlaterek had kept his grimy mouth shut.

"He has no power here," Zlaterek said, spitting a glob of phlegm into the corner, "Nor does that blasted council of his."

"I'm fairly sure they had the power to throw you in here in the first place."

Zlaterek frowned at him and puffed out his chest, even trying, in vain, to move unruly strands of wild hair out of his face, "I was once a Ruin Lord, you know, you should show some respect."

Krothus rolled his eyes, which Zlaterek seemed to take as an encouragement to keep speaking. Krothus reminded himself to throw something at him instead, next time.

"I had earned an audience with the council," Zlaterek began, his voice pumped full of pride, "There had been a slave rebellion out in the jungle quarries, led by some Ruined with delusions of grandeur. I led a task force to stamp it out on behalf of the Emperor. I slew the rebellion's leader in single combat, taking his runeblade as proof of my glorious victory."

"You clearly didn't kill them with your humility."

"Silence, I'm not finished. At this audience, I intended to give this runeblade as a gift, a display of what happens to all those who defy the Empire, the Council, and the Emperor himself. But I was overwhelmed being in the presence of such powerful Highlords, and I made a critical error. I ignited the runeblade by mistake. As a last ditch effort, I tried to play it off as a demonstration of my gift."

"I assume that didn't go well."

Zlaterek smiled, revealing his gapped teeth once more. "Perhaps they simply didn't like my performance."

Nothing more needed to be said, Krothus knew the kind of consequences for openly brandishing a weapon near the Council. He was only surprised Zlaterek hadn't been executed on the spot. Perhaps sparing his life was a final show of favour for Zlaterek's part in putting down the uprising. Maybe it was a far worse punishment.

Zlaterek stretched as best he could while chained up and then attempted to lie down, which actually looked less comfortable than sitting.

"Now that I've shared my tragedy, are you going to share yours?"

Krothus shrugged, he had no qualms about the nature of his accusations.

"I was falsely accused of slaying a Ruin Lord," he said simply.

Zlaterek's eyes lit up. "Not your master?"

"No."

"Not an enemy of your master?"

"No."

"Tell me, damn you," Zlaterek said, tossing a pebble at Krothus for good measure. It bounced off his skull and clattered away into the shadows.

"He was the master of someone I am familiar with," Krothus conceded.

"And did you kill him?" Zlaterek pressed.

"I don't know," Krothus admitted, "It was an indirect chain of events at best."

His fellow prisoner began to applaud, his claps echoing around the cell in dizzying fashion.

"Well, well, well," he laughed, "Who could have expected you to *accidentally* kill a Ruin Lord. Expertly done, I'm sure."

"Shut up."

Zlaterek ignored him. "Of course, as a reward for proving yourself strong, for slaying a Ruin Lord above your station, you were sentenced to imprisonment. None of it makes sense from in here, does it?"

"Weren't you listening? He wasn't my master, and I didn't succeed him, I was merely present when he died," Krothus said, his limited patience drawing to a rapid end. "So no, it doesn't make any sense. Why would I try to kill an established Ruin Lord when I have no power base to defend myself? I am reaping the consequences of something I didn't do.

"Sure, and I only wanted to swing my runeblade around, didn't I?"

Krothus gave up. He did have enough energy for another verbal joust, he had done enough already. He could only wonder when he would be released from this hellhole.

As if in answer to his thoughts, the grate above them screeched as it was moved to the side. The rationed light from above disappeared as one of their jailors shifted his heavyset frame into view.

"What do you want?" Krothus snapped.

A long instrument descended from above, like an impossibly long arm with a cup at the end of it. As it drew closer, Krothus was assaulted by an awful stench emanating from whatever liquid it held, like someone had boiled rotten food into a neat past. The scent was so strong that it was burning his nostrils, and it nearly caused him to wretch as it was brought closer.

"Drink it, or they won't let you out," Zlaterek said as he waved up at the shadow above them.

"What is it?" Krothus asked, hating every aspect of that suggestion.

"It temporarily dampens any Ruin abilities, but more importantly, it has an amazing texture, only slightly offset by the taste and smell."

Delightful. He would have rather slapped it away, but Krothus couldn't stand listening to Zlaterek any longer, so, hoping the unknown mixture would put him out of his misery, he grabbed the overgrown ladle and slurped it down.

Not only was the smell so overwhelming that it threatened to knock him out, but the taste was the foulest thing Krothus had ever had the displeasure of encountering, and the texture, like a thick chunky paste, made everything even worse.

As Krothus struggled to swallow it down, he felt his chains unlock themselves and clatter to the floor. A ladder dropped down from above.

"Enjoy the exercise," Zlaterek snarked, watching Krothus stagger to the ladder and struggle with every rung.

Not too long ago, Krothus would have thought climbing a ladder a trivial task. Now, it was a lesson in humility. Each rung felt like climbing a mountain, each shaky pull upwards just barely managed. Only after his willpower was thoroughly crushed did he manage to crawl up past the opened grate, head spinning and drenched in sweat. His mind felt like it was submerged in mud, his senses dulled. When he tried to reach out through the Ruin, peer around him for some sense of understanding, it wasn't there. The only thing Krothus could feel was its absence. It was like he was peering into the pitch blackness with his eyes wide open.

It was terrifying. The Ruin, his blessing, was gone. If this was what it was like to be a normal man, then he could only hope he never became one.

Then he found himself whisked away by strong hands, weightless in their grip, only to be thrown into a chair in a damp room. Across a desk in front of him was a familiar face.

"It's about time you showed up," Krothus snarled as best he could. His body was assailed by an alternating barrage of deathly chill and intolerable heat.

"You are always so affectionate," Dedri said. "How has your stay been?"

Krothus assumed that looking at him, covered in grime, unwashed for a considerable amount of time, and barely staying lucid despite the horrid poison he had just drank, she already knew the answer.

"A pleasure."

"Good," she said, "But remember, this is only temporary. On paper, you are a reckless Ruined who has brazenly conspired to kill a Ruin Lord out of his remit in a cowardly way, and you are being treated as such."

Krothus would have loved to make a biting comment in response, but he was struggling to stay conscious, let alone speak properly. His defiance was reduced to an unhappy glare.

Dedri seemed to understand his misgivings. "It's required procedure for prisoners to ingest blocker serum before being privately interviewed. It's only temporary, you should feel back to yourself in about thirty minutes."

Krothus' glare continued.

"Anyways," she said, clearing her throat, "Officially, I am here to obtain your confession. But unofficially, I am advising you against this, as that would result in your immediate execution. My sources are working day and night to find enough evidence to exonerate you, or at least reduce your sentence, but until then I must keep up appearances to avoid any interference from outside forces. I hope you can understand that."

"Your professionalism is inspiring," Krothus managed to slur through clenched teeth.

Dedri clearly didn't appreciate the tremendous effort required to make such a witty retort, as she completely ignored it.

"Do you have anyone who would testify on your behalf? Someone you absolutely trust?"

"Vyrion. He was there for Ruin's sake. So was Jarek."

Krothus could only hope Vyrion had figured out where he was and was already concocting some sort of plan to liberate Krothus from this torturous imprisonment. Any alternative was too depressing to imagine.

"That's what I suspected," Dedri said, her lips pursed thoughtfully, "I have already attempted to get in contact with him, but Callida keeps him under close watch, surely hoping he doesn't cause any complications to her delicate situation. If there is an opportunity to safely catch his eye, we will do so, but until then, you need to uphold your part of this arrangement."

Before Krothus could make any demands, or perhaps request a different cellmate, Agent Dedri snapped her fingers and the wide shadow of his imposing jailor loomed over him. And just as an unruly child would be sent to his room, Krothus was carried back to his own personal hell.

As the grate shut above him, sentencing him to his fate, Krothus looked up at wild-haired Zlaterek, who was watching him with a grand smile.

"No matter what they say," the disgraced Ruined said, almost giddy, "You'll never leave, they won't let you."

Krothus said nothing. Zlaterek laughed and laughed.

Vyrion had better be on his way.

Chapter 24
Deal

"I'll never forget the first time I was this close."

"I don't think anyone would," Vyrion agreed. He and Jarek both had to crane their necks to get a full picture.

The Dark Pyramid already looked like an unbelievable feat of Imperial engineering from afar, an impressive symbol of the Empire's advanced minds, but up close, near enough to drink in the full view of its size, the thought of mortals being involved in its creation seemed impossible. So great was its terrifying splendor that Vyrion could only think that the structure had been forged by Gods and dropped to the earth.

The gargantuan shape was separated from the rest of the city by a massive fissure, an earthly maw waiting to swallow up any fool who tried to cross anywhere but the lone bridge that led across. It led to a grand entryway, the one blemish on the Dark Pyramid's otherwise spotless carapace, its strange spikes, endless edges, and bizarre geometry making the way into the monument look like a portal to an unsettling new world.

Jarek nudged him. "Did you come all this way just to stare, or are we actually going to deliver what we need to? This place sets me on edge."

"I know what you mean," Vyrion said. On edge didn't even begin to describe how he felt. He felt truly disturbed, like he was somewhere he was never meant to be, some unworthy intruder about to be quashed by the pyramid itself.

For the hundredth time that day, he looked down at the featureless metal box he held. It was impossible to tell what was inside, let alone how to open it - there were no handles, locks, or marks of any kind on its surface. If Vyrion hadn't been told by Callida it contained something he was not allowed to look at, then he wouldn't have known it was a container at all.

He cleared his throat and gave Jarek a forced smile. "Let's go, then."

Both of them stepped onto the bridge. Thankfully, the thing held their weight.

But as they continued, Vyrion felt himself grow increasingly restless. He could feel an endless flow of Ruin energy passing right through him, a powerful current rushing into the waiting portal in front of them.

"I don't like this." Vyrion wasn't sure as to the cause, but it seemed like something was drawing in the Ruin from all around, like an invisible ocean spiraling down a drain.

"I once heard that the Emperor himself sits atop the Dark Pyramid, drinking in the power from the whole of Thanaton, gathering strength for the next war," Jarek said.

"Has he ever fought in one?"

"How should I know? No one's seen him for years."

They continued up the bridge, enveloped in a procession of Thanaton's finest. High-ranking Ruin Lords, generals, sorcerers; they all looked at Vyrion the same way, like he was a mistake.

They could all tell he was a fraud, that he had no business being there.

Vyrion silently wished for the brazen confidence that Krothus had. He never seemed scared, nor nervous, just being nearby was enough to put Vyrion at ease, an island of steadiness in a sea of anxiety to tether himself to.

But Krothus was gone.

In an effort to distract himself, Vyrion made the mistake of looking over the side of the bridge into the chasm below. Gazing into the endless blackness, he could have mistaken it for the depths of hell itself. A single bead of sweat ran down from his painstakingly tidy hairline, just waiting for him to jump.

"Come Vyrion, now is not the time for distractions, not when Lord Callida has given us such an important task." Jarek had a careful hand on Vyrion's shoulder.

"I know, I was just seeing how far down it went," Vyrion lied.

"Some say to the entire side of the world!" Jarek said cheerfully, clapping Vyrion on the back. Vyrion wobbled, but managed to steady himself before the worst happened. He made sure to stay in the middle of the bridge.

The guards milling about at the entrance were an odd mix. Most were the usual Imperial guards, with their bucket helmets, piercers, and crimson tabards, but there were others that Vyrion had never seen, covered head to toe in some elaborate, gold-adorned metal, more like the shell of some cursed insect than armor, who wielding twisted, spiked spears. All of them were at least a head taller than their counterparts, and had the bulk to match.

A guard approached them, the triangles appended to her breastplate marking her as a most unhappy Captain.

"What business do you two have here?"

Vyrion smiled at her, for all the good he thought it would do, and tried his best. "Good afternoon, we're here to-"

"We don't need your babble, soldier," Jarek interrupted, "Lord Callida has already sent word ahead of our arrival. This is a peace offering for Highlord Malus, aiming to keep things peaceful. Our master is not without honorable diplomacy."

She looked between them, then at the metal box Vyrion held. Vyrion barely noticed, he was busy glaring at Jarek. Why let him speak at all if he was just going to interrupt?

"Fine. But this had better work, the last thing I want is a boring posting becoming a dangerous one." Then she stepped aside.

"Of course," Jarek said, with his most irritatingly charming grin.

The pair quickly made their way through the checkpoint. One of the larger guards stared at them as they passed by, their gaze unflinching until they passed out of sight.

The moment they were past the guards Vyrion made his displeasure known.

"Why do you never tell me what's going on? It's ridiculous to expect me to keep up with whatever convoluted scheme Callida is cooking up when you set me up to be some bumbling fool to be interrupted the moment I speak!"

Jarek, to his credit, didn't raise his voice to match, but he certainly wasn't happy. "It's not your job to know why - it's mine. You carry the package, I do the talking. Callida has reasons for everything and this is what she's said. You can complain all you want but that's just how it is."

Vyrion sighed. What use was there in anger? Jarek was the one person he had left, he couldn't lose him too.

"Then bring us to where we need to go," Vyrion muttered, "And I will be the glorified courier."

"That's the spirit!" He really was making it difficult.

They moved from the richly carpeted antechamber hallway, passing under a low doorway and into what turned out to be the main chamber.

If the outside of the pyramid had been the outer skin of some imposing creature, the inside was as if it had swallowed the grandest, most opulent palace Vyrion could possibly imagine; the walls were plastered with oil portraits of Ruin Lords past, relics encased in glass cases, and an endless amount framed runeblades. An impossibly large room flanked by massive corridors, the main chamber was a stone courtyard built around a glass vault, housing nearly manicured gardens and a quaint water fixture. The courtyard was all Vyrion could see, its multiple levels and unnatural corners like the enclosure for some terrible monster, hidden somewhere out of sight.

Above, lurking within the narrowing ceiling of the pyramid, was a room with a floor of tinted glass, looking down at all below. Within, Vyrion could sense a terrible mismatched collection of Ruin power, some force that dwarfed any he had ever encountered.

He knew without asking, that this was where the Ruined Council sat.

But despite the impressive surroundings, Vyrion liked nothing about it. It was grand, yes, but it held an undertone he didn't like, some nefarious element he couldn't put his finger on.

Walking along the outskirts of the vast open room, they passed dozens of battlegroups, Ruin Lords and guards, all drawn up into loose camps. There were so many tabards that Vyrion was quickly overwhelmed. A shattered bone on a backdrop of azure blue, a trio of lightning bolts on a dark night sky, black teeth grinning in some demented smile - to Vyrion it seemed like half of Thanaton's Ruin Lords were in attendance.

"Highlord Malus is certainly not taking any chances, massing his forces here," he mused aloud, "It's a wonder that the city isn't empty."

"I'm not surprised, peace is nothing but an idealist's foolish hope, everyone knows where this is going," Jarek said.

"Then what's the point of this?" Vyrion asked, frustratedly shaking the metal container he held. "Didn't you say this was a peace offering?"

"Victory is the best way to peace, isn't it?"

"And here I was thinking I was helping people," Vyrion sighed, already regretting coming.

Jarek's smile soured. "Don't complain. We are helping our master, as is our duty. Besides, I'm sure it's better than moaning about Krothus."

"Tread carefully, Jarek." That came out of nowhere, and it had only managed to leave Vyrion fuming.

Thankfully, Jarek backed down. Though he didn't apologise. "Consider me treading in a most careful manner."

Then Jarek pointed to some alcove nestled into the side of the cavernous courtyard, completely devoid of the same guard presence that permeated the rest of the Dark Pyramid. The quiet corner was home to a lone Ruin Lord, perched atop an opulent chair, looking like she had somewhere else to be.

"There she is," Jarek said, "I'll go speak with her and make sure the handover goes smoothly."

"And what am I supposed to do?"

"Keep watch. Maybe it will improve your mood somewhat."

But before Vyrion could give Jarek the smack he wished he had, the senior apprentice was already gone, shaking hands with the Ruin Lord in the chair moments later. What had gotten into him? Jarek seemed bitter, annoyed, and doing a poor job at hiding it.

"What a great use of my time," Vyrion muttered to himself, scanning the surrounding area. He wasn't even sure what he was meant to be looking for, Callida surely had the guards here in her pocket just as well as anywhere else.

It wasn't long before he started feeling vulnerable, standing out in the open, gawking at every passerby as he held whatever valuable payload he had been entrusted with. So he found a seat nearby, keeping Jarek and the other Ruined in his gaze as he continued to watch for something, whatever it may be.

Most of those walking past his lone seat were Ruin Lords, all varied in their appearance and station, but all of them certainly allied to Malus, at least on the surface. Why else would they be hunkered down here?

Not one paid Vyrion even a passing glance. He was clearly beneath their station. Occasionally some patrol would march by, but he didn't catch their attention either.

Only when a trimly uniformed Imperial Agent strut past did Vyrion catch his eye. It was only for a brief moment, but it felt deliberate, measured almost, like he had come down that way specifically to look at him. Whatever the reason was, Vyrion was immediately suspicious. He saw the Agent cast one last look behind, no doubt meant to check if Vyrion was still there, before casually entering a nearby door.

He turned his gaze back to Jarek, who was now explaining something to his contact off some piece of parchment. The Ruin Lord seemed much more engaged than before.

Vyrion was going to try and get closer for a better look when another Imperial Agent, her stride stiff and her hair cut short, walked past. This one waited until the very last second to flick her eyes Vyrion's way, only for the briefest of seconds. Vyrion glared back, watching as she went further past where the other agent had been, walking through a different door.

If he had been suspicious before, Vyrion was now completely paranoid. Did Imperial Intelligence know what they were doing? Was this some elaborate way for Callida to get rid of him?

In fact, Vyrion was so engrossed in these imaginary scenarios that he only noticed someone was sitting next to him when they spoke.

"The Master is pleased you have come."

Vyrion nearly jumped out of his skin, but settled for jumping out of his seat.

The stranger was adorned with a crown of horns in place of hair, their face emerging from their black robes like some ivory mask sculpted to perfection, androgynously beautiful and terrifyingly emotionless.

"You may sit," they said, patting the seat where Vyrion had been only moments ago.

"I think I'll stand."

"Suit yourself," they said, giving Vyrion a smile of razor sharp teeth.

Vyrion looked back and forth, checking for anyone else, possibly an ambush, but it was deserted; no guards, no Ruin Lords, no agents.

"The Master does not wish us to be disturbed," the stranger said, "So we will not."

"Who are you? What do you want?" Vyrion snapped, not appreciating the intrusion. He had enough to deal with today, even without some lunatic appearing at his side.

"I am only what the Master wills me to be, I only want what the Master wills me to," the stranger answered unhelpfully, "But this is not important, and our time is short."

"It really will be short if you don't tell me anything. Who is this Master? I already have a master."

"Indeed. The Master has already chosen you, whispers to you. You have heard it, yes?"

Vyrion frowned. "I don't know what you mean."

"You have, you have," the stranger said, waving a bizarre hand with only two fingers and a thumb, "The Master speaks few words, and only when it is needed. But now there are more words needed, too many, so I will tell you in his stead."

Vyrion's own thoughts faltered as the familiar presence filled his head, the same that had been watching him all these months. The same one that had used his mind as a second home, offering vague words and passing unrequited judgment.

The truth, it boomed, louder than Vyrion had ever heard it, shouting right into his ear.

The stranger was suddenly on their feet, their face a hair's width from Vyrion's own.

"You are at the center of a web of lies," they whispered, "It is wrapped around the Empire's throat, threatening to end the careful balance that the Council has forged. You must free the gray one and act - else you will be too late to stop it."

"Gray one?" Vyrion asked, trying to understand, "I have already been trying to find Krothus, but nobody knows where he is."

"And answers await you," the stranger said, baring their fangs once more.

Vyrion's runeblade was already in his hand. "I've had enough of being some pawn in whatever game is being played here. Whether its Victus, Callida, or you - I am through being told nothing but riddles. Either tell me what you want or leave."

To his surprise, the stranger just stepped back and bowed. "The choice is and has always been yours, the Master only informs."

"The choice to do what?" he pressed.

That earned a final fanged grin from the stranger. "Open it, or do not."

They tapped the featureless metal box with a single claw. A single line had appeared around its edge, a crack in its armor, a way to access what was held inside.

"Why? What's in it?" Vyrion asked.

But the stranger was gone.

Vyrion turned around, looking for some sort of sign of their departure, but there was none. The only others were Jarek and his contact, still engrossed in their parchment down the hall.

Vyrion sat back down, pulse running wild. The box lay next to him, the single line around its edge inviting, encouraging, him. Just one peek couldn't hurt, could it?

But he couldn't. Lord Callida would surely be able to tell if he opened it. And Jarek was right there, anyone could come by and see him.

It was his choice. That's what the stranger had said. But what could possibly be in it that would help him? Callida, or Jarek at the very least, thought it could put an end to the conflict that currently had the city balancing on a knife's edge. Vyrion hardly shared the same optimism.

Truth, the voice boomed again, more insistent.

He could do with a bit of truth. Vyrion looked around, and after seeing no agents or strangers of any kind, he did it. The lid slowly raised, a slight creak eeking out, the last gasp of the secret within.

Inside, nestled in a bed of silk, was a small metal pyramid and an inky black tome.

For a moment, Vyrion could only stare.

He didn't understand, the pyramid relic had been lost in the catacombs, crushed under tons of stone when the tomb had collapsed. He'd seen it. And Jarek had said that the tome had been hidden away in Victus' compound, impossible to find. How had Callida got ahold of them?

Maybe someone else had. His eyes briefly flicked to Jarek, finishing up a conversation that had been quite lengthy for a simple exchange of pleasantries. Vyrion looked back down at the box's contents. As far as he knew, these two items together had a very particular purpose, one that now only he and Jarek fully knew.

Anger bubbled up inside him as his mind latched on to the only possibility that made sense. He snapped the case shut as Jarek came over.

"Sorry to keep you waiting," Jarek said, all smiles, "But everything should be in place. Just give the case to me and I'll hand it over."

Vyrion didn't move. His jaw clenched in a silent fury..

"What?" Jarek seemed confused.

"You gave Callida the artifacts from Victus' ritual, didn't you?"

Vyrion said, "You went back and searched for them."

Jarek shook his head. "Vyrion, please. Why would I do that?"

Vyrion felt like he was going mad. There was nobody else who would have known, it had to be Jarek.

"I know you did. Don't lie to me. You gave the most dangerous woman in the city two artifacts of limitless power."

Jarek let a long sigh leave his lips as his smile slowly deflated. His eyes, normally masked with a twinkle of mischievous charm, hardened. His mouth, usually just on the cusp of twisting into a light-hearted smirk, set into a heavy frown. He now looked like a completely different person.

"You weren't supposed to open that. Callida was testing you."

"I don't care. You still haven't answered my question."

But Jarek just looked at him. Vyrion felt his face grow hot as tears swelled in his eyes.

"Answer me, damn you!"

"I did it," Jarek said quietly, "But I don't expect you to understand."

"And what is there to understand? That our master hadn't been dead for more than a few hours before you decided to gift Callida the artifacts that killed him on a silver platter? That you deliberately kept this from me, only to use it as part of some test?"

Jarek looked like he was choosing his words very carefully, his eyes coldly evaluating Vyrion, like he were nothing more than some deviant equation that required a different approach.

"I was securing our positions, ensuring Callida would actually take us in. It wasn't a guarantee, but it was the best we had."

"And how far in advance did she know about this bargain?" Vyrion pressed, "She had enough time for a fucking parade when we got there didn't she?"

"Vyrion, calm yourself, it's not like that."

"Then why were you so insistent on joining Callida the moment Victus was dead?"

Jarek's frown deepened. "I planned ahead, that's all."

"And I bet you know where Krothus is too, don't you?"

Jarek let out a frustrated groan. "Like I've already told you, I don't know where he is. Callida sent Krothus away, and that's all I know. Why are we even talking about him? You can't even focus on one thing without it all somehow turning back to Krothus, it's exhausting."

Liar, the voice in Vyrion's head said, rumbling through his skull.

"Where is he?" Vyrion asked again, his hand wrapping tightly around his runeblade.

Jarek stared at him in silence, a dark cloud passing over his face. Then he blew up.

"You are obsessed! You are obsessed with this grey brute, and ignoring all the good you have *right in front of you!*" Jarek shouted, frantically jabbing his thumb into his chest, "*I* secured our positions, *I* stopped Victus' ritual, and *I* have been trying to protect you. But no, all you care about is *Krothus*! You even sleep in his fucking bed."

He was suddenly right in Vyrion's face.

"For years, I have clawed my way up the ladder. But for everything I did right, Victus, the bumbling, senile fool, would send me sliding right back to the bottom. I'm glad he's dead. And I'm glad Krothus is gone too. They're cut from the same cloth, two idiots who don't know a damn thing about how to survive in this city, trying to drag us down every chance they get."

It took every shred of willpower Vyrion possessed not to break down, and he hated himself for it. He wanted to feel nothing, to make his heart stone, to tell Jarek to go to hell and walk away. But he couldn't.

"So you're not going to tell me," he said, voice shaky.

"No," Jarek growled. He strode over to the box and yanked it out of Vyrion's grip.

Vyrion had so many things he wanted to say. He wanted to scream, to shout, to swear, to curse his name. Maybe he just wanted to understand. But he did none of these things.

Instead, he just walked away, cursing himself as a coward with every step.

Jarek pounded off in the other direction, cloaked in rage.

How had it come to this? Jarek had been someone he thought he could trust, someone he told everything to. But clearly it hadn't gone both ways. Vyrion felt like a curtain had been drawn away, revealing the true man underneath, someone just as power hungry as every other Ruined in this city. Was that his future, too? The Ruin was in all of them, molding their bodies, marking them with its favor - who was to say it didn't didn't do more?

It was power manifest, but there was never enough of it. Every Ruined wanted more. Needed more. Now, this desperate desire had resulted in Callida possessing the relics that led to Victus's downfall, two objects of unknown power. Vyrion didn't want to think about what she would do with them, but he knew it wasn't good. And whatever the consequences, Jarek was responsible for it all.

Vyrion, feeling like an empty shell of himself, made his way back through the vastness of the main chamber, past the guards, and the Ruin Lords, and everything else. Into the gardens.

There he found a bench by a quiet pond, surrounded by reeds, perfectly still. He sat there for a while. At one with thoughts, at one with the Ruin, for all it was worth. But the peace, much like anywhere else, wasn't to last.

"Excuse me. Vyrion?"

He looked up. It was the two Imperial Agents he'd seen before.

"What do you want?"

The woman handed him a neatly bundled stack of papers. "We might be able to help you."

Vyrion caught two words on the front page.

Deephold.

Krothus.

Chapter 25
Allies

The grasping claws of the jungle canopy scratched up against the Donovan's metal form as it descended through wood and vine, snapping branches and setting their denizens howling. Only when the landing gear squelched into the soggy soil did Inissa finally relax. Flying was hardly her favorite activity, but that was to be expected when her first trip involved climbing up a vine mid-air.

Victus stood next her in the cargo bay, an unmoving hill of muscle in the shadows of the emptied hold. He had said nothing the entire trip. And with Captain Fareese piloting above, it had been a silent, lonely journey, exactly the opposite of what Inissa wanted. She had felt worse and worse the further into the jungle they got, each second taking her closer to her former home. To her mother.

The best Inissa could do was take a nibble of a blueberry tart every time it crossed her mind. She was on her fifth.

The cargo bay ramp let out a hiss as it fell into the mud below, just as Fareese's boots could be heard clacking down the ladder behind them.

"Those trees better not have scratched up my ship," she muttered, "The Navy won't reimburse me for off-hours damages."

Victus glared at her. "I must have given you a small fortune over your years of service, did you squander it with dice and whoring like every other pilot in the Imperial Navy?"

Fareese gave him a wink as she ripped a piercer off the rack in the cargo bay. "If only I knew."

She shoved it into Inissa's hands before grabbing another for herself.

"Have you used one of these before?" Fareese asked. She held a piercer bolt clip in her teeth as she looped a few more clips into slots on her belt.

"Once," Inissa said. On one of the worst nights of her life.

"Better than nothing," the Captain said, handing her a clip, "You know where you're going, Victus?"

"I do."

"Good. Lead the way."

Without waiting for either of them, he strode off the ramp and into the jungle in only a few steps. Inissa and Fareese right behind.

"He was a lot easier to follow with one leg," Fareese complained.

Inissa, already feeling the nauseous effects of her tart therapy mixing with a sudden burst of speed, tended to agree.

Victus continued his breakneck speed through the foliage, with Inissa and Fareese trailing him like hunters at the heel of some gigantic bloodhound. Unfamiliar sounds pressed in from all sides; the constant symphony of buzzing insects; the accompanying harmony of singing birds, and some deep rumble of something larger in the distance, leaving Inissa silently praying that Victus was not leading them into something dangerous.

So dense was the jungle that Inissa didn't notice Victus had stopped until she crashed right into him.

She bounced away in spectacular fashion, but as the ground rushed up to meet her, she stopped. A crimson claw held her tight. Fareese stopped just next to them with significantly more grace.

Victus held up a single claw to his tusked lips, urging silence. Then, still holding Inissa, kicking her legs about as she tried to regain their footing, he slowly parted the vines and leaves in front of him.

Forty paces behind the wall of greenery was the entrance to the Nightshadow Grotto. It was just as Inissa had remembered it; an otherwise forgettable collection of stones piled around the lip of the crater, with a winding path lurking just behind. A handful of orkathi warriors stood in front of it, keeping watch with golden weapons and crude shields at the ready. But, as Inissa's scrambling feet finally found a suitable perch, she saw what Victus had stopped them for.

Just in front of them lay a full platoon of Imperial soldiers, their black armor camouflaged in a thick layer of jungle grime, their piercers trained on the warriors ahead. Inissa counted at least two dozen lying in ambush among the ferns, enough to easily overpower her and the others. But that wasn't the worst part.

Dozens of masks, her mother's mask, grinning at her from every tabard they wore. A nightmare come to life.

The only good thing out of all of this, if Inissa could even call it that, was that none of her mother's soldiers had noticed them yet.

So the trio stayed perfectly still - Victus watching intently, Fareese holding her piercer in a firing position, and Inissa's shaking fingers threatening to drop her own weapon and give them all away. Emperor above, she needed to calm down. They still had a chance. Sure they were outnumbered, severely outgunned, but there was always a chance.

After a while, one of the Nightshadow warriors walked a bit closer, more a boy than a warrior, judging by his small stature and stubby tusks. The soldiers didn't move. He casually scanned the trees, his yellow eyes passing right over the soldiers, over the foliage hiding Inissa and the others, nothing seeming to catch his interest. He started turning around.

One of the soldiers adjusted himself; a tiny, miniscule movement, no more than the stretching of a numb shoulder. But it was enough. The boy warrior stopped, looking back into the jungle.

The rest of the soldiers were still, but Inissa could sense their anxiety, their eagerness. They were waiting for just the right moment.

The orkathi boy took a hesitant step towards them. One of the soldiers raised his piercer.

There was a click to Inissa's right. The soldier's helmet exploded outwards as a bolt smashed through it.

Fareese unloaded the rest of her clip with lightning speed at whatever target she could find.

The rest of the soldiers followed suit, some shooting at the orkathi, others panicking, shooting into the jungle all around them like the trees themselves were on the march.

The orkathi boy ran. Ran far and fast, hollering as he did. The rest of the warriors charged.

One of them, tentacles dangling down past his waist, took a bolt to the shoulder as if it were a gust of wind, ignoring it completely and cleaving his axe through some unlucky soldier's chestplate. Another, a gold ring through his nose, took two bolts to the chest and collapsed, but not before he had ripped a man's arm right out of its socket. A third managed to stick a soldier clean through with a weapon that looked closer to a log than a spear.

Everything else was lost in the chaotic whirlwind of battle.

Fareese would keep firing until she was empty, before slapping in another clip. Victus charged out of their hiding place, using his new mighty strength to snap a soldier's neck. Inissa could only stand there, willing herself to pull the trigger. But her hands refused to cooperate, too busy trying to shake themselves off her arms entirely.

She found herself staring at a bloodstained tabard as the sounds of battle faded from her mind. The crude mask embroidered on the fabric stared back.

Somehow, her mother had known. She must have. She sent these men to bring her back. Inissa could already hear her mother's raspy voice, echoing out from her mask.

"Now, now, Inissa. Did you think I would forget? Did you think I would forgive? Nobody gets away from me, not even you."

A hand grabbed her shoulder.

"*No!*" Inissa shrieked, whipping around. Her breath was short, her head pounding.

She didn't even check who it was.

It was a reflex, something deep within her mind, like when an animal, no matter how domesticated, reveals its true nature. The Ruin embraced her, drawn by emotions raw and unfiltered. Then she struck.

As if he were a discarded sheet of paper, the soldier in front of her crumpled inwards. Bones shattered, tendons snapped, organs exploded.

What used to be a human was left a horrific puddle of bent metal and lumpy tissue.

He didn't even have time to scream.

Inissa felt sick. The Ruin rushed back out of her, its interest diminished as all her aggression evaporated.

She couldn't even look at what she'd done. Inissa forced her eyes away, looking for something, anything, else.

Someone stood just in front of her. The orkathi boy had come back, a mob of Nightshadow reinforcements in tow. Inissa tried to smile at him, but he made no move to return it. In fact, his eyes wide and his face pale, he looked on the verge of vomiting.

They stared at each other for a moment. Then Inissa emptied a wave of half-digested blueberry tarts into the jungle grass, and everything went dark.

By the time Inissa woke, the skirmish was over. Human and orkathi bodies alike were strewn about, the newest additions to the jungle foliage, victorious Nightshadow warriors sifting through them for whatever loot they could find. Victus, or Spinebreaker, was having an animated conversation with an older orkathi covered in scars and golden trinkets just in front of the entrance to the grotto.

A bloodstained hand suddenly appeared in front of her.

"You alright, kid?" Fareese asked, spattered with so much mud and blood that it looked like she had rolled around in it on purpose.

"Feeling great," Inissa lied, her head spinning as she was yanked to her feet.

Fareese took just one look at Inissa's face and sighed. Digging deep into her pockets, she pulled out a rag only marginally less grimey than the rest of her.

"Here, wipe off your mouth before you scare someone. It looks like you ate a bucket of blue paint."

Inissa felt her cheeks burn. She snatched the dirty cloth and did as she was told, wiping her face down so hard that it hurt. But when she tried to return the rag, Fareese was already gone, walking back to Victus with her piercer lazily slung over her shoulders. Inissa followed, careful to avoid any of the suspiciously blue puddles on the ground. She left the rag in the mud.

"It doesn't matter, I need to speak to Headcleaver," Victus growled, sounding not at all happy with how his conversation had been going. He carried some spiked spear, no doubt taken from one of the fallen.

"And like I said," the older orkathi said, "I will not take you to see him with these outsiders in tow. Fira strikes us day and night, her spies are everywhere. Times have changed, Spinebreaker. "

"Changed?" Victus scoffed, "Do not play me for a fool, Ironscar. I haven't been gone for more than a few months."

"A few months was enough to change you, that much is sure," Ironscar said, looking over Victus like he had sprouted a third arm, "I hardly recognise you. And who are these strangers?"

"They are friends of the gray one, who has sent me to carry a message to our Chieftain. Its urgency cannot be understated," Victus said, then stopped for a second, like he had said something wrong., "It's important, I mean."

Ironscar laughed. "You've spent too much time with the Imperials, you're starting to sound like one. But if the gray one has sent these two, then they will be allowed in, at least until Headcleaver speaks with them. He has been expecting news for some time."

"I wonder if Krothus knows we're his *friends*," Fareese asked to no one in particular.

Inissa could only imagine his objection to such a moniker for any of them, especially Victus.

Ironscar moved aside, his wide frame unveiling the pathway beyond. "You can find him in the Chieftain's tent."

"Thank you, old friend," Victus said, before giving a nod to Inissa and Fareese and beginning their descent.

Inissa had remembered the interior of the Nightshadow Grotto being full of orkathi celebrating their recent victory; drums, fires and feasting. But now, that seemed nothing but a faraway dream. The place was nearly deserted, the occasional orkathi face briefly emerged out of the shadows of the caves, only to fade away when their curiosity was sated. The rest were nowhere to be seen. Debris; a mixture of dented metal, shattered wood, and broken piercer bolts was scattered across both the path and the rock faces of the grotto as though some terrible storm had passed through.

"I thought you said a few hundred warriors lived here," Fareese asked.

"They do," Victus said, but even he seemed unsure.

"Mother was never going to let them get away unscathed," Inissa said. Say one thing about her mother, she was not the forgiving type.

"Lovely woman, Lord Fira," Fareese said, "A paragon of virtue."

"Don't remind me," Inissa said, desperately wishing she had brought more food with her.

"Lucky for us, she is most likely far away from here," Victus said, "Lord Fira knows that the time and manpower required to fully stamp out the Nightshadow is significant. The jungle itself is their home, any campaign would take months, if not years, to get any kind of result. All for a tribe that is no threat to a Ruin Lord of her power, and therefore no threat to her holdings here."

"Unless she is no longer there," Inissa said quietly.

"Correct," Victus said with a nod of his tentacled head, "She's no doubt been summoned to Thanaton by Highlord Malus, along with the majority of her forces for the battle to come. Her remaining troops have likely been told to keep the Nightshadow contained to their home and slowly whittle their numbers to a manageable level."

A manageable level. Inissa looked at the depressed state of the grotto, the overgrown grass and half-burnt hovels built into the rock, wondering how many of these orkathi would have to die for her mother to deem them *manageable*. When she was a child, they had been a constant presence at the compound, laboring day and night to construct the massive walls that now kept the jungle tamed. Inissa had never been permitted to speak to them.

"Do not fool these creatures into thinking we are their equals," her mother had said.

Equals was an amusing notion to come from such a witch. Inissa doubted that any of the Nightshadow would have chained their children up and left them as some demon's plaything.

She saw a curious orkathi child peek out of a doorway as they walked past, trying to catch a glimpse of the newcomers, only for their mother to wrap them in a close embrace and drag them back into the safety of the cave-hut, the child giggling all the way. Equal or not, Inissa couldn't help but feel a pang of jealousy.

Before long, they arrived at the bone foundations of the Chieftain's hut, nestled next to the pool of water at the foot of the grotto. Where the pool had once been so pure as to be nearly translucent, it now looked in a sorry state, murky and overloaded with floating debris. Victus gave it a thoughtful frown before pushing through the tent flap, Inissa and Fareese close behind.

Inside, the Chieftain and his shaman sat on the floor, looking over tablets, writings, maps, all illuminated by the light of a dwindling fire. Headcleaver's axe rested off to one side, flanked by two of the Chieftain's huge bodyguards.

"Spinebreaker! It's good to see you," said the young chieftain through a tusked smile. He got to his feet and closed the distance in two strides.

Victus clasped his forearm. "And you, Lokk."

"Tell me, how are our Ruined allies faring?"

Soultotem's enthusiasm was notably absent. But even Headcleaver's expression soured when he saw the two humans among them.

"And why have you brought these two?"

Before Victus could give any sort of explanation, Soultotem hobbled forward, her arms gripping her staff tightly, her aged eyes seeming to pierce through flesh and bone.

"What has happened to you, Spinebreaker?"

Inissa felt a knot in her stomach, one that desperately called out for food she didn't currently possess. Fareese lit up a smokestick.

"Nothing," growled Victus.

"Soultotem, stop with your prodding," Headcleaver snapped, "He looks no different."

"But he is," she said gravely, her tentacled hair shivering. Her staff began to emit a soft crimson glow and Inissa felt a small ripple in the Ruin as Soultotem probed the orkathi in front of her.

The glow faded and the old shaman's face became grim indeed.

"He is Spinebreaker, but possessed by another."

That was all it took for Headcleaver to grab his axe, his bodyguards instantly following suit.

Inissa gulped. Fareese took another drag of her smokestick.

"What is this then?" Headcleaver snarled, "Fira's latest assassination attempt?"

Victus sighed and set his salvaged weapon on the floor, before raising his claws in as unthreatening of a manner as he could. "If it is, then it would be a spectacularly poor one."

"You seem to think possessing one of my warriors is funny, is that it?" Headcleaver spat.

Inissa took a step back. The Chieftain's hands were strangling the handle of his axe, his eyes burning wild. Of all the people for Victus to be bargaining with, a son whose father had been possessed and warped beyond recognition was not a great option.

But Victus, whatever his reasons, still valued his chances.

"I am still Spinebreaker, that hasn't changed," he said softly, "But, now, I am more. Through a coincidence, a one in a million chance, a ritual that both of us were involved in failed. My body was destroyed in the process, but my spirit was not. Now, this body hosts us both."

"Sorcery," one of the bodyguards muttered, her brow furrowed so deeply that Inissa wouldn't have been surprised if they had just learned the word at that very moment.

Headcleaver, for all of Victus' explanation, looked seconds away from violence, but Victus continued, his words pouring out like a great river bursting its banks, unable to be contained.

"Spinebreaker's spirit remains just as well as mine. And, though he may not speak too often, we are one. And as one, we came to you because we need the help of our Chieftain. There is no assassination, nor is there any reason for any of us to come to blows. I should have been truthful from the beginning, its true, but-"

"Silence!" Headcleaver shouted.

His great chest was heaving with the effort of what Inissa could only assume was resisting the urge to chop Victus down where he stood. And she could hardly fault him, her own reaction had hardly been understanding.

"Who are you then?" the Chieftain whispered, "Because despite all your drivel, you haven't told me."

Victus sighed. "You're right. Knowing your hatred of Ruin Lords I figured it a fact best not to mention."

"A *Ruin Lord* thinks he can possess one of my warrior's bodies and pass it off as some miracle?" Headcleaver spat, "I've heard enough,"

"This is exactly what I meant." All Victus could do now was take a hesitant step back as Headcleaver advanced upon him, murder in his eyes.

The Ruin flickered once more, Inissa felt it. Barely perceptible, like miniscule ripples of a pebble thrown in a vast lake, but it was there. Soultotem was reaching out. Some invisible tether of energy went from shaman to Ruin Lord, a feeler desperately searching for something to grasp.

The moment it found Victus, a link jolted to life, an explosion of Ruinous energy that invisibly erupted through the room, passing through Inissa's mind like the sudden remembering of a moment long forgotten.

Images blasted through Inissa's mind, a hazy nightmare of shapes and voices. Victus's compound burning. Tons of stone crashing down upon some altar. Spinebreaker and Krothus, knee deep in muck, cleaving through muddy foes.

Each scene was revealed only briefly, but it was enough for Inissa to realize this was not her nightmare, but someone else's. The further she delved into these scenes, the more this cemented itself.

She saw herself, training blades clashing in vain against Spinebreaker's defenses. Victus' one-sided duels with Vyrion in a grassy courtyard. Spinebreaker, embracing Headcleaver and Ironscar, celebrating the successful hunt of some monstrous creature. Lord

Victus at the head of a vast host, endless ranks of soldiers hanging on his every word.

The lives of both on display.

A final vision lingered just a second longer than the rest, like hesitating on the final page of a good book. A woman and child, one a light haired Imperial, the other a small orkathi with stubby tusks, laughed and smiled in a singular moment of joy. But they faded away like dust in the wind.

Inissa felt like her heart had been plucked from her chest, a sense of loss so intense it threatened to bring her to her knees.

Then, as quickly as the connection was forged, it shattered, and Inissa was instantly dragged back to the waking world. Soultotem had seen enough.

"Lokk, wait!" The shaman forced herself between the Chieftain and his prey. It seemed like no one else but Inissa and Soultotem had seen what had just unfolded, even Victus remained unmoved.

"Get out of the way," Headcleaver growled.

"He speaks the truth, I've seen it."

Headcleaver's axe lowered a few inches. "What?"

"It is as he said, two spirits within one body," she said.

"Impossible. Only lies."

But before Soultotem could plead her case, someone else beat her to it. Victus dropped to one knee.

"I may have been a Ruin Lord, once," he said, his voice hoarse, "But no longer. My connection to the Ruin is broken, my power base shattered, my reputation in tatters. Now I am only myself."

Then he looked up at Headcleaver. "But know I am also Nightshadow. I have performed the sacred rituals in the Crystal Caves, I have carved my name into the roots at the heart of the jungle, all with the ancestors as my witness. And now I come now to you, my Chieftain, my friend, to beg for help."

Inissa reflected on his words. His connection to the Ruin - shattered? How was that possible? She had suspected something amiss before, seeing as he had not called upon it a single time in their time together, but she had assumed it was far more to do with lying low than a lack of ability. To be cut off from the Ruin was inconceivable, a fear that, until now, was an entirely unfamiliar thought to her.

The Ruin was not something she could imagine losing. It was a sixth sense, another pair of eyes and ears and hands, a way to see and feel and sense the world around her. No matter how terrible her tortures had been under her mother's direction, the Ruin had given her an inner strength, a hidden way to reach out and see the world beyond that dark hell of a room. For it to be taken away would be no different than being blinded or deafened.

Headcleaver just stared for a moment, any trace of certainty long gone. His bodyguards mirrored his hesitation, their weapons lowered and loose in their hands.

Inissa held her breath. Fareese took another unconcerned drag from her smokestick.

Eventually, the Nightshadow chieftain gently brushed Soultotem aside and knelt down in front of Victus.

"I may not know you, Ruin Lord, but I know Spinebreaker. So I speak now to him alone." He reached out a thick arm wrapped in black tattoos, grasping Spinebreaker's shoulder. "You have been a noble member of our tribe. And a good friend, even before I became Chieftain. I was proud to have you represent us at the grey one's side, and I am proud now to see you have the strength of will to keep your mind intact despite this sorcery. So I will help you."

"Thank you, Lokk," Spinebreaker said, clasping his forearm.

The Nightshadow Chieftain then gave him a hideous tusked grin, "Now tell me everything."

Headcleaver, to his credit, understood the situation quickly. Krothus imprisoned, with Lord Callida set to wreak havoc through the city in pursuit of her goals, threatening the Empire itself. But he had not seemed truly interested until Victus explained a key aspect; Lord Fira was expected to be in Thanaton. If she were to be preparing for battle, then it was a battle that Headcleaver wished to be part of. So under his command, the Nightshadow lent their aid.

Hours after, Inissa sat with Victus and Soultotem around the final embers of a dying fire, sheltered from the evening rain in an alcove near the top of the grotto. Fareese, out of smokesticks and patience both, had already gone back to ready the ship.

Below them, a steady stream of Nightshadow warriors shambled up the winding path out of the grotto. They had heeded Headcleaver's call in droves, filing out of the caves like an army of overgrown crimson ants, savage axes and golden ornaments glinting in the rain. But despite their impressive appearance, Inissa could only watch with a burden of dread. She knew what foe they marched towards better than most.

"If this doesn't work," she said, "This grotto might be empty for a long while."

"We are no strangers to war," Soultotem said, peering out into the rain as though it were a window into the past itself. "I have heard the call many times, and I expect it will be heard countless more long after I'm gone. Our future, our children, will be cradled safely in the Crystal Caves, and the ancestors will watch over them until we return from our journey. The Nightshadow tribe will remain, as we always have."

Inissa wished she shared Soultotem's optimism. She wasn't sure how effective these orkathi ancestors would be at minding children, if at all, but what did she know?

If Victus had any thoughts of his own, he kept them silent. He sat at the dwindling fire, a silent mountain, staring down into those glowing embers with a look of mournful indifference. Hardly the reaction one would expect from successfully recruiting the help he had so desperately sought.

Inissa had already attempted to speak with him, at least to take his mind off whatever was torturing him so, but her words might as well have been silent for all the good they did. Silent shrugs were the only answers she received. But as any other teenager, stubbornness came easily to her.

"Staring at that fire won't repair your connection to the Ruin, you know."

His eyes, yellow and predatory, briefly flicked over to her. That was progress.

"Am I wrong?"

He huffed through his tusks. "Unfortunately not."

Inissa smiled, a gesture he did not return. "But you do have all your limbs now. That's a change to be thankful for, no?"

Victus glanced down at the tree trunk of a leg he now possessed, then gave it a tap, as if checking it was still there. "A cruel joke, nothing more. When I gain what I desire, I lose something far more valuable, as it always has been. A curse of one step forward, two steps back. A curse that has now made me an old man, taking up space in another's mind and body, with the Ruin nothing more than a sad, distant memory."

"It may not be permanent. You don't know that."

"Does it matter? My failures are far greater than just one botched ritual. The Empire crumbles as a direct result of my disregarded reputation, no one has listened to my warnings, my pleading. Even now, our allies heeded my call only because of the body I now reside in."

"We can still make a difference."

He snorted. "You speak with the optimism of the young. We will try, make no mistake, but we cannot stop Callida with two hundred warriors. Not even with a thousand. This is nothing more than our final gamble, a last roll of the dice to unbalance the scales." Then Victus sighed and drew his ragged cloak closer around his broad shoulders, like keeping warm would bring back everything he had lost.

Inissa felt an anger rise up in her. They had come all the way here, and now, when he got what he wanted, Victus was acting as if they had already failed.

Soultotem watched him, lines etched deep on her face. If she wanted to have a go at it instead, then she would be Inissa's guest, her patience was already wearing thin.

"I am far from young," the shaman rasped, "And far from optimistic. But until you let go of the pain you feel, all those regrets that burden you, you will never become the man you once were."

And before Victus could retort with what was most certainly an insult, Soultotem pushed herself up and hobbled out into the rain with a twinkle in her eye.

She joined the slow-moving column of Nightshadow warriors and disappeared.

For a long time, neither Inissa nor Victus said anything, the only sounds were the steady footfalls of orkathi warriors and the never ending patter of falling rain. Inissa felt that brief flare of frustration faded, replaced with a tiredness, a want for this all to be over, a need for a quiet existence free from all this.

Victus eventually looked toward her, his tentacles flat and unmoving, his tusked jaw set in a thoughtful frown. "Tell me, and be truthful. Can one good deed rewrite so many mistakes?"

She blinked, not expecting such a question. Why he thought that she was the authority on such matters was beyond her; she was no Ruin Lord, not yet at least, and her experience at life had so far been nothing but brief and chaotic. Was he just searching for an easy source of reassurance?

"I don't know," she said eventually, "I guess it depends."

"On what?"

She thought for a moment. "On the mistakes that need correcting. On the good you bring trying to fix it. Everything."

She mentally kicked herself. An unhelpful answer which didn't actually address anything, and one Victus didn't seem satisfied with, as he just went back to staring off into the rain.

Fine. She took a deep breath and gave it another go. "When I was trapped in that dark room at my mother's compound, host to a demon, I wished every day that someone would kill me, put me out of my misery. But when Krothus came, he spared my life. He freed me. I don't know what he's done in the past, but to me, that action alone was enough to make up for all of it."

That at least got him to look at her, the cage of his frown slowly opening up.

She continued, sensing her moment. "Mistakes are only in the past, the future can rewrite all of them."

And for the first time in what seemed like weeks, in a wet cave in the jungle rain, Lord Victus smiled.

Chapter 26

Breakout

Vyrion struggled against the restraints biting into his wrists, fidgeting in vain as the gargantuan metal bird of a skyship that had brought him there climbed back into the air. He could barely see; the interior of the fissure around the Dark Pyramid was home to a thick fog that seemed to block out all but the slightest sliver of light from above.

A young man in guardsman plate approached, his torch scarcely cutting through the haze. He wore no helmet, probably to protect what little visibility he had in the darkness, and kept scratching at some rash on his neck like some flea-ridden cat.

"What is this? I wasn't notified of any prisoner transfers."

Vyrion's captor looked down his nose at the guard, briefly combing what little was left of his hair before speaking.

"I didn't have time to notify anyone ahead of time, as this was an urgent, pressing transfer," he said, his chinless mouth barely bothering to open with every word, "This Ruined had a direct hand in countless murders against the Code, so I hope you understand that he is extraordinarily dangerous."

The guard paused his scratching to move the torch close to Vyrion's face, peering through the flickering flames as if looking for evidence of the claim. Satisfied with nearly burning Vyrion's nose off, he moved the torch away once more, being sure to catch a glimpse of the other man's rank on his uniform before doing so.

"I'll still need to see some transfer papers. We're on high alert today with the Council hearing above."

It was an unlucky coincidence that the day Vyrion finally arrived at the Deephold was when Lord Callida was having her 'peace' negotiations with Highlord Malus. From what he had heard, the Council had insisted upon it, a discussion to keep from further conflict in the city. But he strongly doubted Callida would back down due to a mere conversation.

There was a brief silence, only broken by guard's incessant picking of his rash. "If you want, I can bring you to the warden, Captain...? "

"Farke. Captain Farke," Vyrion's captor said, still playing his part well, "And there will be no need for that, corporal. I've been insulted enough already, the warden will hear of this regardless."

That got the guard's attention. "Look, like I said, you have to have transfer papers or I can't let you in. Warden's orders. I'm sorry, sir."

Farke lowered his voice to a hissing whisper. "I don't give a shit about your warden's orders. Do you want me to bring up your insubordination to Commander Noruss ? What about General O'zel? I have friends in high places that are *very* interested in this transfer being confirmed, one word to them and your career is over. Or worse."

The guard looked terrified. "I-Im sorry, sir. We can go talk to the warden, then."

"No," Farke spat, his few remaining strands of hair rattling loose, "I've heard enough. Hail down another skyship for me. You'll be hearing from your warden soon enough."

The guard quickly cast a concerned glance back into the haze behind him, then whipped back around, panic plain on his face. "Fine! I'll let him through, just stay quiet about it. If anyone asks, you showed me your papers."

Farke's expression shifted immediately, smiling like nothing had happened and leaving Vyrion wondering if he had a part time job in theater. "Good. Lead the way, corporal."

The guard turned and began cutting through the smog with his torch. Farke gave Vyrion a nervous look, dabbing a cloth on his now sweaty forehead, before following. That was the Farke Vyrion recognised, hidden under all that temporary bite and bluster.

The mist steadily thinned as they approached the entrance of the Deephold itself, a small array of torches forming an oasis of light in the dark. The platoon of guards there paid them no mind, staying behind their bolt thrower turrets and fortifications, leaving some officer to talk with the guard Vyrion and Farke were following.

The Deephold was supposedly one of the most secure prisons in the Empire, but entering had been going smoothly, at least so far. Vyrion didn't know much about it; only that Krothus was one of the countless prisoners relegated to these dark dungeons. His unseen ally within Imperial Intelligence had given him very limited information, but enough for Vyrion to formulate a plan, one that involved calling on a favor owed. Even as an unwilling accomplice, Farke had proved useful thus far.

After some agitated, hushed words and a variety of rapid nods, they were waved ahead. A mighty metal gate crawled aside to reveal a tiny doorway wide enough to only allow for a single man. They squeezed in past the rashy guard, the edges of the door pinning Vyrion's arms to his side as though it were final inspection before letting him through.

Inside he found himself on a raised metal walkway, looking over an endless cramped maze of corridors. Vast rows of identical doors stretched up and beyond in all directions, the distant torches of patrolling guards like far away stars in a sea of dimness.

Their rashy guard wasted no time, leaving a trail of flakey skin as he led them down and off the walkway to one of the identical ranks of doors. Numbers and letters were scrawled across each of the reinforced entryways; *AB823*, then *CB1132*, no rhyme or reason to any of the designations.

Disinterested guards passed them by. Occasionally one might toss a half-hearted salute Farke's way, but otherwise they might as well have been invisible. Vyrion kept his eyes peeled for Imperial Agents, but they were nowhere to be seen.

Not for the first time, he found himself wondering if this was merely an elaborate way for Callida to get rid of him. It wouldn't take much effort; convince a few agents to give him incorrect information, and let him blunder his way through the rest. A fittingly disappointing end to a disappointing tenure as a Ruined, one that would not be missed by anyone.

Especially not by Jarek. Not anymore.

They stopped at some cell virtually identical to any other, a boring hunk of iron with a meaningless label on the front. The guard struggled with an extraordinarily large ring of keys before eventually unlocking the door, sending a series of clunks echoing down the hall.

"Right," the guard said, resuming his scratching, "This is where he'll be spending the rest of his days, I can assure you of that."

"Excellent," Farke said, sounding all too eager about that.

But just as he was about to grab Vyrion, the guard turned back to Farke, "When was the last time you gave him blocking elixir? He looks very alert."

For good measure he gave Vyrion a rough slap across the face. As a test, or just because he had wanted to, the resulting stinging pain was just the same.

"Thanks, asshole" Vyrion snarled.

"Oh," Farke said, frowning as if he were remembering a distasteful joke, "I provided some only just before we arrived. He is still blocked, I can assure you."

He, too, gave Vyrion a slap across the face. Whether he was committing to the part, or just because he wanted to, the resulting throbbing pain was just the same.

Vyrion retorted with an angry glare, but Farke hardly paid him a glance.

The guard just shrugged. "Another dose, just to be safe. We have to remove his restraints before I leave him in there, and I'm only doing that if he's blocked properly." He was already pulling some panel out of the wall, revealing a rack of vials filled to the brim with some vile looking liquid. In one swift movement the guard racked his torch and pulled out a vial, uncorking it to reveal a terrible acidic stench.

Vyrion and Farke shared a quick look. Blocker elixir is the last thing he needed right now.

Farke cleared his throat. How can I be assured that he won't escape from here? My superiors are concerned."

The guard stopped, holding the vial inches away from Vyrion's face, the odor making his eyes water.

"You're joking, right, sir?" he said, smiling to reveal a lovely set of blackened teeth to accompany his neck rash, "This is the Deephold, nobody escapes from here. Not even Ruined." He transferred his revolting smile over to Vyrion. "Yes, not even you."

His fingers were suddenly mashing Vyrion's cheeks together, forcing his mouth open like he were a troublesome toddler refusing a meal. The vial swooped in. Vyrion twisted and struggled, trying to reach out to the Ruin, to mold it to his defense. But he couldn't. It somehow felt distant, faded, like its normally vast ocean had all dried up. The cuffs bit into his wrists as he tried to shake them off.

"Wait!" Farke said suddenly.

The guard stopped his manhandling of Vyrion's jaw and looked up.

There was a dull thunk and he dropped to the floor with all the grace of a bag of bricks. Blood pooled around him, oozing out of the bolt lodged in his heart.

Farke gently coughed and holstered his piercer pistol. He retrieved his comb and began to tame his rebellious strands, his hands trembling.

Vyrion blinked as the piercer shot seemed to echo endlessly through the Deephold, amplified with every passing second.

"Emperor above, Farke. Could you do that silently?"

"I panicked, okay?" snapped the disgraced Captain. "I didn't know what to do. I already told you I never wanted to come here."

Vyrion shook his bound hands behind his back. "It doesn't matter - the restraints, quickly!"

Farke did as he was told and started emptying his pockets, fishing for the key. Why he didn't have it to hand was anyone's guess.

A low gong rumbled through the hall, rattling Vyrion's bones. Another bell joined its chorus, and another, until the entire hold was echoing the same steady beat.

"For the Emperor's sake," Vyrion muttered. His plan was failing spectacularly.

He could hear the key scraping against the restraints, desperately waiting for them to find their bearing.

"Can you hurry up?" he shouted, struggling to be heard over the bells.

"I'm trying!" Farke's shaky hands were fumbling the key up and down the restraints.

A series of thunks rose above the drone of the alarm, the clunking of moving metal. Then, all at once, hundreds of doors opened.

Faces hesitantly peered out into the hallway. Like captive animals being released into the wild, they slowly crept out from their prisons. Thanaton's worst first displayed curiosity, disbelief, excitement.

But that didn't last.

A woman covered head to toe in tattoos pulled out a sharpened stake of wood from somewhere, then plunged it into someone's belly. Others were happy to be armed only with their hands. A burly man with no teeth rushed to the cell across from him, slamming a fist into the unlucky denizen's jaw and then snapping his neck round. The hallway descended into chaos, and from the terrified screams and raging roars echoing around the place, so did the rest of the Deephold.

Vyrion and Farke were still struggling with the restraints when someone burst out of the cell in front of them. A gargantuan orkathi leered at them, one arm cut off just at the elbow. His lips slowly drew back, revealing a mouthful of broken, jagged teeth. Just what they needed.

"The restraints, Farke!"

"I'm *trying*!"

The orkathi prisoner took a step forward. Then another. His singular claw swept down, talons outstretched.

Click. Vyrion felt the restraints fall away. His hand was up in an instant as he desperately called upon whatever faint elements of the Ruin he could find. He was not about to die here.

But just as he felt traces of energy heed his call, coalescing around his outstretched palm, he stopped. Like flowers in the first thaw of spring, feathered darts blossomed out of the orkathi's skin. He only managed a second of surprise before he collapsed.

The tattooed woman met a similar fate, darts stuck into her back as she passed out, hand still wrapped around her wooden stake. All around, prisoners dropped like flies.

"What's happening?" Farke asked, a mixture of relieved and terrified.

Vyrion tapped him and pointed down the hall to their saviors.

A neat squad of Imperial Agents slowly advanced down the hallway, a blur of aiming, shooting, and reloading, faces deathly calm and movements silky smooth. Had Vyrion seen them in any other context he would have thought them dancers, dancers leaving piles of unconscious bodies in their wake.

At their head was a severe woman with hair of an uncompromising grey, looking more like a drillmaster than a member of Imperial Intelligence. She gave Vyrion a tight lipped smile as she approached.

Her agents continued their work, circling around Vyrion and Farke as if they were simply obstacles to be avoided and continuing on. Farke, apparently feeling the need to preemptively surrender, already had his hands raised into the air.

"Vyrion, I presume," the woman said, extending a tidy hand.

Vyrion shook her hand firmly. "Thank you for the rescue, Agent…?"

"Dedri," she said, "And this is no rescue, this is merely a prison riot. A very convenient one at that, especially when most of the security is focused above."

The way she spoke made it very clear that this particular riot was far from organic. Convenient indeed.

Vyrion looked up at the countless tons of stone between them and the interior of the pyramid. "Callida has not stopped her campaign. Now the Council has had to step in to force her and Malus to negotiate."

"As if that would do anything. Callida is dangerous," Dedri said, the name uttered like it carried with it a foul taste, "She's brought a large proportion of her power base into the pyramid along with her. Whether for intimidation or just assurance, it's only a matter of time before she decides conquest is a better option. The Imperial Intelligence Agency has elected to stay neutral, but I have elected to actually do my job."

"So you are breaking Krothus out," Vyrion said.

"No," she said, gesturing for them to follow her, "You are. For all intents and purposes, I am merely here to control this riot."

Her brisk pace carried them quickly through the maze of the Deephold. Slumbering prisoners lined their path, grim markers denoting a recent visit by Dedri's men. Vyrion couldn't tell which were Ruined and which were not; dirt, grime, and unkempt hair common across every unconscious body. Imperial and Ruined, only equal when they couldn't sink any lower.

Dedri suddenly stopped, looking down at some man with a wild beard and a fiery skull tattooed on his chest. The skull stared back at Vyrion, as if some macabre request for help.

"I've been looking for you, Yordu," Dedri said.

In a single motion, she pulled out her piercer and cut the man's slumber short with two bolts to the head. She then re-holstered her weapon and kept walking as if nothing had happened.

Vyrion just watched her do it. He had already been put to sleep, why bother killing him? He was here for Krothus, but that didn't mean he had to go along with every questionable choice Dedri made too.

He caught up with her. "What kind of agent executes unarmed, unconscious prisoners? It's abhorrent."

"The pragmatic kind. Martyrs aren't made in prison riots," Dedri said, giving him a shrug, "But now is not the time for moral grandstanding."

Vyrion was about to object to the accusation of 'moral grandstanding' when Farke stumbled into them, already out of breath.

"How much longer?" he gasped.

"Ah, the former Captain Farke," Dedri said, looking him up and down with harsh eyes, "Why are you here?"

"He owed me a favor," Vyrion interjected.

"Yes I - Wait, you know me?" Farke's face was suddenly very pale.

Dedri snorted. "Of course I do. You performed your duties so incompetently that you were flagged as a potential Republic saboteur."

Farke started sputtering, his lack of chin folding with anger. "How dare you accuse me of such a thing! I would never-"

She leaned in close. "Just be glad being an idiot doesn't carry the same punishment as being a traitor."

Farke fell silent immediately. Dedri continued on.

Vyrion couldn't help but wonder if he was in over his head. Dedri hardly seemed the type to have either his or Krothus' best interests at heart. If things went wrong, it seemed far more likely that she would put a bolt in his back and slip away. No loose ends. But perhaps this was just what he needed. Pragmatism. No more naivety on his part, or blind hope. He was doing what needed to be done. He was doing his part to help Krothus, help the Empire.

Though he was sure Callida thought she was doing the same thing.

"Here," Dedri said, quickly disappearing into a cell that initially looked like any other.

No, this one was different, Vyrion could feel it.

He ducked into the cramped room, empty except a moldy grate strewn across the floor. Dedri had already flung it open to peer into the cramped pit beneath. First, she dropped down a metal ladder that had been sitting nearby, then she tossed a key down into the depths. This caused quite the commotion; jostling and rustling and swearing. Then the click of restraints being unlocked.

Vyrion watched the lip of that pit like he had never watched anything before. The familiar feeling of emptiness clawed its way into his stomach, filling his head with worst-case scenarios. He could be too late. He could see it in his mind's eye; Krothus mutilated or dying, his final words decrying Vyrion for taking too long. If he was a better Ruined he would have been able to save him.

But as he desperately waited for a grey hand to appear on the top rung of the ladder, bringing his search to an end, someone else got there first.

A filthy man crawled out of that pit, rebellious, dirt-caked hair running off in all directions, a crazed, manic look in his eye. The moment he saw Vyrion, he dropped into a deep bow.

"Zlaterek, falsely convicted terrorist, at your service."

Vyrion cleared his throat and put on the best smile he could muster, pretending he didn't want to toss this man aside and peer into the pit himself. "Vyrion, not yet a criminal, at your service."

Then, from just behind Zlaterek's wild mane of grime-smeared hair came a weak voice, a wispy shadow of what Vyrion had known.

"Not yet? What has got into you, Vyrion?"

He finished climbing those final steps, emerging out of the pit like he had been reborn out of the dirt itself. Grey skin caked in a layer of muck, unshaved hair rising up like a field of untrimmed grass, body withered and deflated like his strength had been drained right out of him; Krothus looked the worst Vyrion had ever seen him. But he was smiling.

"I knew you would come," Krothus said, "I knew you would."

Vyrion didn't say anything. He didn't have to.

The two embraced. He felt all those imagined tragedies evaporate, all the predictions of his failure vanish. Even the near-constant feeling of dread was whipped back into its den.

And for the first time in weeks, Vyrion breathed a sigh of relief.

Chapter 27

Rising

When Krothus had pictured his liberation, he had always assumed there would be a grand battle, a host of Krothus' admirers leading the charge, Vyrion at their head. They would break down the prison door and drag him from that blasted pit to wreak havoc on Callida's deluded plans.

But reality was often disappointing.

Vyrion had made it in the end, but far from triumphant liberator, he looked exhausted, dark rings lurking under his bloodshot eyes, like he hadn't slept in weeks.

And as for that army of his supporters, they must have gotten lost. There was just Dedri, wearing the same humorless expression she always did, and some officer with such a lack of chin that it seemed like someone had punched it right back into his jaw. The buffoon was sweating so much that Krothus briefly thought he'd been for a swim.

Zlatarek was currently blowing air at the officer in what could only be some deranged attempt at drying him. This only seemed to make the chinless man sweat more.

"We have ten minutes before the whole prison wakes up," Dedri said, "So let's make haste, I would rather not be trapped in a prison riot of my own creation."

Krothus had no idea what she was talking about. But Dedri was one of the rare cases of someone he trusted, at least now she was. He'd doubted her before - leaving him trapped in that hellpit of a cell, arresting him in the first place, but Vyrion being here was proof that she had followed through just as she said she would. That was more than could be said of most of Thanaton, of which he had heard decidedly little.

"Speak then, what has transpired while I've been locked away?" he asked, "Last I saw was the aftermath of Lord Victus' compound."

"A tragedy," the chinless man said glumly, combing what limited excuse for hair he had back in place. Zlaterek continued his mad crusade of blowing air into his face.

Krothus frowned and stepped away from the fools, turning to the others instead.

Vyrion sighed, "Where to begin? Currently half of the Deephold has been forced unconscious as a cover for your escape, and we are on the cusp of civil war as Callida continues to press the limits of Thanaton's stability."

His master had been busy. "And what of Inissa? Spinebreaker? I saw no trace of them before I was captured."

He had thought of his apprentice and bodyguard a surprising amount during his stay. Mostly of what grim fate had no doubt befallen them, left at Victus' compound without him being there to protect the pair. He had failed them both, a rare event by Krothus' measure, but a failure nonetheless.

Vyrion caught him in a searching gaze, reminding Krothus briefly of Callida's intrusive probes into his mind. "I'm sorry, Krothus. I searched everywhere, hoping there would be some sign of them. But …"

Krothus clenched his jaw, struggling not to give away his disappointment, suddenly disgusted at himself. Masters shouldn't feel attached to their apprentices, nor to their bodyguards. Anything he currently felt was a weakness.

"We'll proceed without them, then" he growled. Vyrion gave him a look, but Krothus ignored it. He did not need his sympathy.

Dedri pressed on. "Your master has ushered the majority of her forces into the pyramid. So has Malus, all to try and make a show of these negotiations. But the truth is, this idiotic demonstration of power is only going to enable a bloodbath."

Krothus could only guess at how many soldiers and Ruin Lords those two power bases would entail. Thousands, tens of thousands. A conflict of that scale, in the heart of Thanaton, would be nothing short of a disaster. "I would have assumed negotiations were a good start to de-escalation."

Dedri shook her head. "I wouldn't count on it. Not with Callida."

"There's more," Vyrion said suddenly, "I was there only a few days ago. With Jarek. He handed off the two relics Victus had used for his ritual to some Ruin Lord I didn't recognise, saying that they were key to Callida coming out on top."

"The same ritual that killed Lord Victus?" Dedri asked. She did not sound happy.

"Yes, but the ritual didn't kill him. Not on its own," Vyrion said, "It somehow severed his soul from his body, extracted it almost, with the intention of taking over the body of another. But when others interfered, his soul was lost."

Krothus knew the word 'others' was pulling a tremendous bit of weight in that sentence. It had been Jarek and Vyrion both. And, knowing Vyrion, he was still feeling guilty about it. Though Krothus was certain this guilt was nothing but wasted energy since Victus was surely not dead.

Krothus had poured over countless tomes and passages, searched his master's library top to bottom. He was as sure now as he was that morning, just before he was taken - Victus' spirit had not been destroyed. As to where it had gone, that was something else entirely.

"Changing bodies," Dedri snorted, "The lengths you Ruined go to, it will never cease to amaze me. Why would Callida need to do that?"

Krothus didn't understand it either. Callida was an imposing, powerful woman, her body a perfect tool for both combat and intimidation. And in rare cases, flattery. He refused to believe she had any urge to rid herself of such an advantage.

Vyrion looked down at the floor, like the moldy gaps between the stones held all the answers. Only once he had gleaned whatever secret knowledge they held did he look back to them.

"She could be using them for something else. When we were

preparing for the ritual, Victus instructed us to use a different spell beforehand, one that captured the essence of Ruin Lord specter that dwelled in the catacombs. It split her spirit and stole its energy, leaving nothing left."

Dedri frowned. "Could this be used on a Ruin Lord who is still alive?"

"It is a possibility, yes."

"Perhaps she means to absorb Malus' power for herself," Krothus suggested, "Split his spirit and take his power for her own, somehow." If this was her goal, he couldn't help but admire the ambition. Unconventional methods, yes, but if the result was becoming the strongest Ruin Lord in the Empire, who was he to critique them?

"Victus had to use crystals to store the energy, but I never saw how it would work without them," Vyrion said, "That might work."

"Damn it all," Dedri whispered, "She's going to be in the Council Chamber."

They all fell silent, the implication clear. Were this sorcery to work as Vyrion claimed, then this was magnitudes worse than any of them could have imagined. Forcibly replacing Highlord Malus was an ascension, a step up the hierarchy of the Empire - an ambitiously large step, yes, one which could destabilise and weaken the Empire's structure in its bloody aftermath, but a step within the reason of the Code nonetheless. To try and do the same with the Council was nothing short of heresy. The mere suggestion was absurd, like a disgruntled merchant deciding the best way to highlight their grievances was to burn down the Merchant Guild with the board of directors inside. But if Krothus knew his master, she would not stop, not consider herself victorious, until she stood above all the Ruin Lords, above the Empire itself. Even if she had to build her throne out of the rubble of Thanaton and the bones of its denizens.

"It's insanity to even consider this," Dedri said. "An open clash between Callida and Malus could level half the city, but the resulting power vacuum in the absence of the Ruined Council would rip the Empire apart." She jabbed a finger in Vyrion's direction. "Are you *absolutely* sure she could even use this sorcery?"

"I am," Vyrion said, looking more tired than ever. "Jarek was the only other person besides Lord Victus or myself who knew the specifics of this spell, and he was the one who retrieved the relics and gave them to Callida. He would have told her everything."

Agent Dedri, who Krothus knew to have seen more than her fair share of politics, wars, and rebellions, looked shaken. It was an odd sight, as if one day seeing a familiar sculpture had changed its pose. But just as quickly as the cracks were revealed in her mask of composure, Dedri took a deep breath in and out, and then she was calm.

"We're out of time, Ruined. Let's go." She was outside the cell in an instant.

Krothus turned back around to Zlaterek and the chinless man, still engaged in whatever buffoonery two idiots would enjoy. "Congratulations, you've just volunteered to help save the Empire. Now move."

"I do love a good redemption story," Zlaterek said, grinning as he pawed a handful of greasy hair out of his face and started dragging the Imperial outside.

"Is it too late to go home?" the chinless man asked, pointlessly dabbing at his forehead with a now-soaked handkerchief as he was forcibly swept away.

Krothus ignored them. Leaving the cell was only a journey of a few steps, but one he had dreamt of for weeks. Freedom.

As he stepped out of the cramped room and into the area beyond, he felt like instead of the Deephold's endless criss-cross of corridors, he was setting foot in an expansive grassland, boundless and open, the memories of that cramped pit nearly forgotten. But his wistless daydreaming didn't last long.

Slumbering bodies were scattered across the corridor, as if the prison riot had somehow coordinated a designated sleeping time. The perpetrators were easy to spot.

A handful of Imperial agents, some of their faces familiar, were lounging around in the area just outside the cell, their grey uniforms trim and tidy, their weapons pristine.

Krothus gave them a nod. "Agents."

"Ruined," one of them said, returning the nod. She gestured to one of the others, and they tossed something small and metal through the air.

Krothus caught it. His hand wrapped around the familiar grip of his runeblade hilt, the handshake of an old friend long absent. Every notch on the pommel, every scratch on the godrium guard, told a story. His story. Now not just a story of a grand destiny, but of saving the Empire itself.

Though, looking down at himself, his armor absent and his dark robes stained and ragged, he hardly looked the hero. But such was the way of things.

Dedri cleared her throat. Her agents stood at attention.

"Agents, the Ruined Council is under threat, and the battle between Callida and Malus may have already begun. We need to ensure the Council's safety above anything else. The fate of the Empire is at stake, so success is an absolute imperative. This is a Code Black; no records, no consequences."

"And no backup, no commendations," an agent muttered, shifty eyes searching amongst the others for agreement. He found none.

"That's the spirit, Erik. Now gear up, we're leaving."

Like one well oiled machine, Dedri and her agents grabbed their weapons and double-timed their way down the corridor. Krothus and Vyrion followed behind while Zlaterek brought up the rear, still dragging the chinless Imperial along despite his protests.

The Deephold's maze proved easy to navigate with the agents at the helm, weaving around corners and traversing identical hallways with a practiced familiarity. Their journey briefly slowed at some door stuck into the far end of the cavern. With only minimal fiddling, the agents picked the lock to reveal the longest set of stairs Krothus had ever seen, spiralling up into the darkness like it were eventually set to meet the moon and the stars at its peak. A trio of torches were lit up, courtesy of an agent's satchel, and up they climbed.

As Krothus went up the endless steps, his legs burning as they powered through their first activity in weeks, his mind wandered to his master's plans. He would never have said it in front of Dedri, but to make the Council nervous enough to get personally involved in this power struggle, to threaten so many powerful Ruin Highlords, it was a level of strength that he wished he had.

It was not just raw power, either. The political capital and strength of arms needed to draw the Council's attention was considerable. Disregarding their Ruinous abilities, Highlords, even those not on the Ruined Council, had power bases that could easily take the city multiple times over; tens of thousands of soldiers, dozens of Ruin Lords, hundreds of Ruined. Highlords surely could have founded their own nations and broke away from the Empire if they wished, but still, all of them, their combined powers inconceivable, served on or reported to the Council, all in service to Emperor.

Krothus could only imagine why the Council chose to stay second best to a figure that no one had seen in years. Perhaps they were satisfied running the Empire in his absence, happy to be the de facto rulers and leaving the Emperor to his own devices. Maybe the Emperor's own abilities were so impossibly powerful that they dared not step out of line. It was possible that the constant power struggles and politics did a fine job of keeping the Council too preoccupied to consider such things.

"We're here," one of the agents said, not sounding the slightest bit out of breath.

'Here' apparently denoted another door, unmarked and unremarkable in an otherwise bare staircase. The stairs themselves continued on above for what seemed like forever.

The door creaked open and they stepped out into what could only be described as the exact opposite of the darkness of the Deephold. The endless cell doors were replaced with artwork and treasures, the bleak stone with neatly architectured vaulted ceilings and rich crimson carpet.

"Impressive, isn't it?" Vyrion asked.

"Impressively disgusting," Krothus said.

He had never been inside the Dark Pyramid before, and seeing it now, he was glad he hadn't. The interior was everything he hated; dysfunctional decorations, pointless pleasantries, and unnecessary opulence. Even the size of the hallways was absurd, built for giants instead of men.

Luckily, Krothus didn't have to stare at it for long, as the agents already had them on the move. They fanned out into a loose circle around the rest of the group, like hounds herding livestock, and led them down the carpeted hallway.

Things seemed calm for the time being, but as they continued, the Ruin Lord detachments began to appear.

Each detachment had apprentices and hundreds of soldiers tow, the size of the Dark Pyramid a testament to how easily such groups fit in only a single passageway. But despite the numbers, Krothus was left wondering where the rest of the forces at hand were, small skirmishes of hundreds within the pyramid was dangerous, yes, but not quite at the level Vyrion and Dedri had been fearing.

Such thoughts were quelled when they entered the largest room Krothus had ever seen.

In a grand internal courtyard, thousands of soldiers, Ruin Lords, and Ruined apprentices had gathered, countless banners and tabards marking out forces from across the Empire, all thrust into the melting pot within. There was scarcely enough room to move, let alone form ranks, but the forces of both Malus and Callida had attempted it nonetheless, packed together like weeds and flowers in some overgrown garden. It was the most people Krothus had ever seen in one place, and the thought of them erupting into battle when standing in such close proximity was a nightmare waiting to happen. He could see multiple avenues of escape; the gaping entryways of several adjoining corridors leading elsewhere, as well as the multiple levels of the gardens and floors above, though these too were controlled by some Ruin Lord or another, their banners waving about as if each hallway were some newly conquered land. Above them all was the glass floor of the Council chamber, positioned perfectly for a grand view of the battle lines being drawn up below.

At one end of the courtyard was a vast wall of stained crimson glass, warping whatever sunlight managed to seep into the pyramid a dark blood red, while at the other was a small antechamber guarded by grand, hooded statues.

This antechamber seemed to be the agents' destination, the grey uniforms pushing through the sea of armored bodies with all the grace of a shovel through sand. To say tensions were high was an understatement, even the most gentle of movements from the agents caused soldiers and Ruined alike to flinch as if struck. But despite this, not one protested. Imperial agents, especially seen in such numbers, were not to be argued with - making enemies of Imperial Intelligence had a habit of drastically decreasing one's life span.

Krothus kept an eye out for any familiar faces. He saw Lord Grandis, his half-burned face easy to pick out in the crowd, and Lord Ora, her soldiers sporting the sign of her stag-horned crown.

But one banner in the distance caught his eye, a black mask on dark fabric, its lifeless gaze seeming to follow him from across the crowd.

Lord Fira was here. His master's plan to keep her secluded away had failed. Krothus could only pray that they would not cross paths.

It was not long before Krothus realised that keeping a low profile would have been a great deal easier if he had left Zlaterek rotting in his cell. While Krothus and everyone else in their group had elected to stay in a determined silence, the rogue Ruined was subject to outbursts. His latest one left Krothus ready to wring his neck.

"I should have known to find you here, Partos," Zlaterek spat, pushing some Ruined with glowing yellow eyes, "You double crossing son of a whore, I spent years in the Deephold because of you!"

"My name isn't Partos, idiot. I'm Edrad," the yellow eyed Ruined snarled back.

"Oh," Zlaterek said, eyes wide, "Sorry about that."

Thankfully, Dedri delivered a swift kick to Zlaterek's rear, sending him scurrying back on track.

"Malus and Callida should be meeting in the antechamber ahead of their hearing with the Council. With any luck they are still there," she said.

"We can only hope it will be that easy," Vyrion said.

"It never is," Krothus muttered.

As they drew closer to their destination, the endless ranks of soldiers and Ruined thinned out into a no-man's land, a gap so recognised that there very well could have been an invisible wall. On the other side of this cloaked fortification stood a loose collection of Ruin Lords standing guard, motionless as the grand statues of stone looming above them. Krothus recognised some as those directly under his master, trusted lieutenants and zealous disciples both. They stood apart from a grim band of what must have been Lord Malus' own retinue.

Krothus couldn't sense anything inside, but then again, he was struggling to focus the Ruin on anything at all. The whole area was drowning in tension, flooded in the anxiety and potential violence of the thousands present; trying to pick anything out was like trying to find a single fish amidst the heavy seas of a great storm.

A Ruin Lord stepped out from the formation on Lord Malus' side, her skin feathery and birdlike.

"What is going on here?" she trilled, stopping the agents and their group, "No one is allowed entry, especially not two of Lord Callida's apprentices. Leave."

"Lord Sanata," Vyrion said with a respectful bow, "Krothus and I are not here to assist Lord Callida, but to stop her. She plans to conduct a ritual that will kill Highlord Malus and the Ruined Council if we don't."

Blunt and to the point, Krothus could appreciate that.

Sanata's eyes narrowed, but she seemed far from convinced. Her avian eyes turned to Krothus.

"You must think me a fool to believe such a tale, especially when your reckless friend here was the one who killed Lord Victus, a master who was not his to slay"

Krothus didn't like being accused of something so false, especially when Victus surely still alive, and defeated by nothing other than his own hubris, his own apprentices. But before he could sneer back at her, he was interrupted.

"Cut the political bullshit, Sanata," Dedri said, pushing past, "This isn't some game. The Council could be in very real danger. Malus, too. The last thing either of us want is this boiling over into violence, so open these doors for Imperial Intelligence immediately."

Lord Sanata bristled for a moment, feathers askew, before seeming to calm. "If there is anything that can be done to avoid this bloodbath, then I would gladly assist you. But these doors must stay closed, the very act of opening them would be enough to start exactly the conflict Callida wants."

Before Dedri could offer a rebuttal, another Ruined joined the conversation, an apprentice wearing a set of elaborate godrium armor much too big for him. A Ruined that Krothus would have loved to cut down where he stood.

"What a load of nonsense." Amar's holier than thou tone already set Krothus into a simmering rage, "This is all just a ruse to interrupt my master's attempts at a peaceful resolution."

"And you are?" Dedri snapped.

"I am-"

"Nothing but a useless apprentice who doesn't know his station," Krothus interrupted, "Keep silent, adults are talking."

Amar shoved his face inches away from Krothus' own, that toothy grin filling his vision. "Why don't you go back to rotting in your prison cell where you belong?"

"He does belong there, doesn't he?" Zlaterek piped up from behind them.

Krothus was practically strangling his runeblade hilt. Emperor above, how he wished he could wipe Amar's stupid grin off his face.

But he knew doing so would be a disaster. Everyone around them was watching what was unfolding with an increasing anxiousness, the tension growing so thick that Krothus could feel it pressing down on him, wrapping itself around his throat. They were making a scene.

So he took a deep breath, lowered his runeblade, and stepped aside. Amar would get his comeuppance some time soon, but they needed to keep things calm. As long as they kept the situation under control, then they could talk their way through this.

Dedri took up the space with sheer presence alone, poking a finger into Amar's set of stolen armor. "Imperial Intelligence is demanding that you step aside. There are matters of supreme importance to the Empire which you are-"

Her words kept coming, but Krothus was no longer listening. They faded away into the background.

Someone approached. A Ruin Lord, their presence throwing itself to the forefront of the Ruin's tumultuous storm, blasting out a warning of what was to come. An endless dark pit of paranoia. Cruelty and delusion and disdain, all vying for equal position. A hateful bloodlust for all things. Krothus felt a chill run up his spine.

There was a commotion behind them. Then a woman's voice rang out, warped and distorted. "Who dares to interrupt the negotiations?"

Krothus turned, only to wish he hadn't.

A wall of guards had been parted, tossed to the floor as if nothing but scenery. She stood in the midst of them, frighteningly tall and concernedly thin, swaying on the spot, like she were a stalk of wheat drifting in a wind only she could feel. Her face was obscured by an expressionless mask of metal.

Lord Fira.

Dedri huffed, clearly not appreciating the interruption. "As I keep saying, this is Imperial Intelligence business, we need to-"

Lord Fira held up a gloved hand, and Dedri froze, the Ruin corking the words down her throat. Another wave of her hand, and the other agents were paralysed where they stood.

"Enough from you, Imperial." Then Fira crept closer, her movements like those of a giant spider, approaching her prey with limbs spindly and eyes without soul.

"Lord Fira, good that you're here," Lord Sanata said, sounding like it was the exact opposite. "Highlord Malus may be in danger. The

Council too, if these two are to be believed."

Fira said nothing. Her mask's gaze rested on Krothus and Vyrion both.

"Fira?" Sanata pressed.

Fira ignored her. "You two. Have we met?"

"No," Krothus said.

Vyrion cleared his throat in a most unconvincing manner. "Not that I recall."

"Fira, now is not the time," Lord Sanata insisted.

But Fira was not satisfied. She cocked her head to one side, the blank eyes of her mask piercing through them.

"No. I *do* know you," she breathed, like the very act of speaking calmly required some tremendous restraint.

Then she bent down, contorted, her wiry form twisting and shifting.

It took Krothus a moment to realize that she was crying. Sobs wracked her gangly body, each one warping her posture further and further inwards, threatening to bend her in half completely. To watch it felt deeply uncomfortable, though Krothus couldn't put his finger as to why.

As quickly as it started, her weeping ceased. She drew back up to her full height like nothing had happened.

"You took my daughter from me," she whispered, frantic. "You. *Took.* Her."

Krothus had no idea what to do. What *could* he do? They were trapped.

"There must be some misunderstanding," Vyrion said calmly, "Sanata, perhaps you could help us work this out?"

Ever the diplomat. But Lord Sanata was already backing away, as though Fira was the carrier of some deadly plague that she was desperate to avoid catching. The agents remained stuck in place and Amar, the damn coward, had used the momentary distraction to slip off. Unless Zlaterek was hiding some incredible power under his disheveled exterior, Krothus and Vyrion were left alone.

"There is nothing to work out, whelps. You sullied my home. You took my daughter from me. Destroyed my master's vessel."

Fira called the Ruin to her, the invisible force twisting into great swells of power. Krothus braced for the worst.

But the worst never came; no blast of power, no bolt of lightning, even Firas runeblade remained inert. Instead, all that gathered energy erupted above them, expanding out over the entirety of the courtyard like a great cover of clouds, a spider casting its web over thousands of jittery, battle-eager soldiers and power-hungry Ruined.

And when she spoke, they all heard. A single word, amplified through the Ruin, through the air, bouncing across the walls and echoing down the halls. Fira's metallic voice carried through the entirety of the Dark Pyramid like it was coming from the Emperor himself.

"*Betrayal!*"

Like the pounding of a great drum, the word rippled through the assembly. Heads were turned. Weapons readied.

Dedri and her other agents were released. They fell to their knees, desperately gulping for air.

"*Deception!*"

Krothus didn't understand. Fira was goading the two sides to battle, but why? Surely, she wanted Highlord Malus, her superior, to succeed in his negotiations. This ran entirely against that.

Vyrion and his pet Imperial were trying to help Dedri to her feet. Krothus saw something outside through the wall of stained glass across the courtyard. A distant plume of fire, flashing in the sky.

"*Lies!*"

Soldiers and Ruined all around were being whipped into a frenzy, Fira's crazed shrieks seemed to come from everywhere at once, hinting at some unseen double-cross. Krothus, too, could feel the rush of battle pouring into his veins. They were just about to cross a threshold they could never return from.

Again, his eyes were drawn to the far side of the courtyard. He saw a speck, growing fast, a low hum filling the air.

"*Slay them all!*"

A steady roar rolled forth, summoned forth from thousands of throats. This was it.

The speck was close enough now to reveal its shape, a skyship, trailing smoke and fire. And it wasn't slowing down.

Lord Fira swiveled her head, her voice only now a low hiss. "I will see your heads are mounted on spikes for what you've done. Your souls will feed my designs."

"Just get out of our way you crazed witch," Krothus snarled. Flames erupted from his runeblade, accompanied by Vyrion's own weapon.

He couldn't see behind Fira's mask, but he knew she was smiling. "The Nightmare Lord will feast on many today. It is all proceeding as he told me it would."

That was when the skyship smashed through the grand hall's stained glass like a vengeful comet, leaving a trail of glass shards raining down behind it. Metal screeched in protest as it plowed into the courtyard floor, crushing hundreds into a red paste, the deadly meteor carving a fissure through stone. Hundreds of tons of rock erupted around the skyship as its momentum drove it, shrieking all the way, further and further.

Any semblance of rank was lost as everyone scrambled to get out of its path.

A path Krothus realized was headed right for them.

The Ruin Lords, everyone, they all scattered.

Krothus scarcely had time to jump out of the way before the skyship smashed the area to rubble, clouds of dust filling the air and clogging his lungs. Coughing and choking, he fell to one knee as the dust enveloped him, drowning in a flood of dry air and grains of earth.

He could just barely see the cause of it all. The wreckage, all smoke and torn metal, was steadily burning, a grim silhouette amidst the darkened air.

Something about it that looked familiar.

Then, somehow, its doors shuddered open, and the world descended into chaos.

Chapter 28

Reunion

Inissa, mouth dry, head pounding, struggled to her feet. The violent tremors had finally stopped, but she'd been tossed into every corner of the *Donovan*'s hold. Hardly the smooth landing they'd planned.

It was cramped and dark, the smokey air thick with sweat and fear, a prime proportion of which was her own. Inissa was gripping her piercer so tightly that it felt like her fingers would break off. What she wouldn't do for a snack right now.

Then the hold doors managed to shudder open, a single ray of light beaming in. Not that Inissa could see anything more than that, her view was entirely obscured by crimson flesh on all sides.

"Nightshadow!" someone shouted.

"Huah!" came the reply, accompanied by a crash of weapons that sent Inissa's headache throbbing all over again.

It only got worse as the hold doors inched open and a continuous dull roar rolled in, like everyone in the Empire shouting at all once.

"Nightshadow!"

"Huah!"

The slams were louder this time. Inissa winced, her weapon nearly slipping through clammy hands.

There was a final groan of metal and the doors screeched to a halt, halfway open. It looked like the opening mechanism hadn't quite made it. But the Nightshadow didn't seem to care.

They charged, Inissa caught up in it all, sweeping through the half-open doors as though a breach in some fortress walls, whipped on by their drive for battle and bloodshed. It took all her concentration to keep her balance, each shove sent her spinning, each nudge threatened to bowl her over, ever closer to being crushed beneath the stampede.

A clawed hand clutched her shoulder, an anchor that kept her steady as the tide crashed over her.

"Focus, Inissa," Victus said, "Battle is an unrelenting storm, and it can break even the most steadfast ships. But you must weather it."

"Easy for you to say. I'm not exactly built for weathering storms." If she were a seven foot monster of muscle too, then perhaps she would have shared his optimism.

Victus cast a quick glance at what used to be the *Donovan*. "Neither is our vessel, it seems. One bolt to our thrust orbs was enough to send us crashing into this chaos. They must have imposed a no-fly zone over the pyramid during Callida's hearing. Rescuing Krothus now takes second priority to stopping her madness."

Crash or not, those with them would have hardly noticed the difference. Chieftain Headcleaver had already shoved his way to the front, his huge axe delivering its maiming bite to whoever was unlucky enough to get in his path. The rest of the Nightshadow warriors poured out of the skyship, tossing themselves into the battle with reckless abandon.

Inissa barely even knew where they were, only that they were in the Dark Pyramid somewhere, surrounded by a field of broken stone and mountains of rubble. The centerpiece of this wasteland was the *Donovan*, now nothing more than a twisted hunk of metal and fire. Inissa could only guess what kind of compensation Fareese would expect to make up for such catastrophic damage; it was a wonder she'd managed to land the ship at all, especially with its cargo intact.

The battle was everywhere. Orkathi fought soldier, soldier fought soldier, Ruined fought Ruined, there were no battle lines, no grand maneuvers, only a brutal melee and aimless violence. She stood on the precipice of it all, contemplating falling in.

"What's happening here?" Inissa asked, feeling a tightness in her chest, "This is pandemonium."

"Exactly as Callida wants," Victus said, his tentacle beard writhing, "A spark that will burn down the Empire. We must find someone, anyone, that can help us stop her. Krothus or Vyrion would be our best bet, but I will settle for any Ruined I recognise. Time is vital, because-"

Victus' words quickly faded into muffled grunting, the battle a dull rumble, as Inissa felt like she had been plunged underwater. All of this felt like a terrible dream, a nightmare she could barely comprehend. The Ruin, normally a gently shifting ocean, had drank in the storm of emotions, swelling into a tsunami of rage and fear that crashed into her like she were the lone lighthouse at the edge of a hurricane.

Inissa gasped for breath as everything spun around her. Bodies pressed against each other in an endless struggle. An orkathi warrior took a piercer bolt through the chest and dropped to the ground. An Imperial soldier was engulfed in a storm of Ruin lightning, smoke floating off his armor. Two Ruined dueled atop a hill of rubble, their runeblades clashing in a flash of flame and sparks.

The world and all its sounds came rushing back to her in an instant.

"- and that is where the root of this all began. Especially because-"

"Victus, look," She pointed up at the dueling Ruined.

Victus looked at her, confused, but followed her gesture regardless.

Perched atop the rubble, his blazing runeblade clear as day, was Krothus. What was left of a ragged black cloak billowed behind him as he danced back and forth, surprisingly nimble for a man of his size. His opponent gave as good as he got with his own weapon, engulfed in the absorption runes' sluggish yellow glow, catching some blows on the ornate set of armor he wore, far too big, tied down to ensure it didn't fall off.

"That bastard has my armor!" Victus snarled.

"Then he must have assaulted your compound," Inissa said, bringing her piercer around.

The pair started to push through the melee.

The Nightshadow did most of the heavy lifting for them, easily making themselves the priority target of any Imperial soldier in their path. Their shields were already scarred and dented, evidence enough of the countless bolts flying their way.

Inissa pressed onwards. Seeing her master had given her a clear goal, a destination in the madness. So Inissa followed Victus, lining up piercer shots as best as she could in the mass of bodies, while the former Ruin Lord carved a path of red ruin through Imperial guards with a borrowed orkathi axe. Inissa barely had time to register her next foe, let alone if any of her shots met their mark; the dizzying mash of color from different tabards and banners was making her head spin.

Formations were an idea long absent; everyone fought everyone else. Inissa could only imagine what was running through the minds of the Ruin Lords and their forces, they must have thought that the Nightshadow were a wildcard force of some Ruined or another, else they would have banded together against a common enemy. She could only pray that never happened.

The crowds thinned out as Inissa and Victus clambered over the hill of rubble, the heaving mass of battle partially obscured by a light cloud of dust. Chunks of masonry and crushed rock had transformed the area into a mountain of difficult terrain, the duel atop it the only contribution to the conflict.

"Come now, Krothus, this pathetic display can't be all," the armored Ruined said, "I expected more!"

Krothus roared and swung his flaming runeblade down at the man's head, but his opponent ducked out of the way, the golden glow around his runeblade growing brighter.

"When are you going to fight, Amar? I've had enough of your dancing," Krothus snarled.

Amar smiled wide. "And be robbed of the satisfaction of slowly draining your Ruin energy? I think not. You don't stay in Callida's good graces for as long as I have by tossing away your advantages."

He held his arms out, oversized metal plates strapped to them. "Take it in - overpowering, wonderful chaos. Our master will have us use it to rebuild this Empire as it was meant to be. For too long the Empire has floundered, happy to let the Highlords dictate the status quo and keep themselves above all, while the lesser Ruin Lords are happy to squabble amongst themselves. No longer."

Inissa slowly brought her piercer up to a firing position as she crested the hill of rubble.

"You really like to hear yourself talk, don't you?" Krothus yelled back at his opponent.

Amar shrugged. "A little bit."

She fired. The bolt flicked off an armored shoulder plate.

Amar's eyes flicked in her direction immediately. Krothus turned to check who had intervened as well, but Amar was faster. He blasted Krothus back down the slope and out of sight with a burst of Ruinous energy. Then he raised his hand at Inissa, fingers trembling with gathered power.

With a feral roar, Victus charged from the other side, swinging his axe wide. But Amar saw him, taking his focus away from Inissa to block the blow with his runeblade, Ruin-forged steel versus orkathi craftsmanship. The axe shattered on impact.

"Nice try, brute," Amar sneered. He effortlessly lifted the much bulkier orkathi into the air, the Ruin swirling around them as Victus' legs dangled helplessly above the ground.

Victus struggled, grasping at his throat, grunting out what little words he could. "Give me my armor back ... thieving whelp. Nobody ... urgh ... steals from me and lives."

Amar stopped for a single second, his surprise clear. "Your armor? You lie, creature, this belonged to-"

But the apprentice had committed a critical error. He'd gotten distracted.

Krothus' blazing blade cut once, severing Amar's arm at the elbow, then again, lopping off a leg. The armored plates, too big for their wearer, were unable to prevent the damage aimed between them.

Amar dropped, shrieking, as he clutched his cauterized stumps.

The moment Victus dropped back to the earth, he was upon him, crimson claws wrapped around his neck.

"Think twice before stealing my armor and killing my men," Victus hissed.

With a slow gurgle, Amar had the life squeezed out of him. Then his head lolled to the side, his long hair brushing through a layer of dust on the ground. Inissa would normally have looked away, not one for such displays, but she remembered that terrifying night at Victus' compound, and Lorren's sacrifice. She wasn't proud of herself, but she was glad as she watched the color drain from his face.

When she looked up, Krothus was looking down at her. His face was bruised, caked in dust and sweat. She had never been happier to see him.

"Where have you been?" he croaked.

"Getting friends," Inissa said, jerking a finger back to the crimson bodies fighting below them. "It's good to see you, master."

Krothus had the hints of a grin sneaking through his near-permanent grimace. "I hadn't heard anything for weeks, I feared the worst."

Despite everything going on around them, Inissa was smiling, "So did I."

"I-" Krothus started, but stopped. His face darkened as Victus stood up from his neck breaking.

The two stared at each other for a long time, Victus standing tall and proud in Spinebreaker's form and Krothus looking him over as if inspecting a troublesome piece of art.

"Exactly as I thought, then," Krothus said, pointing his runeblade at the orkathi, "You are not so easily killed, Victus."

The Ruin Lord gave him a tusked grin, almost seeming proud.

Krothus briefly jerked his head in Inissa's direction, still glaring. "Did you know this?"

"I did, and he has been watching over me ever since we escaped his compound," she said, trying to rapidly defuse the situation. "Please, master, the only way we were able to get the Nightshadow's assistance here was through him."

The last thing Inissa needed was these two killing each other, especially now. She silently prayed that logic would prevail.

But Krothus still kept his runeblade leveled at Victus, the threat clear as the flames lazily drifted across the weapon.

"Time is short," Krothus finally said, "Are you here to stop Callida, or do I need to go through you too?"

Victus nodded, head tentacles writhing as he looked up at the Council chamber. "She must fall, for all our sakes."

"Then I will let you live." Krothus lowered his runeblade. "But if you get in my way, or if you hurt my apprentice, I will end you without a second thought."

Victus nodded again. Krothus, deeming that a suitable response, tossed Inissa something off the ground. She only just managed to catch it, too busy thanking the heavens for the best possible outcome of the exchange.

"Take this, he won't be needing it any more."

Inissa inspected the runeblade hilt, a stocky metal grip with an elaborate handguard above it, "Thank you, master. But, I've never used one before, how am I meant to-"

To her surprise, Krothus put a hand on her shoulder.

"Don't think. Feel," he said quietly, "You are a gifted student. I would not trust you with this if I didn't think you could handle it. I need your help, and you are here now, and that's all that matters."

"I -" Inissa started, struggling to find the words, "... thank you, master."

Victus was next to them, wasting no time in ripping his godrium armor off of Amar's dismembered corpse, removing the ties that had kept it to the recently deceased apprentice's slim frame before expertly strapping each piece over the crude leather he had been wearing. Despite the radical change in his physique, the elaborate black plate fit surprisingly well, leaving Inissa wondering how much Victus had looked in his prime.

She looked back down to the hilt in her hand. She had never touched a runeblade, let alone used one, and the middle of a battlefield seemed like a terrible place to start.

But this wasn't a choice, it was now or never.

Don't think. Feel.

Inissa took a deep breath and reached out to the violent storm of the

Ruin all around her, feeling the suffering and the rage and the fear as she had before, but this time, she no longer resisted it, no longer stood and waited for it to break her. She felt it crash over her in great waves and she let herself be swept away, carried along into the storm. She embraced the Ruin as it was and molded the turmoil into her own calm, her own imprint of all the pain, all the anger, a reflection of the torrent that surrounded her.

And inside it, she felt at peace.

When Inissa opened her eyes, the runeblade had sprung out of its hilt, the dual blades pulsing with the runes' bright yellow energy between them. The Ruin flowed through her like a conduit, feeding the blade power.

"Well done," Krothus said, his tone betraying a rare hint of pride.

Inissa felt like she could take on the world.

But the moment didn't last long. Krothus looked past her, watching the disorganized Nightshadow warband wildly attacking anyone nearby, directionless.

"We need Headcleaver and his warriors with us," he said, "They are helping no one being left to their own devices. They should be forcing a path to Vyrion and the others."

"Do you know where they are?" Victus asked, "We've seen no sign of them."

"Neither have I, your grand entrance caused quite the mess," Krothus said, "But it's time we found them."

Before long, they were following him down the hill of rubble as Krothus began rallying any Nightshadow he came across. With each wave of his fiery blade, each deafening command, he would rip the warriors back from their mindless bloodlust. One by one, they would form up behind him, a shepherd and his deadly flock.

"Ranks, form ranks!" Krothus was shouting, to limited effect.

"Shields at the front, spears behind!" Victus added, shoving warriors back and forth to fit with his instructions.

"Stop pushing me!" Inissa called out, flung about with every new recruit.

Despite the slow start, the Nightshadow rallied under their harsh direction, evolving from a frenzied mob into a brutally effective meat grinder. The ranks of warriors smashed their way through whichever unlucky collection of Imperials they came across, the battle between Malus and Callida's forces keeping any skirmish to at least two fronts.

Their advance only halted when a Ruined would emerge amidst the turmoil. Krothus would push through the lines to fight them one on one, his relentless assaults breaking through whatever defenses they could muster before they would be chopped down by an orkathi blade.

Eventually they came across Headcleaver and his entourage, pushed far ahead of any support, leaving a trail of severed limbs and crushed skulls in their wake. The Nightshadow Chieftain was completely immersed in battle, ripping apart any Imperial he could get his hands on, no thoughts towards anything else. But even he slowed when a new challenger appeared.

A barrel-chested Ruined stood in his path, wearing an unyielding sneer. Some apprentice to some Ruin Lord, a nobody in Ruined terms, another level entirely to anyone else.

"Where is Lord Fira?" Headcleaver snarled.

He received no answer.

Inissa could only watch as the Ruined, a big slab of anger, chopped through one, then two of Headcleaver's bodyguards with a jagged emerald runeblade. They had no chance, the weapon swept through metal, flesh, and bone. Headcleaver charged anyways. The Ruined shot up a hand, snaking the Ruin round Headcleaver's thick neck and hoisting him into the air with a choked shout.

The Chieftain's yellow eyes bulged, his tongue flailed around his mouth like it were looking for an escape of its own. The Ruined started laughing as he began choking the life out of him.

But before Krothus could intervene, there was a great flash of crimson. The Ruined's hand shot back like it had been burned, and Soultotem appeared out the frantic melee, crystal-tipped staff glowing.

Headcleaver dropped back to the earth like the world's ugliest falling star, a star that was still holding a hefty axe -as he fell, he twisted round and sent it cleaving down at his foe. The Ruined, distracted by his hand, by the newcomers, was not able to dodge away fast enough.

The blade sunk a deep fissure into the Ruined's skull.

"How easily Ruined fall," Headcleaver hissed, spitting on what was left of his handiwork.

Already, he moved towards new targets, his face painted in blood and his eyes playing host to some dark pleasure. But Krothus blocked his path with one gray arm.

"Stop acting like a mindless animal. There are more important things at stake here than thrill seeking."

Headcleaver, still entrenched in battle frenzy, looked seconds away from striking him. "Gray one. I am here for Lord Fira, nothing else. Don't get in my way."

"Then you will be happy to discover I know where she is," Krothus said, expertly straddling the line between authoritative and condescending, "And I will need your help when we run into her again."

Victus appeared at his side, "Count yourself lucky not to have encountered a Ruin Lord proper as of yet, Lokk. Slaying apprentices may be within our grasp, but it will take all of us to even stand a sliver of a chance if we run into one of their masters."

"Battles must be picked," Soultotem added.

A fire without fuel, the battle lust slowly faded from Headcleaver's eyes. He looked around with a newfound clarity, his eyes lingering on the bodies of his two slain bodyguards, cut into bits like they were nothing

"Lead the way," he grunted.

While the rest of their group moved along, Inissa felt like she had been plunged into a bucket of ice water, shivers crawling up and down her spine. Had Krothus been lying? Was her mother so close? Inissa couldn't sense her presence, but with the battle all around her, she could barely feel anything further than a few feet away. Maybe that was good, maybe it meant her mother couldn't sense her either.

Her thoughts were temporarily brushed aside as the warband, now united and driven, began to push to the where Krothus wanted, an area devastated by fallen stone and massive shards of masonry. They scaled the hills of rubble before gently sliding down the other side into the jagged canyon of stone below, where broken statues and crumbled ground had transformed the area into a shattered wasteland, deathly quiet compared to the riot elsewhere in the courtyard.

Just ahead, a few dozen guards looked on as a handful of Ruined carried giant chunks of rock away from the entrance of some structure, half buried under rubble. Each of the boulders was raised up by the Ruin and cast away, adding to the mounds of debris all around that isolated the crater.

The excavation halted the moment the guards pointed out the warband, and the Ruined halted. They formed up to face them, with one stepping ahead of the rest, one with a tremendous aura of power. A Ruin Lord.

Inissa tightened the grip around her salvaged runeblade, but there was no assault, no bolt of Ruin lightning that flew their way. Instead, the Ruin Lord just stood there, arms crossed, feathery skin scorched and bloodied, patiently waiting for Krothus to approach.

"Lord Sanata," Krothus said, his runeblade ignited but held low at his side, "I implore you to hear our warnings properly this time."

Sanata's apprentices, covered head to toe in a coat of dust and dried blood, moved to take out their own weapons, but their master waved them down.

"We both want to stop Callida. That makes us allies, for now," she said, eyeing the Nightshadow column as it shambled towards them. "Though we have vastly different motivations for doing so, I imagine."

Krothus shrugged. "A pointless distinction."

"I suppose so," Lord Sanata said, sounding like the distinction carried far more weight than Krothus awarded it. "Help us remove the rubble blocking the antechamber doors and then we can see whether this ritual of yours is based in reality. Time is short, I can already sense something nefarious within."

Krothus nodded and motioned for Inissa to join him.

How Lord Sanata could sense anything at all with what was happening around them was beyond Inissa's understanding. The battle might have been out of sight, but the crashes and roars, the invisible chaos thrashing through the air was very much apparent. Even forming a single thought felt like trying to read amidst a shouting match.

She lined up next to Krothus, ready to lend her aid. But everyone was looking up.

Something flew down like a gift from the heavens.

It crashed into the stone nearby, armor scorched and smoking. An Imperial soldier, recently fried. A Ruined staggered into the crater shortly afterwards, sparks of power on his fingertips and neat hair askew. Vyrion.

Inissa was briefly about to praise their luck, to run to Vyrion and celebrate the fact that he was still alive after all their time apart, but she made the mistake of taking a glance at the slain soldier's tabard first. Her mother's black mask stared back. Watching. Judging.

Her mother was here, not yet in sight, but already looming large. Inissa always knew she would find her again. Her stomach rumbled, both demanding food and recoiling at the thought of it. The glow of her runeblade flickered, threatening to disappear completely.

An odd mix of allies followed behind Vyrion; a collection of bruised, battered, and bloodied Imperial Agents, a Ruined who looked like he hadn't bathed in months, and an Imperial officer that Inissa immediately recognised. Farke had been a frequent sight at Victus' compound before he was demoted, though Inissa was surprised to see him here, scared out of his mind and wearing his old uniform.

"Krothus, thank the Emperor we found you," Vyrion breathed, gulping down air as he finally got down to them. " Lord Fira's forces are running rampant, destroying everyone they come across regardless of what side they're on. We only just escaped her.'

Vyrion then noticed the orkathi warband, his surprised gaze quickly moving between Soultotem and Headcleaver.

"Nightshadow? But-"

He stopped when he caught sight of Inissa, freezing up like he was trying to decide if her being there was a trick of the light. But it passed quickly, and he covered the distance in seconds, wrapping her in a tight embrace.

"You're alive. I knew you were."

"It's good to see you," Inissa said, putting on a brave face and smiling back at him. Her mother was so close. Maybe she was watching them at that very second.

Vyrion gave a friendly nod to Victus as they parted, "I am glad you recovered as well, Spinebreaker."

Victus only gave him a grunt of acknowledgement. He seemed content to keep Vyrion in the dark about his condition, at least for now, a decision that Inissa felt was not her place to dispute.

"Then we're all alive, for now," Krothus said, impatience creeping through whatever initial relief Vyrion's appearance had brought. "The *Donovan*'s impact managed to displace much of the antechamber guardians, but I have no doubt the rest of the Ruin Lords will soon return to see what has truly happened here. We need to hurry."

Lord Sanata, looking particularly annoyed, added on, "Are you going to continue having emotional reunions, or are you going to help us? We need to remove this debris or all of this will be for nothing."

"All of you stop talking and start lifting then, we're asking for trouble out here," snapped one of the agents, grey-haired and grim. She was holding up one of the others, a piercer bolt stuck in his shoulder.

Wasting no more time, Vyrion and his unwashed Ruined ally joined Inissa and the rest. A great wall of rock stood in their way, a barrier that could have held up legions of soldiers for hours if they were to dig through it. But they were Ruined.

Like the cogs of some great machine, each of them found their part of the formation, their strength melding into one, their movements a part of a single grand gesture. Inissa could feel their energies flowing around her, a great pool of power that slowly reached out to the mountain of rubble and stone that blocked off the entrance to the antechamber. It slipped in between every crack, every crevice, like they were sending a flood of the Ruin crashing against its rocky shore.

In one voice, they heaved. Then, like a noteworthy pebble plucked off the floor by an invisible hand, the debris flew into the air.

Inissa could feel the tremendous strain pushing down on them, tons of rock begging to be released back to the earth below. Her arms trembled as she forced herself to resist it. Had she attempted this alone, she would have been crushed by the strain of such a task, but she was only one of many.

They groaned and struggled as the barrier hovered away, until, with a great crash, the mountain of stone dropped back down. Inissa's arms were nearly numb, her heartbeat racing through her tired muscles. One of Sanata's apprentices dropped to his knees. They had done it.

The antechamber, dented and crushed, stood revealed in front of them. Heavy doors were bent inwards, other parts peeled back, the shed skin of some metal monster, leaving just enough space for entry, albeit one at a time.

Beyond that narrow gap, Inissa felt something. A feeling of wrongness, some echo of the unnatural. Inissa sensed it clear as day, feeling as though she were seeing water flowing upwards, or flame burning icy cold.

Lord Sanata pointed at Krothus and Vyrion. "If you truly have some idea how to stop this ritual, you go first."

"We'll do what we can," Vyrion said, "And thank you for being the one sane Ruin Lord we have encountered today."

"And what a reward I have received for my good nature. Go, before I change my mind."

Krothus nudged Vyrion forward, remaining next to Inissa as the agents queued up to go in behind. Vyrion wasted no time in squeezing between the cramped gap, and one by one, the Imperial Agents followed close behind.

Over the dull roar of the battle outside their oasis, Inissa heard a faint whistle, the rattle of airborne metal. Then there was a clatter of objects hitting stone.

An agent, halfway through the gap, cried out as a piercer bolt slammed into his back and punched out his front. Another got one in the side. All around them, bolts bounced off the rubble, grunts and shrieks of pain following wherever they met their mark.

Inissa swung around.

Soldiers were pouring over the mounds of rubble into the crater as if a dam had burst. Volleys were sent out again and again.

"Defend yourselves!" Krothus shouted, already chopping through the waves of projectiles as they came down.

But there were too many. Everyone scrambled for cover as bolts pounded their position. One of Lord Sanata's apprentices had scarcely recovered from moving the boulders when a bolt ripped through his throat. An unaware orkathi warrior dropped, two holes in her chest.

"Nightshadow, shields!" Headcleaver was shouting, pushing his warriors into ranks again. The wall of shields went up. Sanata's soldiers slipped in behind.

Inissa wanted to run, to flee so far that nobody would ever find her. She stood next to the narrow gap the agents were filtering into, a primal fear compelling her to push them out of the way and hide in there herself. But she couldn't while Krothus was standing there, he would think her a coward.

He was shouting over at Soultotem as he waved the remaining agents through. "Tell your Chieftain to hold them off while we get inside. Then follow behind us when you can."

"We will try," she croaked.

Next in line was the unwashed Ruined, emitting an odour partway between a barn and a latrine pit. "I'm hungry. When can we eat?"

"Shut up and go inside." He did.

Farke hesitated, looking once to the advancing wave of soldiers, then to the blackness of the antechamber.

"If you don't go in I'm going to kill you myself," Krothus snarled.

Farke squeezed into the gap immediately.

More and more were crossing over the hills of rubble. Inissa wanted to pry everyone out of the way and disappear.

But then she heard it. A sound straight out of her nightmares.

"Do you think you can escape me so easily?"

There she was. Inissa's worst fear stood at the crest of the crater. Looming down, terrifyingly tall, an aura of death behind her.

Inissa began to shake, tremble like she never had before. She couldn't help it, she couldn't make it stop. Her mother walked down the hill towards them.

"Inissa, quickly," Krothus said, trying to push her into the gap, "Let Lord Sanata deal with her. We need to leave, now."

"I can't," Inissa found herself saying, ripping away from him. Her mother's mask smiled down at her, like it was all some joke.

Krothus' voice softened. "There's nothing you can do, not now. She is beyond any of us."

Inissa shook her head and wiped her eyes. Emperor above, she could use a snack right now. But more than that, she was tired; of the fear, of the nightmares, the worrying. That primal terror had faded, replaced with an emptiness, a resignation to what lay ahead.

"I can't keep running away from this, Krothus. She will haunt me the rest of my life if I don't do something."

Krothus frowned, clearly not happy, but Victus appeared at her side, resting a clawed hand on her shoulder. "Go, Krothus. I'll watch over her as best I can. You have my word."

Her master hesitated a moment, his scarred grey face looking much younger than Inissa remembered it, at least for just a fraction of a second.

"May the Ruin watch over you both." Then he was gone.

Inissa let out a shuddered breath. This was it.

Soldiers charged into the orkathi lines. Lord Sanata and her apprentices, runeblades ignited, joined the battle.

Inissa watched as mother drew ever closer, effortlessly drifting through it all like she were being carried by the wind. That blasted mask bobbing up and down, never blinking.

"Is this the end?" Inissa wondered aloud.

Victus shook his head, "Not just yet."

Chapter 29

Even

Just as Krothus squeezed his frame into the antechamber, Vyrion heard a huge commotion back outside; shouting and screaming, the screech of arms clashing hitting a high note above it all.

Krothus frowned and brushed dust off his armor. "We have less time than we thought."

He certainly had a talent for understatement.

"Then we'd better hurry," Vyrion said.

Everything that could go wrong already had, but that gave him little comfort. If he knew one thing, it was that no matter how bad things got, the Ruin always loved to throw one last test, one final trial, his way.

The antechamber was dim, poorly lit by the lazy flames of half-burnt out torches, letting shadows run rampant. It reminded Vyrion of the catacombs, musty and cold, with a hint of something hostile, but instead of those ancient stone walls, the room was covered in rich paintings and opulent gildings of gold.

And as the centerpiece, face down on the floor, was a corpse.

Dedri was already peering down at it. "I think we found Highlord Malus."

The body was that of a small man, shriveled and shrunken, like it had been left in the desert and deprived of all moisture. His skin was rough and leathery, clinging to bone as if only painted on, the dark pits left where eyes had once been stared off into the void.

"Are you sure?" Vyrion had never met a Highlord, but even the name itself evoked a certain strength, a dignity that was not at all met by the husk in front of him.

"Absolutely. And you weren't wrong about the ritual. Looks like he was drained for all he was worth."

But being right was little consolation. If that was true, then that was that. Highlord or not, he was gone, the same as any other mortal.

"All this time spent playing politics and picking sides, and he's dead," Krothus complained, "We never even met the man. What a spectacular waste of time."

"A waste for us, maybe," Vyrion said, "But I'm sure Callida doesn't see it that way."

"Hmph," Krothus grunted. Whether it was in agreement or not was impossible to say.

"More importantly, if this is what she could do to Malus," Dedri stood up and pointed a finger above them, "We had better stop her before she gets up there. The last thing we need is the Council turning into *this*." She gave the withered corpse a nudge with her foot, encouraging a giggle from Zlaterek.

Krothus nodded. "Then we need to figure out how exactly she did it. Quickly."

Vyrion was already halfway there. The moment they had entered, the remnants of the ritual had emanated a tremendous wrongness, an unnatural chill that crawled along his skin and burnt his nostrils. Only the center of the room, next to Malus, was devoid of it.

So Vyrion went to the edges of the room, where the temperature was the lowest.

He ran a hand over the floor, so cold that he expected it to be covered in a layer of ice. Instead, his palm came away covered in a black chalk, nearly invisible in the dim light. Just rubbing it in his palms was enough to send a jolt through his mind, an echo of some terrible power.

"There's a ritual circle here, drawn on the floor in chalk," he said, "Can anyone find another?"

Agents, Ruined, disgraced Captains; they all searched, some on their hands and knees.

"One here," Krothus said.

An agent called out from the other side of the room. "Another one here."

Vyrion thought for a moment, remembering how the instructions he and Jarek had received, all that time ago. It seemed like just yesterday; going into that tomb, fighting for their lives, their night together afterwards.

He cleared his throat, focusing his rebellious thoughts only on the task at hand. "A ritual like this needs powerful objects to focus it, to keep it from spinning out of control. From the looks of things, Callida has three. I'm not sure what they are, but they must have been innocuous enough that Malus wasn't able to notice them himself."

"And if these are destroyed?" Dedri asked.

"It all comes apart." Krothus sounded excited at the suggestion. The rest of the group hardly shared his enthusiasm.

"Then we have our objective."

"We do," Vyrion confirmed, "Taking Callida head on won't work, so we have to be clever."

But despite the confirmation of such a plan, not one of them seemed confident about their chances.

"Did you say *we*?" Farke stuttered. He was dabbing his brow with a cloth that desperately needed to be wrung out.

"Yes, all of us. We are the only ones who know about Callida's plans and are in a place to act on it."

A small part of Vyrion had hoped for a rousing speech, a cheer, anything that wasn't quiet uncertainty from his audience. But Vyrion was left wanting. He looked out at the faces staring back at him; Farke, scared out of his wits, Zlaterek, off in his own strange world, and Krothus, disheveled and withered, almost unfamiliar. At least Dedri and her agents seemed calm and collected, but even then, the concerned glances, the furrowed brows; the cracks were beginning to show.

And they were so few. A group of hopeless hopefuls, up against a now-empowered Ruin Lord, outmatched, and worst still, looking towards Vyrion for some kind of leadership. They must be truly desperate to think a Ruined who spent half his time floating from one failure to the next would be their best choice. But still, they looked to him as if he held the answers.

Vyrion would be happy slipping into the background and letting someone else take charge. Krothus, maybe Dedri, they both had the presence for it. And Vyrion had already done his part to help them along. But despite all his second-guessing, all his reasons why he shouldn't, Vyrion had to admit he liked it. He wasn't flinching away, wasn't passing the torch to someone just because he couldn't handle the pressure. No, he felt like he was made for this. Felt like for the first time, everyone else was burdened by an anxiety he was used to, inoculated against it through a lifetime of experience. Like he was chosen for this moment.

But just as he was finding his mental footing, a rumbling pain started in the back of his skull, pounding through his mind, reverberations sending aftershocks down his spine. That presence, the one that watched him, the one that never left his side, it was suddenly overwhelming.

It spoke, louder than he had ever heard it, rattling his bones and threatening to split his head open.

Hurry.

Only once the presence faded and the pain wracking his head ceased was Vyrion able to continue. "We're running out of time. We need to go."

So without another word, his motley band of allies were on the move.

The chamber fed up into a series of grand stairways, the gigantic proportions looming down at them as if they were nothing but tiny insects. The staircase curved around itself as it spiraled upwards, a helix of striking marble that seemed to defy gravity, providing a view of the courtyard below through a window of splendid stained glass.

Vyrion only briefly glimpsed down towards the carnage below. It was all he could stomach, he had seen enough violence for a lifetime.

As the angle of the spiral stairs softened and leveled out, the space grew wider, each new level opening into a gilded door, flanked by statues of some hooded figures Vyrion didn't like the look of. The stone's veiled, shadowy eyes seemed to follow his every step. And beyond each statue-guarded door, the sounds of battle filtered through. It was already spreading from the courtyard.

Zlaterek poked Vyrion with a wildly untrimmed fingernail, "I think your Ruin Lord has paid them a visit." He nodded up the next part of the stairs.

It was nothing short of a massacre. A dozen of the council's guards had been torn apart; cleaved in two, burned by lightning, ripped apart as if a gargantuan hand had grown tired of its latest playthings. Their crimson armor was nearly invisible, such was the gim cascade of blood dripping down each stair. And all around, like a foul stench that lingered, Callida's aura permeated the very air. Wild glee, murderous joy.

"She's not taking chances," Krothus growled, "These won't be the last ones we find."

Farke was looking down at the mangled bodies like he had just seen glimpse into his own demise. Vyrion could understand the hesitation; some of these guards had been Ruined, chosen specifically to protect the Council and their interests, disposed of like they were no more than thugs off the street. Their chances were looking worse all the time.

"At least we know we're headed the right way," Vyrion said, pushing his own misgivings aside to try and keep everyone else on track.

"I wish we weren't," Farke muttered.

Again, they climbed. Vyrion and Zlaterek brought up the rear while the others pressed on ahead, Vyrion's legs protesting their ascent almost as much as the section of his mind screaming out for self-preservation.

They passed by another pair of those cloaked statues, Vyrion felt their stoney gaze on his back, as though he shouldn't have been there.

"Ironic isn't it?" Zlaterek said, eyeing the figure as they went by.

"What is?"

"The Council are supposedly more powerful than we can possibly imagine, yet their fate is in our hands," Zlaterek continued, in a rare moment of lucidity, "Apprentices and criminals, saving those that rule over them."

Vyrion thought for a moment. "That's true. But these apprentices and criminals may become Highlords themselves, one day." Though he didn't have high hopes for himself, nor Zlaterek for that matter.

"That's what they would have you believe," Zlaterek said with a wink. Vyrion wasn't sure who 'they' were, and he didn't have time to ask.

Another turn of the staircase brought about a sudden chaos. No longer muffled behind a stone seal, the next statue-flanked door had been forced open, and the clash that had taken over the pyramid spilled into the stairway.

The black sun of Callida was everywhere, on the bloodstained tabards of soldiers packed shoulder to shoulder, stitched onto a ragged banner that waved above the mass of armor, signaling some impossible advance. Vyrion wasn't even sure who they were fighting, such was the melee's mayhem. He only knew that they were blocking their way.

"We don't have time for this," Dedri hissed. Her and her agents already had their weapons at hand.

"Then I'll be fast," Krothus said, already climbing the stairs, runeblade in hand.

But Vyrion yanked him back. "No, Krothus. We need to be smart about this, a Ruined would fully draw their attention to a greater threat, and the last thing we need is a whole division of soldiers after us."

Krothus didn't seem fully convinced nor happy about this logic. He looked to Vyrion, then back to the carnage ahead, then back to Vyrion, twisting his runeblade hilt in his hand all the while.

"I agree with Vyrion," Dedri added, "A distraction is needed, but not from you."

With a wave of her hand, the agents began creeping up the stairs, their piercers searching for targets, silently bobbing up and down as if lost at sea.

"My men and I will carve a path, keep any pursuers at bay. You need to continue up to-"

Someone cleared their throat. Vyrion and everyone else stopped what they were doing and looked towards the perpetrator.

Farke had straightened out his ill-fitting uniform and was standing at an even more ill-fitting attention. "Agent Dedri, I am sure we would all appreciate your noble sacrifice, but there is no need. I will stay and hold the line in your stead." He sounded sure, or as much as he could with a wavering, shaky voice.

Vyrion found his sudden bravery suspicious.

Dedri raised an eyebrow, not convinced either. "Really?"

Farke nodded. "I am. I don't know a thing about Ruin sorcery, or rituals, I would much prefer staying as far away from that as I can. If that involves getting my hands dirty here, then so be it." Then, with a rather guilty look, he continued. "And of course, if I survive, I'm sure there would be talk of a commendation for bravery, granting me my previous rank?"

Dedri rolled her eyes. "I'll look into it."

Krothus, still staring longingly at the combat ahead of them, let out a dismissive burst of air.

But Vyrion was never one to overlook a noble deed, even if the nobility was very much up for debate. "Good luck, Farke. We will remember your help today, and I hope to see you after this."

"I very much hope for the same." With a trembling hand, Farke combed his hair back into place one last time, then he unholstered his piercer pistol and moved up with the agents, their advance frozen halfway up the steps.

Dedri nodded at her troops and motioned her hand forward. A dozen piercers went off. A handful of armored bodies dropped to the floor, opening up the beginnings of a gap in the chaos.

"Go!"

Vyrion wasted no time, he was already sprinting as fast his burning legs could carry him. There had been enough stairs in one day to satisfy him for a lifetime.

The soldiers were firing back now, at least the ones that had noticed the new angle of attack. Bolts clattered off the walls, the stairs, metal shards flipping into the air; but Vyrion didn't spare a single second of hesitation. He and Krothus quickly left it all behind, Dedri's disciplined footfalls and Zlaterek's uneven shambles at their backs.

The burst of adrenaline rapidly carried them up the remaining stairs at a rapid pace. Vyrion didn't think he had run so fast in his entire life. His legs quickly realized this too, their screams of protest eventually dragging him to a halt.

"We're here." Dedri was breathing hard, the same as the rest of them.

They had made it to the end of the stairway, to the top chambers of the Dark Pyramid. The passages had already started closing in on them, cramped and crowded, like the architects of the mammoth structure had suddenly started running out of room. It still carried the same gilded elegance; gold and crimson decor, lined with grand paintings of vague shadowy figures, ancient runeblades mounted in glass like bizarre museum exhibits, but Vyrion was focused on something else. He could sense it in the air, in the walls.

Power.

Amidst the courtyard below, the Ruin had felt like a great whirlwind, whipped into a frenzy off the violence, the fear, the anger. But in the upper reaches it was different. It was an apocalyptic flood, an overwhelming force that felt like it could easily sweep away the whole of Thanaton in the blink of an eye. He couldn't see it, but Vyrion knew it was there, it ran over his skin and through his hair, always flowing upwards. Like something was drawing it in. But he couldn't focus too much on it, it felt as though he were staring directly into the sun - do it for too long and it was bound to cause some permanent damage.

Krothus didn't seem to share the sentiment. He was just standing there, eyes closed, basking in it all. Zlaterek was busy inspecting the glass cases nearby.

"I've never seen it so quiet. There should be a full company of guards here," Dedri said.

Not that they would do much good, judging by what they had seen earlier.

"Callida has misguided friends in high places," Krothus muttered.

The corridor was silent, the sounds of combat a distant memory. At the far end, it split left and right.

"Where does that go?" Vyrion asked.

Dedri was peering around, as if Calida could be hiding in plain sight just next to them, "It's the walkway around the council chambers. One big loop."

There were only four of them left, with three relics to find. Two routes, but only one real choice.

There was a sudden musical twinkle. Glass shattering. Zlaterek sifted through the broken shards, picked up the hilt of some runeblade, no doubt belonging to some hero passed. "Sorry, been trying to find one all day."

Dedri sighed and pinched the bridge of her nose.

Time was short. Vyrion could already feel his anxiety bubbling up within him, worries of failure and death, all he could do was try to stay one step ahead of it. "We still need to find and destroy those focusing relics. You two go left, we'll go right. I doubt Callida has been as obvious this time. So no chalk circles, she should be powerful enough that she only needs them to be nearby. She will have tried to mask the relics' presence somehow, so make sure to look carefully for anything amiss."

Zlaterek nodded, only half paying attention. He was busy inspecting his salvaged weapon, wildly muttering to himself like he were having a conversation with the thing.

Vyrion looked to Dedri, hardly seeming happy about her assignment. "Make sure he does it properly."

"I'll try. I can't say I rate our chances very highly, but good luck."

Vyrion wished he could say that he had a great certainty in their success, that he could sense that they were on the right path. But he couldn't.

"And you," he said lamely.

"The Ruin watches over us, we don't need luck," said Krothus.

Whether he truly believed that was unclear, but Dedri didn't stick around to debate it. Grabbing Zlaterek by the arm like he were an acolyte about to be reprimanded, she dragged him down the hallway and out of sight.

Vyrion and Krothus followed, taking the other turn.

"The Ruin seems to be far more supportive of Callida than to us, or she wouldn't have got this far."

Krothus shrugged. "Everyone has a destiny, the Ruin just helps you get there. Perhaps she was always meant to make it here. Perhaps we were always meant to stop her. Or try to, at least."

"I never took you for a deep thinker."

"Anyone is a deep thinker compared to all those Ruined below, mindlessly throwing their lives away as a part of someone else's game. I can at least say that my thoughts are my own."

It was a good point. Vyrion had to wonder how thoroughly the forces of Callida and Malus had contemplated their position before they had jumped into the fray. Probably not a single passing thought. Even before Fira had goaded them all on, before the *Donovan* had plummeted through the courtyard, every Ruin Lord there had been waiting, if not praying, for violence. He could feel it in the air the moment he had arrived. Whether they believed it would grant them a higher status, an excuse to dispose of rivals, or just to sate their bloodlust, it was all irrelevant. To Callida, they were nothing more than a distraction, a gang of useful fools laying their life on the line for her to realize her ambitions.

It left him wondering, were he and Krothus the same? Tools being used, risking their lives for someone else? If they were, he wasn't exactly sure who their wielder was.

The hallway kept wrapping around, no end in sight. Vyrion was nearly ready to turn back around when a side passage seemingly appeared out of nowhere. If the Ruined Council were going to have an entryway, he figured it would be this. A huge door of gold was flanked by two of the largest people Vyrion had ever seen, covered head to toe in armor so bright it hurt his eyes to look in their direction. He would have thought them sculptures if he couldn't see the tips of their monumental spears swaying with every breath.

But there was someone else there too. The sight of which instantly turned Vyrion's stomach upside down.

A man silently paced back and forth in front of the silent guardians, his messy mop of hair bouncing along with every step, a hefty satchel carried on his back. His face lit up the moment he saw them, splitting into a half-mocking grin. "Vyrion! Glad to see you're still in one piece."

"Jarek," Vyrion said, struggling to keep his tone even, "What are you doing?"

Jarek threw his arms up at the door behind him. "Waiting for the results of the council hearing, of course." But if he was, he hardly seemed concerned about it. He quickly closed the gap between them. "It's... good to see you. After our last talk, after I hadn't heard from you in days, I was a mess. I looked everywhere for you, fearing the worst."

Vyrion felt the beginnings of a smile force itself across his face against his will. He hated how easy it was. "I'm fine, Jarek."

There was a loud cough, breaking up the conversation with all the subtlety of a skyship crash. A shadow passed over Jarek's handsome features.

"Krothus," he said, sounding like he wanted to spit on the floor as he said it.

"Jarek," Krothus said, spitting on the floor enough for the both of them.

Vyrion moved in between them. "Enough you two. Jarek - where is she?"

He jerked a thumb towards the golden door behind him. "Lord Callida is already inside. If you're here to try and stop her, I'm afraid you're too late. It will be over soon enough."

The words felt like a cold dagger to the gut. Too late?

"And do they know her plans for the Council?" Krothus growled, nodding up at the luminescent guards flanking the doorway.

Jarek laughed, a sound that used to brighten Vyrion's day all on its own. Now it only stoked his anger.

"The Council Guardians are glorified doormen," Jarek explained all too happily, "They only grant entry to those who have been invited by the council themselves, never permitted to leave their posts. I could confess Lord Callida's entire plan to them right here, and they wouldn't move. But if I tried to *force* my way through for whatever reason, then that would be another story entirely." He paused, letting the inferred violence hang. "So just stop here, our master has won."

"Your master," Vyrion corrected, "Not ours, not anymore."

Jarek's ever-present smile seemed unbreakable. "You can argue semantics all you want, but when she is finished, you will quickly rethink your position. You'll see."

"I doubt it," said Krothus.

But Jarek ignored him. "Not even the Emperor himself will be able to challenge her. Think about it." He was suddenly clutching Vyrion's shoulder. "The best place we can be is at her side, Vyrion. We will be catapulted up Thanaton's ranks in an instant, finally having the recognition we deserve. Just, please, give it a chance."

"That's nice," Krothus snarled, "Now get out of our way, or we'll kill you."

"I'm talking to Vyrion, you grey thug," Jarek snapped, ripping his hand away from Vyrion to grab at his runeblade hilt. "The next time you threaten me, I'll have your tongue."

Krothus just took out his own weapon and looked to Vyrion, as if asking permission. Vyrion waved him down. He could get through to Jarek, he was sure of it. He didn't need any more death today.

"Don't make us do this, Jarek," he said, what little pride he had stopping him just short of pleading, "Please. Callida is manipulating you, using your knowledge of Victus' ritual to get what she wants. She reads your thoughts, promises you the world, but she only cares about herself. You don't need to die for her."

Those emerald eyes looked back at him. "Do you take me for an idiot, Vyrion? I'm not some dog following whoever promises the finest scraps, my destiny is my own."

"No, I meant ..." He hesitated, trying to find the right words, "I meant that you want to rise up through Thanaton, as any Ruined would, but it does not have to be at the expense of the entire Empire. There are other ways, you know this. She's led you believe there is no other way but-"

"You think so little of me." Jarek interrupted. "You really think I believe in her crusade? Of course not. But it's a means to an end. The only way we can rise from the muck without being dragged back down by the soon to be drowned is by rising far, far above them."

Vyrion felt like he was treading water, going nowhere. "I don't understand. You're willing to let everything burn. Everything. Just for that?"

Jarek was getting frustrated. His smile wavered, his voice grew louder. "You don't need to understand! I made the choice for both of us. You'll reap the benefits whether you can wrap your mind around the gravity of it all or not."

"Jarek, please, I just want to-"

"I don't care. It's done."

Krothus interjected with a mighty sneer. "Delusional *and* a traitor. What nice company you keep, Vyrion."

"No one was speaking to you, brute!" Jarek shot back. A vein was bulging in his forehead, ready to burst.

Krothus ignored him. "We don't have time for this, Vyrion."

"I'll make sure you have all the time in the world," Jarek barked, "I hope you enjoy rotting back in your cell."

Even Krothus fell silent, just for a moment. Vyrion just stared.

He had wanted to understand Jarek's poor decisions, to help him see some manipulation, some deception. It was the only way he could think of that would have placed him outside the Council chambers. The Jarek he knew wouldn't have gone this far just for power, would he? Perhaps Vyrion really wanted to find a reason why Jarek had treated him poorly, anything that wasn't Jarek himself. But now, with one statement, Vyrion realized that the only one being deceived here was himself. The Jarek he knew didn't exist. He doubted it ever had.

"You knew where Krothus was the whole time didn't you?" Vyrion asked slowly, "Every time I asked where he was, begged you to tell me, you lied to my face."

He was calmer, but Jarek looked different somehow. His smile was gone, a mask discarded, its purpose served. He nearly looked relieved.

"Of course," he said, without a hint of shame, "Doubly so

considering I was the one who got him arrested in the first place."

Vyrion felt sick to his stomach. "Why?"

Jarek waved a dismissive hand. "Someone had to take the fall for Lord Victus' death, risk the wrath of what few allies he had left. It wasn't going to be me. So who better than the oaf currently leading you astray? And with tensions so high, all it took was a few words to the right people, an informant spinning tales of murder outside the code's rules. You wouldn't understand, but this was what was best. For both of us."

Krothus was silent, but his fury obvious; his eyes nothing more than burning embers set in a twisted scowl.

Vyrion laughed, he couldn't help it. A single croak, laced with so much disbelief it could have been fake altogether. "For both of us? This was mere hours after we became Callida's apprentices, Jarek. It could have been a blank slate. Why not blame Lash or Partha? They-"

"I've been serving Callida for years." Jarek spoke like he were in a courtroom, correcting the record of some false accusation. "While Victus spent his days digging through the dirt like the lost fool that he is, I found someone who had the power I needed to climb above him."

Vyrion didn't know what to say. Had he really been so blind? Victus too, if this was to be believed. His most trusted apprentice had been pledged to another for who knew how long.

But Jarek wasn't finished, frantically vomiting words as if finally given permission to confess his sins, "I told her about Victus' relic being delivered, and I hired those mercenaries to attack the skyport and force Victus' allegiance. I killed Jayn Reed when she was about to talk. The moment Victus started planning his ritual, I informed Callida and decided to sabotage it. All of this was done to set me free. Set *us* free, Vyrion."

"Free ... from what?"

Jarek hesitated, like he wasn't sure himself. "From the Empire's failings. Free to gain the power we deserve."

For just a moment, Jarek's drive seemed to falter. Like he was saying the words without fully understanding the meaning behind them.

Vyrion took one last shot. "Jarek - stop with this nonsense. Just walk away, let Krothus and I through. We can pretend this never happened." He knew that could never be the case, but they were running out of time. Jarek needed to move, or be moved.

But Jarek didn't seem to be going anywhere, in fact he was suddenly furious all over again. "Oh you're an expert on pretending, right Vyrion?" He pointed at Krothus with his runeblade hilt, teeth bared. "Pretending he's anything but a brain-dead mongrel that should be put down."

Then he pointed it at Vyrion. "And pretending you weren't crying and whining like some lost puppy with him gone. It was pathetic. Weak. When this is all over, I'll make sure his head is mounted on some spike somewhere and you can get a long look at it. Then you'll realize that I'm the only one who could ever put up with someone like you."

There was a sharp intake of breath from Krothus. Then deafening silence.

Vyrion had sometimes thought about what it would be like, when he lost someone he had once cared about. He had always imagined himself looking out at a sunset, sat on a well-worn chair, reflecting on the good times and the bad, the conversations, the arguments, the laughter. He had expected to feel emotions crashing down on him; a sense of loss pulling on his heartstrings, a profound sadness bringing a tear to his eye, possibly even a wave of nostalgia, a wish for better times.

But now, he felt nothing. A hollowness had carved itself into his chest, a gaping cavern that he was half expecting to tumble into himself. Nothing. Lorren died for this?

Then, like the breaking of a vast dam, that hole in his heart was suddenly flooded. Anger, hatred, rage; it all rushed through him, filled it to the brim and just kept going. He felt it craw across his skin and set his fingers trembling. The Ruin feasted on it all, enveloping him, surging through him like he were struck by lightning.

Jarek took a step back, his bravado cracking. But Vyrion didn't care.

He shot his hand forward, hurling a blinding bolt of energy out of it. Jarek ignited his runeblade, catching the bolt in a clash of emerald and red, sending it crashing into the wall.

Shards of stone skittering across the floor. The Council Guardians watched, but did not move.

Krothus was trying to step between them. "Vyrion, let me-"

"No!" he hissed. It didn't even sound like his voice. He shoved Krothus out of the way.

One bolt. A tooth-rattling crash of thunder. Two. Another crash. But Jarek was deflecting them one by one, drawing closer as he did.

His blade crashed into Vyrion's, nearly ripping the thing from his grip. Vyrion rolled to the side, swinging wide, stabbing forward, anything he could to try and wipe that stupid look off Jarek's face. Self-preservation seemed a far off fantasy. He wanted to kill him. Needed to.

Their runeblades crashed together again. Jarek's emerald power runes hummed like a horde of angry bees, energy crackling off them, sending white lights skittering through Vyrion's vision.

"You never knew what to do when you got up close," Jarek sneered.

He knew he was taking the bait, but Vyrion couldn't stop himself. He ripped his blade away, tried to send a cut swinging down from the other side. But Jarek slammed into him, knocking him off balance. There was a screeching wail as his runeblade carved a gulley through Vyrion's chestplate.

The follow-up came down like an executioner's sentence. So bright, Vyrion could scarcely look at it. That should have been it, a quick skirmish, a valiant effort, a noble death. Some might have been satisfied with that.

But Vyrion wasn't. It only made him angrier, the force of it pushing into his skull, like a kettle desperate to spill over.

He raised a hand. The blade stopped mid-swing.

Then he roared, a yell of frustrated fury, of raw, animalistic violence. The type he never knew he had. Crimson lighting erupted from his palm, the bolts like the tentacles of some terrible creature, flinging themselves in every direction with reckless abandon, desperate to grasp Jarek in their terrible embrace.

Jarek danced back, panic creeping in. He blocked some of it, sure, but each bolt that snuck past singed his clothes, burnt his skin. The smell of roasting flesh filled the air, accompanied by frantic yelps of pain.

This was what Vyrion wanted. He had never wanted anything more, to rip Jarek apart, make him pay for every happy memory that would now plague his mind, corrupted beyond recovery. Each brief image that flashed into Vyrion's mind opened a new avenue for the Ruin to pour in, warranted a new explosion of energy out his fingertips.

Evenings spent drinking plum wine on the roof of the compound. A bolt smashed through whatever feeble barrier Jarek had constructed, a rock through glass.

Their morning walks atop the walls of Thanaton. A jagged streak of power sent Jarek sliding backwards as it caught his runeblade.

A chance meeting in the library that night. But it wasn't chance at all, was it? He seared off a chunk of Jarek's shoulder.

But Jarek had one last trick up his sleeve. Burnt and bloodied all over, he rolled under the next bolt. He swept Vyrion's probing jab away. Then a shockwave sent Vyrion slamming into the wall.

The impact sent Vyrion's vision spinning. His head throbbed, knees wobbled. Jarek's runeblade was already flying down at him. Vyrion, addled and acting only on instinct, blocked it poorly, sending pain arcing through his wrist. And the runeblade kept coming down. Battering his last, desperate defense. Shocking his arms, rattling his bones.

His runeblade flew out of his grip and careened down the hallway.

Krothus was running towards him, but he was too far to help. Vyrion cursed himself. Why did he think he could do this on his own? He had given it everything he could, and it had done nothing but delay the inevitable.

Jarek leaned in close, his ragged breaths hot on Vyrion's face, "You always did care too much."

Vyrion stared back at him, unflinching. "And you never got the bigger picture."

Jarek's runeblade came down. Vyrion didn't move. He just gestured with his left hand.

There was a sudden squelch, like slop into a bucket. Then Jarek's confidence evaporated, color drained from his face as his runeblade retracted and fell out his hand. He tried to stifle a cough, only for blood to pour from his mouth.

He looked down. Two twisted points had thrust themselves through him, like seedlings wriggling up through soil above. Vyrion's runeblade. He had sent it sailing back the moment it flew away from him.

Vyrion nudged his hand, its invisible grip on his runeblade forcing it deeper. Jarek groaned, took a shaky step back.

"I never knew what to do up close," Vyrion said quietly. He nudged his fingers and the blade thrust all the way through Jarek's chest and back to his hand.

Jarek managed one last look, his mop of hair slicked in blood and sweat and burns. Then he fell.

Vyrion had expected to feel a satisfaction, a weight lifted off of him. He got no such pleasure. The emptiness just felt worse.

Krothus reached down and pulled him up to his feet.

"That was impressive," he said simply.

Vyrion was looking down at Jarek's body, angled oddly, still smoking from the lightning blasts, the hole in his chest. "I'm sure it wasn't for him." Adrenaline kept him calm, pushed it all out of his head.

"His opinion is irrelevant. Always has been. But his arrogance might just help us."

He carelessly ripped Jarek's satchel off him, roughly shaking the contents loose. Papers, trinkets and provisions dropped out and clattered across the floor, the grand finale in the form of a glowing, runed skull. It bounced twice, then gently lolled over on one side, its sunken eyes staring up at the both of them.

"One of Callida's relics?"

"Must be," Vyrion said. It certainly looked the part.

Krothus shrugged, then stamped on it. The skull splintered with a satisfying crack, sending a light plume of smoke wafting up.

"That should do it."

"Good. But we still need to get to the Council," Vyrion said, nodding at the massive guards flanking the door ahead of them. They remained utterly still.

"I have no problem going through them," Krothus growled. Vyrion hardly shared his confidence.

Someone behind them cleared their throat.

They both whipped around, runeblades at the ready.

"No need for such things," the stranger said, flashing an unnerving smile of pointed teeth.

Vyrion recognised the crown of horns, the three-fingered appendages. He didn't lower his weapon. "What do you want, creature?"

"The Master wishes you entry, so it will be granted," they said, already pushing past them and up to the guards.

Krothus shot Vyrion a look. "Who, or what, is that?"

"A friend. I think." He still wasn't sure, but they were a bit short on friends at the moment.

He scarcely had a single moment of silence when the presence shouted into Vyrion's skull again.

GO. NOW.

Vyrion had to hold his head in his hands, such was the tremendous pain from the voice's yells. He was already going as fast as he could, what else could he do?

The Council Guardians watched with interest as the stranger stopped just in front of them. "The Master commands you grant them entry."

The Council Guardians looked at one another, helmets blank, and then, without a single word or objection, they stood aside.

The stranger gave the guardians a pleasant nod and then turned back and waved an open three-fingered hand. "The master's Council will see you now."

Chapter 30
Mother

There was no way out. The mountains of rubble closed in on them like a pen around cattle, the warband's shield wall nothing but a feeble mockery of the impregnable ring of stone rising up around them. All the while an endless tide of soldiers poured into the crater.

There was no way out.

Inissa stood among the orkathi at the entrance to the antechamber, trying her best to put on a brave face. It proved to be a near-impossible task.

There were just so many. Bolts pattered against the shield wall like rain on concrete, a constant onslaught that never seemed to end. Inissa closed her eyes, pretended she was waiting in the compound kitchens, listening for the great rainstorm to pass by.

A bolt struck a Nightshadow warrior next to her. He emitted a sound halfway between a gurgle and a shriek, not very common in Thanaton's rainstorms, and collapsed.

There was no way out.

"Stay alert, girl." Victus was standing over her, a great shield of armor and flesh.

"I am."

"You aren't."

Why did it matter anyways? She was hardly their best asset in this fight. She wasn't even second, let alone third.

Lord Sanata stood just ahead, squawking instructions to her three remaining apprentices, each flap of her feathered arms scattering stray feathers into the air.

"Kol, stay to the north, near that boulder. Don't leave the shield wall, but try and stop as many bolt volleys as you can."

"Yes, master." Worryingly pale, looking like he was wearing more blood than left in him. But still he went.

Next was a woman burdened with an expression of permanent surprise. Whether she was as terrified as Inissa or instead cursed with unnaturally high brows was unclear.

"Saurine, left flank. Don't let them break through."

"As you wish, master."

"Ba-foru, find that oaf of a Chieftain. Make sure he doesn't rush out to an early demise."

"Mmm, mmhmm." There wasn't much else to say when your jaw was bandaged shut.

Sanata briefly had a look at Inissa, like she were evaluating her use, or lack thereof. The latter seemed more likely. Inissa was inexperienced and scared out of her wits, yet here she was, trapped in a battle far beyond her ability, with her mother bearing down on them. She had disappeared into the crowd, for now, but Inissa knew she was still out there. It was only a matter of time until she found her.

Sanata waved Inissa over, her evaluation completed. "I do not know you, young one, but my advice is to stay out away from the front line. It is no place to learn."

"Where else is there?" It was a bit too late for a personal retreat. There was no way out.

The avian Ruin Lord looked around, like she were noticing their surroundings for the first time, then shrugged. "A good point. Remain within the shield wall, then. And keep your head down."

So just what she was doing now. Sage advice, then.

"And where will you be, Sanata?" Victus asked, "Acting as a doomed general, overseeing the end?"

That earned him a look, one of curiosity more than anything else. Victus still spoke like a Ruin Lord, despite his outward appearance. "For now, yes. But someone needs to stop Fira's madness. She has no care for the Council, the Empire, not even her own allies. Her paranoia is the only thing that drives her."

"So you aim to challenge her directly."

"If she ceases to see reason, then yes. The goal is to buy enough time for Callida's plan to be stopped."

"Hhmph," said Victus, grunting like he was giving her permission. He leant down and ripped an axe free from the Nightshadow warrior with a bolt through his neck.

Inissa tried her best to build a smile out of her crumbling facade of calm. "Good luck, Lord Sanata."

But she was already gone, lost behind the shields and crimson muscle of the Nightshadow formation.

"What chance does she have?" Inissa asked, to herself as much as anyone else.

"I wouldn't count her out. Not yet," said Victus. He was looking above them, like he had suddenly developed an interest in the courtyard ceiling. Inissa followed his gaze.

A swarm of hundreds of piercer bolts held their position above them, frozen mid-air as if they had forgotten how to fall. Other bolts would fly into the swarm, only to be ensnared in its grip, swelling the shadow above to ever greater size. And it was moving, slowly drifting like a lone cloud on a summer's day. Drifting in the direction that Lord Sanata had gone.

Victus steered Inissa away, pushing her back into the midst of the Nightshadow mob. "Come, girl. She has her job, and we have ours."

Inissa snorted. "And what is that? Hide and wait for this all to end?"

"No. Your mother will have apprentices of her own here. And when they join the battle, the Nightshadow will need a Ruined at their side."

He said it like she was the same as any of Sanata's apprentices, or Krothus, or Vyrion. As if she weren't a teenager who had picked up a runeblade for the first time only moments ago.

"There is a huge difference between them and me, Victus. I won't be a help at all."

"That is yet to be seen."

They were suddenly in a small clearing amidst the crimson bodies. Headcleaver stood surrounded by his bodyguards, massive brutes who looked more scars than sense.

"We won't simply wait here for Fira's cultists to bombard us with their coward's weapons!" he shouted.

The bodyguards crashed their fists into their chests in a salute that looked far more painful than necessary.

"We come for Lord Fira!" Headcleaver continued, triumphantly thrusting his axe up into the air as if it had struck her head off already.

Roars erupted from hoarse throats, weapons rattled, shields smashed together - Inissa realized too late that Victus had brought them to the soon to be front of the Nightshadow offensive. The last place she wanted to be.

The shield wall broke. They charged.

Despite her protests, Inissa was carried along the crimson tide. It broke its former banks and swept beyond, a great wave crashing into the waiting shore of soldiers. The impact showed no mercy. Not for anyone.

Pressed in on all sides, Inissa could scarcely see, let alone move. A warrior to her left caught a bolt through the eye, shrieking as he fell out of sight under the forest of trapped bodies. An orkathi axe caved in a soldier's helmet, unleashing a river of red as it was ripped free. Combat was a distant memory, cast aside in favor of wildly lashing out at whatever moved first, jostling and pushing on either side to get enough room to do so.

Inissa kept her runeblade close, unignited. The Nightshadow were too close. The last thing she needed was accidentally cleaving someone's arm off.

But her passivity seemed destined for a quick death.

As a gap opened up, a window that revealed itself only when two warriors hacked their way through half a dozen outflanked guards, she saw them. The one thing worse than her mother. Her apprentices.

If the Nightshadow charge had been a hammer, all force and momentum, the counterattack was a spear, razor sharp and precise. The six Ruined fell upon the orkathi advance like a pack of rabid animals, runeblades sweeping through flesh and metal like it were nothing but paper. Ripped and torn, dismembered and mutilated; the fate of their victims was the same regardless of whether they were Nightshadow warriors, Sanata's soldiers, or even Fira's own troops. They stopped the orkathi attack in its tracks.

Inissa watched them slaughter their way through the lines. She could feel her hand trembling, runeblade rattling. She needed to do something.

Someone else seemed to agree. Ba-Foru, bandaged jaw and all, appeared out of the chaos, runeblade at hand. But far from a triumphant saviour, the moment she revealed herself she was forced on the defensive. One of the counter-attacking apprentices, so fast as to be nearly invisible, sent a blow crashing into her, such strength behind it that it nearly sent Ba-Foru to the ground when she blocked it.

Inissa twisted and turned, trying to free herself from the throng, trying to help. But as she stumbled closer to her mother's Ruined, she noticed something that stopped in her tracks.

There were crystals. Protruding out their skulls like an unnatural growth, carrying an ever-shifting aura of sickly green; it was a sight Inissa had hoped never to lay eyes on again. But there they were - six crystals. Six vessels. Six living nightmares.

Any thoughts of helping evaporated as a chill enveloped her. She could only stand there and watch, gripping her runeblade hilt tighter than she had ever done, like she were keeping it from fleeing, and not the other way around. Why had she managed to lose Victus in the charge?

She saw Ba-Foru fall to one knee, crying out as her weapon flew off into the air. Her opponent, a withered, feral beast of a man, smiled down at her.

But then, like Inissa had called out to him, the man turned, still smiling.

His pupils were gone, his eyes a blank white.

Inissa starting backing away slowly, at first. But when that runeblade plunged through Ba-Foru, when her killer turned that terrifying gaze back to her, Inissa's retreat quickly turned into a rout.

She needed to get away. Somewhere, anywhere else, just not there, not amidst those demons. So she ran. The kind of desperate, frantic running where there are no thoughts besides fear, no feeling other than a pounding heart and heaving lungs.

She had made a mistake. She shouldn't have stayed, wasn't ready to face any of it. Not her demons, not her mother, not her past.

Her foot caught on a crushed helmet, sending her sprawling. She hit her head on something hard, setting her vision spinning, filled with warped images of bodies and blood and death.

Someone reached out a hand. It was Saurine, surprised as ever. Inissa reached up to grab it, but stopped. Something was wrong.

Hands with gnarled, long nails were holding Saurine in place. Her look of surprise was genuine, her hand reaching out as a desperate lifeline.

"Please help-"

A runeblade punched through Saurine's chest. The flesh around it blackened and died, like an unseeable fire raged around it. Then it was ripped away, and Saurine tossed aside as her killer stepped forward.

Blank white eyes stared down at Inissa. The possessed Ruined's mouth opened, filled with half-rotten teeth, but their voice seemed to come from elsewhere, from inside the crystal affixed to their forehead, a hideous whisper that he felt in her very mind.

"*Nobody escapes me.*"

Had she been able to, Inissa would have screamed. But fear froze her in place, stronger than any spell. The demon apprentice slowly reached out, a putrid aura coalescing in its palm, calling Inissa back to the past, to the darkness.

Then something flung the demon thing back, the Ruin blasting it away in a sudden surge. Inissa found herself being hoisted to her feet by powerful arms.

"Come child," Soultotem rasped, "This is no place to die."

Inissa could only meekly nod her thanks, her eyes still transfixed to the creature in front of her.

The blast had left it stunned, just for barely a moment, long enough for two Nightshadow warriors to try their luck. A spear thrust right through its leg, ripping away muscle and tendon, while a blow from the other warrior's axe stuck deep in the creature's shoulder.

That should have killed it. But the demon didn't seem to care, didn't even seem to notice.

As Inissa was pulled away, the last thing she saw was the demon raise its hand, then twist. Both the warriors fell, their bones shattered. It was still smiling.

Then it all passed out of sight. Soultotem didn't allow Inissa more than a second to process any of it, she only continued dragging her through the battle, pushing through bodies, both living and dead, in her march away from the front. Inissa just let her do it. Her mind was busy torturing her; images of those blank eyes, the fatal runeblade punching through Saurine's chest. She felt herself be carried away, caught in the current.

Only when they stopped behind the crumbled arm of a fallen statue did Inissa find her voice again. It came out strained and hoarse.

"I need to leave. I'm not helping anyone here."

She knew it sounded childish the moment she said it. They were fighting for their lives, for the future of the Empire, and she was already panicked and trying to run away. Why, because she was scared? Everyone was.

But if the old shaman shared the same sentiment, she didn't show it. She just put a gnarled claw on her shoulder. "We only do what we can. No more, no less."

"But I can't do *anything*, not when my mother is so close. She knows I'm here. Her apprentices know. That demon knows."

She felt panic rising up within her again, but Soultotem's claw gently squeezed her shoulder, sending it crashing back down.

"There is no escape from the past, child. The further you run, the more you fight it, the stronger it's hold on you becomes." She gave her a tusked smile. "Only when you find yourself old, like I have, you realize that the past is not an enemy. Nor is it an ally. It simply is. It is lessons to be remembered, mistakes not to be repeated. You are who you are because of it, but you must not let it control you. You must remember that yesterday has already happened, but it is not the same as today, nor tomorrow."

Inissa looked down at her dormant runeblade. It felt empty and lifeless in her hand. Probably not much different to its previous owner. Even if it was just a thing, a weapon, it had a past too.

Hers haunted her day and night, the memories of that dark room, that demon's touch. For so long she had pushed it away, fleeing from the memories, filling the void with treats and distractions. But now there was no easy escape, no running away. Her mother was here.

Deep down, Inissa still remembered the woman beneath that mask, and despite all her power, all the demons she summoned, Fira couldn't change that. She was a woman, a mother. A mortal. And a mortal could be stopped, Ruin Lord or not. Those demon-infested apprentices too, Inissa had seen a creature far worse than any of them meet its end.

So it was possible. The matchup hardly seemed fair, but it wasn't like she had much of a choice. She turned the runeblade over in her hands, feeling its rough metal caress her palm.

"Do you think we can win?"

Soultotem's smile faltered a bit, though she tried not to show it. "Only the ancestors know the answer to such things. But anything is possible."

Anything was possible. It was a statement meant to cover all avenues, cloak the near-certainty of failure with a hope for some miracle. Far from convincing. But Inissa didn't see it that way. She would have never thought it possible to flee her mother's fortress, become a Ruined, wind up here, wielding a slain foe's runeblade. Yet here she was.

"Anything is possible," she echoed. The runeblade ignited, bursting to life in her hands, a renewed sense of purpose driving it.

Soultotem watched her carefully. "You are strong, for an Imperial. You remind me of my daughter."

It felt good to know that not all mothers were monsters.

They returned to the fray.

It wasn't long before Inissa's arms were screaming in protest, slicked in sweat. She had forced her way back through the throng one sweep of her runeblade at a time, destroying any black mask tabard that crossed her path, aiding wherever she could, Soultotem hobbling always just behind. Each impact sent Inissa's teeth rattling, her clammy hands threatening to toss away her only weapon as she struggled to hold it firm.

But as much as she tried, nothing seemed to change. There were always more soldiers, always more bodies, but progress was elusive. It only seemed to be delaying the inevitable.

And one inevitability could be delayed no further.

Inissa was knelt down, checking a Nightshadow warrior for signs of life that she knew she wouldn't find. That's when she heard it. A runeblade's hum, a screech of metal halting its path.

It only took moments for her to find them.

Victus blocked another strike with a section of his armor, wrestling the demon to the ground. They struggled and floundered like two lovers in a spat of passion, twisting and turning, kicking up dust as they each tried to gain the upper hand. Victus had the brute strength, columns of muscle pressing down, but the demon was a trapped animal, feral and desperate. It quickly found a better solution.

The Ruin swelled around them and Victus slowly raised up in the air, meaty legs kicking. He clutched at his chest, trying to remove a hand that wasn't there, a hand crushing him to death.

The demon was on its feet, wheezing out a breath that might have been a laugh. Inissa was already running. Victus' eyes were bulging out his skull.

She couldn't lose him, not like this. But she just wasn't fast enough.

Someone leapt out of the muddle around them, sailing through the air as if tossed from the upper reaches of the courtyard. His huge axe came crashing down, and in one fearsome blow it caved in the demon's chest, slamming it to the ground.

As it fell, so too did Victus, the Ruin's hold dissipated.

Inissa skidded to a halt, nearly toppling over. It had been close, frighteningly so. But Victus seemed fine, rubbing at his chest, taking deep breaths, looking far more like he had nearly choked on his dinner than the Ruin itself. But Headcleaver, his savior, was focused on something else, something just in front of Inissa.

The demon was crawling towards her, clawing at the ground in a desperate bid at her legs. Inissa froze. Its blank white eyes stared up at her, the shattered bones in its collapsed chest rattling as it dragged itself closer, all the while it gasping out breathy wheezes. She just kept staring, caught between wanting to send her runeblade swiping down or running the other way.

Headcleaver lent down and wrapped his claws round the crystal in its forehead. He plucked it out, like removing a tick, then crushed it in his palm. "Abominations."

The demon shuddered, then finally lay still.

"Ones that can't seem to understand when they're dead," Victus muttered. He clasped Headcleaver's arm in thanks, then turned to Inissa, to Soultotem. "Good to see you are both still breathing. We are trying to push through to Lord Sanata."

Inissa had to rip her gaze away from the shattered body in front of her. One ragged hand still reached out, unmoving.

"I'm sure she can handle herself," she said eventually, though it was more a hope than anything else.

Victus kicked the demon's corpse. "That might be true if these creatures weren't lurking about. A few of them getting involved in Sanata's plans could prove to be a fatal distraction."

"Just another reason to end any of the creatures we come across," said Headcleaver, sounding very happy about such a possibility. His bodyguards lurking nearby seemed less keen on the idea.

"Then we should get on with it. Time is short." Victus said.

Soultotem pointed her staff ahead. "Then you may be pleased to know that I can sense something nearby. It might be her."

Inissa could feel it too. But it wasn't just Sanata. It was like the Ruin were crashing into itself, two great waves colliding, hammering into one another in tremendous fashion and sending great splashes of power echoing all around.

Inissa knew who else must have been involved. And were she on her own, she would never have drawn closer, might have tried to ignore it entirely. But she had the others, she had her runeblade. It had to happen now, or it never would.

She had to see her mother.

A no-man's land had formed in the midst of the crater, a wide circle where the combatants of both sides seemed happy to avoid. The amount of singed and dismembered bodies left within the area indicated such a lesson on positioning was harshly learned.

At the center of it was a dizzying dance of swordplay. Their runeblades crashed together in bright arcs of crimson and purple, each touch met with a terrible crackle, each strike sending sparks cascading into the air like they were celebrating the act of combat itself. Something smelt like burning, and Inissa wasn't sure what.

There she was. Inissa's mother was right in front of her. Cuts and burns had sprung up across her wiry limbs, but her mask betrayed nothing to their effect, its blank face unreadable as ever.

Lord Sanata was hardly as lucky. In some places, she looked to have been touched by death itself; her feathers had withered, armor rusted, and even flesh had rotted away. But decaying or not, she still fought on.

"In the name of the Emperor, stop this, Fira." she squawked, "We both want to stop Callida. Save your grievances for the Council, call off this delusional struggle."

It sounded more like begging than a reasoned request, and Inissa's mother clearly saw it as such.

"The Council, the Emperor, they are nothing more than false idols. I only have one master, and he does not answer to anyone within this crumbling institution. The Ruined who defied me will die, as will you."

Hearing that metallic, echoey voice was enough to send Inissa's heart pounding away.

Victus nudged her. "Look there." She followed his pointed claw.

Just on the edge of the circle, a pack of demons prowled along the boundary, lurching along in frightening unison. There were five left.

"Focus on our task. Put your mother out of your mind for now. Understand?"

"I do." Easier said than done. She looked at the orkathi with her; Headcleaver, Soultotem, the bodyguards, Victus too. Her hopes weren't high, but they had to try.

It wasn't like they had a choice regardless, the demons had already noticed them. Like hounds called to heel, they had bounded over, fanning out, penning them in. All those blank eyes watching them carefully.

One of them tossed a battered corpse to the ground. Kol, no more blood left in him, nothing more than an empty husk. That was the end of Sanata's apprentices, then, reduced to nothing but trophies to taunt with.

"It's time to put that runeblade to use, girl," Victus said quietly. He shifted the axe in his hand.

Fear was all around, it felt like Inissa was drowning in it. But all she could do was swallow it down. This was it.

The demons closed in on them, circling round, eyeing them up, each of their movements janky and unnatural, like puppets on strings.

In a raspy croak, they spoke all at once.

"*No escape.*" They were all looking at Inissa.

Then they struck. Runeblades hissed and hummed, the Nightshadow bellowed their war cries, everything came together all at once.

It was madness. One demon cut clean through a nearby warrior, lopping off half his torso. Inissa felt drops of blood spatter across her arm. Headcleaver caught a runeblade in the head of his axe and threw its wielder to the ground. Victus blocked a strike with his godrium armor, then ripped the runeblade out of its grip and tossed it away.

Inissa quickly found herself pressed in close to one of them. The demon stabbed and jabbed at her, the point of its runeblade ripping right past her face. She dodged back as best she could, but very strike was hair's width from ending her life.

She thought back to her lessons with Spinebreaker. With Krothus. The demon was charging at her, dedicated solely to offense. She needed to get it to overcommit.

She feinted a clumsy strike right. The demon took the bait. Its stance too wide, its torso twisted around too far as it swung in to punish the mistake; it was vulnerable.

Inissa's runeblade cut one of its arms off at the elbow.

But if losing appendages was something the demon was concerned with, it didn't show. Its white eyes stayed blank, its unnerving smile stayed wide.

"*Come back to us, little one. You are a long way from home.*" The presence within the crystal in its forehead flickered back and forth.

If the goal was to intimidate her, then it had spectacularly failed. It only made her angry.

She crashed into the demon's defense, two arms to one, her weapon's absorption runes leeching energy from her opponents weapon as they struggled. It hissed and snarled, but it couldn't break the stalemate. Then Inissa kicked out at one of its legs.

The demon grunted in surprise as its knee buckled. As it stumbled back, Inissa's weapon unleashed its stored energy, a flash of blinding light that overwhelmed those soulless blank eyes, forcing its maimed stump up to cover them. The crystal called out to Inissa for mercy.

Inissa's mercy was chopping her blade right into the demon's skull. The crystal exploded into a million pieces. Her foe seemed surprised more than anything, shuddering as though uncovering a startling revelation before collapsing into a heap.

She wanted to shout and cheer, celebrate her victory, show that she was no pushover after all. But any thoughts of celebration were cut short the moment she remembered where she was.

One of Headcleaver's bodyguards fell, his body a mess of deep gouges, dressed in a cloak of slowly seeping blood. Inissa briefly saw an image of their killer; axes and spears stuck in, fatal wounds collected like scars but rushing at her still despite them.

It was already right on top of her. Too late to bring up her runeblade.

Krothus would have been disappointed, death by distraction was hardly a noble one.

But as its runeblade came down, as this new demon's grin grew wider, Inissa found herself thrown to the side, stumbling just out of reach. Someone had shoved her clear.

She looked up just in time to see Soultotem standing there, holding back the runeblade with her staff. Holding back an executioner's axe with a bit of string.

The staff shattered. The strike cut right through, acting out its sentence with brutal efficiency. And just like that, Soultotem was gone. Inissa felt it. Felt the shaman's presence snuffed out, carried away into the Ruin's endless ocean. Gone, because of her.

But before Inissa could do anything about it, the tide of the skirmish shifted, sweaty bodies and bloodied weapons opening avenues as quickly as they closed them. A stray elbow caught her in the back, sending her flailing into the edge of the Ruin Lord's duel.

"You witch!" Sanata was shrieking. Smoke billowing from one of her hands, she waved it around in vain as it withered and died, suddenly no more than a blackened husk.

Inissa didn't need to see her mother's face behind that mask for her to know she was smiling. One more touch of her decay empowered runeblade and Sanata would look no different than her hand.

"The Council will put you down when this is over, Fira, like they should have last time."

"They have no power over me. The Empire eats itself time and time again, a flawed, broken relic, the Council blind to untapped power right under their nose. You continue to believe their lies. So does Callida, Malus, the Emperor himself. I've been shown the truth. The future."

Lord Sanata snorted. "If you're going to kill me, spare the ramblings. I would rather do it in silence."

Inissa watched, frozen, as her mother took a step forward.

"I will. But know your soul will serve a higher power."

She tried to look somewhere else, look to something comforting. But all around her, they were losing. Headcleaver's bodyguards had dwindled to a fraction of their original number. Victus and the Nightshadow Chieftain himself were cut off from them, facing a demon with half its face ripped away, neither looking confident. All around, the Nightshadow were being driven back by relentless piercer fire.

Inissa saw Soultotem's body, hunched over in the middle of it all. Three demons stood over it, staring her way. Grinning, taunting. Then they ran straight for her.

"Agh!"

Inissa risked a glance. Her mother had speared Sanata right through the middle, the purple aura of her runeblade's decay runes turning her feathers to dust.

Too much, it was all far too much. Inissa's heart raced, her vision faltered, her head swam. The runeblade in her hand flickered, sputtering on and off with each shuddered breath. There was pressure building and building, all of it pressing in on her skull, hammering at her head. It hurt, filled her whole body with an agonising pain.

All she could do was scream. Scream as loud as she ever had, ever could.

And screamed she did.

The demons tried to come close. But they should have fled. Any semblance of form or life was lost as they were crushed into oblivion, folded into pieces so tiny they might as well have been dust.

Inissa screamed and screamed until she felt her throat would burst, that the pressure in her head would make her entire body erupt. People ran, desperate to escape. The slow ones were blasted away. The battlefield was thrown apart.

Inissa had no idea how long it lasted. Only that it wasn't forever.

By the end she was on her knees, alone in an empty circle. Alone, except for her mother, looming down at her, a gangle of stick limbs and ragged cloth.

"My daughter, I thought I had lost you."

Inissa didn't respond. Her runeblade was still in her hand, maybe she could-

Her mothers arms wrapped around her, a mantle of unwanted affection. Inissa froze up.

"I missed you. I thought the worst, I thought ..." To Inissa's surprise, her mother choked out a mask-muffled sob, but recovered quickly. "You look different. Grown."

Inissa still said nothing. But she wanted to. Wanted to ask her how she could have treated her the way she did, how she could live with herself every day knowing the horrible things she'd done. But she didn't.

There was a click and a hiss as her mother removed her mask. Inissa looked away, not wanting to see whatever lurked underneath.

"My child, please. Speak to me, let me know you're alright." Her voice was softer without the mask. Familiar, almost comforting. Just hearing it made tears begin to flow.

Inissa still refused to look up. "What do you want?"

"What's best for you, Inissa. As I always have. Please come home with me, we have so much to make up for."

As she always had. What a load of nonsense. But Inissa had a chance to make things better, not for her, but for everyone else.

Inisa took a deep breath. "I will go with you. But only if we leave right now. Only if you forget all of this, only if you leave the orkathi be."

"You are in no position to bargain," her mother said, her voice hardening, "I must do my work, you know this. The Empire has run its course."

"Please, mother. Take me, but leave them."

Against her better judgment, Inissa finally looked up. She couldn't remember when her mother had started wearing the mask, and she didn't know what she expected to see under it now, after all these years. Some horrible demon, its skin rotted away? Some terrible wound, the source of her mother's madness?

But there were no blemishes, no mutations, no terrible curse. It was just her. It was always her. A few wrinkles more from when Inissa had seen her last, but just as the sun rose every morning, her mother was her mother. Like a spell all too familiar, Inissa was instantly transported back to better times; laughter and contentment and love. A past she knew deep down was nothing like the nostalgia would have her believe.

The idealistic child within Inissa was begging, pleading for her mother to see reason, to prove she was a changed woman and just walk away. But one look was all it took to see how much of a fantasy it really was.

Fira held her by the shoulders, one step away from shaking her. "Come, child. I will take you home, but you know I cannot leave work undone. I follow a higher cause."

"Please, mother. Listen to me, just this once."

Inissa was on her feet now, her mother's vice grip nearly bending her shoulders inwards.

"You know I can't."

"Please!" It was nothing more than a desperate wail.

"No. You must understand, I only want what's best for you."

What's best for her? Inissa tried to wriggle out of her grip, to force her mother's hands away from her. But she couldn't no matter how much she twisted and turned and thrashed. Her mother tried to hug her close, stop her struggling.

It all happened so fast. A runeblade ignited. Inissa felt blood seeping down.

Her mother always had such beautiful blue eyes.

Chapter 31

Trial

Krothus was getting tired of being constantly reminded of his insignificance. Though he supposed entering the Ruined Council's chambers was the one time he was meant to feel small.

The chambers were housed in a large dome, ringed by nothing but columns and shadows. At the center were thirteen seats, closer to thrones than chairs, in a crescent around the glass floor in the middle of the chamber, overlooking the carnage below as though they sat high paying spectators at the fighting pits.

The centermost seat, grand and prominent, was empty. The Ruined Council occupied the others.

Just standing in their presence was overwhelming. Krothus felt like he needed to look away, to avert his gaze. But he refused. If he was there to save them, then he had earned the right to bask in their power. And power it was. If Krothus could feel Ruin Lords like ever-burning furnaces, emanating great waves of their strength with each pulse of their inner flame, then these Highlords wielded barely restrained firestorms, the kind that could leave entire cities nothing but burnt timbers and ash. The kind that Krothus could only dream of possessing.

But that wasn't all. The Ruin's vast blessing had made its mark on the twelve Council members, its favor evident. One Highlord was covered in green scales, forked tongue curiously flicking out their mouth, while another, her legs withered and lame, hovered above her chair, carried aloft by the Ruin itself. A third was more machine than man, whirring gears and clockwork limbs manufactured into a heavy frame, a pair of eyes all that Krothus could see under a heavy helmet. The rest were a menagerie of mutations, rich robes and haughty expressions. They certainly fit the part.

For all their oddities, Krothus knew the twelve were second to only the Emperor himself; their abilities incomprehensible, their pledged forces as vast as a small kingdom, the Empire under their collective thumbs. This made it all the more amusing seeing Lord Callida stood defiantly, staring up at them like an unruly child in the center of the room. Had she been anyone else, Krothus would have laughed at their boldness.

But even watching her from across the room, he could sense a change. The Callida standing before him and the master he had once served were different in orders of magnitude; she now crackled with barely contained energy, as if she had been struck by a bolt from the heavens and was struggling to contain it.

And despite all their power, none of them, not the council, not Callida, noticed Krothus and Vyrion enter. They continued unimpeded and unaware of their presence.

"And you would think yourself worthy of the title of Highlord purely because you have brought chaos to our doorstep?" the Highlord hovering about her seat croaked. She looked impossibly ancient, a floating bundle of wrinkled skin.

"You and Malus were supposed to settle your matters privately. *Quietly*," the mechanical Highlord added in a voice like grinding metal. "Involving your power bases has only served to fuel your ego and stoke a conflict that will rage through the city. This madness is not what we agreed, nor is it worthy of a Highlord."

Callida laughed, a condescending twinkle that was far more an insult than anything else. Krothus knew it all too well. Tensions were already running high, but his former master always knew how to push the right buttons to escalate it even further.

"Of course, Achima. You would prefer we kept our combat confined to your rules, so even when I emerge victorious, we could still be stuck talking about whether I am *worthy*. Malus is dead, and I killed him, that should be reason enough."

Her statement resulted in a wave of murmurs sweeping across the Council, none of whom looked too pleased about this development.

Highlords were few, a death of even one was a significant event. It would take a tremendously gifted Ruin Lord to slay Highlord Malus, even if they had procured such ancient weapons as Callida. The Council had clearly misjudged the situation.

Krothus felt a tap on his shoulder.

"Look," Vyrion whispered, "The relic, it's there in her hand."

Sure enough, amidst her fine crimson robes, Callida was clutching the small pyramid tightly, holding it close, like she were worried it would fly off.

"So she hasn't used it," Krothus said.

"Not yet."

It was only a matter of time.

"You forget yourself, Callida," hissed the scaled Highlord, his forked tongue doing a furious dance all on its own. "You think you can simply walk away from all this with a new title, just by demanding it be so? Who do you think you are?"

"I am the future, Obra," Callida said, smiling wide. "The Ruined Empire no longer follows the code that it was built upon. It is broken. The strong rule the weak, but if the strong are not permitted to rise, to rule, then the status quo is weakened with every passing day. The Empire has become a fat, bloated carcass, slowly rotting away as this Council sits idly by, comfortable and untouchable."

If the Council had been agitated before, they were now absolutely furious. Krothus felt the tension in the room grow thick with the risk of glorious violence, the Ruin whipped into an excited flurry as a result. Things were about to come to a head, and with that relic in Callida's hands, it was not going to end the way the Council expected.

If he and Vyrion were going to intervene, the time was upon them. Krothus was prepared of course, he had imagined this moment countless times before; crushing Callida's plans with a smile on his face, watching her wail, defeated, as he ended her scheme with a few clever words.

But before he could waltz in and charm the Council as he had always envisaged, some fool started clapping. Slow at first, building and building as the domed room amplified it a hundred fold, making it seem like a hidden audience was making their appreciation known. The Council and Callida all looked about, bewildered. Vyrion gave him an odd look.

That was just about when Krothus realized it was him clapping. Not quite how he wanted his entrance to be, less towards superior mockery and more towards childish interruption. But it got his point across. He cleared his throat and stepped forward.

"What a speech, Callida. You are truly a representative of the everyday man, nobly bringing reforms to the upper reaches of the Empire. I am sure the Imperial citizenry are honored to have such a magnanimous champion."

Krothus wasn't sure he could have coated his words in any more venom if he tried. He was half expecting to feel poison sting his tongue with every syllable.

Now came Callida's realization, her plan discovered, her understanding that all was foiled. The Council watched him with a mixture of outrage and confusion, as she slowly turned round.

Krothus had never truly seen pure, unadulterated hatred before. The kind that burned from the soul, the kind that wouldn't rest until every trace of you was wiped from the earth. But he could see it now. Callida's eyes could have burned a hole right through him.

He was ruining her moment of final, glorious victory, and no doubt had she not been in the Council Chamber, surrounded by Highlords, she would have killed him instantly. Krothus felt the whisper of death in his ear. His imagination had hardly considered that part.

"Who dares to come here uninvited?" the ancient Highlord growled, bobbing up and down in the air as she shook a wrinkled fist. As amusing as the gesture was, Krothus knew he had only moments to explain his presence or his glorious intervention would come to a rapid close.

"I am Krothus, former apprentice to Lord Callida," he said loudly, "And this is Vyrion, former apprentice to Lord Victus."

"We are here to stop Callida," Vyrion added. "She is attempting to use an ancient ritual to betray you all, the same tool she used to slay Highlord Malus."

Their reaction was yet another deviation from Krothus' imagined victory. Some simply laughed, no doubt finding the notion of such a thing absurd, while others remained in a silent stew of anger; though due to their uninvited entry or the suggestion that the Council were weak enough to be slain by Callida, Krothus wasn't sure. The only thing he was certain of was that none were as furious as his former master.

"These intruders are nothing but traitors," Callida spat, "They are speaking out of turn and I will scrub them from your presence." Her hand reached out, a halo of lightning crackling around it.

Krothus got ready. What for, he wasn't sure. He was quite sure there would be no dodging that.

"They are guests of the Emperor himself, and will not be harmed," a voice called out.

The horned stranger had appeared, crawling along the impressive seat in the middle of the Council empty like an ugly fly over a corpse. Krothus still failed to understand the creature's involvement with the Emperor, or more importantly, how Vyrion was tied into it, but he was willing to overlook such connections if it kept him in one piece.

The mention of the Emperor caught the Council's attention. Several shifted in their seats, and those that had been laughing had a rapid change of heart.

After a surveying glance around the room, Callida retracted her hand. Stolen power or not, disobeying the Emperor's will and facing the wrath of a dozen Highlords at once was clearly not something she was keen to jump into. But the look on her face said it all - she wasn't done, merely circling back into the undergrowth, looking for another opportunity to strike.

"Speak, then, if the Emperor wills it," Highlord Achima said, gears in his chest creaking and clunking as he leaned forward.

Krothus looked to Vyrion, who cleared his throat and raised his voice to address their newly attentive audience.

"My lords, Lord Callida is in possession of a stolen artifact that allows her to conduct a ritual. A ritual that -"

Vyrion stopped. The Highlords looked to one another as the silence lingered.

"Vyrion?" Krothus whispered. He was just standing there.

Vyrion's mouth was moving, forming some silent words, but speaking seemed beyond him. Krothus was left wondering what he was playing at, at least until Vyrion finally gurgled out a stuttered gasp, a man drowning on dry land. He clutched at his throat, clawing at some invisible assailant.

"These two are nothing but delusional criminals, responsible for killing a Ruin Lord on the orders of the Republic," said Callida, smirking as she watched Vyrion squirm. "They have obviously deceived the Emperor to gain his protection."

The Council were on their feet in an instant.

"You dare disregard the Emperor's protection?" Highlord Obra hissed. His runeblade was already held in his scaled hand. The rest of the outraged mob followed suit.

Meanwhile, Vyrion was turning blue. Krothus' stomach was wound so tight that it felt as if he were being strangled too. He had to do something.

The hovering Highlord waved a wrinkled arm at Callida like she were swinging a gavel, "The Emperor's word cannot be broken. The penalty is death."

"Where is the Emperor, then?" Callida snarled. "His seat sits empty, just as it always has. You look to a ghost for leadership."

Unable to break the invisible hold around Vyrion's throat, Krothus ran at Callida. He wasn't about to lose him, not now, not when they were so close. But an instant later Krothus found himself blown back, sailing through the air and crashing into the polished floor.

"You insult the Council and the Emperor both!" Achima whirred.

Callida had cast Krothus aside without moving a muscle. Like she hadn't even noticed, too busy slinging insults to the Council. That enraged Krothus even further. Fury gnawed at his heart as he got back to his feet. He would kill her, kill her if it was the last thing he did.

Vyrion, on his knees several strides away, eyes bulging, pointed above them with a shaky finger. Krothus looked up.

The relic had left Callida's hand, now hovering high in the air, barely visible. If the Highlords had noticed it, they made no indication, no doubt blinded by the tempting promise of removing a troublesome thorn from their side. Krothus was quite sure he saw the tip of the pyramid folding open. That was far from good.

Callida too, looked up. "Perhaps the Emperor needs some competition."

There was a great flash, forcing Krothus to avert his gaze or risk being blinded. Even so, the light seeped through his fingers, his eyelids, like the morning sun bearing down on his face but a hundred times worse. Only when it reached a critical point, so bright that Krothus could feel it searing into his brain, did it stop. A low hum buzzed all around.

When Krothus opened his eyes, he could only wish that he had kept them shut.

Tendrils of ghastly energy stretched out from the artifact, waving about like the tentacles of a vast monster, the ethereal limbs seizing whatever unfortunate soul was within reach. Krothus held out some hope that the Highlords would simply be too powerful to be caught in the sorcery, but for all their seemingly limitless might, they were swept up as easily as any other. Achima tried to cut through a tendril with his runeblade, only for it to ignore the gesture completely and yank him up into the air; Obra was slithering away, at first, before attempting to crush a spectral tentacle with the Ruin, which it ignored and ripped him away.

Krothus could only watch as the most powerful Ruin Lords he had ever seen were captured. He remembered Victus's ritual, the deathly chill, the helplessness he had felt being dragged into the waiting arms of whatever lurked within that metal pyramid. The creators of the ancient device, whoever they had been, had certainly been thorough if

Highlords were rendered just as useless.

Two of the ethereal tentacles swung down down at him, impossibly fast, impossible to avoid.

Options fluttered through Krothus' mind; fighting, running, using the Ruin to blast them back, but in the end, he knew he could only sit and watch as the things came at him. If the Highlords couldn't avoid this fate, then he was just as doomed as them. All his ambitious plans, his glorious destiny - it was all a waste. He closed his eyes and waited for the tendril to sweep him away.

But Krothus waited, and waited, nothing happened. He opened one eye, then two. Like a hunting dog that lost a scent, the tentacles were circling round, searching for something they could no longer find. Krothus hadn't hardly done anything to conceal himself, he was just standing there, yet the spectral limbs acted as if he had suddenly vanished.

A brutal cough rang out just ahead, the kind that would normally herald the end of a life, but for Krothus it only inspired hope. Vyrion was massaging his throat, deathly pale but very much alive, as a tendril too lurked just above him, blind and deaf to his presence.

As he sat up the ethereal tentacles retreated, drawn back within the artifact without their prize. The others, far more successful, remained suspended in the air, a dozen Highlords struggling within their grasp.

Krothus walked over and hoisted him to his feet, triggering Vyrion to unleash a mighty outburst of coughing. "Ugh ... I have a feeling our benefactor is ensuring our survival, somehow."

How useful. "If the Emperor truly wanted to help us, why doesn't he strike Callida down himself?

She stood just under the activated artifact, looking up at the terrifying display with a fanatical enthusiasm, arms raised up like she were expecting an embrace from above.

"The world is full of mysteries, Krothus," Vyrion rasped. He sounded like he'd been shouting for hours, his voice hoarse and withered. "But we still need to stop her. We've destroyed one of the focusing relics already, if another one is nearby we could destabilize the ritual. We have to try."

Even with only a single relic destroyed, the ritual was far from stable. Bolts of unrestrained power occasionally crackled across the ceiling like a half-forgotten thunderstorm, while a maelstrom of energy whirled and flashed around the tip of the pyramid artifact, barely contained within whatever sorcery Callida was channeling. The cracks were there, they just needed to push it further.

Krothus watched her, perched at the center of it all.

"She would probably be carrying one herself," he suggested, "There is no way she would entrust the entirety of her plan to underlings, Callida wouldn't gamble on something like this."

He knew Callida as he knew his own mind. If you wanted something done right, you had to do it yourself.

Vyrion cleared his throat, not that it did anything, "We can only hope that Dedri and Zlaterek will find the third, then. Because I don't think we will be able to take Callida's from her."

Krothus smiled, feeling the familiar excitement roll across his back. "But we're going to try anyway, aren't we?"

"Of course we are," Vyrion said, smiling right back.

Their runeblades ignited at the same time, flame and metal, strength and sorcery. In any other time, drawing a weapon in this room was a crime punishable by death, but such things were leagues away now. They charged towards the center of the ritual.

It didn't take long for Callida to notice their presence, the brief flicker of surprise flashing across her face giving Krothus the smallest burst of satisfaction before her smugness returned in full force.

"It's too late. I could have easily disposed of both of you even before Malus unwillingly surrendered his power to me, but now? Now it would be nothing more than swatting flies." Her runeblades flew into both her hands, the blades simultaneously igniting into two pillars of crimson. "Come then, toying with two whelps will be a perfect way to cherish the final moments of before this Empire is remade for the better."

She didn't wait for their response. Callida moved like lightning, faster than Krothus could even make sense of. It was only instinct that brought his runeblade up in time. And when Callida's weapon struck his own, the force of the blow turned his arms numb and sent him sliding backwards.

Her other blade, forgotten in his desperation, hovered just next to his head. One swipe, and it would be over. He hadn't even lasted longer than a single moment. But Callida just laughed, whipping the blade across Krothus' cheek instead. His face burned as the Ruin sharpened metal cut a shallow gash up the side of his head. Krothus didn't have to look to know it was already bleeding, the waves of warmth cascading down onto his neck face telling him as much.

A bolt of Ruin lightning flew at Callida from the left, not that she seemed to care. A single glare was all it took to dissipate it into nothingness, a single move of her finger sent Vyrion sailing towards her. A swift headbutt sent him sprawling.

Above them, the tendrils were slowly dragging their unwilling captives towards the artifact at the center of the storm.

"You're going to have to do more than that," Callida purred, "Otherwise this won't be any fun."

Krothus, face still afire with the pain of his new wound, wanted nothing more than to see her smug face smashed in. He roared as his flaming runeblade flew out the previous deadlock and swept downwards, only for the other of Callida's runeblades to effortlessly catch it. A strike from Vyrion was met with a similar result.

The trio stood there for a moment, Callida smiling, no doubt savoring her inevitable victory, while Krothus and Vyrion were struggling just to keep their blades from being ripped out of their grip. Then Krothus suddenly felt something crash into his chest and toss him away.

He had no idea whether it had been a punch, a kick, or the Ruin itself; but the ringing in his ears and the sharp pain of a broken rib hurt all the same. Vyrion hadn't fared much better, clutching his leg a short distance away. Callida looked like she was thoroughly enjoying herself.

"This isn't working," Krothus grunted.

"Obviously," Vyrion said, "But what choice do we have?"

Krothus looked up at the great storm of energy above them, the ethereal tentacles slowly dragging their payloads painted across it all like a dozen shooting stars. Vyrion was right, there was no choice here, it was either fight or watch it all burn.

They both got back to their feet, sharing the same hard look; determination and desperation both. Krothus had known Vyrion for as long as he could remember, and in all that time, Krothus had never felt the rot of doubt seeping into his heart like it did now. Did they have the strength to do this?

Again and again, they threw everything they could muster at Callida. Blasts of the Ruin, bolts of lightning, flurries of runeblade strikes; she rebuked the two of them as if they were children. Too slow, too weak; she was barely interested and still they were vastly outclassed.

Soon, Krothus was back on the floor, his lungs heaving, his body battling the inferno of pain flaring up from fractures and cuts all over. He could deal with the pain, that wasn't something new; he'd been beaten senseless, stabbed and cut, even choked to the point of blacking out in the past. And he had dealt with it as a Ruined should; growing stronger, unleashing the same fate on those responsible. But humiliated? To be cast aside so easily, so pathetically, that hurt more than broken bones ever could. What was the point of all of this if it was only to lead here?

Vyrion seemed to be thinking the same thing.

"Damn it, If you sent us here to stop this, then *help us*!" he shouted, smacking his head repeatedly, as if the secret to victory was locked deep inside.

Krothus found this crazed behavior concerning, Callida found it amusing.

"No one is coming to help you Vyrion, no matter how hard you hurt yourself," she sneered in between laughs, "You are alone in your failure."

But she wasn't quite right. Krothus felt some presence raise the hairs on the back of his neck, an unsettling feeling of something, some*one* casting their eye upon him.

"You're the one standing here on your own," Vyrion spat back, "That's your failure."

Callida rolled her eyes. "Falling back on words to do the fighting for you? Pick better ones - I'm far from alone. Just look below us, countless apprentices and Ruin Lords throw their lives away at my command, while your good 'friend' Jarek lurks just outside these walls, at my beck and call. "

"He did, until Vyrion killed him." Krothus spat on the floor, a hefty proportion of which was blood.

Callida's mask slipped for a moment, concern briefly rearing its head. Not for Jarek, no, she looked up at the chaos above as if noticing it for the first time, the ritual her only focus. Only now did she see the fragile stitches holding it all together were frayed.

A boom echoed across the chamber, audible even over the hum of the sorcery at work. The trio stopped their exchange, all looking in the direction of the noise. The doors on the opposite side of the chamber had swung open.

Two people stepped into view, one in a battered grey uniform, the other in nothing short of rags, both looking particularly pleased with themselves. Krothus felt the rare stubborn smile begin to force itself across his face as he saw Dedri give him a wink. All the while, the presence he had felt was gaining strength.

Callida looked back to Krothus and Vyrion. "You can bring as many weaklings as you want, this changes nothing."

"What if we have this? " Dedri called out, pulling a glowing talisman out from her jacket pocket, "Does that change anything, you *bitch*?"

"Bitch!" Zlaterek echoed, his ancient runeblade at the ready.

Callida had no witty retort for the newcomers. Any trace of humor she had found in toying with them had vanished completely, replaced with an animalistic hunger, a fury in her eyes that Krothus nearly cringed away from. He wanted to warn them, to prepare Dedri and Zlaterek for the power they had just provoked, but Krothus already knew it was too late.

Callida sprinted forward like a gust of wind, faster than any of them could even comprehend. Krothus did the only thing he could in that single moment. He tried to stop her.

He willed the Ruin to wrap itself around Callida, to halt her relentless advance and pull her back, to slow her just long enough to buy them time. Krothus didn't have to look to know Vyrion was doing it too - he could feel it; the fear, the adrenaline, the last desperate gesture to stop their plan from falling apart at the seams.

Even together, they were nothing more than flies buzzing about the head of a charging bull; an annoyance, a distraction, only enough to take her attention for a fraction of a second.

But that was all Zlaterek needed. Armed a wild grin and his stolen runeblade, he cut through the amulet, shattering it with a crash like a thousand breaking windows.

Krothus felt like cheering, but he settled for falling to his knees, exhausted.

Callida stopped her charge short, skidding to a halt a few strides from the newcomers, her arms stretched and straining above her as the ritual threatened to spin out of control. Jagged cracks of light were bleeding through the maelstrom above as sparks of unbound power shimmered into being, sending great claps of thunder echoing through the chamber. But despite the dazzling firestorm and Krothus' brief glimmer of hope, the Highlords remained ensnared, dangerously close to being drawn into the epicenter of the maelstrom. And once that happened, once the Council's power was stolen away, it wouldn't matter how many relics they destroyed, Krothus knew Callida would be unstoppable.

He considered taking advantage of the brief moment of vulnerability as Callida held the ritual in place, but something made Krothus hesitate. Whether it was some hidden wisdom, or just a gut feeling, he wasn't sure - but whatever it was, Zlaterek didn't possess it. His former cellmate took a single step forward, weapon raised high above his head.

Callida only had to flick her finger. Zlaterek blasted away as if he had been struck by an explosion, flipping through the air like a reckless acrobat before cracking into a column with such a force that chunks of masonry scattered across the floor.

He didn't get up.

"No more games," Callida said.

Dedri was already backing away as Callida's attention went back to maintaining the ritual. Krothus couldn't blame her, an Imperial Agent was nothing compared to such power, even he and Vyrion weren't any more useful, after only a few minutes of Callida's toying they could barely stand. There was no way they could steal away the last focusing relic she possessed in this state.

"This is it then," Vyrion said.

The sad certainty in his voice felt like a cold dagger to Krothus' gut. "So it seems," Krothus managed to mumble out, "It's been a pleasure, all these years. No one could deny our ambition."

Vyrion seemed surprised at the defeat echoed in Krothus' tone. Maybe he expected Krothus to be in proud denial till the end, but if Vyrion was disappointed, he didn't show it. He just smiled back at him, putting on a brave face. "One last try?"

"One last try."

The Highlords were nearly at the artifact now, their ethereal vessels swaying like voyagers navigating a wild storm, all while Callida was managing to hold the heaving ocean together. Krothus couldn't bear to look up any more. What point was there? Time was short, and he and Vyrion both already knew the fate that awaited them.

They charged. There was no battlecry, no brave speeches, only the quiet breaths of the determined.

Krothus led, as he always did. If Callida took him out first, then perhaps Vyrion would get some opportunity to avenge him.

Each step into his eventual doom cleared Krothus' mind. He didn't think of the future, of the new Empire that would be forged out of their failure, nor the past, how he could have changed things. No, he only wondered how close he would get to Callida before she would snap his neck.

Closer and closer.

Something caught Krothus'seye, some figure in the periphery of his vision. He could have thought he saw someone lounging on the center seat of the Council's chambers, but when Krothus tried to get a better look, it was empty, the figure absent. But despite this, a single image was burned into his mind's eye, like Krothus had caught a glimpse of something he shouldn't have, some dream that he could scarcely remember. A hollowed face burning with crimson flame, sitting atop a suit of ancient armor. One arm outstretched, one bony finger pointed directly at him.

Then he felt it.

It swelled into him like an injection of lightning. It wasn't just power, it was a force unlike Krothus had ever experienced, like the Ruin itself had been refined, purified into some nectar with such potency that every pump of his heart threatened to rip his body apart. Raw vengeance and fury burned through his veins, his muscles so pumped full of otherworldly strength that Krothus felt as if they were going to burst at any second.

This was what he had always wanted. No, what he *deserved*.

Each step propelled Krothus forward a dozen strides with ease. He felt invincible, undefeatable.

A quick glance to Vyrion, easily keeping pace with Krothus' frightening speed, eyes bleeding crimson sparks, revealed that he too had received the same gift.

Callida barely got her runeblades up in time. Krothus crashed into her defenses like an avalanche, an overwhelming cataclysm that even he could not contain. His first blow sent her stumbling back, the next nearly drove her to her knees, all the while the flames within his runeblade whirled with the force of a hurricane, singeing her clothes and burning her hands.

"What power is this?" she managed to growl, forced to rip her attention away from the ritual to defend herself, the storm above intensifying the moment she did.

Krothus didn't know what the power truly was, nor did he care. All he could think of was gleefully continuing his burning crusade, his mind disregarding any other thought.

Amidst his continued clash with Callida, Krothus' nostrils were filled with the smell of burnt ozone as a rush of air whirled around them, heralding the arrival of a supercharged bolt of lightning burning past. Callida managed to just whirl away, causing Vyrion's strike to impact one of the Council seats, utterly demolishing it, blowing it to smithereens. Another near miss shattered a pair of columns. They were no longer toys to be tortured.

Callida looked far from confident, almost fearful at the sudden turnaround in circumstances. Krothus barely registered the change, so intent was his bloodlust. His runeblade smashed into hers over and over, his vision tunneling, each unsuccessful strike followed by a new jolt of energy flowing into him.

So much power, so much strength, Krothus felt it all, deserved it all. But a sudden realization rippled through his body, like a final misjudged bite at a feast's end.

It was too much.

Krothus' heart was racing at a frantic pace, his arms so tense that they threatened to break in half. His runeblade was burning the hand that held it, but like a rabid beast he relentlessly pressed on. His will no longer felt his own, so enthralled with his singular task that his body was destroying itself just to see it done. Callida's defense was frantic, desperate, its only purpose buying her the few final seconds needed for her plan to come to fruition. Her runeblades were gripped by blackened, burnt hands, but still they were holding.

Krothus didn't just want her to fall, he needed her to. Tears streamed from his eyes, his head threatened to collapse in on itself, and still more power was thrust into his body.

This gift was going to kill him.

And if that weren't enough, Vyrion's bolts of Ruin lightning were growing more powerful by the second, each one now bringing the possibility of bringing the whole room crashing down on their heads, each one slowly draining their wielder of life and soul. But still their foe remained.

Callida parried another of Krothus' blows, sending a shock of agony up his burning arm, the pain sending him to his knees. He couldn't help but look up. The Highlords were right at the center of the ritual.

"You've failed," Callida cried, "It's over. The new era of the Empire has arrived."

The artifact glowed bright white, illuminating the room. Callida reached out above her, as if she were welcoming a new dawn.

Vyrion wobbled, then collapsed. One last bolt smashed through the domed ceiling, sailing off into the grey sky, burning clouds as it went.

Then Krothus saw it. The soft glow of a rose, cast in amber. Worn around Callida's neck. The final relic keeping the ritual together, it had to be. The final chance he had, the only way to win, despite all of this.

Krothus willed himself to his feet and burst forwards, trying to focus his failing body on one final attack. Callida saw him, crossing both her runeblades in an attempt to withstand the blow. But he couldn't do it, he couldn't break through. His body, previously so powerful, was shutting down, poisoned by his mightiest desire. In a last ditch effort, he flung a final wide strike at her as he lunged forward.

Callida laughed, surely recognising Krothus' failure as her victory's beginning. His guard dropped, impossible to keep up while being so reckless. Callida took up the opportunity. The waves of pain already washing over his body almost drowned out the feeling of the runeblade as it burned through his flesh. Almost. He still felt his arm being severed.

Warmth gushed down his side and his runeblade clattered away. Krothus would have felt relieved if pain wasn't ripping through every atom of his being.

The light of the ritual grew impossibly bright. Callida looked down at him, lying in a growing pool of his own blood.

"It seems like you won't get to see my new Empire after all," she sneered.

Krothus took a deep shuddered breath, then smiled up at her. "It certainly seems that way."

Seeing that smug look being wiped off her face, he knew it was worth it. He held her necklace in his remaining hand, stolen away while she'd pounced on him.

As his vision faltered and everything slipped away, Krothus realized his burden had been lifted.

His grand destiny had been realized.

Then he squeezed his hand and crushed the necklace to bits.

Chapter 32

Ruin

When Vyrion woke, his breath caught in his throat. The council chamber was half-destroyed; seats shattered, columns scorched, even the ceiling had been partially blown out. He could barely stay conscious long enough to figure out if they had won.

The maelstrom above had dissipated. Callida was nowhere to be seen. And Krothus was-

Vyrion shoved himself to his feet with wobbling elbows. Krothus was there, a grim talisman at the center of the room.

He limped over to his fallen partner, feeling more drained with every step. The power Vyrion had been given was too much for any mortal to bear. It had nearly killed him.

Krothus wasn't moving. Perhaps he had not been as lucky.

Vyrion refused to believe it. Krothus couldn't be dead. What was the point of all of this if Krothus was gone at the end of it? He knew it was all his fault; if he had only figured out Jarek's plan earlier, if he knew where the relics were, if his attacks had brought Callida down. Then it might look different.

His stomach sank when he made it to the bed of blood Krothus rested in. As though he had walked through a curtain of fire, he was burnt and scalded everywhere, a gouge down the side of his head, cuts and bruises everywhere else. And worst of all, his left arm was severed at the elbow, the stump neatly cauterized as the one lucky result of whatever firestorm had crashed into him.

Vyrion unsuccessfully swallowed his horror as he knelt down.

"Krothus?"

No response. Vyrion put a hand on his chest, desperate to feel some sign of life. Tears stung at his eyes as he waited and waited. But there was nothing.

Maybe he should have been honored, grateful for Krothus to have met such an heroic end. But Vyrion felt nothing but a burning anger - he and Krothus had given everything for this moment and yet Vyrion stood here alone. If they had been deemed worthy of such power, worthy of saving the Empire, then why was Krothus not worthy of being saved himself?

The presence that had been with Vyrion since he had arrived in the city was still there. Vyrion knew he was listening.

Krothus needed to live. Vyrion didn't care how it happened, or what he had to give in return, it just needed to be done. And if the Emperor himself could not make it happen, then Vyrion would find someone who would.

Someone appeared next to him, someone with a horned head.

"The Master is grateful for your work here," the stranger said, "Without such worthy vessels, all would have been lost."

"His gratitude is not something that can help me right now," Vyrion snapped back. He was tired, so very tired.

The stranger smiled, light glinting off their sharp teeth. "The master's gratitude opens many doors, some of them impossible to comprehend." Clutched within their three-clawed hands was that small pyramid of metal, deceptively harmless and plain within their grip.

Vyrion narrowed his eyes. "Where is Callida?"

A claw tapped the hard face of the artifact, and that toothy grin grew wider. "Every ritual incurs a cost, regardless of whether it succeeds or fails."

Trapped. Consumed, the voice in Vyrion's head whispered.

One less unknown to worry about, Callida's plans had faltered, her ambition only bringing her death. But Vyrion still felt on edge, thinking of what lurked within the artifact, how close it had been to sending the Empire crumbling. Worse still, the thing was only one of two artifacts he had uncovered, there was still no telling where the Black Book was, who had been in possession of it.

The stranger pushed past him, kneeling at Krothus' side.

"What are you doing?" Vyrion asked, not sure why he was objecting. It wasn't like it could get any worse.

The stranger looked down at the stump where Krothus' forearm used to be, then at his unmoving chest. Their horned head twitched briefly, as if someone were whispering in their ear, and their toothy jaw began to move, silently mouthing words Vyrion didn't understand. Only when they finished their one-sided conversation did they turn back to him.

"The Master gives a token of thanks, in return for such a gift." It tapped the pyramid again, then placed it on Krothus' chest, a ghostly circle of unfamiliar runes slowly fading into being around it.

Vyrion didn't know what to do. Nothing good had ever come from that thing. Was it stealing away Krothus' soul, imprisoning him away within its metal facets? He did not deserve such a fate.

He lunged for the pyramid, desperate to stop whatever was happening. But the stranger locked him in a three-fingered grip, far stronger than Vyrion would have expected.

There was a flash of light. Krothus's chest kicked up and back down. A wisp, smokey and so faint as to be barely visible, ripped itself out of the tip of the pyramid. For a brief second, Vyrion thought he saw a screaming face emerge from the vapor, silently wailing before it dissipated into nothingness.

With a great sputtering gasp, Krothus woke. He sat straight up, eyes wild, gasping for breath.

The moment the stranger released their hold, Vyrion was embracing him. Krothus' remaining arm was pulling him tight, squeezing him as those panicked, rapid, breaths slowly calmed. Of course, once Krothus seemed to gain his bearings, Vyrion was quickly shoved off.

Krothus looked down at the stump of his left arm. He stared at it for a good while, frowning, as if his disappointment would somehow mend it.

Vyrion cleared his throat. "I can ask who made Victus' leg, if you're interested."

Krothus' frown lessened, which was close to a real smile as Vyrion knew he could give. He was looking up above, towards the noticeably maelstrom-less ceiling. "Callida?"

"Defeated, I think."

Vyrion didn't know where the artifact was being taken, but he could only hope it was somewhere far, far away, out of reach of whoever next tried to exploit its secrets. He looked for the stranger, hoping for some additional cryptic explanation, but they were gone, vanished without a trace.

Instead of the stranger, there were a dozen other faces looking down at them; still emanating all that superiority, all that distinguished stature, despite nearly being forcibly removed from power only moments prior. The only evidence of the Council's previous struggle were the damages to the Council Chamber itself, a battlefield all its own.

The floating, ancient Highlord hovered over her shattered seat, not seeming too bothered by the change of scenery. "You two have done the Empire a great service, and for that we thank you. Callida's insane plans have failed."

"Agreed," whirred Achima, gears happily clunking away. "You have proven yourselves worthy of the Emperor's favor, it is not every day we see Ruined with such potential, such drive."

Krothus had gotten to his feet, clutching his stump as he stared the Highlords down, "So make us Ruin Lords, then. We've proved ourselves as such."

Vyrion would have never been so blunt, but he shared the same thought; they had done more than enough to be considered.

But it was never that simple.

Highlord Obra's forked tongue flicked out his smiling mouth. "One victory does not make you worthy of such an honor. You have potential, yes, the kind that merits us watching closely, but you must find your own way to such a title. You cannot be made a Ruin Lord, you must become one."

"There will be many opportunities for such things in the coming months, many Ruin Lords have lost their lives and their holdings today," added Achima, "If you can exploit these vacuums of power for your own ends, we may yet see you as Ruin Lords."

"Now leave us, we have much to discuss," the floating Highlord rasped.

And after all that they had done, that was it.

Krothus looked furious, but Vyrion just sighed and led him away. The Empire might have been saved, at least for now, but with that came all the same rules, hidden or not. The strong ruled the weak, as they always must. It had seemed simple before, but when two lowly Ruined apprentices manage to be the ones to save the lives of the Ruined Council, the lines blur, the logic cracks. The longer Vyrion stayed in Thanaton, the more he had come to realize that the rules were only the justification for taking what you wanted. Only this time, he and Krothus lacked the bargaining chips, the power, to follow through.

Below them, through the glass floor of the Council Chamber, the results of the Empire's decrees were clear to see. The courtyard looked like a vast colony of ants from this height, half its population laying still. The only positive Vyrion could extract from it all was that the fighting had stopped. Perhaps word of Callida's defeat had somehow already reached all sides, or more likely, they had simply lost too many to continue on. He tried to push any thoughts around Inissa or the Nightshadow out of his mind. They were fine, surely. He only needed to go down and find out himself.

He and Krothus limped out to the way they had come in, protesting with every painful step. As they passed by a shattered column, Agent Dedri emerged from the shadows, looking as close to happy as Vyrion had seen her.

"The Empire lives for another day, Ruined. We are all in your debt."

"So we keep hearing," Krothus muttered.

Dedri's face fell as she saw his arm. "There have been many sacrifices today, count yourself lucky you get to walk away from yours."

"Oh I certainly feel *lucky*," he sneered.

"At least the bloodshed below has stopped, if just for now." Vyrion was trying to stay positive, but even in victory it was far more difficult than he needed it to be.

Dedri nodded. "Good. Never thought I would prefer Ruin Lord scheming over anything, but I would take that over battling in the streets. If this never happens again it will still be too soon."

"It would be a long way off," Vyrion said, not believing his own words in the slightest. "Callida has been made a clear example of, and I doubt the Council will be advertising how close she got."

"You're right about that. And neither will either of you - what happened doesn't leave this room."

"Understood." They could be as quiet as they wanted, but there wasn't much to stop someone else from doing the same tomorrow, or the day after. There were no shortage of ancient artifacts, nor overambitious Ruin Lords, someone was bound to put two and two together once more.

"We won't have to worry about Zlaterek telling anyone," Krothus said, nodding at the pile of rubble nearby.

Zlaterek was crumpled into a heap, wrapped in a stoney coat of column fragments. His head was twisted off to one side in a bad way, his crazed eyes staring up and far off. All that from one wave of a finger.

Krothus was frowning down at him, mulling it all over as if he had just eaten something bold and wasn't sure what to make of it.

"He did his job well," Dedri said quietly, all that professionalism washing out, just for a moment. It looked like she had aged ten years since they'd entered the room, the lines on her face so deep-set that they could have been cut with a knife. "We found that relic hidden in one of the glass cases outside, masked as some trophy of the Council. He insisted on coming in here to help, the fool. The guardians let him through, somehow had an outstanding invitation from his last visit. Need to have a word with their handlers about that."

"He will be mourned," Vyrion said. An easy lie, one he was telling as much to himself as anyone else. Who would mourn him? Would it be Vyrion himself, only after knowing him for a few hours? Dedri? Krothus knew Zlaterek for longer, and he didn't seem to care. He almost seemed amused by the notion.

Dedri quickly left the subject behind. "We should leave, I still have my men to check up on."

Vyrion could have objected, said they needed to say a few words more about Zlaterek, and his sacrifice. But he didn't.

They made their way out the doors, the Council's gaze burning at their backs.

To Vyrion's own surprise, he barely felt anything when they passed Jarek. Whether it was their victory, the realization of his betrayal, or simply exhaustion, Vyrion walked past with only the slightest flutter in his chest. There was no feeling of satisfaction at justice served, only a hint of melancholy. A waste.

They descended down the grand stairway, observed only by the hooded statues that lined the passage, their stone gazes seeming almost grateful. Before long, they were back at the site where Callida's forces had interrupted their ascent.

There were bodies everywhere, piercer bolts stuck into them like strange growths expanding out of armor and skin. In the area beyond the huge doorway, there was an exhausted calm as previously warring forces recovered together as if nothing had happened. Say one thing about Thanaton, the conflicts changed like the tides.

What little remained of the soldiers wearing Callida's banner were rounded up and under guard against a nearby wall, only a handful at best. The remainder of her contingent lay on the ground, a carpet of black armor and black sun tabards.

Dedri was already sifting her way through the sea of the dead, looking for islands of tattered grey. They were there, hidden amongst the black, each surrounded by a ring of slain foes. Bolts through visors, in weak points in soldiers' armor - they hadn't gone down easily. But they had nonetheless, and Dedri's face darkened with every agent upturned.

Vyrion watched her with a heavy heart, his own search a brief one. Farke was propped up against a pillar, his hair a mess, uniform marred by the two bolts in his chest. His weapon was still clutched in his hand, braced for an enemy that would no longer come. From what Vyrion had seen through both trials and experience, Farke had never been a good officer, but today he had played the part of one perfectly. Lorren would have no doubt had some positive words to say, had he been around. But he wasn't. And now neither was Farke.

"I'm going to stay here," Dedri said, her voice hoarse, "I need to count my casualties. There's going to be a lot of letters that need to be written home when I'm done."

"I'm sorry," Vyrion said, not sure what else to say, "They died honorably."

"Died fighting fellow Imperials," Krothus added on unhelpfully, almost like he was mocking the whole thing. Vyrion shot him a look but he just shrugged, as if someone was going to say it anyways.

Dedri gave a purse-lipped smile. "Letters need to be written regardless, letters that always say they died as heroes. Heroes fighting the Burning Head Cult, the Republic, anything but the truth. Who would trust Imperial Intelligence if they knew that Ruin Lords were our biggest threat?"

She didn't wait for their response, going right back to her grim census among the drove of bodies. Vyrion and Krothus continued back down the steps.

Vyrion hoped the same didn't await them in the courtyard. Inissa, Spinebreaker, Headcleaver, Soultotem; there were many that they had depended on to hold back Fira. One or all of them could have met the same fate as Dedri's agents. An unwanted image of their bodies, savaged and ripped apart, filled his mind.

"Vyrion?"

They were in the antechamber now, dim and cold. The withered corpse of Highlord Malus lay where they left it.

Krothus was staring down at it, stone-jawed, single remaining fist clenched. He looked closer to the drained body than to the man Vyrion knew; one arm gone, ragged and burnt and torn down everywhere else. It was a wonder he was still standing. "Is this it?"

Vyrion didn't understand. "Is what it?"

"*This.*" He waved his half-arm at him. "Is this the only reward I get? Weeks in that cell, I give everything I had to stop Callida, and I get *nothing*. No, worse than nothing, I gave the Council my damn arm and that still wasn't enough."

"I know. And it's not fair." Vyrion tried to reach out, put a hand on his shoulder, but Krothus shrugged it off.

"Spare me your pity."

Vyrion sighed. "It's not pity, Krothus. I understand your frustration. Really, I do."

"But?"

"But nothing. That's it. You are completely justified in feeling the way you do, I would too."

Krothus stared at him, teeth clenched, like he was looking for something to snap at, something to latch onto, drive his anger further. But Vyrion hadn't given him much to work with.

"Gah!" he grunted. He gave the corpse a good kick.

Vyrion wished he could help him, trade his arm for his, even. Krothus was far better a Ruined than Vyrion ever was, to see him worn down so far was like seeing his own view of the future getting washed out right in front of him. The best he could do was try and keep him focused on what they could do.

"Your apprentice still needs you, Krothus."

Krothus looked back. Then he gave a heavy sigh and trudged to the antechamber doors, as if he had only just remembered they were there for more than kicking corpses.

They passed through the narrow gap in the antechamber doors and out into the crater. Vyrion felt his stomach sink the moment he caught sight of the field of death and destruction beyond. Bodies blanketed the rubble, the bodies of Nightshadow warriors poking through like great crimson hills. Gone was the roar of combat, instead replaced with a quiet hush of the grave, the air filled with the smokey scent of a battle fought; stale fear, fresh death, and a hesitant relief.

The remaining Nightshadow, barely half of the warband that had intervened out of the crashed skyship, were draped across one of the rubble hills nearby, exhausted, but blanketed in an aura of thankful victory. Seeing any at all was a good sign; Fira had not succeeded.

In the middle of them was a singular figure surrounded by a moat of empty space. Chieftain Headcleaver sat alone; no bodyguards, no blustering speeches, only armed with his axe and a contemplative stare. If not for his tremendous size, Vyrion could have mistaken him for a lost boy, unsure of where he was or why he was there. In front of him was a body, her arms carefully crossed over her broken staff. Soultotem.

When Headcleaver noticed them approach, he put on a brave face and hoisted himself to his feet. "Ruined. Is the witch dead?"

"She is," Krothus said, clasping Headcleaver's forearm with his remaining hand. The Nightshadow chief returned the gesture, briefly glancing down at Krothus' other, mangled, limb but otherwise ignoring it. Krothus noticed the look, tucking it back under his ragged cloak as one would a hidden blade.

"What happened?" Vyrion asked. A stupid question. She died, that's what, and all he was doing was rubbing it in.

Headcleaver had to force his words out, like each one was an admittance of her demise. "Soultotem died a warrior's death, ensuring a future for our people. She wouldn't have picked any other way."

He stopped, just stared down at the old shaman in silence. It took a few moments before he was able to rip his gaze away, looking to what remained of his warband instead. "I will take my people home. We have fought long and hard for this moment, and it will be a difficult road ahead of us if we are to rebuild and adjust to a life without fear."

A life without fear. Vyrion liked the sound of that, an existence unburdened by his anxiety, his constant catastrophizing. But he was still a long way off such a thing, especially when he had yet to inventory who else had made it.

"Fira is gone then," Krothus grunted, "Where is Inissa?"

"See for yourself," Headcleaver said, pointing a claw further down the crater. A few survivors milled about in scattered groups.

Krothus headed that direction immediately, but Vyrion lingered for a moment.

"Thank you for your help, Headcleaver. For your sacrifices."

Headcleaver gave him an ugly tusked smile. "Our sacrifices are timeless. We are bound by blood now, Ruined. This won't be the last you see of us." He let his words linger for a moment, all before he looked back down at his shaman, wiped that grin off his face and fell back into silence.

Careful to avoid trodding on any bodies, Vyrion slowly navigated his way through the battlefield, a good distance behind Krothus, stomping through the wasteland as though it were nothing more than a field filled with troublesome weeds. Only when he drew closer did Vyrion recognise who the group was.

A pair of automatons, scratched up and dented, turned their unnervingly human-like heads at the two Ruined as they arrived, whirring and clicking in greeting. The autos flanked a very unhappy Captain Fareese, her arms crossed defiantly, listening to Spinebreaker, encased in what looked oddly similar to Lord Victus' old armor.

"Like I said, the ship will be repaired in good time," the orkathi said, "I'll see to it personally."

Vyrion almost laughed, seeing Spinebreaker trying his best to negotiate with Fareese. It seemed an odd pairing, and he was certainly confused as to why the warrior would care.

Fareese was not nearly as amused. "You'd better. The Imperial Navy won't, I'm sure. If you factor in the damages from the crash, the ammunition we had to use sniping out of the hold, the emotional trauma, plus the reputational damages of course, then I think a neat sum of-"

The orkathi had never looked happier, seeing Vyrion and Krothus appear, immediately using the opportunity to leave Fareese mid-swindle. "The men of the hour! We all felt Callida's demise, Ruined or not. As a result of our intervention the Empire limps on, wounded but very much alive. I hope you understand what a tremendous debt this city owes you."

"Cut the patriotic nonsense, Victus," Krothus snarled, "Where is

Inissa?"

Vyrion initially thought he hadn't heard right. But when Spinebreaker's tusked smile dwindled to nothing, and a shadow of guilt draped itself across his face as he saw Krothus' arm, Vyrion knew.

"Over there," the orkathi croaked, pointing to a clearing nearby.

Krothus left without another word. Leaving just Vyrion and Victus.

Vyrion had imagined a final conversation with his master many times. Asking him why he had to choose Krothus for his ritual, why he hadn't asked Vyrion to help him find someone else, *anyone* else. Why he had never told him his plan. Sometimes Vyrion imagined himself offering an apology for what happened, sharing war stories, a handshake of mutual respect. Business was business, they both did what a Ruined should do, defend their goals and fight for their future. Victus would have understood that. But now, with Jarek gone, with the revelation that he had been manipulating everything for months, if not years, Vyrion wasn't sure what to think.

He certainly hadn't imagined Victus looking like this. They both stared at each other for a long while. Measuring up, guessing what came next.

Victus spoke first, all in Spinebreaker's deep growl. "For what little it's worth, I am sorry." He looked at the sea of bodies around them. "I have lived a long life, and like any long life, I could build cities of my mistakes, pave roads with my regrets. I cannot right all of them, but with this I can try. I am sorry."

An apology was a good place to start. Vyrion took a moment to look at him, to truly look at him. Victus occupied Spinebreaker's body, yes, but the uneven stance, the hands clasped behind his back, even the pensive look on his face, there was no denying it was him.

Victus noticed his staring. "You don't have to believe me, but it is a mutual arrangement with Spinebreaker. We are one, now."

"You think that justifies what you did?" Vyrion snapped, realizing too late that it was a far harsher tone than what he intended. "Your lack of foresight gave Callida the tools to cause all of this mayhem in the first place, Victus. You spent so much time overthinking the past that you were blind to the present, blind to the future. All of this was your doing."

The Lord Victus Vyrion knew would have bellowed defiantly, snarled at such a presumptuous suggestion as he limped around shouting profanities at anyone who would listen. His hip flask would have no doubt made an appearance.

But now, he only gave a sad bob of his tentacle-haired head. "I agree. And my punishment has been watching the world pass me by, watching my beloved Empire slowly wobble closer and closer to the cliff-edge. All my work has been dismantled, my compound burned, my legacy shattered. I have been powerless to stop any of it. But not for one moment do I expect any sympathy from you, Krothus, or Jarek. Ruin knows I don't deserve it."

He looked defeated, so deflated that Vyrion wouldn't have been surprised if he fluttered to the ground.

But Vyrion added on an additional burden. He had to tell him.

"Jarek is dead. He was serving Callida the entire time."

For all the bulk of his new body, Victus looked small, shrinking even further at this news.

"That boy always wanted to climb high. Living under a weak master with such ambition as he had breeds frustration. I knew deep down he wasn't happy, but I had no one else."

Vyrion hadn't felt a shred of sympathy passing what was left of Jarek earlier, but he did now. Not for Jarek, but for Victus. It was the type of pity that crawled out when seeing old beggars on the street, seeing someone cry alone. Pity for the lonely.

"I know you two had a mutual fondness," Victus continued, clearing his throat awkwardly, "I'm sorry."

"Not close enough, or I would have been able to see his true self," Vyrion said, unable to keep the bitterness from his voice.

Victus gave him a familiar look, the kind he would have during their lessons. Vyrion half expected him to start correcting his stance. It all seemed so long ago, now.

"It would have been an impossible task. Most do not know even their own true self. Some delude themselves with an idea of what it might be, how their intentions mask their actions, but it is for your choices to demonstrate who you are in the end."

It made sense. Perhaps it was as much a condemnation of Victus' previous obsessions as it was a reassurance of Vyrion's current situation. Victus seemed to be genuinely remorseful, but Vyrion wasn't sure that it was enough to overwrite the stories he had been spinning before all this. For all that talk of saving the Empire, he had been pursuing a new body for no other reason than to extend his own life, and he was willing to sacrifice Krothus to do it.

But was that so different to Vyrion himself? He actually had saved the Empire, supposedly, and had expected a boost to his reputation, an improved title, as a result. He could try to convince himself that wasn't the case, but when the Council had denied him that, he certainly felt cheated. And Zlaterek, Soultotem, perhaps even Inissa; others had been sacrificed on the way to that goal.

Vyrion found himself extending a hand. "Maybe these actions can change that inner self, make it better."

Victus took it in his claw, "One can only hope."

They shook hands, a silent acknowledgement of their past, a bridge rebuilt for the potential of the future. Then Vyrion went to join Krothus.

#

Krothus never understood families. Never had one, never needed one. And he was staring at a grand example of why they were a bad idea.

Inissa sat beneath him, face painted in dried tears. She held an overgrown bundle of spindly limbs tight in her arms, a woman with a blackened, bloody hole through her chest. An iron mask lay on the ground nearby.

Fira was dead. Inissa lived. Krothus would have considered that a victory, but his apprentice had left logic far behind.

"She was a terrible mother. A blight on the Empire," he said.

Inissa sniffed and wiped at her eyes. "I know."

"She would have killed everyone here had you not stopped her."

"I know."

"She was allied with demons, set to destroy-"

"I *know,*" Inissa snapped, those ugly tears dribbling down again. "But I still killed her. She was holding me. And I stabbed her in the back while she held me. My mother. Can you not understand that?"

Krothus felt it wise to hold his tongue. Wise, but difficult. He wanted to shake her, shout and yell, say she should just be thankful that she still has all of her limbs. He would have gladly killed his own mother five times over if it had made him a Ruin Lord, if it saved his arm. Instead, he had saved a dozen fools, blinded by their own arrogance, deafened by their hubris.

He looked down at the thing, a ghoulish stump of marred flesh where his left forearm used to be. There was a dull ache there, like someone had clubbed his missing limb with a rock. An ache that never got better. It just throbbed and throbbed, a constant reminder of his humiliation.

He tore his eyes away from both arm and apprentice as someone approached. Vyrion. The man of the hour, only losing a former lover for his troubles.

He just gave Krothus a nod before he lent down to comfort Inissa, the two of them sharing some meaningless blather about emotions, and mourning, and family. Krothus wasn't listening, it was all nonsense anyways. Like Vyrion knew anything about family. He wouldn't know a thing about-

"Krothus?" Vyrion asked.

Krothus frowned. "What?"

"Did you not hear me? I asked if you knew about Victus."

"I did."

"And you didn't tell me?"

Krothus was coming dangerously close to blowing up. It wasn't like he had kept it from him. He hadn't told Vyrion because he had been locked in a cell the moment he had an inkling about it. Trapped for Ruin knows how long while Vyrion was running around like a headless bat. And did Vyrion expect him to tell him in the midst of the chaos here earlier? No doubt some absurd moral clause in Vyrion's delusional psyche demanded it.

His raging thoughts were interrupted by a tug on his cloak, so ragged it was in danger of disintegrating completely.

"Are you okay, master?" Inissa had left her mother where she lay, finally up on her feet.

"I-" He stopped, took a breath. His anger drained out of him like he'd sprung a leak. He wasn't okay. He was mutilated, disgraced, and disappointed. And now he was a Ruined without a master, without a way forward.

Vyrion was looking up at him. "This isn't the first time we've started over, Krothus."

"And what comfort is that? How is the Empire supposed to move on from this? How are we?" He wanted Vyrion to understand. To know how he felt. What little shreds of pride he still possessed prevented him from confessing his weakness outright, telling them how far his convictions had dipped, how he realized his destiny had been a lie.

But as he saw into Vyrion's eyes, and as he lightly squeezed his burnt shoulder, Krothus knew he understood.

"We press on," Vyrion said, quiet but firm. "The Empire presses on. Look at how far we've come since that day we forged our partnership. We started over then. We started over when we arrived here, and we start over today. And each time we do, we grow stronger."

He gestured behind them, to the Nightshadow warband resting amongst the rubble, to Fareese and her automatons, to Victus. "Every power base starts somewhere, forms out of something."

"And you aren't alone," Inissa added.

Vyrion was smiling now. "No, you aren't."

Krothus wanted to scoff, to laugh in Vyrion's face, throw out every insult he could to try and justify the emptiness he felt. But at the end of it, Vyrion would still be right. And deep down, an ember deep within Krothus' heart was excited at the prospect. At the challenge.

He knew Callida's power play would have ripped a hole through

Thanaton's political structure. Hundreds of dead Ruin Lords, slain Ruined, empty fortresses. Each and every one of them was an opportunity. A rung to climb the ladder. A way up.

There would be others, of course. All trying the same thing. But Vyrion had spoke the truth, they had started over before, they would again. And what better way to begin anew than to start climbing, kicking down anyone trying to follow behind? The smoldering ember inside him was steadily burning now. Perhaps his destiny was not finished with him just yet.

He looked out through the shattered glass of the Dark Pyramid and into the sky beyond. Skyships floated by, a hint of blue just visible between the usual gray of Thanaton's clouds, looking like a gateway, a portal to the world beyond.

"Ruin Lords, then. I think we could manage that."

Vyrion was full on grinning. "Oh, I'm certain of it."

Chapter 33
Epilogue

Krothus stood alone.

He had been staring out into the swamp for hours, watching the sun rise above the expanse of ugly muck, casting its indiscriminate rays on those working within it. In fact, he had been there long enough, watching the draining crews, that the sun was already on its downward path.

He had been sick of Muckbron and Cresslog before, but after months of thinking it over, plus the day's already wasted hours, that latent irritation had metastasized into fully realised hatred. He despised the rotten scent drifting up from the slowly draining tide of stagnant water, the lumbering fools below singing their off key disharmonies as they set up more drainage platforms, and resented the crashes that emanated from the in-progress bridge between the two now-Imperial affiliated settlements. What was the point when the swamp was to be drained anyway?

But detestation of the place and its denizens aside, Krothus had to stay there, waiting, or everything would come tumbling down. All he had worked for. All he had sacrificed for.

As his simmering fury boiled over, he had to work to unclench his good hand. He had to work even harder to unclench his metal one, if he could even call it a hand.

Krothus was not used to the thing and probably never would be. He drew his scowl away from the unfortunates saddled with their pipes and their mudsuits to glare instead at the metal mockery of a lower arm he was now burdened with.

It was a crude, ugly thing. An artificial substitute for what had once been his well muscled forearm, his cherished runeblade wielding hand. He had no idea how it worked, only that it was temperamental at best, its grip strength tremendous, its dexterity severely lacking. It had four fingers and a thumb, yes, but whatever sorcery allowed his mind to give commands through the plates and gears and tubes had yet to allow anything but the most basic of actions. He'd replaced what had once been a masterwork blade with a brutal hammer.

And that was his reward, his burden. But one he would far prefer it to the curse that he'd been host to, the reason why he had to return to this blasted swamp.

It was when he looked back up at said swamp that the skyship came.

Krothus had never seen a Republic skyship. Where the Imperial ones he had seen, the *Donovan* included, had been like flying fortresses, prickly with bolt throwers, squinting through small viewports whittled out of their armor plating, the Republic vessels seemed to scoff at such utilitarian design.

Its descent was a graceful flutter, arcing down across the ridge like someone had gently placed a cup of tea on its coaster. The vessel itself was small, a bulbous arrangement of seamless spheres and overlapping ovals, glass and armor melding together in an almost artistic display. And as it nestled into the ground, Krothus could sense something about it, much like he could sense a jumble of Ruin energy running through Imperial skyships. A feeling of controlled power, a restrained calmness that thrummed through his senses at a constant, perfect pitch.

Krothus immediately decided he disliked it. And he would have been satisfied when the skyship powered down, dismissing the presence of the annoyance, if not for the man who suddenly appeared.

He came out of a hatch which had opened with a hiss and formed a neat ramp. The man looked just the same as when Krothus saw him last - bushy brows and a shell of battered armor.

"You're late," Krothus snarled.

"Avoiding Imperial patrols takes time," Commander Oar said, not appearing too bothered about the solitary vigil Krothus had to endure. "Besides, you're the one who won this swamp. Why not savor it?" It was clear from his tone that he as well as Krothus had no fondness for the place.

"It was your surrender, not my victory. The Empire's prize was nothing but a multi-year development project."

Oar briefly looked at the drainage platforms, at the teams setting them up. "My idea. Winning the place back once your Empire has foot the bill will be a far better investment of our resources."

"And was your investment in me your idea too?"

"No. Master Seefa's recommendation."

Krothus frowned, remembering the woman's power, how she had frozen an entire battlefield's worth of fighting with her presence alone. "Where is she? Seefa must be happy hearing of my former master's demise."

"Busy. But Master Seefa, along with the rest of the Republic, are pleased at the result, with your performance. The Ruined Empire is most tolerable when it is predictable."

His *performance*. Krothus felt his eye twitch, his mangled, metal hand drift towards his runeblade.

"Careful, Ruined," Oar chided, bushy brows drawing together, "Remember what my message said about being on your best behaviour."

Krothus briefly weighed the choices he had.

He could surrender to his fury, give it what it desired and chop Oar to bits. He was from the Republic, so it was justified, and he was no Ruined or Deus Master, so it would be effortless plus Oar was also incredibly irritating, so it would be fun. But then the Ruined Empire would receive an official diplomatic message declaring Krothus to be a traitor, an attempted double agent who had been spying for the Republic all this time. He wouldn't last a day, self proclaimed hero or not. Worse, he might even take Vyrion down with him, as the sentimental fool would no doubt try to clear his name and get himself killed in the process.

Or Krothus could stand there and listen to whatever Oar had for him. Krothus would not get the satisfaction from the man's death, but neither would he get dissatisfaction from his own. An even trade.

"Just get to the point, Oar. I've come all this way, alone, as your message dictated. Why?"

"Because we aren't done with you, Krothus."

"Who is *we*?"

Oar flashed him a fierce grin. "Me, Master Seefa, the Senate, the Archminister - every citizen of the Republic. We own you."

There was a creak as Krothus's metal hand clenched. "No one owns me."

"Oh I'm sure. Do you know what leverage is, Ruined?"

"No, I was actually lobotomised in between reading your message and getting here."

"Funny. But smart comments or not, we have all the leverage we need on you. There are enough of our double agents across the Empire to confirm any evidence we need to provide, enough of your own enemies to carry out the sentence. You work for the Republic now."

Krothus was furious, of course, but no amount of anger could change the fact that Oar was correct. He had been given a poisoned chalice, he could gulp it down for a swift end or slowly sip at it until he built up the strength to survive the whole dose.

So Krothus clenched his jaw and calmed himself. He had no choice.

Seeing that there were no more objections, Oar clapped his hands together. "Smart. Seems lucky for both of us that your lobotomy was not very effective. Besides, working for the Republic isn't all bad - the further you rise up the Empire's hierarchy, the more useful you are as an asset. So we will help you get there, provided you do enough of what we tell you. This can be a mutually beneficial arrangement."

"Oh? I wonder why more Ruined don't take you up on such a generous offer."

One bushy brow raised mischievously. "If only you knew."

Oar then tossed Krothus a blue gem, which he caught with his good hand. It felt warm to the touch. "This is how we'll reach you. It only works one way, so don't go talking into it or anything, it won't work." Then he turned around and started walking up to his skyship.

"You still haven't told me what you want!" Krothus called out after him.

Oar only stopped and turned around when he was up the ramp. "We'll be in touch. In the meantime, I would suggest you prepare yourself - gather allies, apprentices, power, whatever it is you Ruin Lords do best."

"What do you think I've been doing?"

"Well you'd better hurry up, or you won't survive what's to come. We need a piece to be played. The game has already started and you are far, far behind."

Then the hatch closed and the Republic skyship jumped back into the sky.

Krothus watched it get smaller and smaller until it disappeared.

Then he looked down at his metal fingers. They creaked open and closed under his command, the sound like grating laughter in his ears. He had once thought it the price paid for breaking Callida's shackles over him, for forging his own destiny. But here he was, stuck in the same game, a piece that had only changed players, the board reshuffled.

Krothus thought of the Ruined Council, the unfathomable power he had been given to prevent disaster. The kind of power that had almost destroyed him.

That was what he needed. The only way to win the game was to be a player, not a piece. And Krothus would gladly trade all the rest of his limbs if that's what it took.

He wouldn't just settle for Ruin Lord, or even Highlord, they were only higher, more valuable pieces. No, the Emperor was the true player. He was not beholden to the Republic, the Empire, Seefa or Oar or anyone else but himself. Krothus had felt that power, knew it was true.

But the Emperor's turn would end eventually. The Ruined Code demanded it.

And with that chair would not remain empty for long. Someone was

destined for it.
    Someone like Krothus.

Printed in Dunstable, United Kingdom